In the
HEART
of the
GARDEN

LEAH FLEMING worked in teaching,
catering, running a market stall, stress
management – as well as being a mother
of four – before finding her true calling
as a storyteller. She lives in the beautiful
Yorkshire Dales but spends part of the
year marinating her next tale from an olive
grove on her favourite island of Crete.

Also by Leah Fleming

The Olive Garden Choir
The Wedding Dress Maker
The Daughter of the Tide

In the
HEART
of the
GARDEN

LEAH FLEMING

HEAD
of
ZEUS

First published in the UK in 1998 by Hodder and Stoughton,
a division of Hodder Headline PLC
This edition published in the UK in 2019 by Head of Zeus Ltd

9 7 5 3 1 2 4 6 8

A catalogue record for this book is available from
the British Library.

ISBN (PBO): 9781789543278
ISBN (E): 9781789543384

Typeset by Adrian McLaughlin

Printed and bound in Great Britain by
CPI Group (UK) Ltd, Croydon CRO 4YY

Head of Zeus Ltd
First Floor East
5–8 Hardwick Street
London EC1R 4RG

WWW.HEADOFZEUS.COM

*For David and that corner of the world, above all others,
which holds a smile for us.*

'This blessed plot, this earth, this realm, this England'

—*Richard II*, WILLIAM SHAKESPEARE

Prologue

For Sale.

The sign is fixed above the gate post. The deed is done. Miss Iris Bagshott takes a deep breath to mark her decision, gulping in the green silence outside. It's a Samuel Palmer evening, bronzed and enamelled with gold around the edges, one of many in this Vaughan Williams folk song of a summer, haunting, harmonic, memorable. Why should she be feeling so agitated when the pipistrelles are darting into the shadows and the bees drone and the night air smells of stocks and honeysuckle? Time to take the tour. That might ease all her misgivings. Time to do the nightly inspection of sunshine borders and shade corners, water in her seedlings, let the dog stretch its legs in the fields beyond now the sheep have been shifted from the meadow...

Slow down, Iris, follow the golden rule, slowly, don't rush the tour or you'll miss something. It's not that difficult these days to creep at a snail's pace.

The sign above the gate should please that blessed builder. Now he can make me a generous offer, stop pestering me to sell up and downsize... what sort of word is that? If Arthur Devey's a cutting off the old stock he won't be able to spell it either! What about buying one of his new bungalows indeed!

He keeps harping on about the value of a cherry orchard with planning permission, the premium of having such an ancient barn suitable for redevelopment, the size of my cottage for just one old lady and her dog. Well now, let's see if he puts his money where his mouth is. How dare he think that at eighty-five I don't know the stairs are getting steeper and narrower, and that two acres of garden is a bit too much for arthritic knees? Really… I can still remember flaying his dad's backside with a slipper when he was a nipper in my classroom. The Deveys are mere Johnny cum latelys to Fridwell village while Bagshotts are rooted in its soil like the oaks in the forest. Some say we've been here since Domesday.

Miss Bagshott sips from the smooth rim of her china mug as she surveys her kingdom from the bench seat by the kitchen door. The tour always begins at the homely end of the garden where the salmon pink rose, Albertine, climbs up the warm wall and the studded oak door looks out on the oldest part of her kitchen patch, with not a square inch of its soil vacant. Nothing seems more simple or more beautiful to her at that moment than a well-stocked kitchen garden where even the brick path sprouts seedlings, lemony thyme and velvet moss amongst the weeds.

Into the rows of green lettuces, spinach, chard, cabbages and carrot ferns, chickweed, thistle and couch grass muscle in like thugs but in such well-manured red soil anything will grow. What a riot of plants for the pot stuffed into beds edged with alpine strawberries, glistening in the moonlight like a Sultan's rubies, mixed with bronzy sage leaves, lobelia and any stray herbs which can grab a spot. Silver-green foliage, blues and pinks all spilling out over the path in front of her favourite peonies whose heads flop like ballerinas curtseying in pink tutus.

Peonies shouldn't really be in a kitchen patch but I like it when plants find their own place in the sun. The sweet peas dance up the cane tepees alongside an arch of scarlet blossoms from the runner beans. They give height and interest to the bed.

Her eyes drift beyond the boundary wall where the rhubarb has gone to seed and spirals of golden heads lighten the shade. Why shouldn't some of her umbellifers stick their feathery heads in the air and feed the hoverflies? It takes away the regimented look from the borders, gladdens the eye as it rises over the wall up to the Chase. Here the great oaks sleep in the dusk on the high ridge, silent witnesses to centuries past silhouetted against a marigold sky.

Nothing like trees to cut you down to size, outliving each generation in the end, and Miss Bagshott wonders: Is it true, do her ancestors really stretch as far back as the forest itself? Who cleared this piece and chose this blessed plot to feed themselves?

Then she hears the soft trickle of water over stones. The stream which meanders through her patch is so much a part of her garden that she scarcely gives it a thought. Now, in the silence of evening, amidst the perfume of newly mown grass cuttings on her compost heap, Miss Bagshott smiles. Human kind never strays far from the source and giver of life and Fridwell spring must have been named in someone's honour. But who and why?

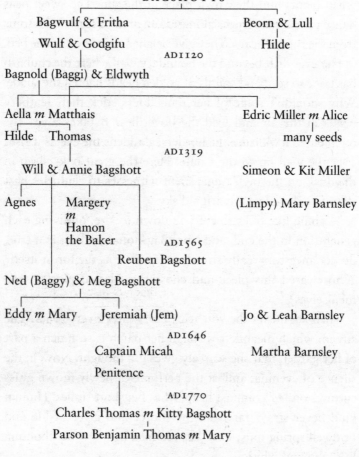

AD912
BAGSHOTTS

Bagwulf & Fritha   Beorn & Lull

Wulf & Godgifu   Hilde

AD1120

Bagnold (Baggi) & Eldwyth

Aella *m* Matthais   Edric Miller *m* Alice

Hilde   Thomas   many seeds

AD1319

Will & Annie Bagshott   Simeon & Kit Miller

Agnes   Margery   (Limpy) Mary Barnsley
              m
              Hamon
              the Baker   AD1565

                    Reuben Bagshott

Ned (Baggy) & Meg Bagshott

Eddy *m* Mary   Jeremiah (Jem)   Jo & Leah Barnsley

                    AD1646

              Captain Micah   Martha Barnsley

              Penitence

                    AD1770

Charles Thomas *m* Kitty Bagshott

Parson Benjamin Thomas *m* Mary

AD1918...

Enoch & Annie Bailey

Jim Bagshott *m* Rose Bailey

Nathaniel   Iris Rose

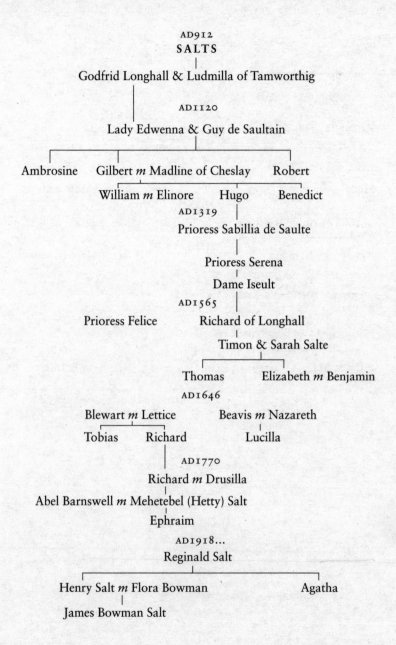

AD912
SALTS
|
Godfrid Longhall & Ludmilla of Tamworthig

AD1120
Lady Edwenna & Guy de Saultain

Ambrosine   Gilbert *m* Madline of Cheslay   Robert

William *m* Elinore   Hugo   Benedict

AD1319
Prioress Sabillia de Saulte

Prioress Serena

Dame Iseult

AD1565
Prioress Felice   Richard of Longhall

Timon & Sarah Salte

Thomas   Elizabeth *m* Benjamin

AD1646
Blewart *m* Lettice   Beavis *m* Nazareth

Tobias   Richard   Lucilla

AD1770
Richard *m* Drusilla

Abel Barnswell *m* Mehetebel (Hetty) Salt

Ephraim

AD1918...
Reginald Salt

Henry Salt *m* Flora Bowman   Agatha

James Bowman Salt

PART ONE

THE CLEARING AT FRITHA'S WELL

AD 912

'All things pass away, so may this'
—Deor's Lament, *The Exeter Book*

'The Peony
The roots are held to be of more virtue than the seed;
the root is also effectual for women that are not sufficiently
cleansed after childbirth, and such as are troubled with
the mother; for while likewise the black seed
beaten to powder... is also available'

Into the Forest

❧

The buzzard circled and coiled high over the forest, patrolling above the treetops, sweeping the air with upturned wings dark against the lavender sky of late spring. The roosting birds hid deep under the branches, wary and silent, until danger passed over. The wolves, like grey shadows, crouched under cover of scrub, watching the lambs graze in a terraced clearing.

The bird was joined by its mate. They swooped down into the vale of the silver river which coiled like a snake, glistening in the moonlight; down to the dark earth clearings and the smoke of man, spiralling up to greet them from holes in thatched rooftops.

The sun was setting low over the thick forests of the west, rays of pink and orange promising a settled spell of weather. To the east lay the grey swamps of the Minster church clearing; more sloping terraces fallen to the foe of woodland, the plough. Further afield stood the earthworks of Tamworthig, open land no longer the domain of wolf or eagle. The buzzards soared back to their roost among the oaks.

Underground, moles were turfing and digging to the surface,

pushing through the bracken fronds. Worms were churning and sucking down the rotten autumn leaves. They could feel the thunder of heavy ox hooves and the rumble of cart wheels. Men were on the move.

The dusk creatures darted into the hazel scrub, but the little spring still gushed and bubbled out from the deep rock, dancing over the pink boulders, carving a path through the thicket downwards to the brook and river beyond. The Forest of Canok was alive, watchful, waiting, while mankind trundled trek-weary over the faint track. Finally the sparse procession of covered wagons ground to a halt before fording the stream.

'Stop right here! I'm not going another foot tonight. This'll do, Baggi. There must be a wellspring ahead – we can rest up here, feed the stock. Me bum's nailed to the boards.'

Fritha jumped from the cart, stretched her stiff joints, shook out her dark braids and the skirt of her tunic and waved to the other cart. There was a scent of bluebells on the dusk air. They were on the edge of a forest and somewhere close by a spring was trickling into this shallow stream. It would be an ideal spot to rest their weary bones.

For two days the travellers had struggled on in heavy rain, ploughing through the mud with restless livestock tethered to the cart, reluctantly dragging their hooves. The rain had lashed on to their covered wagon, everything was soaked, even the boards they sat on. The children were sodden, hungry and tired out.

She lifted her son, a flaxen-haired babe of two summers, from the back of the cart and shook him awake but he lay draped like a mantle over her shoulder. His sister slept, curled up with the hound, whining at being roughly woken.

'Are we here?' she yawned, staring up at the net of black branches overhead.

'Just another stop over, Wyn. It's almost dark, time for supper,' Fritha soothed, hoping to humour the child.

'Can me and Ranulf go rooting?' Wyn jumped up and down, her dark plaits flying. Once awakened she would want to scamper and play, race about and get under everyone's feet. Her father, Baggi, shouted from the other side of the cart.

'Pee in the bushes but stay close by, do you hear? There may be bears, wild boars or wolves lurking in the scrub. We don't know this track and any noise from us may make them edgy. Mam'll light us a fire and get the kale pot on the boil to warm yer innards with broth.'

He turned to untether the goats and the other beasts, moving them on to graze as best they could. He led the animals to the wider verge by the stream, waiting for his younger brother in the cart behind to lift his heavy wife down from the back where she had lain wearily all afternoon. She needed watching that one, not like his woman who was already at her chores.

Fritha took the wooden bucket to draw water. It was still light enough to trace the source, which could not be far, for the stream was still weak. She followed the bank where primroses and purple violets, chickweed and watercress, edged the water. The garlicky scent of ramsons wafted down from under the taller trees in the distance. It was a beautiful setting in which to lie down and rest, with plenty of bracken to stuff a plump mattress. Soon she came to a hidden bank, out of which water bubbled from the rock. This was a sacred spring, of that she was sure, and Fritha squatted to draw the water into her bucket, first sipping it from her cupped hand. It was soft and sweet to her parched tongue. Above her the birds were making their evening noises, piping and chattering, oblivious to her presence. She sat down to enjoy a moment of quietness.

What a bunch of moonstruck idiots they were, striking out

to find a new life for themselves with hopes as tall as spears! Beorn's woman, Lull, looked exhausted, too close to her time to be travelling for three weeks over rough tracks and deserted stone roads. They rattled and bumped, became stuck in ruts and boggy, swampy tussocks, pushed, shoved and struggled to keep moving on to a better site, lighter soil, higher ground. A hard journey for families with young.

Baggi promised he would know when they found the right place to settle but Fritha was bone-weary. All I want is a bed of ferns amongst the bracken, some tree shelter and a fire to keep the wild beasts from attacking our livestock. This place will do, she thought.

It was good to be deep in a forest away from the open stone way of the ancient folks, where ghosts marched with the blood of her ancestors on their swords. They had kept the old east to west street in sight as a guide on their great trek to find new land to clear, a better living for their childer, away from the troubles, away from warring thanes and the Dane folk; savage warriors who skinned folk alive and carried off the women to satisfy their lust. Now they were heading northwards from the old stone street, through dense forest with only the tracks of animals and packmen to follow, rising higher on to ridges with a better view.

Holding the bucket in one hand and a bunch of kindling sticks under the other, she shouted to her childer on her way down from the well to gather more brushwood for the fire. Fritha busied herself setting a circle of firestones, striking the flint and tinder, boiling water in their kale pot for the rootings. The children also gathered cress from the stream and any first spring growth they could find for the pot. Wynfrith was a helpful lass in that way, but disobedient and wilful when the moon was in the other direction.

There were still oats in the leather bag and a few of her dried herbs to add flavour to the broth. The chickens in the wooden cage had not laid an egg for days and were eating up the last of their meal. How she wished she could wring their necks! It was weeks since they had tasted meat. If the hens were let out they would soon disappear into the undergrowth for a fox's feasting.

Lull sat with her back hunched, rubbing her belly, looking low in spirits. For a moment Fritha felt a flash of annoyance at her laziness. Beornwulf was already making up a shelter for her to rest in. If only she were not so swollen in those legs and ankles. It was not a good sign.

'We shall have to stop soon, Baggi, or Lull will drop the bairn in the cart,' whispered Fritha to her husband. He was always the more cheerful, hale and hearty of the two brothers, full of schemes and dreams. It had been his idea to strike out for some better land for the two families. Baggi was always the one who listened to the packmen's gossip that there were rich pickings in the northern kingdom of Mercia, where no thanes had cleared land and the holy men lived in hermit's cells deep in the forests.

Baggi and Beorn were freemen. Poor though they were, they still had the right to leave their thane's service and seek other dwellings. Beorn was happy to strike out, too, but Lull was not. There was a restless streak in the elder brother which made Baggi push them on and on but even he knew it was time to stop for a while, to see Lull's birthing through. They must settle, make a clearing and plant out before the summer's end if they were not to starve or be destroyed by the winter darkness.

The wooden carts were mud-splattered, wheels splintered and in need of repair. Baggi must not risk another upset load. They were worn, crammed with tools, and the precious plough took up most of Beorn's cart. Baggi had brought everything they could barter, buy or make for the life ahead. Strapped to the sides with leather thongs were dry seasoned oak beams for the hut-making.

Nothing was left behind but the tears of the old ones, too afeared to make the journey. Their well-loved voices still rang in Fritha's ear, the parting touch of kin, all the fare-thee-wells stuck inside her chest. It would be the last she would ever see of all of them, as solemn a parting as at the graveside. Her heart held hundreds of misgivings.

Would the provisions last? There was flour, meal, hard cheese, honey combs, dried apple rings, mead in the cask, seeds in the dryest purse, amongst the skins and precious roots and plantings wrapped in damp straw, a bucket of barley sprout-ings for the ale-making, a gift of salt for curing – all that well wishers could spare for them. Fritha fingered her grand-mother's amulet around her neck, a necklace of beads carved from the root of the peony flower; her trusted charm against evil and sorcery, sickness and bad spirits. For extra measure she had a string of peony seeds and her own store of sacred herbs safe in a leather purse tied to her waist girdle. She was taking no chances.

Sometimes as she lay beside Baggi she felt such foreboding. As if by leaving the settlement they would attract evil spirits to follow in the shadows, setting them around with obstacles and mists, luring them into bogs and swamps to be swallowed whole and sucked down into the blackness. Perhaps if she made a wooden cross piece and hung it around her neck as many now did for protection, calling on the High God of Heaven as the priests and hermits taught, that might help them find a fertile spot.

They were baptised in the Christian faith but Fritha

preferred the old ways, the runes, the spells and charms, learned by rote at her own mother's knee. The old gods were more sympathetic to womankind, for Erce was the Mother of the earth and growing things. Fritha always carried the nine sacred herbs: thyme and fennel, full of power; mayweed against skin rot; plaintain, the mother of herbs; stime to fight pain and poison; mint, sage, wormwood and the blessed rue.

She stirred the pot dreamily, wondering as she gazed over at the others, busy about their tasks, if they too had misgivings about striking out alone, without other company to make a stouter band of travellers. They would be easy pickings for brigands and marauding Danes from the northlands.

Poor Lull, little more than a child bride, now so swollen and fearful. Fritha could never tell how a birthing would go. Each of hers had been different. She was glad she had plenty of peony seeds to make a brew for the labour. Lull was a strange, silent girl, friendly and helpful sometimes, then lost in a mist of moods, distant, forgetful.

Beorn would not dream of letting his brother travel alone and forced his woman to leave their hut. It would perhaps have been better if the girl had stayed. She was holding them back by her feebleness. Little Wynfrith at five was more of a helpmate to her mother than this dreamy girl. Wyn would have to mind the baby so that the new mother might spin and weave cloth for them from the hedge rovings they were gathering along the track. In the sack was madder root, woad and onion skins to dye the wool yam, a task which Fritha enjoyed above all others. How she loved to mix the colours! But it would be many weeks before they were settled enough even to think about fancy stuff. There would be so much else to do if they were ever to fill their bellies. Everything looked so grey and drab and unpromising at dusk.

When it was almost pitch black, night calls echoing across the treetops, they sat round the circle of firestones to draw breath and sup their stew with relish. The moon was high and bright; the wellspring gurgled in a soothing sort of way.

The night was calm and mild and Ranwulf slept where he ate. Baggi lifted him on to the mat of ferns and covered him with a thick overmantle. Soon Wyn was asleep and Lull moved closer to her own wagon with Beorn. Baggi stoked the embers thoughtfully.

'It takes some out of you, all this travelling. I'll need no rocking tonight. Tomorrow we'll get a good start. Take the day fresh, keep heading north-west.'

'Must we? Lull can't go much further. She looks off to me, yonderly, as if her time's coming. Why don't you scout around with Beorn, check out the forest edge? Give us all more time to come to, clean ourselves up a bit. I could bake some stone bread, make milk porridge for a change if the goat will drop some milk. Don't you think?'

Fritha touched his leathern arm and smiled her gap-toothed grin. Baggi scratched his head and in his straw-coloured hair and rough wool tunic. Beneath the straps of his leather sandals his feet were black.

'We're all flea-bitten, dust-covered and mud-caked it's true. Go on then, you've twisted my arm. But only the one day, mind. I'll rise at first light and give this place the once over.'

'Thanks. You're a good man, Bagwulf. Even if you're a slave driver, moon-touched and as restless as the sea tide!'

Fritha supped from the mead beaker. She was proud that her man wanted more for his family than sharing a cramped hut with his kin; thought more of himself than to spend his nights at the ale bench. The two brothers had sawn and hammered and fashioned tools, sometimes until cock crow.

She was touched by the quality of his handiwork. With this soothing thought, her eyelids began to drop.

The travellers slept soundly, undisturbed until the cockerel stretched its neck in the cage and crowed. Fritha woke with a start. Baggi was gone, Beorn still snoring. Wynfrith and Ranulf were nowhere to be seen. Trust them to tag along with Baggi. His little henchmen, he called them. It was turning into a beautiful sunrise, everywhere decked in spring green, that special freshness of new growth. The dew sparkled on the leaves and the scent of the forest bed was as good as a feast to her nostrils.

Fritha built up the fire to get the stones hot for baking and searched in the cart for the flour cask. When she turned round Baggi had returned dangling a cock pheasant, its bright plumage brilliant in the sunshine. 'Look what I've found for us. It fell into my path.' He laughed. 'Get that in your stewpot before any one sees it.' He turned towards the stream. 'Where're the bairns?'

'With you… I thought you'd taken them with you?'

'No, they were fast asleep, dead to the world when I left. They must have gone rooting for you downstream. Our Wyn is good at finding mushrooms. They won't have gone far. The hound must be with them too.' Baggi smiled but it was a thin smile and he struck out along the path briskly. 'Wyn! Ranulf! Come and break your fast… now!' There was no response.

Fritha ran to the other cart and shook the couple inside roughly awake. 'Quick! Rise up… the kids have gone off the track somewhere. Just wait 'til I get hold of that little mischief… she'll get such a wallop! I told her not to wander.' But Fritha felt an icy coldness in her heart.

'Don't worry, they won't have gone far. Their bellies will guide them back. You'll see.' Lull tried to be a comfort but Fritha was having none of it.

'You stay here and keep shouting. I'm going back the way we came. Perhaps they'll be laiking downstream. Little Ran loves to splash about in water.'

She headed down to the ford, grasping her overcloak around her. Suddenly the sky was overcast and the chill wind bit into her face.

'Come on, childer, come back now! This is no time for hide and seek,' she called desperately.

By the second nightfall there was still no sighting of child or hound. All day Beorn and Baggi combed through the undergrowth, beating with sticks, calling out, penetrating further and further into the thick forest, leaving runic carvings on tree trunks as sign posts back to the carts. Only the scattering of birds disturbed the air, and black ravens watched silently from high in the branches.

Lull paced round and round the fire, reciting the old charm and adding new exhortations:

Erce, Erce, find each child, fetch the childer,
Bind those rascals tight and bring them safe back.
No ground shall keep them stuck or hidden.
No dragon's feast are they.
Whosoever steals them shall never thrive.
May they wither as fire withers wood,
As bramble and thistle hurt the thigh.
Show us thy power, thy skill to protect.
Thrice round the fire I go...

She felt sick in the stomach but kept up her vigil. Soon they would stroll back hand in hand, unaware of the anguish they had caused. They would be beaten soundly for their naughti-ness by Baggi, though he was tearful with thanks for their return. Then they would set off and leave this cursed place and journey onwards. Soon they would laugh at their fear. That was how it must be. But as the shadows lengthened and the weary men returned, fearful now of the worst, only Fritha remained hopeful.

'Wyn is a sensible lass. She'll find shelter in a cave or hollow, give Ranulf water from the stream. With water they will live and the nights are not cold. And the hound will guard them. He's old but his teeth can still draw blood.'

She sat hugging her knees, half in a dream, letting the fire go cold, watching the water bubbling from the spring. We must wait by this spring until they return.' She refused to see the worried looks of the two men. Two lost bairns and now a mad wife, that was all they needed.

No one slept that night, taking it in turns to pace around the fire. They could hear the howl of a she wolf, the screech of a vixen, but not the sound of children crying to be found. By the third day Fritha had eaten nothing. She tied strips of hemp cloth to the branches of the wellspring as votives to the water spirits to help in the search.

The men circled and recircled, each time taking another direction, hearing only the echo of their voices in the valley. Until finally, to their joy, a voice called back up to them.

Baggi tore excitedly through the bracken and found a wattle and mud hut, a hermit's cell, where a hoary old man stinking of rancid neglect stood with staff upraised, ready to defend himself.

'Peace, brother! Why such a rush on such a beautiful morn?'

'Have you seen our childer, a boy and a maid, this high?

They wandered off from our cart. I heard you calling... thought 'twas them.' Baggi sagged with disappointment.

'Nay, brother, my eyes are misty. I see no one but scent the air like a deer. I will pray for their souls and safety. How long did you say they've been gone?'

'For three moons since dawn.' All the strength was seeping out of him as he saw Fritha waving frantically from the high bank, waiting for a response, hoping with every breath for good news. How could he share what was in his heart, the fear that his bairns were lost, never to be found? That some cruel fate had lured them into the depths of the forest and it was all his fault.

'Fret not about what has befallen them. Search and ye shall find. Trust in the Lord Jesu and His Saints, pray to the Blessed Chad for a miracle. He will find them else bring you consolation. You must bear what must be borne. Travelling is a mighty dangerous thing even in the summer months. Perhaps someone from the clearings high in the far forest has found them – the shepherd or the woodburners. They are kindred folk. Word will travel down with the pedlars and packmen, holy men will pray for them and pass the word. Stay awhile until you have proof of their fate.'

The hermit made signs of blessing but Baggi took no heed. He plodded back up to the ridge with a heavy heart.

'Who's that down there? What news? Is there hope?'

'There is always hope, Fritha, while we have breath.' He sighed, trying to hide his fears from her. How he cursed himself for risking this trek. It was all his idea. He had forced the pace, bullied them into this madness. How could he ask them to move on now?

Fritha's cheeks were hollow, her bony figure hunched and suddenly shrunken. She was his helpmate, his breadmaker and latchkeeper, following him so trustfully. He had torn her from her kinfolk, and now something had torn her bairns from her hearth. He could not look her in her grey starved face. He could not face those burning dark eyes. She was of British stock, had the knowing without words, that gift of truth-divining as if she was feeling his thoughts.

'Are they are lost to us?' she croaked in a thin broken voice.

'The holy man says we must pray to the Saviour God for help. Our bairns may be safe in a sheep clearing with the wool gatherers. The forest is holy land, a wilderness of heath and scrublands stretching far to the west. We are still in Mercia. Over the big river is Dane law. We will not be welcome there. You must be brave.'

'Are you telling me to stop the search? That all is lost and we must leave our bairns to the mercy of the wolves, for the ravens to peck their unburied bones? Bagwulf, I'll not move one inch from this spot until I know their fate. Go on yourself but don't expect me to get in the cart. What's the point of making a homestead if there's no son to plough it after we're dust? Don't think I'll go on another measure. I'm rooted here where you brought us all and here I must stay.'

Baggi crumpled at her words as if stabbed by spears. Fritha stood dry-eyed and ice cold in her fury. 'Time enough for tears when we find their bones but I'll never come with you. I make my homestead here.'

It was Beorn who broke the silence, hearing their raised voices shouting, blaming, punishing each other. 'I didn't want to have to speak of this yet but on my last circle far out… there was fur and blood, the remains of a hound – a grey hound with brown streaks. I saw nothing else. I didn't want to dash your hopes that the hound was still guarding them. The ground is torn, he must have fought to the death… with something.'

'Let's see it, show me! Up where?' cried Fritha, suddenly alive, tearing at his grey woollen sleeve to drag him away.

'Stay, lass, there'll be nothing to see now. The ravens were waiting to finish their feast. Come sit with Lull. She fears her pains are coming. Help her bring new life to us all. The shock of this has let down the birthing waters. Please, Fritha, we'll not give up hope yet. Baggi and I must build a shelter round the fire.'

'This is no place to build a homestead.' Baggi shook his head, all the strength leaking out of his belly.

'Brother, you've had your say long enough. Here we stop for the summer at least. This will clear well enough for me. It's high, away from swamps, the ground is solid, there's water and sun from the south. Scrub is always easier to clear at the edge of a forest. I'll travel no further with you and Fritha is too heavy in heart to move on. Get the tools out of the cart while I gather sticks. We can plait some walls, build up the firestones.

'It's better to be busy and doing. Better than roaming the forest on a fruitless chase. I'm sorry but you know what I fear. I wanted to shield you from the truth.'

For the first time in his twenty summers, Beornwulf felt he was in charge, making the decisions for all of them. Cruel fate had stopped them on this trek. Here was where they were meant to stay. If he wished to go on Baggi must travel alone and that, he was sure, his brother would never do.

Fritha was sitting hidden from the others by the wellspring, her wellspring. Her prayers hung in tattered rags on the overhanging branches of the willow tree, the water spirit deaf to her pleas. Her heart was filled with yearning for her kids. In her imagination she was clasping them to her bosom, feeling their hot breath, the soft down of hair on Ran's head. Never to see them again... Her heart was numb with shock. She could see no colour only darkness and trees. Heavy was the wound she bore, like a knife thrust in her side. Soft sounds of a lullaby stuck in her throat as she rocked her empty arms. Gazing deep into the water she thought she could see their faces glimmering up at her. She cried out and turned away.

Suddenly there came another cry. The groan of a woman straining in labour. Fritha turned from her hidey hole as if in a trance. She was living in a half-remembered dream, a tale sung by the minstrel with the lyre in the mead hall. The cries grew louder, pulling her back, and she made for the cart to aid Lull.

This was a good sign surely, thought the two men as they nodded together. Now they must set to work on their homestead. By sunset with a bit of luck a wattle hut would be raised, a fire lit and a new bairn would be at Lull's breast. How Fritha would react to that, did not bear thinking of.

The Search

In the days following their fruitless search Baggi and Beorn gathered staves and prop posts, cut and lopped down branches, plaited wattle walls, fixed them into a ditch of stone footings, criss-crossed the roof and wove in heather and ling to thatch over the roof, leaving a hole in the centre for the smoke to escape. Lull nursed her baby daughter whom they sprinkled with dew, raised to the moon and named Hilde. It was a strong name for a girl but any baby would need to be tough to survive here. The bairn was swaddled in tightly to its mother in a makeshift sling, close to her breasts. Lull was afraid to let the child out of her sight.

Fritha took no interest in the baby once it was delivered safely. She could hardly bear to look into the soft pink face and blinking blue eyes. Every waking moment she busied herself with a hundred tasks and the rest of the time roamed alone over the tracks, searching, searching, for her lost children. Once she saw a traveller, rushing upon him like a mad beast and badgering him to tell her if he had heard of any children rescued from the forest in other clearings. He was almost scared to reply that he had not.

As the moon waxed and waned and high summer burned through the leafy branches on to the clearing, her spirits sank deeper into hopelessness. She withdrew into a sullen silence but worked like an ox, following the plough as it churned over the dark red soil, picking out and clearing away stones, gathering furze and kindling for the fire, tying them into thick prickly bundles. She scooped up the precious dung for the midden to feed the winter soil, letting it stink and dry in the open air. No wonder she fell asleep on her feet as she stirred the supper pot.

The men chopped down trees, split the timbers and loaded them on the cart, trundling the wood off to harden and dry in the clearing. This would make the stout walls for their winter dwelling. It would be a race against the season to plant out barley and peas, beans and oats, flax, hemp and linseed. The hens, fenced off in their own croft, clucked over a brood of chicks and soon there were spare cockerels for the pot.

Lull busied herself collecting rushes for the bed straw and lamplights, carrying water from the stream to douse the dry plantings, taking care never to stray far from the site or disturb Fritha at her digging by the well. She cured animal skins, carded goat's hair rovings into balls to spin from a shoulder spindle. They would need more cloth for the baby's wrappings and fresh undershifts for their rough cloth tunics. She was not fit yet for heavier work, feeling faint and weak if she walked too far in the sun.

It was Fritha who tended to the fire and the cauldron, gathered greenshoots, nettles, fungus and herbage for the pot. Often she found herself yearning for the old huts far away, for her kin whom she would never see again, for the Maytime feasting and dancing, the time of visits and merrymaking when hawkers peddled their gossip from clearing to clearing, relaying messages and greetings from far-flung members of family. Here it was all back-breaking hard slog in the heat of the sun and she could see no point to it. Beorn was their leader now. He had a child even if it was only a girl to marry off and find a bride gift for.

They had all helped to make a patch of bare earth for her, closer to the water and her spring; a leek and kale plot for the sowing of winter vegetables and pot herbs, for onions and greenshoots. Digging over the soil, clearing away roots and stones, flinging them on to a heap, was strangely satisfying. Raking over the tilth, planting out her precious seedlings and cuttings occupied her hands but not her mind. There was only the memory of Wynfrith tugging at her skirts, wanting to help, to share the task. The child would wait for the plants to rise straightaway and grew fractious when everything took so long to appear out of the soil.

Fritha turned her sunburnt face southwards to the sight of the oxen plodding forward, the iron plough biting into the earth, cutting neat strips across the cleared earth, the ridge made by the furrow deep and straight. The two men must work from dawn to dark to finish their ploughing if they were all to survive to next summer. Each night they returned with sweat like dew on their foreheads, ready only to eat, drink from the last of the mead cask and sleep.

Fritha woke every night before dawn, creeping out to sit with her loneliness by her spring. It gave her comfort to be there away from Lull who crooned over her newborn, suckling her contentedly whenever she stirred. It was strange that such a feeble maid had birthed so easily and brought forth such a strong baby with sturdy plump limbs, showing that her milk was rich enough.

There was no one but the deaf spirit of the well to hear

Fritha's woes. She sat under the grove of high trees pouring out her troubled thoughts on to the water. Sorrows bound her heart tightly like the hoops of a cask. Only here could she clasp and kiss her children, rest their heads on her knee as in the olden days when they were all together in the wagon.

As each moon set and each sun rose slowly over the forest, as deep shadows lifted, she wept for the pain to go away, for the earth to swallow her into itself as it had done her bairns. How she longed to be suckling her own babe at the breast again. The moon blood had never returned since Ran was birthed and now she feared she was dried up inside, as barren as thin soil. Only the moon blood brought a quickening in the belly and the swelling of new life.

She fingered her necklace of wooden beads, tearing at the leather thong to throw it away. What use had it been to her, bringing only bad luck and foul deeds? Her grandmother swore by the power of the peony charm but something stronger had taken away its strength to protect and now it would shrivel the soil, kill the growing things. They would all starve or die of the swamp fever.

Only then did she recall Grandmother's words: 'All things pass, so may this.' But would this feeling ever pass from her? It was like a weed which bound itself around berry bushes and blossom, sucking out the strength and goodness. Sitting here in the dark time when wild beasts lurked she felt like the sad-minded woman whose sufferings were endless in the minstrel's song. All things pass, so may this… How could she ever forget her own flesh and blood or stop her search for them in the wild wood? Would it ever be bearable?

But if she were to defend them all against the dark ones she would have to bestir herself, take heed of the other advice her old grandmother had given many times: 'Nothing grows from nothing. You must bless your labours, honour the earth, sprinkle it with water and blood for it to yield up its strength to your stock and flavour to your food.' A blessing of words and deeds, that was what she must offer if they were to survive. Hilde must live, thrive and multiply, if the loss of her own children was to be borne.

Fritha kicked her feet in the cold water, splashing away the dust and grime from between her toes. Her skin was like tanned hide, dark and tough as good feet should be, strong soles without blisters. I must grow with my plantings, feed them all well. For the first time in weeks she could face the dawn with determination and resolve. This now was her piece of the middle earth; she would make it rich with fruit and grain. Only then did she notice the blossom on the hedge-rows, the white of the may bending its branches like snow, the carpet of daisies and dandelions, buttercups and lady's smock, the pink dog roses peeking through the scrub and the humming of the bees about their morning business. The seasons went their way whatever a woman's suffering but here she would stay put, just in case...

Baggi woke with a start, feeling no body beside him warming his backside. Fritha was like a shadow, rising silently early each morning. He knew where she would be sitting and would not disturb her sorrowing. He had his own worries, feeling a frown as deep as a furrow across his brow. It was all going too well. Not, of course, the terrible loss of his bairns but Fritha mourned that enough for the two of them. Men must keep busy, not dwell over their troubles. They could not talk of it together. There was a high wall between them now and neither would tear it down. For Baggi it was a shield to hide behind so that he could get on with sowing, hoeing and keeping the livestock safe.

It was all going too well, though. He was having to admit that the site was good and Beorn right for once. The soil was clay mixed with sand and the rich loam of season upon season of rotted leaves. Virgin soil of the best quality. As long as the rains came regularly his plantings would survive. Yet still Baggi felt uneasy. Land such as this was often cleared for common grazing, on which to raise sheep and cows. The edge of the deep forest offered the advantages of shade and rich leaf mould as well as protection from the wind. Why had no one ever cleared it before? Surely they were not the first to pass over the ford and see its possibilities?

Did the land belong to the Kings of Mercia? To a bishop or earldorman, some thane in his great hall? Or was it land once tilled, now overgrown and forgotten, ripe for exploitation by young peasants like themselves? Was it part of the ancient hunting forest where the nobles chased the deer and boar? If so they were already trespassers and could all be hanged. He was sure at first that some thane's reeve would ride up one day and demand an explanation, rent, services and tithes for the honour of being permitted to better the land. But he had seen no one but the hermit and when they had returned to ask more of the holy man, his cell was abandoned and deserted. Baggi even wondered if he had dreamt their encounter on that fateful day.

What they needed was a thane, a shield protector, someone to replace the kinfolk they'd left behind. One lonely homestead, a few kine and ploughed fields could easily be destroyed by raiders, their harvest stolen and their wives carried away as slaves. He argued to Beorn that thanes in wild lands must be eager to find new settlers for their rough scrublands. The two of them had just seized an opportunity, being freemen not runaway slaves, but had no proof of their status only their own word.

This forest was so vast you could walk for days and nights and never see another clearing. They were treading over no one's hearth, and surely doing the owner a liege man's service by their careful husbandry? He could not bear to think that all this would go to waste for the want of somebody's permission.

Beorn thought him daft even to think of going looking for a thane. 'We can't pay rent or do services yet. There's too much to do here as it is.' They nearly came to blows over the matter in the heat of the midday sun.

Baggi sometimes sensed uneasily that they were being watched from a distance and that their presence was reported back to someone. They were too close to the thin edge of the forest to go unnoticed. What if they did all the work and then the cleared land was confiscated or given to someone else while they were branded thieves or hanged for their efforts? Better to be safe now than sorry later.

Somehow he would have to make it his task to seek out the owner and plead his case. He would have to journey back to the Minster in the swamp where the monks prayed in the clearing they called the 'Field of Martyrs'. He was sure he would find an answer there. But how to convince his brother it was the right way to go about things was another matter. Beorn could be as stubborn as an ass when the wind was in the right direction. Baggi would have to bide his time and seize the moment.

Lull and Beorn stood in the shadows. The baby had been restless, crying hard, and would not be shushed until they walked her up and down in the moonlight. It was then that they noticed Fritha, moving in her kale patch, etched naked against the midsummer moonlight. She was bending over, busying herself. She seemed to be digging in the dark.

'What's the crazy woman doing now?' Baggi joined them, watching her antics with concern.

'She's digging for something or else burying it. We can't see for sure. Tell her to come inside and rest. Time enough to delve and hoe when it's daylight,' whispered Beorn, shaking his head in amusement.

'Shush! Don't disturb her. She has a purpose. Don't laugh at her,' said Lull, hugging her baby. 'Who knows what I would do if I lost my bairn? Let her be. Whatever it is, she's doing no harm. She likes the old ways and the old charms. Come, inside, the baby is asleep now.'

They crept back into the hut silently but Baggi's heart was bursting with sadness. Why did his woman have to be so secretive, so odd, so silent? What on earth was she doing out there in the dark? Something she didn't want them to see, one of her granny's old tricks, some conjury or witchcraft? He should go out and stop her now. But Baggi sank back on to the ferns and straw. He hadn't the stomach to order her about. One look from those sad black eyes was deterrent enough. He was the slaughterer of Wyn and Ran. How could a father ever forget that?

First she dug up four sods from the corners of the growing patch and then Fritha carefully began to pinch out the top shoots from plants coming up, gathering green herbs, cabbage leaves, radishes, everything except burdock – she must not gather any of that. Next she placed some greenshoots in each hole, bits of each in turn. She could not add oil or honey or yeast yet for there was none to spare but a beaker of goat's milk was dropped in for good measure. A sprinkling of precious rock salt, hairs from the beasts and some from her own head too, peony seeds, fennel seeds, all fell on to the pile and as she walked from corner to corner she prayed the old prayer:

Eastward I stand and pray for your mercy.
Guardian of the heavens, Earth and sky.
Raise crops for us,
Fill the fields for us,
Let our seed double,
Fill this patch with food for all.
In the sprinkling of blood and water
Guard against witchcraft and foul deeds,
Make this land fruitful forever.

Slowly she paced around the tilled ground, sprinkling spring water into the holes, then carefully dug back the soil. Fritha was doing her best, following the old charm, and prayed she had missed nothing out, nothing important which might spoil the spell. If Baggi and Beorn would bless their plough and mattock, axe and hoe, then the meadows would surely flourish with pasture and the crops never fail. Just for good measure, though, she placed four cross sticks on top of the holes, hoping the Christian Gods, Father, Son and Holy Ghost, would add their power to the spell. She promised that when the harvest time came around she would bake a loaf filled with all the grain seeds she could muster and bury it under the ground as a thanksgiving. You had to put back what you take out, or crops fail. For the next three nights she must repeat the prayer at each corner or the charm would not be strong enough to see them through the winter.

Fritha returned to the hut and crept back to Baggi's side. For the first time in many moons she would sleep until first light and wake with no tears running down her cheeks. Yet she could sense danger on the wind. Why was the forest alive with the screeches of birds disturbed from their roosts? She thought she could scent woodsmoke on the air, the sound of hooves thundering through the bracken. Danger on the way! She could hear the sound of hounds somewhere to the west of the clearing. Raiders were coursing through the forest in search of plunder.

Wake up!' She tugged at Baggi's bare arm and kicked him. 'Wake up! All of you... Take the bairn to the bear pit... Can't you hear them? Hurry before we're roasted alive. I smell fire!'

Strangers

The settlers peered out cautiously from the wolf pit, lifting up the bracken to see if the raiders were gone. Lull crouched over Hilde to protect her and silence her crying. Beorn was already climbing out to see what havoc the robbers had left. They had stayed all night in the foul hole in the ground, terrified to move for fear of capture or worse. They stood up and stretched themselves, damp, chilled and sickened by the sight before them.

'Look at the hut, it's just a pile of ashes! All that work...' Beorn kicked the burning embers in disgust.

'But at least we weren't all roasted inside it. Thanks to Fritha we're safe.'

Baggi touched his wife's arm gently. How could he confess to nearly beating her black and blue for yanking him out of his bed, disturbing his slumbers?

Scattered around them were the feathered corpses of the hens. It looked as if a fox had run amok in their pen. The goats were scattered and their kids gone, the hut torched and the crops trampled over, but Fritha's kale patch stood unscathed; the rows of vegetables upright and still fit for the pot. Thanks to her sorcery she had heard hooves and night noise close by, allowing them to escape until the danger had passed. They owed her their lives and Baggi was proud of her. He would never smirk at her spells again, even if the sight of her testing the soil with her bare bum still made him roar with laughter.

'Shush! Someone's coming again! Look, the clearing...' cried Fritha in alarm. They all hid as best they could to see whether the raiders had left stragglers to mop up. A bedraggled girl crept out, examined the devastation, saw the kale patch and started to gather plants into her skirt.

'Hey, you! Where do you think you're going with my greens!' yelled Fritha, storming from her cover like a wild woman. The girl stepped back, caught in her thieving.

'I thought this hut was deserted, that you were killed or fled from the Danes. We're lost and in need of food. I was sent to gather what I could...' No more than a youngster, she dropped the plants at the sight of four dirty faces, four angry bodies, lined up against her. Fritha snatched them back but seeing that the young girl was afraid, softened her voice. 'Who are you then, wandering alone in the forest? Did they leave you behind?'

She fingered the cloth of the girl's gown in all its wondrous colours, seeing the bright scarlet of her leather boots and her red-gold braids bound with copper wire, the soft tissue veil edged with gold though torn and stained. This was no peasant woman.

'I am the Lady Ludmilla, daughter of Thane Wulfrun of the Tamworthig... my churl is not far away. We lost our horses and fled into the forest to escape the raiders yester eve. The tracks are afire from river to forest with Dane men from the Peak Lands. I'm much afeared that all my kin were lost on our journey to Thane Guthrie's hall. I have never been in such a great forest and you are the first woodfolk I have met. I am at your mercy, but pray don't harm me. My father will reward all who come to my aid. Who is your liege lord here?'

Ludmilla was shaking. She had never been so close to peasants before; such bedraggled wild woodfolk with fiercesome faces.

Her voice was cultured in an accent it was hard for Baggi to understand but he recognised her fear of them.

'You're welcome to rest by our fire. That's all the devils have left us, as you see. We too escaped into the wood. They've killed and stolen our stock, our harvest is not yet ready and much is destroyed, but what we have we will share.'

'Who is the Hlaford, the breadkeeper, in this forest?' asked the lady again.

'We're new to this homestead and as yet have come across no lord. Naught but travellers such as yourself.'

'So you've no protector to help you with your losses?'

'No! And no one to make us do services or pay rent either. We stand or fall by our own efforts,' Beorn was quick to add. Ludmilla smiled. She could not understand a word he was saying; his dialect was lilting and thick, not a Mercian sound.

'Come,' said Fritha gently, 'sit by the spring and take some water. It has been a long night for all of us. You will not be used to such humble and hardy people as we. We fled to escape from warring chieftains and here we are back in the middle of it again.' She brought Lull and her baby to show to the lady.

'See – eyes like bluebells and sturdy limbs, Hilde should do well,' Lull mumbled to the lady who was unused to such small creatures, backing away awkwardly from the child. Lull gazed in awe at her tattered gown. 'This cloth is so soft and the threads of gold embroidered so richly.'

Fritha ventured to finger it softly, 'I've never seen such colours nor touched anything so beautiful. Like the petals of a silken rose I seen once on a wreath in the old church.'

'It was to have been my betrothal gown but now it is ruined,' said Ludmilla, brushing it down and examining the mud stains tearfully. She fingered the clasp of her leather belt with long nails as sharp as eagle's claws. Bracelets jangled at her wrists and she wore a necklet of twisted gold. Fritha and Lull stared in wonder at her adornments.

'Is that so, you are to be wed?' The women smiled.

Suddenly Lady Ludmilla found herself weeping with tiredness and disappointment, telling them about the old thane, Guthrie, a friend of her father, to whom she was promised, her reluctance to wed him, and then the terrible journey and fear that her poor brother Edgar was captured or slain. Then she noticed that the shadows were deepening and the sun had long passed overhead. 'My churl, Osbald, will be waiting for me downstream where we hid. I am too tired to walk back. My servant will think me dead and go on without me. What should I do?'

'Baggi will go and tell him you are safe with us here. He can join us. Perhaps he'll help us in the fields and we'll cook something in the pot. Tomorrow you can return. Rest by the spring for now.'

Fritha could see that the girl was quite faint with hunger and fear. The pot would have to feed them all somehow.

Later, as the sun set behind the oak forest, the weary group sat around the firestones as they had done on the very first night of their arrival. The two strangers sat alongside them, sipping meagre broth from a wooden bowl in their turn. It was the only utensil left beside Fritha's bucket. Osbald offered his helmet to his lady to sup from but she turned up her nose at the smell of his damp sweaty hair. He boasted about the Great Hall at Tamworthig while his lady nodded off, full of ale from the cask. This rescue was turning into an adventure now, but soon the maid must face her father and the fate awaiting her.

They dozed by the spring, watching the prayer cloths flutter, and Fritha told the lady about her lost children and how she found comfort by the water. How she planted marigolds with buttery petals and flowers from the hedgerows. Ludmilla was reminded of the shrine at the Minster where the Blessed Chad performed miracles for the faithful at his holy well. If she prayed to the spirit of the spring, would it help St Werburga rescue her from marriage to an old man?

She went to rinse her face and her arms slipped gently into the spring and sank down, waving under the surface. As the evening drew on and the ale weighed down her eyelids she accepted that her fate was sealed. There was nothing more to be done.

Close by a horn blew, loud and confident. They had no time to scatter before a posse of horses rode into the field followed by a flurry of running men with shields and spears who surrounded them quickly. The terrified group faced the thick thighs of an armed man on horseback who peered down at each of them in turn until his eyes caught sight of the girl's silken veil. 'Are you of Aethelflaeda's kin, daughter of Wulfrun the ring giver? Have you been kept against your will by these ruffians?' The servant stepped forward, trying to defend her.

'Sire, I'm Osbald, churl to Wulfrun. My lady's come to no harm. We have been fed and watered by these kind folk, settlers in the forest. Do them no harm, I beg you.'

'Let the lady speak for herself.' The leader pointed his sword and lifted her veil to see the fine square face with its flushed cheeks and ale-sparkling eyes, the rosebud lips and shapely outline of the young maid. He was well satisfied by what he saw there. She in turn saw the strong face of a warrior with a scar across his cheek, hair the colour of harvest corn, the bull-like figure of youth and strength. She bowed meekly in submission.

'My servant speaks only the truth. How come you know of our plight and of my kin?'

'Your brother awaits in my hall. Those raiders did not get far before we clashed swords and brought them low. Others, I see, took their revenge in the forest. He asked us to hunt for you, knowing you had taken flight. This part of the forest is mine, together with all who dwell therein. Even now the Lady Aethelflaeda of Tamworthig is on her horse, sword in hand, ready to chase the northmen back over the Trent. You will return with us to the hall and afterwards to your father's house. Until these brigands are gone, it is not safe for noble-women to be abroad.'

'Whom do I address as my escort and lord?' asked the Lady Ludmilla with interest.

'I am Thane Godfrid of the Long Hall, at your service.' The man jumped from his horse, standing firm as a tree trunk. 'In whose service are these?' He looked around at the straggle of settlers and their burnt out hut.

'They are in need of a lord protector, sire, one who will help them replace their stock, build their hut and restore this clearing.' Ludmilla smiled sweetly and Osbald was not fooled. Here be mischief indeed. What was brewing here would upset Thane Guthrie's apple cart. In one fell swoop the Lady Ludmilla found her young liege lord and poor Baggi and Beorn theirs as well.

Along with his gift of cows and five acres of land each, they must work every Moonday on their lord's land, at least three days a week at harvest, reap him an acre of oats, pay the hearth penny and a tax for his church, and besides all that render him such other services as he bespoke. The price of being a freeman did not come cheap.

The settlers waved off Thane Godfrid's rescue party without a word. For months they had seen not a soul. Since that day's sun had risen and set it seemed the whole of Mercia had ridden over their ground and knocked down their door. Who could believe they'd had such company? Now it was back to weaving lattice branches and bracken fronds. Would their fortunes ever change?

Miracles

꩜

There were hundreds of tasks for the homesteaders to finish by the time of harvest moon. Sometimes Fritha looked out proudly at stooks of hay, sacks of beans and peas stored for winter porridge, oxen fattening with the swine on acorns and autumn nuts, hens scratting in her kale patch which was thick with cabbages, onions, leeks. She was bone weary though from all their efforts.

Baggi and Beorn worked late into the dusk light to make crofts, clear more land, gather brushwood for the women to bundle and store. They dug ditches and soakaways, coppiced under the trees, gathered the hard dried beams brought on the cart for the winter dwelling. Together they raised them, arched over like the upturned hull of a boat, and sank them into stone-lined trenches before carefully weaving and filling the wattle walls.

The thane of the Long Hall sent his reeve to set terms and conditions of tenure, leasing them land and grazing rights, inspecting their work and telling them to be ready for service for their new thane's harvest. Each day they set out early for Long Hall, over the ridge and down into the valley where his fields lay alongside a fine wooden church and the thatched hall dwellings, which made their own little hut seem very small. Here they joined other peasants to bring in grain, peas or barley, whatever was demanded of them. At dusk they tramped wearily home, bringing the women, starved of gossip, news of the courtship of the Lady Ludmilla by the young thane. The field men were fed with harvest loaves and ale, salted herrings and goat's cheese, and often saved bits in their pouch for Hilde to pounce on. Sometimes they fell asleep as they sat by the fire.

The past season had sped by so fast; the visit of Lady Ludmilla, the raid and Fritha's lost children seemed like a far off dream. Yet as she lay in the darkness, hearing the harvest gales rattle and moan through the forest, she often heard her little ones crying out: 'Ma... am.' Then she rose quickly, dreaming they were safe somewhere, just waiting for her to collect them and she must run through the storm of whirling leaves to seize them in her arms. But they always disappeared into the mist. She would waken feeling sick and shaky. One morning the sickness overwhelmed her so fiercely that she swooned with dizziness. Fritha knew then her prayers were answered at last. This was perhaps a sign of life, not death.

By Martinmass she was sure that there was a child growing in her belly which was firm and round, a child that squirmed and kicked, making her back ache, her breasts swell and itch more than usual. It was difficult to reckon when it would be born. Please Gods, make it in the spring when food would grow again and the hens lay eggs. Fritha feared the long darkness of winter. Would they survive the cold and wetness of this damp ridge? Had they cut enough kindling for the hearth? Would her pot herbs last out?

The women took to wandering through the woodlands with the small babe, picking blackberries, beechnuts, crab apples, sloes. The last of the harebells nodded in the breeze and the scent of smoke tinged their nostrils with homesickness for the old settlement and their kin. This time last year nothing but excitement lay before them. But now was no time for regret for there was so much to gather. They had pannage and herbage of their part of the forest edge. Lull caught prickly hogs to bake in mud on the fire while Fritha checked barley sproutings for the ale-making and the hive where a swarm of bees safely captured from the treetops was settling in for the winter. She would sometimes smile with pride at all they had made from nothing.

By a rush light dipped in meat fat they spun wool and hairs and wove on the pegged loom, piecing together bits of cloth, fur and hide into warm bootees. There was no time for fancy colourings like the Lady Ludmilla's red boots. All their cloth was dark and dull as ground oats.

But how Fritha longed for something to wear as red and as bold as the peony petals; as purple and soft as the harebell or the blackberry stains on her fingers. She had gathered more sacred herbs, dried them and shaken them on to a piece of cloth to store in a dry purse. Seeds were so precious, the promise of future growth, but she was sad that the summer flowers were over and the colours of autumn would soon disappear into a uniform brown. Tomorrow Lull must prepare their precious salt for the ox killing.

The pedlar man called for the last time this year with his knapsack of wares. Sadly there was nothing to spare for his coloured trinkets and threads but he brought news of the great battle deeds of Queen Aethelflaeda, wondrous tales of her beating back the northmen again, and of how the fair Lady Ludmilla had begun to ignore old Thane Guthrie in favour of the knight of Long Hall.

The track was wider now and the lord's knights rode past on their way to hunt; sometimes a holy man stopped for water at the well and gave them a blessing. As her baby swelled and grew, Fritha feared all was not well. They laughed at her hard belly which was always outlined by grime on her tunic. Lull was never as big as this. By now Hilde was crawling and would burn her fingers on the hot stones if not watched constantly. Lull became irritable and complained that the hut was too small, the soakways a danger for her bairn, tying a leather thong from her wrist to the babe so she could not wander far. Most of the time the child was tied safely to her back. The women did not find it easy to share the hearth chores but Fritha, usually the stronger of the two, found she often had to rest a while to get her breath, such was the effort of carrying this child.

Soon they were plunged into a harsh cold winter. How Fritha prayed to her well that the babe would stay warm and snug in her belly, until the days lengthened and the frost did not nip so hard on her toes and fingers. Sometimes she would dip them in warm pee to cure their itching. They heated the ale with hot stones and threw in herbs to warm the belly. She also dropped peony seeds into her own brew, along with dried wild raspberry leaves as her mother once did for a quick and safe birthing.

'Have you got a calf in there?' laughed Baggi, patting her bulge. 'How will it get out?'

'Same way as the others – with a lot of cursing and sweating,' Fritha joked, trying to hide her fear. Sometimes she was afeared to sleep in case her belly burst like a ripe pod.

Lull and Fritha talked about the strangers who passed the homestead on their way from the Minster, a full day's walk down into the misty swampy valley. The forest woodburners said it was a dismal grey place, little more than a few hovels beside the monks' enclosure and the shrine of the Blessed Chad. Lull begged to make the journey but Beorn insisted they wait until the spring. She sulked with disappointment but perked up as the sun rose higher in the sky and the daylight hours drew out. Soon the snowflowers lit up the forest hollows with tiny green spears. When would all the other colours come back to Fritha's well?

It was always called Fritha's well. Fritha had found the source, tended the patch, nurtured the soil, and so far it had not failed them even on the iciest of days. No one ever dared speak openly of the terrible night of their coming or of the lost bairns whose bones had no burial. Whenever travellers stopped to take water, Fritha would take them aside quietly to ask if they had heard tell of babes lost in the woods and taken up by strangers. Heads would be shaken sadly and she would fall silent, shrinking into the shadows away from the others.

One day followed another in this way until one fateful morning when Fritha woke with a searing pain across her lower back. It came and went as she did her round of tasks.

This pain was not like her other birthings, squeezing and holding, but sharper, as if her insides were ripped by a rusty blade. It was all she could do finally to seek out Lull and crawl into the hut, to lie gasping until the bearing down began. She squatted and crouched over fresh bedding, trying not to scream and waste breath. It came in its own good time, slithering out, a purple girl child, tiny for the size of her mother. Frith bit the cord and saw to the rest with Lull hovering nervously by. She had gathered the babe to her breast when another sharp searing pain forced her down again to drop the afterbirth. There was a rush of blood and another tiny creature fought its way out of her, lying red and silent before them.

Lull took one look and screamed in horror. 'Two bairns

in one go! She's bewitched...' She ran to call the men folk to witness this strange event.

Fritha stared down at the little creature struggling for life, so tiny, so perfect in form, face screwed up in rage though the sound of its crying was weak and pitiful. Her heart was filled with love for them; one lusty, kicking and strong, the other whimpering like a puppy, struggling to survive. She hardly dared touch the boy child. Then came another afterbirth, thinner and not so rich as the first. These she would bake and eat for herself, to strengthen her milk. Twin bairns, double seed.

The spirit of the well had looked kindly upon her after all, answered the prayer cloths waving in the branches. Her seed was doubled. She found the tears running down her cheeks; tears of love, relief and thanks. Baggi stood in the doorway breathless, his brow furrowed. Lull pushed inside, pointing.

'Look! I told you... take them away, both of them.' She made to snatch the weakest babe but Fritha warded her off.

'Don't you touch them, they're mine! Help me wrap them tight in swaddles.'

'I'm not swaddling them. 'Tis witchcraft or worse. 'Tis against nature.' Lull turned to the men for support.

'Lull! How could you say such gubbins? The Gods have given me back what was lost... See! One of each for Wyn and Ran.' Fritha was feeling unexpectedly strong and full of power.

'Put them by... or at least put the runt away. One must go, sown in wickedness and mischief.'

'What are you on about?' asked Baggi, puzzled by the fuss at first.

'She has taken your seed and his to do this.' Lull's finger stabbed at her husband accusingly. 'How else do you get two? How could you take my man, Fritha? Wasn't one enough?'

'Lull, you're moonstruck! Tell her, Baggi... tell her, Beorn. I've shamed no one. 'Twas the spirit of the well who answered my pleas... returned to me what was snatched away. Wyn and Ran back with me again. Tell her, Baggi.'

Fritha held out her babes to him. The man hung back, knowing this to be a cause of shame whispered about in his family far back. Twins were bad news, a sign that magic was afoot. One must always be put away so the other could thrive. A woman could not feed two. It was against nature. Had his woman been unfaithful behind his back, crept to Beorn in the darkness or the woods?

Anger and suspicion rose in his breast and Fritha, seeing his scowl, held on to the babes tightly. 'Don't you look at me like that! As the High God of Heaven is my witness, Beorn owes you no wergeld, no compensation. These are mine and yourn, both of them. I prayed for double seed for all our crops a while back before the raiders came...

'You all laughed at my charms and spellings but I prayed to the water spirit for double seed and we've been given it. Why should a woman not give birth to twine? We have two breasts or had you not noticed? And these will soon be full of milk.' Fritha pleaded but her man was not sure.

'You've allus been off your head, woman. Two bairns means only one thing. Two fathers.' Baggi turned to his brother. 'A curse on you for bringing shame to us! I demand wergeld – money or blood.' He pushed Beorn hard and stormed out of the hut.

'Hang on there, brother, don't you go a-cursing of me for summat I never did! I've never looked at the track she were on, that crazy wife of yourn. Not once, not ever... do you hear me? I have my own bairn, why should I want of yourn?'

'That's right, you tell them,' screamed Fritha, stunned by the accusations flying about like birds trapped in a hut.

'Not so fast, Beorn. She witched you, that's what. She was so desperate for seed that she got you befuddled with ale so you never saw which woman you were lying with…' Lull was not going to stop the fight now.

'When have we ever brewed ale strong enough to make us legless? It's so watered down as to be only child's beer. You've been careful to make our barley sprouts last through, so don't give me that one or you'll feel my fist in your lughole!'

'LEAVE ME BE!' shouted the mother as she fixed the babes to her swollen breasts. 'See, they can feed. Over my dead body will you take one away. There's been no shaming. Go and calm down Baggi before it comes to a fight. There've been twoers before in your kin, he knows it.'

'Aye, and one was left out for the wolves to devour, to ward the evil from the camp,' said Lull. 'Keep the girl and I'll take the runt out into the wildwood and we'll speak no more of this matter.' She tried again to snatch up the smaller babe who was struggling to catch hold of his mother's teat.

'Don't you dare! This forest has had two of my flesh, it's not going to feast on a third. You're wrong, Lull. It's you who have heard too many old wifies' tales. We've been blessed, not cursed. Let the high heavenly sword strike me down dead if I lie.' Fritha tore at her breast. 'You'll have to kill me first before I yield up a child to you.'

'I'll take no more of your lies!' her sister-in-law screamed. 'Now look what you've done to us all. I'm not staying here a moment longer.'

She stormed out into the darkness, Hilde crying, the babies tugging harder now.

Fritha was so angry she screamed, 'Get out of this hut then, all of you! I'll manage on me own. Get yourself another one and don't darken this door again, any of you... and that goes for you, Bagwulf, if you believed any of them lies.'

Thus began the great chill at Fritha's well which split the clearing into two parts and lasted many moons. Beorn and Lull gathered their belongings and a few bits and pieces which were not theirs for good measure. They made another hut far afield at the bottom of the clearing, out of sight, close to another thin stream. Baggi stayed behind, unsure and saddened. But he had no time to build himself another dwelling. For many weeks, despite sharing their shelter, he never looked once in the direction of his bairns. Fritha still prepared food which was divided up between the two groups and eaten in silence. An icy chill reigned where once was warmth and laughter.

Sadness and silence shrouded the homesteads with the last of the winter snows, blanketing the forest in a blinding whiteness. Reluctantly Baggi studied the dark-haired girl and the flaxen boy. Even he had to admit to himself that they were the spitten of Ranwulf and Wyn. It brought tears to his eyes to see Fritha believing so utterly that her lost children had been returned to her by kindly spirits. She was even calling them by the old names though he knew it was wrong to do so.

'Give them fresh names, woman. This is a second chance for all of us, perhaps. New names for new bairns, eh?' He found himself smiling into the blinking blue eyes of his son.

'Then he must carry your name but we'll call him Wulf. This one is a gift from the Gods and we'll call her Godgifu, or Gifu for short. What do you think?' The thaw was beginning at Fritha's well.

When the pathways were clearer and the spring floods over, Baggi and Fritha took the twins to the wooden church at the Long Hall for a priest's blessing with holy water, just to be doubly sure that they would thrive. Fritha yearned to ask Lull and Beorn to their little feast but they were stranded in their new homestead, fast in for weeks in the snow and wet. She had asked the priest if he thought her bairns cursed but to her surprise he'd smiled and said the Saviour of mankind had twins among his kinfolk, sturdy henchmen in Galilee, wherever that was. If the Saviour did not turn them away then Lull and her kind were wrong.

The priest did, however, whisper that perhaps an excess of zeal on Baggi's part had caused this wonder. They must never copulate when the moon blood was high. It turned hair red and disturbed the order of things. His seed must be rich indeed.

This news put a skip in Fritha's step. The air was lightening, spring was round the corner, but as the time drew close to the season of their first coming to Frithaswell she wept again for Wyn and Ran. Then the joy of two babes at her breast eased the pain in her heart. All things passed and so would this but the memory of her loss would remain with her 'til her last breath.

Strange Harvest

⟨ornament⟩

'I'll never marry an old man now that I have seen Godfrid. He has captured my heart,' Lady Ludmilla had vowed to her parents, stamping her foot. Her mother just sighed and shook her head.

'Whoever marries for love alone? Do you think I felt such passion for your father when we were wed? That may come later if you are favoured… bedding down together, getting used to each other's ways and moods. Love is only the silliness in a minstrel's tale. How can men do battle work with such a weakness biting their heels, child? Now settle down and accept what is best for you.'

But Ludmilla was not going to let the handsome Godfrid, her warrior, slip through the net she was spinning for him. At every opportunity she sought him alone, shamelessly using Edgar as her chaperone. It was not difficult to persuade the thane that she was his heart's desire, sending him off quickly to beg for her hand as her rescuer and champion.

Wulfrun coughed and spluttered that there were difficulties, but as this knight had saved both his son and his daughter then surely something might be arranged to free Ludmilla from her trothing pledge.

'We'll have to soothe Thane Guthrie's pride with silver and of course you must return his betrothal gift. That golden armlet is a rare prize, crafted in the time of the great King Alfred. He told me it was highly valued among his kin.'

Only then did Ludmilla realise that it had not been on her wrist for weeks or even months. She could not recall the last time it had glistened in the sunshine or sparkled on the silken edge of her long sleeve. Her heart thudded. If the armlet were lost, how could she give back word and return the thane's token? She would never be free now to warm the bride bed of her hero.

With heavy heart she found herself riding once more through the great forest, treading the serpent's paths again, bogged down in mud and mire. The snows had melted fast, leaving the tracks flooded and hard to find. She made to turn back but Osbald Halfdane urged her on though both of them knew it would be like finding a bone needle in a hay stook.

'If you leave it much longer the spring growth will cover over the bare ground and the jewel will be buried forever then.' Osbald was in no mood to pander to his stubborn charge. If she wanted to release herself from her pledge she would have to find the armlet.

Ludmilla's riding knights rode with them over mud and swamp, back along the track north to the exact spot where the two of them had escaped the Dane raiders, at last finding the swollen stream and grove of trees lining the bank near Baggi's clearing. It looked so different in the chill air, dark bare branches laced overhead, a covering of rotting leaves on the red earth. There they met one peasant and his wife who greeted them with fear, not recognising the lady in the midst of the fierce horsemen. Ludmilla was wrapped against the chill in a thick blue wool overmantle edged with fur, a warm hood masking her face. This time the party was well prepared with staves and a wicker basket of loaves, cold meat and cheeses. Baggi bent low and asked the purpose of their visit in such rough weather.

Ludmilla reminded him of their meeting and described the jewel she had lost somewhere close by. If these peasants had stolen and sold it, she was sure they would have left this hovel by now to overwinter in the warmth of some township. The poor family looked honest enough and she gazed in amazement at the sight of two babies wrapped in skin pouches tied against the woman's chest. Ludmilla asked her if she recalled whether there had been a golden armlet on her sleeve when she'd come to their homestead. Fritha smiled and nodded. Not one minute of that visit had she forgotten. Lull and she loved to dwell on every detail round the hearth before their quarrel. The terrible raiders, the night in the pit, the arrival of the fine lady and her rescue by Thane Godfrid... who could forget such an eventful day?

'So you did see an armlet on my sleeve?' Ludmilla was impatient to be moving on.

'Aye, a beautiful ring of gold with red stones, the colour of corn poppies as I recall. Yes, we seed it there.' Fritha pointed to her wrist. 'And the twisted ring, a shoulder clasp with a dragon's head...'

'Yes, yes... I have those still. It's the armlet which is lost and must be found, do you hear?'

Fritha bowed low and answered. 'We've found no jewel, my lady, but we'll search our fields and tracks for you when we turn the soil over and broadcast the seed. My eyes are still sharp and always bent to the earth. We'll do our best.'

'See to it then!' The lady nodded briskly and turned her horse to hide her frustration. She had so hoped it would be just lying there waiting to be found. Damn the thing! She had been so besotted with the fine features of her lord, the surprise of his timely arrival and relief that Edgar was safe, that she recalled little of her visit here. Now they must proceed slowly on foot to the Long Hall, searching in the mud. It was a hopeless task.

Osbald thanked the couple curtly. He did not trust forest peasants, who were too proud and independent for his liking. This lot seemed harmless, winter thin and starved enough not to have sold a rare jewel. They were sadly in need of a spring wash. It must be hard to live in such a dreary place. He was glad the High Lord of heaven, in His mercy, had seen him born to churls and not peasants.

The slow trek back to Long Hall yielded no joy and Ludmilla confessed her despair to her lord.

'Perhaps the robber Danes found it and it is now over the Trent. But we will be wed, fear not,' he soothed her. 'Thane Guthrie is a reasonable man. He'll take a fair weight of gold for it. These things happen... Fret not over such a bauble.'

'I wish it were a mere bauble, Godfrid. Oh, it's all my fault! I cared nothing for the old man and so was careless with his jewel. Father has no more gold to spare on my behalf. He says I have drained his coffers enough,' sighed Ludmilla.

'There'll be a way, surely?' answered her love, patting her arm, knowing his own money chest was empty and his purse light. If these were the sad facts perhaps he too would have to look elsewhere and find some rich widow to warm his cold bed.

*

As the spring fields turned to green in the clearing, the fresh growth unfurled. Wulf put on a little weight but Gifu the greedy, plump and eager at the breast, stole what Fritha could offer and demanded extra sops. Wulf's skin was scaly and raw. His mother marvelled the mite survived at all. She gave him fresh milk from the goat in a little pouch which he could suck and soon his limbs fleshed out and he breathed easier, beginning to take more interest in the world beyond her teat, much to Fritha's relief.

Since the lady's visit she was always poking in her kale patch or along the edges of fields, just in case, but found nothing. What it must be like to live so careless of gold and precious stones, to wear expensive blue-dyed wool in the mud and ride a fine horse! It was a world she could barely imagine. Though it did not seem to have made the wench contented with her lot for her eyes were restless and afeared, Fritha remembered.

She herself may not have many possessions but she felt so blessed to have a strong man's aid and two bonny bairns. It was a pity that the harsh words of last winter had never been forgotten. Beorn and Baggi must still work together in the fields but the old joking banter had gone. Tasks were shared in silence whenever she was around. Sometimes she caught sight of Lull digging over her patch in the far distance with little Hilde now toddling behind her, still tied with a wrist thong.

It was good to have the hearth to herself but sometimes she felt weariness overwhelm her. How Lull would have enjoyed seeing the lady again! And there was no one with whom to share her worries over Wulf. He did not gurgle or prattle or smile half as much as Wyn or Ran or Gifu. Baggi was right to give him a fresh name. He was nothing like her lost son. He was special in a strange way. Her heart was stone heavy at the thought and from all the tasks she must undertake to keep them fed and watered; much worse than tending sheep, goats and hens which filled the homestead. Now they had ducks and some geese which gave big eggs and feathers, but they were such messy creatures and it was hard to scrape up their droppings for the precious dung heap.

Baggi and Beorn had a plan to dam the stream and channel it into a big pond; a pool for ducks and for catching fish. It was going to take them all the spare summer hours to dig out and edge the water. She wondered what Lull thought of this bright idea. As if on cue she saw her sister-in-law approach, carrying her child and a bucket towards the well. Lull nodded coolly, trying not to look her in the face, but little Hilde, once set down, scampered across to chase the ducks, falling flat on her face and howling hard. She was at that meddlesome age, no longer a baby but not yet a child, and needed some watching.

'Keep out of the water, Hilde!' Lull called, and Fritha lifted up Gifu to see what was going on. The toddler wanted to reach up, to play and touch. She was too young to sense the coolness in the air between the mothers. Fritha tried to fill the silence.

'We had another visit from yon lady from the Great Hall. Would you believe she was searching for a lost jewel? I thought the knights would beat us and take us away. I think they believed we'd stolen it from her. However will she find her bangle in all this mud? But I said we'd keep an eye out.'

'You did right... Come away, Hilde, don't pester. And keep off them boulders, they're slippery...' shouted Lull, seeing her child hovering by the spring, stretching her hands to the water. A splash sent them both rushing to the bairn who lay soaked and kicking in the water. Fritha grabbed at her tunic and fished the little body out quickly. Hilde was coughing and spluttering but unhurt. Shocked and protesting, she clutched a tangle of weed in her hand.

'Come, bring her to the fire and dry her off, Lull.'

'Thanks... she's such a handful. I don't know how you manage with two of them, I really don't.' Lull smiled and cuddled her daughter with relief.

'You just do. Gifu is easy though poor Wulf is still weak. But then, boys often are,' answered Fritha, smiling back.

'They are so like you.'

'Do you think so?'

'The girl especially, so dark... Gifu, isn't it?'

'Aye, Godgifu... God's gift, double seed.'

'Fritha?'

'Yes?'

'This has gone on too long. It has been a bad winter with no one to chase away the nightglooms. I've missed our hearth-talk and your help winding the wool. Perhaps we were all overwrought and hasty, too easily vexed?' Lull bent her head and fell silent.

'Harsh words are so easy to say and hard to forget,' Fritha said finally. 'It's good to have my own hearth and pot, but you are welcome to call anytime. Two pairs of hands make any chore seem easier, don't you think? Besides, I have missed your company.'

Lull pressed her hand briefly then glanced at Hilde. 'What's that child chewing on now? Spit it out!' Hilde was biting on the weeds in her hand, mouthing at something covered in mud. 'Put that down!' Lull snatched away the object and the child howled again.

She looked more closely at the dirty thing, fingering its smooth surface, feeling the hollowness. She brushed it on her top skirt, rubbing away weed. It was a perfect circle. Fritha gasped when she saw it.

'Lull! See, the armlet... Hilde has found us the lady's jewel!

She must have dropped it in the water. See how it's gold studded with stones. No wonder the Lady was eager to find it again. Look how the jewels are set into the gold, like fine metal wire. The pattern's so delicate. Baggi, Beorn! Come quickly and see what the child has found in the spring... treasure from the holy well... again!'

The women smiled warmly at each other for the first time in many moons.

Fritha took her bucket to the spring, touching the prayer strips reverently as they fluttered in the breeze. First she squatted down to sprinkle herself with a blessing of water in thanksgiving. Their swift return of the armlet to Long Hall had brought great joy to its owner and proof of their loyalty to Thane Godfrid's hall. Osbald Halfdane returned with a bolt of fine cloth, enough to make two over tunics for the women and a shift for Hilde. There were also carved bone rings for the babes to chew on and an invitation to the feasting when the wedding took place.

How Fritha pinched her arm to believe she was awake and not asleep then! There they were, sitting at the feast boards in the Long Hall while the harp was playing and the minstrel singing the old Lays of Beowulf, the battle hero. Above her, woollen hangings wafted from the smoky rafters where smoke coiled up to the roof hole. Hounds were yapping noisily but their babes slept safely in a corner. The boards were full of fine glazed earthenware flagons, the like of which neither woman had ever touched before. They were belly-stuffed with roasted meat and fine mead, honey cakes and thick bread. Their horn beakers were kept brimming as honoured guests at the wedding feast. Baggi's cheeks were as red as hot stones and Beorn loosened his belt before swallowing the last dregs of his beer.

On the high table sat the lord and his new lady, wearing the morning after gift of amber beads as a token of her bedworthiness. Ludmilla was wearing a fine gown of cornflower blue, worked and embroidered with gold lacework, silk sleeves edged in deepest scarlet as bright as a summer meadow. Her veil was like a cobweb of gauzy silk around which she wore a circlet of fresh flowers. Thane Godfrid was roaring drunk with a pink flush on him like a shiny apple. He wore a tunic of darkest brown like tree bark. It was edged with braid, as shiny as his fiery hair, and Fritha giggled to remember the priest's warning about lustful excess leading to a red-haired baby.

The wedding feast had lasted many days; first came the great thanes and kin from the shire hundreds, then the lower kin, and lastly the foresters and tenants. Each group was feasted according to rank and custom.

For days before the feast Lull and Fritha just stared at the gifts they'd received, afraid to soil them or touch anything in case it vanished in a puff of smoke. Then they rinsed their fingers and gently felt over the cloth, trying to imagine what would happen if they did this or that. Could they squeeze something else out of the length? They could hardly bear to take the sharpened knife to it but the thought of the feast and going there naked drove them on to make the first cut. Of one thing they were both certain: the cloth must be dyed a bright colour. No oatmeal, sludge or muddy hue but something to brighten their lives forever, the colour of the peony globe or the corn poppy, buttercup yellow or bright leaf green. There was so much colour to choose from in the green woods as the may blossom covered the field edges.

At last they would have something to brighten the drabness.

It was time to test out last year's dried onion skins with a piece of madder root. Now the metal pot which had fed them all winter must be cleaned out and dried in the sun, filled with spring water and clean hot stones, brought to the boil to soak the cloth, turning it to the richest golden orange. The cloth was then hung out and dried straight on some branches together with a line of dead crows flapping beside it to keep off birds and their droppings.

In the heat of the sun, the cloth dried a little streakily but was soon ready for sewing. Fritha could not wait for the feast day to show off her new finery and her leather belt carved with animals. She rinsed her body in the spring, scrubbing from her face all the winter's grime and oiling her braids to make them shine. She plaited a few flowers into them also. Then over her head she slipped the tunic, drinking in its newness. She covered her head with the last bit of unbleached linen fixed with two bone clasps. For once she felt like a marigold, shining so brightly that all the bees would surely buzz to her scent.

As she stood by the well she could see the men hard at work in their field strips, full of peas and corn. Lull was gathering furze and her own blessed children were sitting safely amongst the rows of leek shoots, kale wort and onions. The walls of the new hut were sturdy and the fresh thatching secure. All around was green growth, bright peony heads, flowers and herbs for the picking; all her own work visibly rewarded. They would survive and their children after them in this place of sunshine and shadows. From scrubby heathland to ploughed fields with a strong liege lord to protect them. Surely nothing would destroy a homestead built at such terrible cost?

Fritha's well and Beorn's field, with water harnessed and earth subdued under the plough. Here was hearth, home and kin. It was spring once more, a time of hopefulness and promise. 'All things pass and so must this,' she said out loud. 'We have scratched and scarred the face of this middle earth with our bare hands, sacrificed with our blood, humbled ourselves before the spirits of the greenwood who raged at our coming.

'Spirit of the living well, guard our rootings here from those who would devour us. Here be sacred soil. All things pass but surely not this "luffendlic stede"?'

By the Water's Edge

Iris

❧

'Ishall miss all this,' Iris whispers to herself as she walks the blue brick paths around the raised beds, stooping to pull out stray thistles, leaving a pink chiffon poppy to brighten up a line of cauliflowers. So much easier to stretch and hoe around these beds, not so far to bend her creaky back. She fingers the broad bean pods with pride, hanging fatly from the stalks just as they should be. The next crop of peas is ready to be picked and the dwarf french beans are doing fine. Beans and peas must have filled many a Bagshott belly before today, surely?

The kitchen garden is the heart of any plot. It's supplied my pots and pans when friends gathered for meals and gossip in the old days at Friddy's Piece after the war. This veg plot saw us through some thin times then. When food was plain and in short supply, soups and casseroles, pies and chutney from this little plot never failed us.

The kitchen patch was never a grand Edwardian walled garden affair, just a simple potager of vegetables and fruit bushes with herbs dotted here and there and a few self-setting perennials. The area was enclosed by an old wall and privy shed at the top, sheltered on the lane side by a rambling hedge of holly, elder, crab apple and hawthorn bushes. To the south lay the old brick and timber cottage itself, while to the west a neatly clipped yew hedge with an arched gateway sealed off the rest of her garden.

It's strange how I never feel alone in here, she mused. It's as if there's always someone just behind my shoulder working away, and a line of cheeky pigeons perched on the elder waiting to pounce on my brassicas. Why do I feel like I'm deserting my post and abandoning them all by selling up now?

Tonight she will do the full tour; around the square kitchen beds, through the yew arch and up the gentle steps to where the spring tumbles down from the culvert. She notices that the boggy patch by the stream needs a bit of sprucing up; the flag irises as sitting tenants are crowding out her carefully graduated line of white astilbes, green and white striped hostas and pink primulas.

They ought to be yanked up and taught a lesson but they've been there so long I haven't the stomach or the strength. Besides the boulders are thick with slime. I might slip. How come it's always this quiet wild bit which gets neglected, like some long-suffering trusty friend who knows I mean well even when I never get round to visiting them? Fridwell Open Gardens Day comes at the end of the week, old girl, and all this lot'll be under close inspection. Cleaning these boulders is a job for Bob a Job boys or George from the village. Better get them in soon.

No garden is alive without the sound of running water somewhere in it. Iris treads the stone steps gingerly up to the culvert which nestles half-hidden by the foliage of ferns and shade lovers. Here the greenery is darker, holly and yew again, silvery barks and foliage; a cool shady corner where the sun's rays scarcely touch. There is a shrine-like feel to the spot, as if some Buddha should be resting in an alcove there to aid contemplation.

How will I survive without the sound of water? And what are those pinks doing here? They must have escaped from the edge of someone's herbaceous border; strays from amidst the 'Hidcotes' and 'Clotted Creams', wild tiny creatures struggling for light. It'll be time to take cuttings soon for my new garden, if I have one.

Iris likes to cheat the garden centre by buying one sturdy plant then creating hundreds of perennial cuttings and transplants to share around and sell at the produce stall; another gem from the Iris Bagshott Gospel of Gardening, her much out of little, loaves and fishes philosophy.

A garden's more full of sermons than any parson in church, she always maintains.

Iris looks down from the top of the sloping garden, following the line of the stream south towards the church tower in the next field and onwards as it curls down in a narrow channel, widening eventually to swell the old mill ponds in the distance. How water glistens and captures the eye, cheers up dull corners, trickles down the stones here in a steady gush and once on level ground slows its pace to a stately flow.

The church has a squat little bell tower which issues a jarring sound even her failing ears can't miss on the third Sunday of every month. Not much of a looker, Saint Mary Fridwell cum Barnsley, restored and reshaped to suit past budgets; built upon the foundations of a much older and larger edifice, as old as Fridwell and her own cottage, with the same foundation walls of pink stone, dating back to the time when monastic life was the closest to Heaven you could get on earth. But why here? Who chose this clearing for its water and grain fields, its protected position and seclusion? Who and why?

PART TWO

THE PRIORY

AD 1087–1120

'For the itch, the stitch,
Rheumatic and the gout.
If the devil isn't in you
This well will take it out'

—Anon

'Clove Gilliflowers
They are gallant, fine temperate flowers...
yea, so temperate... they are great strengtheners
of the brain and heart, and will therefore serve
either for cordials or cephalics, as your
occasion will serve'

The Hut By The Well

Tthe falcon steepened its ascent, circling the forest and passing high above the old clearing by the spring where once Fritha tended her patch. There are no signs of men dwelling here now; the cleared earth has returned to the wild once more. Here and there her peony seeds struggle for light in the undergrowth, the garden reclaimed by the greenwood.

Now the flash of steel is glinting in the morning sunshine. Suddenly, at the signal of the hunters on horseback, the beaters flush up the heath birds from their cover on the wasteland. The falcon banks steeply, plummeting out of the blue to bind on to its quarry in one fell swoop, tearing its neck, feathers flying as the raptor gorges on its kill. This new hawk is shaping up well, sharp-set and plump-breasted enough but hungry for blood. The morning bag of heath birds will please the hunter who lures back his tercel to the glove with titbits and hoods him firmly with a leather cover topped with a plume of coloured feathers.

*

Hidden from view, Bagnold the swineherd, one of the beaters, caught a brief glimpse of his overlord, Guy de Saultain, and spat on the ground. He hated to see the wily old fox on Baggi's shott, the corner of the wood where his own great-grand-sires had once made their dwelling. Beornsley and Friths well meadows now lay waste; fields overgrown with nettles and scrub, tangles of knotted briars laced over ditches and the overgrowth robbing the soil of air and sun. Somewhere deep in the shadows lay the rotting beams of his family homestead. He was sure this was the exact spot from the way the stream trickled from the spring. Here they drew water and here was where his mother grew her pot herbs. Look, there, struggling for light, were some bright red peony heads. He could see his home garth again, bright with marigolds and orderly lines of leeks and onions. Bagnold felt tears welling and sadness aching. He stared around through a mist of tears. After so many years it was all still here waiting... perhaps for his return.

It stirred painful feelings to see such desolation around Frithswell. Only the fierce thought that this bondsman would never bow his spirit to the Lords of the Kingdom calmed his urge to rush out and kill de Saultain. But one day Bagnold would gain back the shott, the place his fathers once held as freemen before they were forced to sell it for food and pro-tection in those bad times of famine and pestilence before the final conquering by fierce men from the south.

Now he lived with Eldwyth and their brood of hen chicks, tending swine by the Longhall, bound in service to the Nor-mandy knight and his sons. One day, however, he intended to go back to Frithswell and reclaim all the wasted land and fine strips, unclog the weeds from the pond and grind his own corn like his ancestors who once sat at the bridal feast of Thane Godfrid. How the land flourished then and prospered by the well; how the daughters of Godgifu grew strong and tall, with high breasts and fair skin, gaining favour with the high kin of Ludmilla's offspring; how Baggi's sons of Frithswell bred strong men who fought alongside Thane Godfrid's sons when hordes of Northmen spilled through the woods like peas from a torn sack and the thane's men stood their ground, repelling the foe – a tale told many times over their meagre hearth to warm the cold bellies of his bairns; that victory feast of roasted meat and flowing mead in silver beakers. Bagnold could see them in his head, studded with bright stones. Sometimes when he ate his special mushrooms he danced among the jewels and flew over the treetops swifter than any falcon or lord on horseback.

This knowledge was the only treasure in this rotten life; the source of his freedom and power. The mushrooms grew secretly on a bank. Only Bagnold knew where in the forest to gather them.

He went in season after curfew, risking his eyes being gouged out and his bollocks cut off if he were caught, but it was his land by right and the only way he knew to defy the cursed de Saultain. The mushrooms were a gift from the tree spirits to take away his pain and for a while after eating them he alone ruled as King of the Forest. The branches would bend to him and whisper in his ear messages of homage and encouragement. Then he could forget that he was little more than a slave with only half of his left arm; useless as a ploughman, fit only for a stockman's task, dressed in rough homespun like everyone in the village of Longhall. Even his daughter, Aella, was stronger and more useful than he was.

He knew they laughed at his bitterness in breeding only wenches. He blamed the overlords for robbing him of strength and cursing his kin with double seed. Aella was thirteen, a wench of strange, fierce looks with hair the colour of rust and green eyes flecked with amber. She was already in thrall to the manor house and his mates often joked that she was too fine of feature ever to be of his breeding. She did not have the bulbous end to her nose, the fiery skin or sweaty sandy locks of her father. At the ale bench, he often drank until he fell over sideways and heard them call him 'the Bagshott's stump' behind his back. Eldwyth would moan at his antics and curse him too.

Lately she turned her back on him under the covers and spoke only when she felt like doing so; trying to tell him things were not so bad under this rule. While she could hear the slopping of fresh milk into her pail, the chewing of the cud, the din from the smithy close by, the swish of the plough in the fields and see the greenshoots of her cabbage patch growing, then she was not grumbling at her fate. But when did a woman know anything worthwhile? She'd told him all this talk of Frithswell meant nothing to her.

'I'm fed up with you yattering on about the old days. What more can we want than our own hearth stones and kith and kin nearby, a church to salve our souls and enough holy days to dance and play games? You're an old misery guts! How can you of all folk change anything?'

Everyone knew he was forest-reared and orphaned young in the great harrying of Mercia after the Conqueror came; found wandering down the track with his hand hanging off. He remembered little of that night or the first coming of the knights with their chainmail coats and steel helmets and fiercesome steeds, slashing, burning, torching everything and everyone in their path. His father had stood in the shield wall with the men of Longhall and their thane's young son. But how could peasants do battle against such armoury, equipped only with leather shields and their courage? Loud were the wailings and beatings of breasts as men were hacked down with their thane, their women left to the mercy of the Conqueror's lust.

For twenty years a white fire burned in Bagnold's chest as he recalled how he was snatched from the wolf pit where his mother had fled with her children as the soldiers rampaged over the tracks. Sometimes the smell of burning or the scream of a child would stir panic in his limbs and he saw himself running, running. And then the searing pain of the hot iron on his stump, being held down in the smithy to endure the cleansing... that he would never forget. The rest was a blur. The fate of his mother and kinfolk was never known. The whole of Mercia lay under the Conqueror's heel after that time. The Long Hall was pulled down, then rebuilt with stone walls and deep ditches; home now of this Norman knight. Guy de Saultain took the old thane's lands and his daughter, Edwenna the Fair, to his bed. There was no one left to gainsay it for their native priest was killed and the new overlord brought his own chaplain to enforce the Church tithes and law in the district.

As he watched the huntsmen ride off to another clearing, another kill, Bagnold spat on the ground again. They were cursed, he would see to it. The tree sprites were his friends and they would see that no de Saultain ever flourished on Baggi's shott. One day... one day. Until then he would scheme and steal, poach and break curfew, for he was possessed of special powers. With his mushroom magic he was ten feet high, dressed in a world of colour and richness finer than the mantles of any poxy Norman. One day all this would be his... one day.

As Guy de Saultain rode back from his morning's hunting, the jessy bells jingled from the falcon's tethering straps and the bell from the peel tower was still ringing out the news of King William's death. Few here would bow their heads to pray for his soul. Many could not forget his triumph over the Mercian liegemen whose thanes were slain at Hastings and Stamford Bridge. Guy himself would shed no tears either. How eagerly he'd left his home village of Saultain to cross over the rough sea; how full of thoughts of glory and battle honour he had been – a silly young pup of a horseman, ambitious to serve the Norman cause. Little did he expect to be put out to grass in this damp backwater, mopping up Mercian treachery and guarding the centre ground. Now his hair was as silver as his helmet, his cheeks hollow, afflicted of late by a weakness in his stomach so that food rushed through him and his breathing was laboured.

He could feel his strength ebbing away. There was little pleasure in hawking now or in his new tercel, Courage. The effort to stay upright and dignified while searching out some-where to relieve his bowels every hour had quite exhausted him. All he wanted was to soak in the bath tub, change his linen and lie on his bed.

No one would mourn his passing; his sons, Gilbert and Robert, were quarrelsome and weak, his daughter Ambrosine too pious for her own good. His saintly wife Edwenna had died in childbirth many years ago. Who else cared a jot about his welfare? He noticed how the beaters bowed grimly to him. The Mercian English were a cussed lot, proud and servile at the same time, bringing him their rents and tithes with sullen dirty faces. The Reeve chosen out of their ranks to chase up any late payers was little better though at least he was cropping his hair short now to show where his allegiance lay. Even his late wife had been none too clean and tidy when they were first wed.

The Saxons liked gaudy colours, so easy to target in battle. Aim for long hair and a brash tunic and you'd bagged another. But there was little satisfaction in such a conquest, racing northwards to dig out traitors and agitators, Danish rebels and raiders, before they could gather to counterattack.

Here in the middle lands he had fought the bloodiest of campaigns to wipe out resistance and was given his estate in recognition of his effort.

This very morning Guy had found himself riding over clearings and tracks he had not seen for twenty years, back over the killing fields where the peasants were gathered for slaughter like a cattle cull, their offspring speared out of their misery, crops burnt and laid waste. They were little more than animals after all so must not feel pain like noblemen or Normans. How could they when their blood was thin and intermingled with that of Celtish brutes? And how dare they resist their superiors and not expect to be destroyed? He was often amazed by how much torture their puny bodies could resist, how stubbornly they defended their hovels and kinfolk before they were piled into the gravepits.

Guy could not fathom why they haunted his dreams with such regularity, those bloodied faces shouting blasphemies and dying curses, spitting into his face so that he awoke drenched in his own sweat like any coward. Why was he always hearing babies wailing for their mothers, the screams and pleas of women as his men bore down on them to silence their impudence? No matter how he drowned his sleep with poppy juice and peony seeds, the long procession of the vanquished haunted his dreams. He had rebuilt the old church and given alms and Masses, praying that his wife would intercede for his soul. It had helped for a while but finally the apparitions had returned to grin at him.

Lately one image came nightly to wake him: the hut by the well, long since returned to bracken and fern beds now, and the terrible scene re-enacted with his own daughter's head instead of... the cursing finger of that old, old man before his soldiers closed in on him, hacking him into joints in seconds. Why did one scene stand out when there was so much else? Just one minor halt on their way north.

At first he took comfort from the words of Bishop Ermenfrid who absolved knights from eternal damnation by suggesting if they did not know just how many they had slain on the battlefield, they could do penance for one day a week for the remainder of their life or else redeem themselves by building a House of Prayer or endowing land to the Church. He had done all of that for a while but a shire knight was far too busy to give up one day a week to religious observances so he paid Father Jerome to say prayers on his behalf. Surely all his building works at Longhall must count for something? Yet sometimes he was gripped by a fear that it was not enough. What if there were a last trump and a Day of Judgement? How would his life's deeds be stacked up? For or against salvation? He had only been obeying his lord the King. That was every knight's sworn duty, to defend the realm against treachery. Now he was the King's representative in this shire and his manorlands were well ploughed and planted. Longhall peasants should have no complaints. He was just but ruthless with villains hereabouts; stealing, fornication, poaching from the hunting chase or running away were dealt with swiftly by the hanging rope.

Yes, his day had gone well enough but he was glad to be approaching the manor gates. It struck him that there was much good land laid waste out there, just lying fallow waiting for reclamation. He had spotted some mangy beasts grazing and foraging on the common land but preferred his serfs close by, at work in the manor fields under the Reeve's watchful eye. They had their own hovels and were easy to curfew and control.

Yet there was something about that spring where they'd cast off Courage into the air; the way it cascaded over rocks covered in moss, the carpet of wild flowers on the banks but above all the blood red globes of the peony bushes struggling towards the sunshine, bruising his eyes with their brightness. It was there, perhaps... Was that the very place of his dreams where shadow creatures disturbed his peace?

Guy was stabbed with a jolt of alarm as sharp as any lance tip. Nothing remained of that day so long ago, no tell-tale bones, no survivors, nothing but the fall of Courage as he crashed down on his quarry to mark the spot. Like a falcon, Guy de Saultain shook himself. Surely there was nothing to fear from the place now?

Ambrosine de Saultain knelt by the bedside praying fervently for the fear to leave her. Her father was dying; his sickness had worsened since the last time he'd gone hawking many weeks ago. Now he was like a skeleton with yellow shiny skin drawn tight over his bones and his eyes had a faraway look. If only she could get him to eat and keep down what the cooks prepared. He lay in the solar above the hall, a private chamber for the family's use, propped up on feather bolsters. Sometimes she sat and mopped his brow while the monk from the infirmary at the Minster offered infusions and powders to ease his pain. She'd hoped for a cure but the monk had shaken his head sadly and talked of weeks, a month at most.

Something troubled her father's soul. He was fearful of

sleep and the poppy juice decoctions. Father had always been tough, as tall as the great oaks in the forest, everlasting and eternal. This man was so weak, so mortal, like a trunk riven by lightning, broken and laid bare. In all of her eighteen years Ambrosine had basked in the sunshine of his approval, his obvious pride in the way she'd stepped so easily into her mother's place even as a little girl of ten. She was his peace weaver, the first born, with hair like spun gold. He'd often pointed proudly to her high brow and straight back, his 'little princess' and 'queen of his heart'.

Her own birth bridged the gap between two opposing worlds, forged links with the proud Saxon forebears of the Long Hall – Ludmilla and Godfrid the Strong. Ambrosine, born on 4 April, the feast day of Saint Ambrose, spoke two tongues: the rich native language of her mother and wet nurse and the French of her father's northern Gaul. He still needed her to translate for him even after twenty years as knight of this manor. Lady Edwenna had been proud of her Saxon forebears and their Gods but Guy de Saultain insisted on Latin names for his offspring. Sometimes Mother had travelled afar to worship at the well shrine of St Chad, close to the Minster. She told wondrous stories of his greatness to her daughter; how he hung his cloak on a rainbow, for instance. Father laughed at such nonsense, dismissing all 'Anglais' holymen as savages. It was he who insisted she spoke the French tongue and learned her letters to understand how the household functioned, giving her the heavy keys of the chatelaine as soon as her poor mother slipped so cruelly from them.

The keys had weighed down her girdle and her spirits ever since. Gilbert and Robert were still young and silly colts, immersed in battle arts. They treated her like a mother and she scolded their tutors for spoiling them and Father for being too busy to bother disciplining them. Even now they would ignore their sister's pleas and ride off with other boys to make mischief among the peasants: teasing old men, flirting with the pretty maids and testing their manhood in the usual ways. She had little power to stop them and Father was in no state to try. They were ignorant of good script, attended worship only when bribed, and drank from Father's cellar without his permission. It was a pity they were too young to find wives and settle down out of her way.

Sometimes she felt as if her own life was slipping away in the care of others. Ambrosine yearned for the peace of a cloister, time to read and contemplate the religious life. The holy rule of St Benedict – that was the life for her. Enough of giving orders, managing the household servants, readying the chambers for guests, making sure they were well provisioned for the winter months, which took so much preparation in the kitchen garden, the orchard, the dairy, the buttery and candlery. Then organising all the clothing to be hung on poles, mended, sponged down and freshened. Now she was supervising her father's last journey in life and wanted to do it as he would wish.

The girl looked around the chamber with satisfaction. The walls were curtained with fine tapestries, some worked many years ago. Others she and her mother had worked together; she sitting at her mother's knee handing out threads and needles, fingering the fine strands between her fingers, sorting them into shades of colour like an arc of the rainbow while her mother sewed such beautiful pictures of flowers and unicorns. It was one of the memories she clung to on sad days for she still missed her mother's gentle touch.

Ambrosine knew that childbirth was dangerous for all but the most robust and wanted none of it. Her own betrothal had been delayed because the boys were too young and too wild, and now her father was too ill to make any decisions. Once he was dead she would quietly disappear into a secluded convent and live life as she chose at last.

She fingered the quilted counterpane with admiration. It was one of Father's treasures, made for his bride in a convent near Arras; the stitching so neat and straight, whorls of feathery patterns so carefully executed. Whoever had made this was an artist of great skill and she longed to have the time to learn such a craft. She had servants to clean and cook, to bake and mend clothes, but no one to whom she could talk as an equal and share all her dreams, no confidant. No one to whom she could confess her fears for she had a little weakness which troubled her very much.

As she glanced over the dark room, she knew she was really looking for movement: scuttling spiders, fluttering moths, buzzing flies, the drone of wasps, the shiny coats of beetles across the rushes on the floor. How God could create such tiny monsters to terrify her, she would never understand. They had no place in her chamber and she tried desperately to remove any trace of their presence. Sweat would pour from her brow as she made her nightly inspection of the room to see if long-legged spiders were lurking in the crevices, waiting to descend on silken threads. If she were alone she would scream and rush out as if they were chasing her, big as she was.

She employed one of the young thralls, Aella, the cleanest, prettiest of the serving girls, solely to go before her into the solar and examine each wall, garment and surface for any intruders. Whether she killed them or not Ambrosine did not wish to know. The evidence must be removed. She herself was too sensitive to crush a flea but felt easier now this delicate matter was being taken care of by another girl.

It troubled her that they must open the doors and window shutters, untie all the knots and bindings around the room, so that her father's spirit would be free to escape from his body when the time came. More opportunities for the winged invaders to trouble her though it was a selfish thought when Father was so weary of life. Her duty was to make him more comfortable, to wash him gently with lavender and balm oils, to plump his pillow and tend to his sores.

Guy de Saultain stirred in his half sleep, muttering to himself, 'Begone!... *Dieu!*'

'Gently, sire, it's only me... only a bad dream.' The girl held his hand. It took him all his strength to pull it away.

'Don't touch me... I'm doomed... evil under the sun!'

'Shall I fetch Father Jerome? He'll guide you through this darkness to the light, Father.'

'No, no priest yet. Take the fear from me, Ambrosine. Give me some peace.'

'What troubles you so? I must fetch the Father, he alone will know what to do... Please?'

'No one outside must hear this, it's for your ears only, child. Perhaps if I tell you, it'll lose its power over me...'

'Tell me what?' She leant over to catch his murmuring. His breath was foul, she could barely stand to breathe in. Guy de Saultain sat up, strangely calm and steady now. 'This happened long ago on our arrival... I was young and proud. You have to understand what kind of man your father was... I want you to meet Guy of the shadows.'

For the first and only time in his long life he told someone about the hut by the well.

Afterwards he lay back exhausted by the effort of confession. Ambrosine sat frozen, ice cold, her face bleached by his words; pictures of that terrible scene flitted before her eyes like glimpses of Hell. She felt sick in her belly, gagging at his description of such vileness. Her back ached from sitting so rigidly, at first hardly daring to move for fear of disturbing his flow. Somewhere out there, close enough to Longhall, this man and his soldiers had done a terrible deed, out of spite, vengeance, even enjoyment, with no thought for their immortal souls or those of the victims they tortured and slaughtered. How could her own father be lying here yet party to such horrors? Now the knowledge of what was done to that mother and her baby was hers too and she felt soiled and sullied, sickened by his words.

'I was young, child. I thought I would live forever, that no harm would come if it was shriven from me. Now I know better. It has never left me and I must take it with me. Pray for me or how can I be forgiven?' he pleaded.

'You must ask Father Jerome. I cannot speak on such matters.' Ambrosine found herself talking in a dull flat voice as if from a great distance away.

The images were still all around her, the cries and the screams. How could she rid herself of them? He had showered them over her and now she was drenched in their foulness. She shifted her stool to draw back from him. His confession had disgusted her but now it was inside her own head, it was as if the shame belonged to her also. This was her father, knight of the shire. How could a Godfearing man do such things to innocents? Who else of their servants was witness to these deeds? Was she also guilty of this crime for being of his flesh? If so she must quickly go and make confession. Father Jerome would know what to do.

The Spider Brusher

As dusk drew its shadows across the woods, gates and shutters were closed to keep out strangers and the foul night air. Aella, Bagnold's daughter, stood waiting at the foot of the solar stairs to see if her mistress needed the room swept; the nightly ritual which was a secret between them. The manor was subdued; people talked in whispers and mouthed their orders. Straw was laid over the courtyard cobbles to deafen the horses' hooves and soothe the final passage of the old knight into the next world.

For Aella, life at the manor house was her entire world and she willingly lingered late to help where she was ordered: fetching, carrying, sweeping, peeling, dunking, serving and clearing away, weeding in the kitchen patch, feeding hens, ducks, geese. Maid of all things, she often thought, but loved it just the same. There was always some task to delay the dreaded moment when she must leave the compound and return to sleep with her sisters in their cottage, listening to the drunken swaggering of her dad as he bickered with Mother late into the night.

In the hall there was bustle, noisy banter, gossip and good scraps to fill her belly. Home was a damp hut, colourless and drab; a few sticks and stools, a wooden meal kist, a pot on the fire, smoke, dirt, bugs and vermin. Aella was confused by the two worlds she must pass between. If only she had been born to a knight not a swineherd with one arm. On the ladder of village life they were almost on the bottom rung and she knew that only her fair looks and tidy manner had won her such a place with the de Saultains.

At the top came the Steward and the village Reeve and his cronies, who looked after the estate for Sire Guy. The ale brewers were popular and the ploughman respected but no one listened to Bagnold. Dad was worse than the crazy idiot son of the miller when he was fired up with juice. Ranting of the way he had lost his lands and freedom to the murdering Normans and his arm to their swords. No one believed a word he said. He was a foundling from the woods after the troubles of many years back though he went on as if it were yesterday, not long before any of them was born. He forbade Aella to work at the hall but had no power to dissuade her other than his belt when she went there all the same. Couldn't he see she was doing them a favour by spending her days there? It left more space for her stupid sisters to pull each other's hair out and spit at each other.

She knew that serfs were not allowed to leave the village, to buy or sell or marry without their knight's say so. All this talk of clearing the land at Frithswell was a load of cow dung. Baggi's shotts at Frithswell, wheresoever that was, meant nothing to her though her father had been full of nothing else since last hawking day; the last time their lord had ridden out.

Bagnold had found the well and his mother's patch, apparently. It was all there just waiting to be dug over. There was no stopping his fancies when he was ale-soaked and puffed up like a rooster. No wonder she never wanted to go home.

Now the door was opening and she could see candles flickering as she was summoned up the stairs. Aella tiptoed through the solar, the stench of many potions in her nostrils. The knight lay still on sunbleached white linen. His daughter glided silently by, beckoning her through into the small chamber where she had her bed.

The four corners were to be inspected. She must kneel on the floor and brush away all that might offend the eye. Those were her instructions. Then inspect each garment hanging from the pole. How she would love to finger the fine clothes, their fur-trimmed edges and silken girdles, but there was no time. Aella took a candle to the wall and watched the flies hop from the hangings. She passed it rapidly through the air to burn the wings off any insects. Next she took a stool to reach into the ceiling corners and brush away any new cobwebs but never touched the spiders where they hid. That would bring bad luck and misfortune on all of them. Live and let live, she thought as she swept them out of sight. Bugs never bothered her, not even when they lived in her hair and on her clothes, you just got used to them. But ladies were different creatures and not used to uninvited guests residing on them.

Aella drank in every detail of her lady's chamber; the wall hangings to keep out the cold and damp, the candle holders with real tallow candles, the pet dog asleep on the bearskin rug, the solid bedstead raised off the ground. On the long oak chest stood a silver and gilt cross before which Lady Ambrosine prayed to the Blessed Virgin, her gold-leaved Psalter, fine carved comb and a bowl of dried rose petals and herbs to scent the air. It was like living in paradise. Aella basked in the sight of it but knew she could never live in such splendour. It was enough just to pass through into this room and be of service.

How lucky she was to have been the chosen one though

the other servants teased her and called her names like 'bug warden' and 'spider brusher'. Everyone knew how terrified the mistress was of creepy crawlies while Aella was as tough as the ploughman's boots when it came to catching, skinning, gutting, ripping off skins, so a few bee stings would mean nothing to her.

Now her nightly task was finished she turned to retrace her steps but her mistress stopped her with a hand on her arm.

'Aella, you must know this domain well... do you know of a wellspring by the edge of the forest?'

'There are many wells in this forest and all have names. My dad used to live by one they called Frithswell when he was a small boy... or so he says. I've been out of this place but once, to the next clearing for a wedding. With your father's permission, of course.' She averted her eyes in case Lady Ambrosine might see she was lying for in fact she had accompanied her father on his many poaching trips and knew the watery banks by the stream better than any lad in Longhall.

'Did your father live long in these woods?'

'He came here as a child in your father's time. All the outsiders were brought into the village after the troubles, or so he tells us.'

'What troubles?' quizzed the mistress, her blue eyes piercing Aella's composure.

'I think it was in the old thane's time or thereabouts. There was much destruction... so he says. My lady, he's a man of many words when he sits at the ale bench, but his arm was cut off before he came to Longhall and seared here by the smithy's iron. That bit is true.' Aella was oddly troubled by all these questions. Never before had her mistress addressed her so earnestly.

'You may go now, Aella. Speak to no one of these matters. The past has a long arm, I fear.'

'My father speaks much of the past too. He wears out my ears!' She bowed and smiled, seeing her mistress's mood lighten at her jest.

Ambrosine tossed and turned all night, trying to rid herself of the fear, the shame and puzzlement of her father's revelation, but it was the parish priest, Father Jerome, the fussy little man with the high voice and girlish manner, who provided the solution with such a simple idea. She had cornered him next morning after Mass, tempting his fast with a platter of honey-baked comfits and asking him how best a troubled soul might redeem themselves for the afterlife.

'Almsgiving, good works, visiting the sick, penance and pilgrimage, Masses for the repose of the soul. They are the tried and trusted route. Flagellation and fasting I prescribe only in extreme cases. Why do you ask?'

'I'm concerned for my father. His time is close and I fear he has little time left to make amends. Is there a sure and certain hope in any one act?'

'To endow a church or found a prayer house or monastery. These should not fail to ensure admission, child. But Sire Guy has already built us a fine stone peel tower with a bell to chime the hours, and given us a stone font and fine silver too. Why such worry in your voice?'

'I fear it's not enough.'

'Then a House of Prayer would top it all, like jewels do a crown. A Priory or some holy House of Prayer, secluded from the world and dedicated to the glory of God. Surely voices ever raised in supplication would be to his everlasting salvation? But I am getting carried away.'

'Go on, Father Jerome. I think it sounds a wonderful way

to cleanse… to redeem his life.' Ambrosine could feel her heart beating like a tabor in her chest. To build a Priory, to lead nuns in worship, to make a sacred and holy place in this wilderness wood. She could see it so clearly.

'Has your father ever spoken of this? He's not a rich man, I understand. It takes land and gifts and endowments to build such a place. Farms to service and provide food, servants to keep, stone to build a chapel… a huge undertaking. And there is so little time. Would he agree?'

'I know my father seeks peace for his soul. Perhaps this is the answer he is looking for.' Father Jerome nodded, no wiser as to why he was being bludgeoned by all this special concern for Guy de Saultain's soul, though it took little effort to know there would be much on the conscience of any warrior knight and especially one who had ridden with King William of the Normans. There was much to which he himself had shut his eyes and ears on his own journey. 'Leave this soul-burdening with me, Ambrosine. If the opportunity arises…'

'It must, Father Jerome. See to it before it's too late – for all of us.'

As he turned from her she was already seeing herself as Prioress of her own convent, basking in sanctity, surrounded by noble nuns. Living simply from the land as St Benedict's rule commanded; a true seat of learning and a source of spiritual refreshment, a wellspring to all around. Suddenly she knew that her Priory must be built there in that dreaded place, the hut by the well in the forest, the very scene of her father's damnation. Only then could the cleansing begin. Only then would the souls of the de Saultains be safe from retribution.

The Bequest

I, Guy de Saultain, of the Manoir de Longhall, having a care over my soul and the souls of my heirs, do petition the Holy See of Liccefeld to release three hides of my land with homage and dues, assarted from the Forest of Canok by the west brook, Bernsleag, and the stream known as Fridswell, for a House of Prayer so that the Church shall forever possess it and none of my adversaries shall detract from it. If it so he that any of mine enemies shall presume to violate these my alms which I give to God for the remission of my soul, let them be alienated from their inheritance of God and damned among the infernal ghosts...

The deed was written, the sacred task accomplished, but Ambrosine de Saultain felt no joy as she headed the horseback procession up the narrow winding track towards the forest clearing. What an effort of will to make her father accede to her wishes, sign the document with his spidery, feeble script and seal the wax with his signet seal. To give back land to the Church – land which Gilbert and Robert would have wished for the estate. Gilbert had sulked and stormed for weeks afterwards, blaming his sister for treachery and sorcery, calling her every name under Heaven for this deed.

With her face set in the warm breeze of the summer afternoon, Ambrosine knew she had done her duty, redeemed her father's soul and cleansed their name. She was not going to justify her action or speak of how she had forced his compliance.

'I'm doing this for *all* our sakes. You would not want the sins of the father visited on your innocent heirs!' Pleading had at first been useless as Guy refused even to consider such a gift. Then she stole into his chamber when he was in great pain and told him that this suffering would be as nothing to the torments of hellfire ahead if he did not agree to her plan. Guy stared stubbornly ahead and answered not one word, clenching his fists defiantly. Finally she threatened to reveal his confession to the Church, make public all that she knew of the acts of massacre and blasphemy, perform a public penance at the shrine of St Chad so that all the world would know of his infamy.

'We've found the very place, Father. I can make sure your generosity is forever honoured.'

She could see he was weakening; his body being little more now than two hawk-like eyes burning above a bundle of stick-like limbs. He waved her away and summoned the priest. Finally he signed the prepared parchment, dismissed them both from his sight and turned his face into his pillow, to give up the ghost a few hours later. Ambrosine had wept at her own hard-heartedness but his eternal life was far too precious to be lost by weakness on her part.

The place was never charted by the old survey, Longhall itself was scarce mentioned in that great Domesday register, but thanks to her all this area was now named and mapped out forever. Frithswell or Frithaswell as the locals called it did not trip easily over the tongue of a French-speaking scribe. Now it was written simply as Fridswell. How that name haunted her waking hours! Planning, dreaming, scheming for ways to make her Priory happen. But time dragged so slowly and no one else was in a rush to build her stone chapel. Today they were going to visit the monks and lay brothers who were clearing the site so that the fields could be reploughed and the ground could yield a harvest again.

Ambrosine was furious that the others cared only about the produce and not for the real purpose of her mission. The procession wound slowly out of the woodland, some mounted on fine steeds like the Bishop's representatives and Gilbert. Father Jerome sat on a mule while his parish assistant, a young cleric, walked alongside. Behind them walked the servants with donkeys laden with victuals for the lay brothers' evening meal and a small repast for the visitors. The sun was blazing down on her half-mourning surcoat and Ambrosine was glad of the white veil which kept its rays from her pale brow. Suddenly the clearing opened up before them and she could hear the welcome sounds of activity at last, the noise of progress.

It would be the ideal site for a Priory, bordered on two sides by streams and brooks and the other by dense woodland, like an island floating in a sea of meadows and pastures. Farther out would be the home farm and a mill with a water wheel and supply of fish ponds nearby. In the centre of it all, close by the wellspring, would stand the chapel and cloister garth, with a guest house for visitors and a little scholarium for young pupils. It would be perfect, so peaceful a setting, but they needed the promise of many extra dowries and endowments to make her dream come true. She was trusting that all this would be provided in due course by followers who shared the same vision.

There had been so many delays: disturbances on site, mischief-making, equipment stolen as if some unquiet spirit roamed free to spoil her plot, but today was far too warm and beautiful to think about such nuisances. Today would be a celebration. The first foundations had been dug and after one long year her dream was finally coming true.

Aella the spider brusher, daughter of Bagnold 'Bagshott', dawdled behind with the other servants. Her grey tunic chafed her in this heat. It was not a day to be outside but rather indoors within the cool stone walls of the manor house still room. Who would want to stick themselves out here in a pen full of holy women? She could not fathom why her mistress, kind as she could sometimes be, was so firmly set on building another church. Wasn't one enough for her? It was making Aella nervous to see how often she herself was included in Ambrosine's plans. I must have all my familiars around me, Aella. My hound, my maids, all my girls.' The lady would smile as if she were doing her maid a favour. Hellsteeth! Would she be expected to brush over the convent walls each night? Suddenly Aella felt trapped by the very thought of it. But she would never return to Bagnold's hut now that the new lord and master was in residence.

Mother had dropped a pup at last, breaking the curse of girl childer. In fact she had dropped two but the runt was squashed behind big fat Edric and did not breathe. All Father's drunken hopes were now pinned on his precious son, who squawled and puked, not understanding that he was destined to be a freeman and reclaim Baggi's shotts at Fridswell. Aella was sick of the babe already while her younger sisters doted on him, constantly feeding him titbits so that he grew round and plump as a piglet and Mother hoisted him on her hip for fear he should drown in the dung heap or the ditchways. His legs were too swollen for him to stand upright. Sometimes she saw them all at Mass, spilling out of the little church, dirty and scruffy in their usual rags.

Aella was determined not to return to that pigsty so smiled coyly at her distant kin, lanky Matthias the farrier's boy, who stared at her longingly like a dog at a bone, clenching his hood in his red hands like a lovesick loon. His leather jerkin was worn and shabby, face scrubbed clean only where it showed, hands covered in grime from the smithy – and the bits no man ever washed soot-smoked like bacon but not smelling half as good.

His mother's kin came from the Beornsley side of the family and had entertained dreams of Matt's becoming a clerk at the Minster. For three days they'd traipsed down the valley to the monks' school but he was found only to have the shoulders of an ox, the strength of a plough horse and no head for scholarship at all. He was soon sent packing to work with the lay brothers. Beating out the horse shoes and repairing plough shares was all he was fit for. There would be no place for him in a nunnery. But how would she ever see another man if she was enclosed behind a high wall? Aella was praying it would take years for them to build the stupid place and that by then she would be long wed with bairns of her own.

They all stood on the ridge looking down at the work in progress. The clearing was full of men in black habits looking like busy ants as they carted, dug, marked out the area with posts. Aella could see the outline of the walls and ditches like a giant game of hop scotch drawn in the dust. Some of the foundations were as deep as grave pits; to the side were neat piles of furze and scrub waiting to be used on the fires outside the monks' cells. Their kale patches were stocked with vegetables separated in a cross shape and bee hives stood in orderly rows. But now the men were gathering around the foundation ditch in a crowd, all peering down and crossing themselves. Something was obviously amiss.

Father Jerome was sent down the slope to see what the trouble was and he too peered down into the pit, crossed himself and puffed his way back uphill in the heat. He shook his head at his mistress and her brother.

'Well? What's the delay?' asked Ambrosine.

'They've found some bones. Human ones, I fear. They were digging a trench along the line marked and found fresh bones, not ancient ones. We shall have to exhume and examine them if they are to be buried properly. I fear theirs was no Christian burial, just a hurried measure to conceal some foul deed. This must be the place where the old family at the well fell to the sword in the clearances... 'Tis a bad omen, sire. Not good news, my lady.' Father Jerome pursed his lips in a solemn look of disapproval.

'What's going on?' yelled Aella from the back of the group, unaware of the grim discovery.

'Shush, she'll hear you! Bad tidings for you kinfolk of Fridswell. The bones of Bagnold's family in a pit... we think.' One of the servants pointed excitedly to the cluster of clergy now gathered to see for themselves.

'What kinfolk of mine might they be then?'

'You know damn' well whose bones these must be. Yer dad's told us all a hundred times.'

'Godsblood! Wait 'til he hears. He'll raise the dead with his din if he finds out the Lady Ambrosine's building on Baggi's shotts. He thinks the land's still his. He's a cracked pot when it comes to this place. I never thought it were that close by. He mustn't find out or else…'

'And do you think that's likely? The whole of Longhall will hear of this by the curfew bell. Father Jerome is a worse gossip than the women by the well.'

Aella scratched her head, at a loss. To think her own grandmother, uncles and aunts were lying all mingled together in that heap of bones.

'It looks as if they'll dig'm out and bury them decent so they can rest in peace, poor beggars. Not that they'll know owt about it, will they?'

Aella had a strange eerie feeling that they were being watched by her dead kin, and shuddered. What would her ladyship make of all this fuss? Aella was going to keep out of her way 'til things were calmer. Shaking her copper curls, she slunk into the shade.

Ambrosine de Saultain leaned against a broad-trunked oak, watching the proceedings as if from a great distance. Her face was flushed pink, her heart beating rapidly at this grim discovery. The Lord had guided the diggers to the exact site of the hut by the well. Now there was proof. The truth was out at last. Here was another Calvary waiting for Resurrection Day, and here her Priory would bring a much-needed cleansing and a blessing. The sooner those bones were interred and sanctified, the sooner the brothers could carry on with their mission. It was a simple matter and there need be no undue delay.

Later Aella brought refreshment to her mistress as she sat in the shade. Ambrosine shook her head, impatient at the delay. 'Isn't this a wonderful site? See the outline east to west where our chapel will lie… Well have a little garden too to sit in, a walkway for quiet times and contemplation. Oh, I can see it all now! You and I will be the first to welcome our sisters, won't we?'

Aella turned away sharply to avoid her gaze. *If she thinks I'm going to live out here…*

Father Jerome returned again to say that they were stopping work for the bones to be gathered and counted. The authorities must be informed of their findings and no doubt an investigation would be ordered.

'Why can't you just bury them quietly when we've all gone?'

'The Bishop won't allow such a thing. These may be holy men's bones. We must honour the martyrs and find out all we can. Then they can all be laid to rest. Dishonour the dead and the place will never flourish or be blessed aright.'

'But surely all this happened long before our time? No one will know anything in Longhall.' Her plan depended on no one from the village being aware of her father's deeds.

Aella overheard the discussion and said nothing. She knew exactly who had once lived here and what he would say to hear of this. Perhaps she should warn her father. He could tell his tale to the Shire Reeve if needs be, and the place would be condemned as unfit for a House of Prayer, unsuitable for her mistress's purpose. Then her ladyship would forget her schemes and Aella would be safe in Longhall. With that comforting thought she began to gather up the baskets and cloths, walking back to the village with a fresh spring in her step.

As Baggi 'Baggshott' watched his stolen fish roasting over the stones under a stretch of sky full of stars, he knew for the first time in his life a moment of pure contentment. His guts were swimming in ale, soon his belly would be swimming in roach, and around him was another harvest of heavenly mushrooms to translate him into the King of the Night Forest. On top of all this was the certainty that Fridswell would soon be his again. When Aella spilled the beans about the cache of bones, he knew at last justice was on the side of the poor man and the Normans at Longhall must swallow wormwood and gall to explain how the remains came to be concealed on their land. It was many months since he'd told his sorry tale to the investigators who sat behind a table and solemnly wrote down every word he spoke about that terrible night.

With help from his dried mushrooms his tongue had loosened and flowed, embellishing the few known facts to heighten the drama of dark deeds, draw pity from his audience and fuel his own sense of injustice into a blaze of indignation. The truth of the matter was that no matter how he strained to recall the events, he remembered nothing much of his ordeal but that did not stop him from giving a first-hand account of how his grandfather, uncles and aunts, mother, brothers and sisters fell horribly to the Norman sword of Guy de Saultain. When cross-examined he had to admit he did not know who the soldiers were who'd executed this atrocity but argued that the Sire must have known that this part of the forest was wasteland and returned to build his Hall. He must have been there before. Since sire Guy was dead there was no one to say if this was true or not.

How he had basked in their attention, and the bucketsful of ale given by the curious to find out more and loosen his tongue. The village Reeve spoke on his behalf, demanding compensation, wergeld for the loss of his kin. Bagnold himself demanded the return of Fridswell clearing for his heir, Edric. Now at last fortune would bless his family. Aella kept her mouth shut and held her head up high in the village. She looked into her father's bloodshot eyes and patted his arm as if for once she thought well of him.

He did not care that there were few old folk to confirm his story or that the ones still alive dared not speak against the de Saultains for fear of losing their huts and livelihoods. He stood alone, the sole survivor of the massacre, shaking his stump for proof. This was his moment of revenge. For a long while after the hearing there was a feverish search for evidence as to who actually owned the clearing. The tenancy charters, documents in the monastery archives at the Minster, proved it was part of a large tract of land made over to St Chad by King Wulfhere and tenanted by the knights of the Long Hall since Thane Godfrid's time, then sub-tenanted to certain freemen on limited leases only. There was no evidence either way to prove Bagnold had any right to reclaim land which seemed once to have belonged to Lady Edwenna.

He was happily ignorant of all these legal wranglings. He wanted only to hear what was to his advantage. As far as he was concerned he was owed compensation and only that parcel of land would satisfy him. No news was good news so the swineherd went about his tasks with a swagger in his gait and a cocky air towards all he met, smartening himself up as befitted the heir to a property. If Eldwyth sulked and bit her tongue it was only because she was miffed at all the attention he was getting. Now he could wander abroad as he pleased, roam the woods, poaching, setting his nets where the brook eddied and flowed, biding his time, confident of good fortune ahead.

All that fateful year and the months following, Ambrosine prayed for a settlement to be agreed. How could her will be so thwarted by a peasant, a serf of the lowest order? Her first instinct was to dismiss Aella from her service for being a relative of that abominable man. At the hearing he'd doffed his hood and winked in his lady's presence as if she was a serving wench. Christian forbearance forbade her to punish Aella for her father's insolence. Yet the sins of the father was something they had in common now.

Not once had she been tempted to reveal her own knowledge of the hut by the well, though. She played her part as innocent bystander and dutiful daughter, defending the de Saultain honour by her silence. No accusation would ever be placed at their door. The hearsay of a drunken serf would stand for nothing in the shire court. Right would prevail.

Then came the wonderful day when the Bishop in his wisdom decided that Fridswell was a place of holy martyrdom in a time long past and would therefore make a suitable place for a house of seclusion. The bones of those innocents found in what must once have been the fish pond should be placed in casks and interred in the stone walls of the new chapel in righteous memorial to the slaughter of innocents by persons known only to God.

It was left to Aella and the Reeve to break the news to Bagnold. He refused to hear their words, pulling his hood over his ears as he ran off. The Reeve tried to tell him that he would be given three extra pigs for his own use as compensation. 'Food for your stew pot, think about it, and no payment to her ladyship!' Bagnold, however, was having none of it, disappearing into the woods for two nights. Eldwyth feared for his safety and persuaded Aella to ask permission to seek him out. She knew exactly where he would be found, hidden in the bushes by the clearing, watching the hermit brothers tending their patches.

'It's not fair! All this on *our* land... She'll never get an ounce of goodness out of it while I'm alive to see to it and I'll haunt her when I'm gone.'

'Oh, Pa! What can you do to stop her ladyship? Her mind is set on her blessed nunnery. Who are we to gainsay it?'

'There'll be no building on my mam's patch. Never. I can still see her bending over them weeds, proud as a peacock when her crops had fat heads on them. She used to tell me this soil was blessed by the well so now I'll make sure it's cursed by that same water.'

For the first time in her life Aella felt compassion for her father who seemed to shrivel before her eyes, drained of colour, his shoulders hunched and jaw sagging. Before her was an old man, as limp and useless as a bolster with no stuffing.

'It's not that bad. With those extra pigs no one will go hungry this winter and Edric will soon take over from you. We, of Baggi's shotts will be freemen again, you'll see. It may take time but one day we'll hold our heads up alongside them de Saultains, just you wait on.'

'I'll not be there to see it! This'll be the death of me.'

'I don't suppose it'll come in my day either but we have to hope that our children do better than us.' Aella patted her belly gently.

'Here, are you telling me you've got a pup in there?' Bagnold sighed for a moment, lifting himself out of his despair.

'Of course not... but one day there will be and I'm going to make sure my childer gets a step up the ladder of life not a kick back like us. That Lady Ambrosine has another think coming if she expects me to rot inside her Priory. She can find someone else to sweep her walls and give the bugs in her corners a fright.'

'That's it, you tell her. You're one of Baggishotts and this'll always be *our* land, *our* plot, *our* place in the sun. No de Saultain will ever thrive on it without our say so and that's my last word on it!' Bagnold doused himself in the spring, rinsing away his anger and disappointment, but Aella to her surprise found herself carrying hers home. They festered and rankled in her head for weeks. She could not shake them off. Only when Matt the farrier's lad hugged her like a bear and patted her with his leathery paws did the sadness melt for a few moments.

Soon the leaves drifted across the clearing once more, filling the half-dug ditches and foundations of the chapel and the Priory walls. The lay brothers returned to the Minster where there were plans to build a larger church in stone, and only three hermits chose to stay on to guard the site. The last bequest of Guy de Saultain lay beneath a covering of ice and snow. Only his daughter burned with indignation at yet further delay. Gilbert was now the master of the house and married to Madline, a wealthy maid from Cheslay who'd brought a handsome dowry. Another woman had taken the solar chamber and already they were building a stone buttery and dining chamber in her honour. The village was full of builders and masons, carpenters and joiners, and all thought of the Priory faded from her brother's mind. There was nothing Ambrosine could do to fulfil the bequest but pray.

The signs were not good. There had been bad harvests when famine and failed crops clawed at the empty bellies of the villagers. Only the most thrifty and careful managed to stave off hunger pangs. All were weakened by sickness and cold. Aella had paid her fine to marry Matthias and begged permission to leave the hall without a backward glance. Such was the ingratitude of serfs!

Robert ran wild around the district, hunting, hawking, wenching. He listened to no one, least of all his sister. On the feast of St Ambrose 1095 Ambrosine found three grey hairs as she combed her thick locks which were no longer spun gold but more the colour of wet sand. For seven long years she had waited for her life to begin, seven years of prayer and frustration and resisting Gilbert's hints that he would find her a suitable match.

To mark the feast she asked the chaplain and her maid-servant to accompany her on her regular route up to Fridswell where she would donate food, oil and candles to the hermits who had so faithfully kept the clearing open, pollarding the forest trees and planting an orchard of apples, pears, cherry trees and walnuts. She knew the men by name, almost as friends. They could read her impatience and frustration and would humour her request to pace over the site, planning this and that, as if it would be built tomorrow.

Ambrosine and her maid came often to the spring. Here she could listen to the trickle of the water and pray fervently that God would turn away from his deafness and answer her pleas. Doomsday was fast approaching as another century passed and still no sign of the King returned in Glory. There were strange portents in the sky of great events to come. The heavens were troubled by a warrior wind which blew into her mind the distressing thought that the year 1100 was fast approaching and then there would be great darkness over the earth. What if her family was caught unprepared on Judgement Day? All she had accomplished so far was promises, promises. That would not be enough to save them.

As she peered into the water, the sunlight refracted into a wondrous star of light on its surface and she thought she saw the face of a girl with dark hair in braids, weeping and rocking something in her arms. Such a piteous sight. Ambrosine reached out to her but the girl vanished, only the ripples on the surface witness to the scene. Had she dreamt such a vision? Was the Holy Maid of Nazareth there before her?

Ambrosine knelt on the bank side and crossed herself. She must be patient. This was a sign meant just for her feast day. She had seen the Lady Mary in the well and the place was sanctified by such a presence. Here at last was her heart's desire, a holy place dedicated to the Holy One. Suddenly she felt a certainty as rich and fulsome as any banquet. Here too would be her own dwelling, her home, her cell, her future joy. Only here would she find peace for herself and those who would surely follow. Here she would live out her days in solitude and prayer into old age and agues, weakness and infirmity, until her last breath.

She must wait no longer for others to decide for her. If needs be she would dig the chapel with her bare hands whatever the cost. Ambrosine de Saultain would become an anchoress and then they would have to leave her in this holy place. How it would all come about was no longer her concern. If it was the Saviour's will then it would happen.

Only after she opened her eyes did she spy a little black spider crawling over the folds of her gown, struggling to climb each mountain of cloth. She watched in wonderment as its separate legs worked in a harmony of movement. Such a tiny piece of God's creation. How could she ever have feared it would harm her? It was so small and she a giant with the power to crush and destroy it.

There had been enough destruction in her family to last

many generations. All the creepy crawlies of Fridswell would be safe in her hands for she would live alongside them and learn their ways with humility and thankfulness.

The Warrior Wind

‘This world's jumping over the moon!' sighed Aella, as she scrubbed the winter grime off the family tunics in the hot tub. Tom's hose with holes in the feet dangled from the branches; rough wool shifts left to bleach in the sunshine lay spreadeagled over the hedgerows like strange blossoms. Everything was changing since that awesome night close to St Ambrose's feast when stars showered the night sky and the villagers rushed out of their huts to witness the wondrous sight of God shooting sparks from His smithy above them. Old Meg the wise woman shook her head and said heaven was preparing for battle. Father Anselm, the new priest, said Doomsday was fast approaching and they must be shriven to await the Coming of the Lord in Glory. How relieved Aella was when dawn kept breaking just as usual without His arrival. Today baby Hilde had risen from her bed, gurgling and full of the joys of spring. The sounds of the smithy next door were as a cock crowing to the child and only the banging of hammers would send her to sleep.

Edric, Aella's brother, was already hard at work with Matt but he wore a sullen expression. His heart was not in his tasks. He was too clever with words, too argumentative with his betters. He lived in his head not by his hands which were clumsy and lumpen. At twelve years of age he still had the plumpness of his early years.

This fat had saved his life when all Bagnold's family were struck with the sickness. Half the village caught the pox, and Bagnold and Eldwyth and Aella's sisters withered and died. Only Edric clung on and now lived with his sister like a cuckoo in the nest, eating them out of house and home. Aella had feared for their own health but the Angel of Death had been merciful to the smithy, passing their door without a mark, and soon another child was swelling her stomach.

At first Edric was suspicious of their strange habits. Aella tried to copy the ways of the big hall: eating with a sharp knife, cleaning her one precious wooden bowl and goblet, a late gift from her mistress. She tried to prepare any meat they could forage with herbs and sauces gleaned from her vegetable patch, spit-roasting flesh on the hearth instead of flinging everything into the kale pot, but Matt complained she was too extravagant with their meagre wood supply and made her stop.

Her husband laughed at her fancy ways even as he wolfed down her meals. She made sure that her face was always clean, hair neatly bound under her head scarf, and clothes washed long before their rancid smelly armpits stank to high heaven. The soot and metal dust were always ingrained in their skin but she insisted that the men should douse themselves in the brook before Sunday Mass. It was the only way Aella could pretend they were not still bound serfs. She smiled to think how some of her father's aspirations had rubbed off on to her.

When the blacksmith caught the fever Matt stepped in quickly to take over the forge. Sometimes they were so busy that it was all hands to the hammers and Hilde was perched safely out of harm's reach while Aella fetched and carried like a slave at the mill quern. The child would observe them all, jumping with glee as the sparks shot up off the hot metal.

The first they knew about the Holy Cross of Jerusalem was when Father Anselm prayed for Pope Urbano and his great pilgrimage to rescue the Holy City from the Infidel – whoever he was. A savage murderer no doubt. The call to all Christian knights to follow his banner meant nothing to the likes of a blacksmith's wife until all the armour at the manor suddenly appeared for sharpening, repairs, upgrading, links to be soldered, shafts tightened. The horses were reshod. No guesses where the knights were heading then.

On the day of their departure the whole village stopped work briefly to wave them on their way. The two brothers, Gilbert and Robert de Saultain, rode out proudly, silver chainmail polished, helmets flashing, and a line of mounted serving men with panniers bulging for the long journey to the end of the world falling in behind. It was whispered they would join up with soldiers from the four corners of the land in a great procession south to the open sea.

Aella caught sight of her former mistress, the Lady Ambrosine, who now looked so severe and pale in her severe garb, like a widow or a nun. Clad top to toe in black, she wore a gold cross on her chest. Sire Gilbert's wife went to the gate to lift up her children for a last glimpse of him. By the looks of her there was another de Saultain growing fast under her surcoat. For a fleeting second Aella felt a twinge of sadness for the poor woman until she thought of how many servants and maids would help her cope in his absence. It would be a relief not to have the Lord of the Manor in residence, and his brother too. The Steward and Bailiff were bad enough, breathing down their necks, checking everything was duly paid up.

Once the novelty of being lordless was over Longhall settled back to its usual pace of life. Edric was so restless and difficult, Aella went to see the priest who suggested that he might join a few scholars to learn some letters and perhaps if he did well he would be accepted as a lay brother at the Minster. Edric was eager to try something other than smithy work but Matt was furious that he might lose even a pair of unwilling hands.

'You're just like old Baggi and his Baggshotts, think you're better than anyone else in this village. Why should Edric be trained up as a scholar? What's so bad about a smith's forge?' Aella could see he was hurt by her eagerness to help Edric.

'Your kin came from the same place as mine. We named Hilde after one of them, way back. They trekked from far away to find a better life for themselves. Surely we owe it to our childer to give them chances when they arise? It's up to Edric after that. He doesn't fit in here, you can see that. He has neither the skill nor the inclination to learn. Inside here will be another true son for you to train up.' Aella patted her belly and smiled, her green eyes pleading, and Matt was silenced by their power over him.

'What if it's a wench?' he mumbled.

'No, not this time. It lies differently and kicks harder.'

'You'll not be able to help me once there are two of them.'

'I'll manage somehow, Matt.' Aella sighed and crossed her fingers for an easy birth. How could she ever have feared being cocooned in a convent of nuns, the one which had always been going to be built but never was? She had jumped into Matt's arms to escape that fate but lately had admitted to herself that perhaps the Lady Ambrosine was the wiser woman after all. Especially at the end of a day like yesterday when Hilde screamed and Matt sulked, the dog stole the bacon hock, Edric dropped the hammer on his toe and somehow it was all her fault.

At nightfall when she collapsed on to the straw mattress, limbs aching with tiredness, Matt's hand would stray in her direction, feeling its usual path down between her thighs… A woman's work was never done!

A year had passed since Ambrosine's brothers rode off without a thought for anyone but themselves.

She knew that neither of them cared a stuff for Jerusalem or the cause. They were spurred on purely by boredom and the challenge. Was this how the Blessed Ambrose had answered her prayer of supplication? Not one stone would be put on another at Fridswell Priory now that her brothers were gone and she was tied forever to Longhall. She did not understand the ways of saints. For years now she had kept her own private vows of chastity and obedience, wore only the habit of a religious woman, kept to fast days and attended services, trying always to act humbly and quietly. But, God's blood, it was enough to make a saint swear when not one of her wishes was ever granted and no decisions would be made without the say so of one of her brothers.

Her sister-in-law Madline now had three boys to rear alone. It was left to the single maid to see to the everyday running of the manor and its estates. Days were taken up with visits and accounts, inspections, household preparations and decorations, maintenance and supervision as Ambrosine glided around Longhall giving orders, checking that all was as it should be. In the little time that was left she would take her nephews aside to teach them their letters, instruct them in good manners, tell them stories about the Saxon warrior knights, Beowulf and Guthlac the saint, just as her own mother once did to their father, and tried to finish pieces of embroidery before the material became grey with dust and neglect.

One day a month she did venture to abandon her tasks to visit the old hermits at Fridswell, taking food and gifts and servants to help them tend their patches.

It was sad to see the clearing so overgrown, reverting once more to scrub and nettles. The men were too infirm for heavy work now. The foundations had long since disappeared under weeds, strangled like her hopes by duties and obligations. The casket of bones was long buried in the church yard and forgotten. But one small patch was always kept tended and clear: the garden by the wellspring where she saw the vision. No thorns would ever be allowed to threaten the simple beauty of the few flowers and herbs planted under the bushes of peonies which bloomed there every year and threatened to swamp all the other plants unless kept pruned back.

Over the years Ambrosine had gathered a collection of sacred flowers – white lilies, briar roses, violets and the herbs of healing which grew in the manor yard like weeds – and transplanted them here. To these she added the cheerful yellow daffodils which now danced all along the banks of the stream, bluebells and primroses which sprang from nowhere each spring time to give her the hope to carry on. Each planting she watched over like a mother with a new born. Sometimes, when no one else was close by, she would whisper a prayer to the Holy Spirit and to St Mary herself: 'Holy Mother, hear my plea. Whatsoever herbs of healing thy power here doth produce, grant good success so that all who receive these thy flowers and tend their souls to make them whole again.' Then she would sneak some soil into a pouch on her waist girdle and take it back with her to the little church to be blessed with holy water, returning it to the plot again on her next visit.

During all of this time only a trickle of news reached Longhall about the faraway crusade, and by then the details would be months old and unreliable. Once a prayer of thanksgiving was announced that the Siege of Antioch was over and the city relieved or stormed. Ambrosine heard rumours from the packman's tittle-tattle fed to her servants about knights returned with limbs missing or stricken with terrible wounds, half starved with hunger, in rags or carried home dead on biers to be buried within their castle walls. For them life went on untrammelled by such worries. Little William, Hugo, and the new babe Benedict raced over the estate like puppies just as Gilbert and Robert had done as children, with hardly a recollection of that fateful morning when the knights rode out to their great adventure.

It was the late spring of the year 1100 when two horses kicked up the dust on the beaten cart track from the Minster Cathedral to Longhall. Heads looked up with interest; men working in the field strips, the women picking stones. No one recognised the dusty horses or their dark-skinned riders. Strangers were always viewed with deep suspicion but the hounds in the manor yard did not bark. It was only as the men rode past the smithy that Aella, the farrier's wife saw the grubby crosses on their armour as she pulled Hilde and young Thomas away from their horses' hooves. There was something in the way one of them slouched in the saddle which made her recall old Sire Guy in his latter days, returning from hawking, exhausted and sick.

Ambrosine was called from her chamber out into the

courtyard. She stood stock still at the sorry sight before her. The first man had skin burned dark with a scar running across his cadaverous face and piercing black eyes. The other was recognisably Robert, but not the brother who had ridden out square of face with blue eyes sharp as sapphires. These were sick men, hunched over like bows. Robert almost fell off his horse with exhaustion and collapsed into her arms, saying scarcely a word above a whisper.

'Where's Gilbert? Is he behind you?' she asked. Robert stared at her, his eyes watering, and Ambrosine knew that her elder brother would never return. 'Oh, poor Madline...'

Two grooms escorted Robert the new Lord of Longhall to his chamber and the noisy children fell silent at the sight of the dirty, smelly strangers. Madline was not to be found so Ambrosine gathered up the children and pushed them out into the park field to play with a ball, telling them to be good for their mother and very quiet.

The other soldier sat by the empty hearth ravenously supping wine and bread, too intent on his task to notice his surroundings. Ambrosine noticed the way his hands shook as he held the goblet. He looked up suddenly, aware of her at last. 'Forgive me... I forget my manners before a lady. It's been a long time. I am Geoffrey Gonville. Robert and I have travelled far together. I'm on my way home too, near to Chester by the old stone road. He was not fit to do the last part of his journey alone.'

'I can't believe this is my brother. He's so changed.' Ambrosine paced the floor, hugging her arms around herself, chilly with sadness.

'We've seen too much, travelled too far, not to seem different and Robert was sore at heart for his own hearth. It didn't go well for us. Oh, at first, yes, there were many places to see and admire. But always the heat, the dust, the terrible sieges. And too much injury and sickness. I'm sorry about your other brother.' Gonville paused. 'We've all lost good friends and comrades.' He shot her a look of pure anguish. She could not meet it for her instinct was to gather the stranger to her like a child and hug him close.

'You must rest here until you are fit to journey on. It is the only way we can thank you for your courtesy in bringing Robert back safely to us.' Even as she spoke she saw his eyelids droop and he slumped over the table and slept where he sat.

Madline crept in like a shadow, gliding across the rush-strewn floor, her face pale, mouth quivering with emotion.

'Ambrosine... he's dead! Gilbert's gone. He got as far as Antioch but the siege was long and fierce. Robert says he did not suffer but he lies. I can see it in his eyes. I've told the boys he now commands the soldiers of Christ, worthy of great honour and love and never to be forgotten here. We shall make an effigy to his memory. I shall see to it straight away. Benedict will never know...' Machine fell into her sister-in-law's arms sobbing.

'We'll not forget him,' whispered Ambrosine, choking back tears. 'How can we? For every time I see one of his sons I shall see his chin, his flaxen hair, the curve of his nose. While we live so will he in our memory, I promise.'

She felt an icy calm. Her brother's return had changed nothing. She must act as head of the household, ministering to them all as she had done ever since her mother died and her own childhood ended. Robert would need nursing and the stranger, Gonville, hospitality as befitted his rank. Madline needed to be kept busy. It was the only way with widows. Now was not a time to mourn and think of what might have been; that would come long years later.

In the weeks which followed their sudden arrival neither knight was fit to be moved or to venture far out of Longhall. It was as if once the burden of their sad news was laid down it gave them both leave to collapse into sickness and fever. Robert slept for a week, sipping only the tisanes of camomile, vervain or yarrow and juice of the soporific poppy prepared by his sister. Geoffrey Gonville was fitter, stronger in mind and body, and soon began to devour roasted flesh and drink whatever was put in his hand, draining the cup with relish. He would take himself off on horseback, roaming around the countryside as if preparing himself for the last trek northwards.

Ambrosine drew great strength from his quiet presence, his gentle, thoughtful ways. He was a man of few words, as if he carefully censored anything which might cause her any distress or concern. He would sit at the dining board, deep in thought, while Madline and Ambrosine prattled over every snippet of information concerning the lost Gilbert. Only when Madline left to see to other matters would he come properly awake. In those moments he would flash his dark eyes in Ambrosine's direction, black as sloes in a bowl of cream, and she was silenced, blushing like a silly maid at the intensity of his gaze. She had never before been discountenanced by a man's presence; with father, brothers, stewards, priests she could hold her head high. But this man made her feel awkward and gauche. There was something in the way Gonville searched her face which was disconcerting and she could feel a flutter of wings in the pit of her belly. How strange that any man could stir up such a turmoil within her. She found herself falling silent, breaking his gaze, looking away.

Robert eventually recovered enough to shuffle around the

manor and take air in the park field. Madline suggested they go up into the forest to give him some cooler air and Gonville, who seemed in no hurry to depart, said he too would be happy to accompany them all.

'Such a strange man, don't you think? One minute so courteous and charming, another distant from us all. But he stares at you, sister, or had you not noticed? His eyes follow you across the chamber.' Madline nudged her sister-in-law mischievously.

'Nonsense! I expect I remind him of his sister or betrothed…' she spluttered.

'Who's blushing now? You *have* noticed then?'

Ambrosine said nothing more and tried to look disinterested but she was aware that her legs were trembling as they dismounted to rest for a while by the well at Fridswell. 'I want to see how my new plantings are getting on,' she said.

Madline looked at her sadly. 'I'm sorry, once again life has got in the way of your plans. You're not meant to be a holy bride of Christ, Ambrosine. I remember how you used to argue with Gilbert until you were both puce with rage. You insisted you would be an anchoress and he said: over his dead body.' She stopped suddenly, the memories flooding over her. 'He wanted only what was best for his sister, I'm sure, and now you will be free to choose your own path. He has no power over you any longer.'

She smiled weakly. 'His children are my life now… at least I have the comfort of being of service to them. And Robert needs us both. Have you heard him crying out in the night like a child? It churns my heart to see him so weakened.'

Ambrosine walked ahead. It was she who rose and comforted her brother in the night, trying to fathom what devil tormented his soul. He was just as his father before him had been and she wondered what deeds lay heavy on his soul.

Was her life ever to be devoted to the religious rule? When would she be free to follow her own crusade?

They spent the afternoon walking in that tranquil place as the children raced through the woodlands, gathering the last of the tired bluebells and wild flowers, splashing in the streams and chasing the deer. Ambrosine took Robert and Gonville to see the holy shrine but her brother was not interested and walked off alone to watch the sun slipping down over the ridge. She told Gonville about the plans for the Priory and showed him the outlines of its foundations. Together they walked back upstream to her little garden, now a profusion of green herbs and flowers which were seeding themselves wantonly along the banks of the stream. Gonville knelt down to sip the spring water.

'This is good water, fresh and clean. When you live in heat and dust the coolness of fresh water becomes very precious. Water is the life giver and many a good man of ours died for lack of it. It's strange how we thought of the Saladin as savage and uncultured when they have ways to harness water in channels, irrigating even the driest desert and growing the most exotic fruits and flowers. They see all green places as holy and construct beautiful fountains in the middle of stone or tiled courtyards to keep themselves cool. Even the clothes they wear are light and free-flowing. We were always so hot under our metal armour. Soon we abandoned our stiff clothes and bathed where we could.

'Lady Ambrosine, if you could see the beauty of those gardens to a parched soul, such peace in a terrible place. It's we who are savage and uncouth, I tell you...' He stopped. 'I forget myself again. You seem to have that effect on me.'

'Please go on. Tell me about the gardens – what did they grow?' She wanted to deflect his growing interest in her.

'Rich fragrances assail your nostrils from roses and jessamine and other plants I cannot put a name to. They mark out beds into regular shapes and fill them with many bushes and plants, the like of which I never saw in a Norman castle. There are shady archways and always the sound of running water in your ear to soothe the senses. They grow herbs too to make medicines and potions for every ailment. There was so much we could have learned, but did we heed them? No, all we did was crush and destroy, and now we are lost.'

'But I thought Robert said you raised the cross over Jerusalem again?'

'Yes, and crucified many innocent Christians in the process. For anything we achieved we paid a terrible price. We are damned for deeds not fit for a lady to hear of. The slaughter we inflicted on the enemy was barbaric. Even the doctors we captured were massacred with the rest, their bodies piled outside the city walls to stink in the sun and so bring more sickness among our own men. There was no one to save your brother. He died in the dust and dirt and squalor of wounds which should not have killed him.'

'I feared as much from what Robert did not say.'

'He feels the shame of defeat, as do we all. Nothing tangible is accomplished and the bitter hatred against us in that land will bring about more bloodshed ere long.

'Can you understand any of this? Could you forgive a man for wanting to forget all of it and take up a peaceful life again?'

He towered over her, eyes beseeching. Ambrosine stepped back from him.

'Only God can forgive us. I will pray for you.'

'Are you vowed as a nun? I thought that was just…'

'A whim? No doubt you know all about my foolish dream

from my brother but it's my intention always to live the religious life.' Ambrosine was glad that this was out in the open between them, like a shield to protect her from the advances she knew to be coming.

'I would wish to take you with me as my wife. You have all the qualities I have long sought in a woman – so honest and sincere, quiet and strong. I need such a lady in my life. You would grace any castle with your skills and you have laid siege to my heart. I fear it will never feel whole again.'

He leant forward but she put up her hand to stop his embrace.

'No more, sire, I beg you. There can be no talk of such things between us. I'm old now, long past child bearing. Under this veil my hair is thin and almost silver. I have never met a man to tempt me until now but I made my vows many years ago, at this very spot, and cannot turn my hand from the plough. Please, think of me no longer. You will need sons now to give you hope. Go home and look elsewhere.'

Gonville bowed and saluted her with his hand. Seeing Robert nearby, he walked away without a word. Ambrosine felt a deep heaviness in her limbs as they rode back, bats flitting and darting overhead and the midsummer moon high above them. It should be a night for merriment and lovemaking, not sacrifice and confusion.

Why now? she asked. Why when I am anchored to this spot, burdened with the care of others? Once I could have ridden away gladly and left them all to get on with their living, forgotten my hopeless dream, but something keeps me here. I cannot deny it. I must not be weak. It's too late for me now.

The very next day Geoffrey Gonville packed up his few belongings for a swift departure from Longhall. Nothing more was spoken between them but pleasantries and farewells but each could feel the other's sadness. Only in the last moments did the knight catch his hostess alone, holding out a package wrapped in hide.

'I brought these from the East. I was going to take them home but now I know they were meant for you. Plant them in your patch and think of me. I found them scenting the walls and paths of every garden I saw out there. Point them to the sun and they will scent and cleanse your plot. The Arabs call them "quaranful" and the Frenchies "giroflee". They will scent everything they touch, flavour food and wine too, whatever you choose.'

She opened the pouch. Snug within were many seed heads. She smiled but could not speak for fear of breaking down. When Madline joined them Geoffrey gave her a phial of the richest fragrance.

'This is Hungary water, made from the most perfumed of all the roses. It'll cool your brow when those noisy rascals over there get the better of you. Robert can tell you how it is made and perhaps one day there'll be roses blooming here to fill the bottle again.'

He hugged his comrade in arms tightly, both men choking with emotion, then jumped on his horse and was gone.

Ambrosine wanted to chase after his shadow, leap on to his saddle and cling to his waist. But she stood silently shading her eyes, blinking back the tears as he faded from view.

The Priory

The day dawned at last, bright and showery first then settling into the most beautiful of mornings with a blue
sky and white puffs of cloud promising a settled spell to
Fridswell. The excitement in the thatched dormitory house
was mounting as each of the vowesses was woken early for
prayers and ablutions, dressing with care for there was still
much to do before the afternoon ceremony began.

Already the lay sisters had gathered bunches of fresh flowers
to garland the pillars of the church, fresh rushes for the porch-
way to strew before the Bishop himself and over the refectory floor. In the buttery there was a flurry of chopping and
pounding and the kitchen patch was raided for the freshest of
greens for the broth. In the little pond close by the fish were
waiting to be caught.

It was to be a simple meal as befitted the rule of St Benedict,
nothing ostentatious or self-indulgent. Fruit from their own
cherry garth and tranches of freshly baked bread made in the
shape of crosses from flour milled in their own granary. Here,
Edric Miller, late of Longhall, querned the flour between stones
powered by a water wheel, which was the wonder of the area

and the bane of all the local tenants who must now take their grain to be milled here.

Soon the Bishop would process through the streets of the Minster city in the valley, flanked by monks and nuns from the new convents flourishing throughout the forest and vales of the Trent. They would carry the great seal and embroidered banner of St Mary's Priory, Fridswell, with its beautiful picture of the Holy Mother depicted in silks and gold threadwork by the nuns for this special occasion.

How brightly the morning sunshine touched the timbers and stonework of the buildings with a salmon pink glow. How firmly the little chapel stood from east to west. The cloister garth enclosed a quadrangle of new mown grass divided by two paths into a cruciform shape, a small pond sunk in its centre. This was only a modest construction, housing ten nuns and two postulants, but in its modesty lay its strength and charm. They were still completing the guest house chamber attached to a small infirmary where the old and sick would be given shelter.

The infirmary had a separate enclosed yard which encompassed the stream and wellspring garden; the original site where Ambrosine de Saultain had received her heavenly vision. The garden was now laid out into borders and walkways edged with stones. Here the elderly took a morning stroll along straight paths, sniffing the aromas of herbs and flowers, loosening their stiff joints in the sunshine and smelling the wondrous fragrance of the pink gillyflowers which edged every border, their silvery spears of leaves spilling over the edges.

It had taken Ambrosine many years to gather together alms, pledges of land and dowries from other noble families in the area. Sire Robert petitioned the Bishop and the Minster many times to honour their ancient pledge to build a House of Prayer and the rest of the family worked tirelessly to make Lady Ambrosine's dream come true at last. At every setback she had come to the shrine and begged for strength to continue in her quest. Now her dream was to be realised. There were crops ready to be harvested in the fields beyond the cloisters and wooden huts for the servant lay sisters who would work their land. The nuns were prepared to do as much as would fit around their religious observance.

The villagers of Longhall and neighbouring hamlets had no choice but to supply food and services to aid this venture. They were summoned to give alms and tithes for the candles and font, vestments and carved choirstalls.

Edric 'Bagshott', late Reeve of Longhall, and his wife Alice were busy dressing their offspring for the occasion. Edric's seed was as prolific as the grain flowing through his new mill. Two sets of twins no less, both delivered safely.

His sister, the widow Aella, watched all the proceedings with her daughters and grandchildren. She alone could remember that first foray to Fridswell with her father and how he'd cursed the de Saultains for taking his land. Now it belonged to the church and many a Bagshott belly would be filled from the harvest of opportunities here in the years to come. While the Priory flourished so would they and she wished her old mistress joy in her efforts. By God's blood, she had waited long enough for this day!

At the manor house of Longhall, Madline and her sons and grandchildren were sprucing up their velveteens for the service and trying to stop Sire Robert from wandering off. He was forgetful and frail these days. Now it was the eldest son William and his new bride, Elinore, who kept the estate from sinking further into debt. Every spare silver penny had gone into the furbishing of the Priory and sometimes Madline looked at their shabby home and wondered whether such a sacrifice of services, tithes and land was worth it.

Hushed voices hovered over the bed of their patron and benefactor, Lady Ambrosine, soon to be professed the first Prioress. She was not in the best of health and far from steady on her swollen legs but nothing was going to stop her from enjoying every minute of the ceremony. She had rehearsed her responses a hundred times, knew just when to sit and stand, had confessed ten times to her chaplain. Now in her fifty-sixth year it was a struggle to dress herself unaided. Her temper was just as fiery as in her youth and the younger sisters hovered anxiously by. This was *her* day. The old battle axe had struggled to supervise every stone laid, every sod cut, every vestment sewn.

'I can do it... leave me be.' They all knew better than to argue. I must be there at the gate to welcome everyone. Just think, after all these years... Hurry, hurry!'

She could still give orders, the old Norman bossiness was hard to lose. Her ears were sharp and her eye bright enough to see slipshod work. It was only her breathing which was laboured and her heartbeat faltering. The nuns scattered from her wrath like fleas before a besom.

Ambrosine smiled to herself as she shuffled slowly up to the heart of her garden on this brightest of mornings to see how all her babes were growing. She sat on the tuffet admiring her handiwork and looking down on to the thatched roof of the infirmary. The gravel paths linking the buildings to one another had all been laid under her supervision; the gentle trickle of the holy spring was like music in her ears. Her lilies were cut fresh for the chapel but some still poked their heads from behind those gaudy peonies. Here was a glory of shape and colour but healing plants too. At the heart of this plot was God's mercy to mankind. Now she had turned her musings into a sermon!

It was a pity womankind was not allowed to speak in church and that it took so many men around to declare a female fit to serve her Maker. If Eve had bothered more with her garden and less with the serpent then perhaps things would have been different. Now they must have chaplains and priests and regular inspections and obey men's rules in order to live their simple religious life. But here at last was a woman's domain.

Her eyes drifted towards Geoffrey Gonville's gift. The clove-scented pink gillyflowers were much admired and had lived up to his promise. She thought of the walls of Jerusalem and Christ's suffering, of her own choice to refuse the love of a good knight. While his blossoms danced in the breeze such remembrances would never die.

But now her dearest wish was to be fulfilled. Out of the seeds of destruction and dishonour came forth this beautiful place of peace; a priory hidden from the world to honour the de Saultains of Longhall, Our Lady of Fridswell, and all the company of Heaven forever. Ambrosine could hardly contain her joy that her wishes had not been in vain. She smiled ruefully. They had only been granted, however, when she had learned some patience; especially the humbling patience of old age for now her very well-being depended on the care and compassion of others in her community. No longer could she manage to dress or work without the others, or go to the latrine unaided, to eat what was offered or sleep like a rock. Only now, brought so low, was she raised high to be honoured as the first Prioress. Ambrosine raised her eyebrows heavenward. There would be more humiliations to come. De Saultains were bred stubborn and the Saxon in her made it even worse. 'Lord, what a trial I've been to you, but thank you for this blessed day and for the promise of grace to this wretched sinner.'

A butterfly with painted wings of red, black and white flitted from flower to flower, catching her eye. How could she once have feared such a beautiful creature? She stood up to examine it closer. She would collect a posy, she decided, just a few choice blooms for the Holy Mother's statue by the well.

'Blessed Mother, who will love this place as I do? It has been my labour of love, a long travail to give birth to this Priory. Long may it flourish to honour you...'

In the excitement of the arrival of the procession, with tabors beating, fiddles and pipes, crowds of villagers pressing forward to catch a glimpse of the Bishop in his robes of gold, so many visitors to squash into the tiny church, the absence of its Prioress went unnoticed.

Only later was Ambrosine de Saultain found, slumped on the path in the heart of her garden. She had the broadest of smiles on her radiant face and was clutching a bunch of pink gilly flowers to her breast. Her own celebrations had clearly begun.

The Ghost Garden

Iris

❧

The dog is bored with Miss Bagshott's slow progress tonight and trots off down the steps to the hole in the hedge to 'do her duty'.

Not so much bounce in your running now, Lady, more a stately limp; your doggy years match my own but your bladder is more reliable. Why is it that running water always triggers the urge?

The clump of purple bearded irises catches her eye, all leaf and little flower this year. I should look after my namesakes a little more, she thinks, and picks out the note pad from her apron pocket to mark them down for 'the treatment'. A plant only gives in proportion to what it receives is another of her Bagshott rules!

Why were my generation given such flowery names? she reflects. There was a vase full of Roses, Daisies, Violets and Lilies in the village school with now and then the odd flicker of imagination – a Rhoda, Marigold or Marguerite amongst our workaday blooms. Now the Katies, Sarahs and Beckys are bussed to Barnsley Green for their education.

What this village needs is new blood, new families, not old coffin dodgers like me. Perhaps that's why I've given in my notice. I might sell up to Devey's Developments after all. I ought to give the children a chance of some greenery and trees to climb. It's selfish of me to be keeping all this to myself.

Yet Iris feels a shiver of revulsion at the thought of some JCB ripping up her flower beds. But now is not the time to debate the issue if she wants to sleep tonight. She must keep on her familiar route march down the windy path, through the wrought iron gate which leads into the herb garden, the most hidden place, tucked away at the back and fed by the stream; a sun trap by day and silver by moonlight.

How many years did it take me to grow my box clippings into such thick edges and still I don't like the smell of it – like cat's pee. Iris dips the watering can into the old water butt and sprinkles the leaves of lavender, rue and thyme to release their scents on to the night air.

This always feels like the oldest part of the garden; a *hortus conclusus*, a physick garden for the nuns perhaps, once full of monkshood and digitalis, pennyroyal and henbane. Centuries of rippings out and makeovers can't erase a slight feeling of menace here, for all its cool smoky blue tones, silvery foliage and green leaves.

Summer warmth lingers still in the enclosure, the thick hedges softened by speckled foxgloves and pale lilies, golden balls of marjoram, feathery dill, tansy and the fading dicentra 'Bleeding Heart'. The delicious smells of bright green spearmint, sweet woodruff and herb robert engulf her. She rubs a sage leaf in her fingers.

'How can anyone die who has sage in their garden?' goes the old saying. Well, quite easily when you're my age but, please God, not tonight, not until I've finished the tour, seen to the Open Day arrangements, tidied up and sold my house.'

Iris sniffs the celery tang of the broad lovage leaves and inspects the tall verbascums, Aaron's Rod, standing like sentries guarding the two standard bays.

What this herb bed needs is a statue, a cheerful Venus in the centre, plump and sturdy, holding up a bird bath shell, guarding the plot from harm, rising from her sea of lavender. The best Iris can manage so far is that chimney pot dripping with ivy 'Gold Heart'.

Why has this never been a favourite spot of mine for all its subtle planting and mystery? There's something creepy about the stillness tonight and the absence of bird song doesn't help. Perhaps it's that pot of *Lilium regale* peering out through the foliage like spectres. But aren't white lilies supposed to keep away ghosts?

The spirit of the past often flows through this garden and now it is returning. The iron gate creaks and groans: in the shadows someone glides by. From the corner of her eye Iris glimpses a chink of light shining into another world, another time.

PART THREE

WITHIN THESE WALLS

1349

From miln and from market
From smithy and from nunnery
Men bring tidings'

—Anon

'White Lilies
The root, roasted and mixed with
a little hog's grease, makes a gallant
poultice to ripen and break
plague sores'

Rumours

The white doves soared from the loft at the sound of strangers opening the hatch of the round columbarium, leaving the fat squabs flightless in their pigeon holes. A flurry of flapping wings rose over the convent wall towards the safety of the barn roof. The birds perched and fussed, observing from their vantage point the busy morning routine around the priory of Saint Mary of the Frideswelle. Out in the far fields a line of harvesters were scything down the last of the corn; a slow steady rhythm of swinging blades flashing in the sunshine. At a distance from them a trickle of gleaners gathered in the residue, old women and children mostly, while a gaggle of nuns in bright holiday dress darted hither and thither, enjoying the excitement of this annual holy day.

Within the cloister quadrangle no one stirred for it was late afternoon in early autumn. Only the long-tailed swallows lined up along the chapel roof, leaving their empty nests in the rafters, preening their feathers for the long flight ahead.

Across the thick forest of the hunting Chase the autumn leaves were browning and curling upwards; a sure sign that the season was closing fast. Already a few leaves fluttered like feathers on to the turf. It would take only one frost to loosen the rest. Deep under cover the fallow deer roamed at will, filling their bellies with greenery, hidden from humankind.

The orchards were dripping with fruit, branches arching with the weight, and bees droned around the ripened crop. Here and there ladders were perched precariously against tree trunks and children were busy throwing costards and pearmains into baskets under the supervision of two old nuns, conspicuous in this riot of colour by still wearing the habit of the black ladies. Soon the cool store lofts would be full of pears, quinces, filberts and apples. The medlars would be left to rot to perfection before they graced the board of the Prioress and her guests.

In the cemetery orchard a few pigs snouted for windfalls under the watchful eye of the holy women laid to rest under the sod, united now in offering their bones to nourish the cherries and damsons each season.

The scent of fruit and ripeness hung heavy on the air. The pink stone of the dorter and refectory walls glistened in the sunshine where crimson rosehips and berried honeysuckle climbed up to the upper casements. The birds cooed to each other across the cobbled courtyard where hens clucked and strutted below.

At their presence a yard girl, daughter of some local villein, looked up warily from her bean gathering. By her side was the wooden clapper which she would lift high and rattle to scare away intruders from the kitchen garden.

In the dovecote, novice Agnes Bagshott, late of the City of Spires, felt the warm dung squelch between her bare toes as she stared into the dark hut. Dame Juliane was bending her ear with dire warnings.

'You'll clean and scrape off this floor and wheel every

last drop of it in the barrow – to me and not to the kitchen garden, do you hear me, child? I don't want the Cellaress getting her hands on this. Dove dung is the very best, better than chicken droppings. It rots down faster, is richer and finer for my herbs. This must come only to the physick garden. Don't allow yourself to be diverted. Be obedient for once!

I don't know how you can get yourself into so much trouble after all your father's efforts to have you accepted here. We don't usually take girls of your menial rank... Well, get on with it! I want to see this floor gleaming before the day's end. Only then will I allow you leave to watch the harvest feast. You can wait on with the servants. That would be your permanent role here if I had any say in the matter.

'Go on, girl! How many times do you need telling? Or are you deaf as well as stupid?'

Agnes turned her back to hide a grimace. She had a round moon face with small green eyes and twisted her mouth wickedly to mimic her superior before her shoulders slumped in resignation. She turned the wheelbarrow into the doorway, tucked her surplice defiantly into her belt, lifted the fork and bent to her penance. Dame Juliane shuffled away, glowing with satisfaction at having given the lazy novice a piece of her mind.

The dove dung was cleared out twice a year so that the stuff had a chance to rot where it stood. The stench was just about bearable and through the slat holes she could see blue sky. The other novices would be parading their finery through the fields all day and feasting all night but not her. It was unfair of them to punish her so for taking a little leave to visit her kin down the lane, hopping over the wall from the 'mount' banked up to one side; her favourite place to hide and watch the world go by outside the cloister wall. So what if you were meant to meditate around the paths and count your sins as preparation for confession before the old greyfriar who trundled up from the city? It was just too tempting to leg it over the wall for a bit of a chit-chat with her cousin Kit while she struggled to help Simeon the Miller bag up the flour in the mill.

Kit had such pain lifting and no amount of Dame Juliane's cold comfrey compresses, bleedings and poultices, had drawn the devil out of his foothold in her bum. Agnes was only trying to help. Anyway she had done far worse things than visit her family, but that was for her to know and them to find out.

'I hate you, Dame Juliane, you big fat cow!' The anger inside her spurred her on and she piled dung into the barrow until it was almost too heavy to lift. She trundled it away, leaving a trail of tell-tale droppings, winding her way through the gates and gravel walkways around the cluster of thatched buildings which made up the small nunnery. Her feet were stung by the sharp pebbles and burnt by the heat of the hot gravel. Then she passed down the snicket to the opening of the small herb shed where Dame Juliane made up potions and lozenges, poultices and concoctions, for the infirmary and the sick of the district, who were always knocking day and night on the outer door.

The physick garden was enclosed by a hedge and a gate which was often locked to keep children away from the poisonous plants; there were boarders crammed into every nook and cranny of the little convent. They would accept any small child, even someone low-born like herself, if the dowry was sufficient to swell their coffers and put a fine fur trim on the nuns' winter habits.

Agnes Bagshott was here only by courtesy of the community chest of the City guildsmen, chosen from among all the other daughters of the worthymen to be trained as a nun because her father was too mean to splash out another dowry on a daughter. He had sold her life away to ease his own pocket and she hated him for that. How assiduously he had worked to convince them that Agnes alone fitted the requirements of the Prioress, Dame Serena, and the other patrons from the de Saulte manor. He had lied through his teeth as the nuns had soon worked out for themselves.

Agnes had already been chided for idleness about her tasks, disobedience to the rule and disinterest in the services. She had been caught loitering in the city market, chatting to old friends and trying to speak to her father to plead for her release. After that misdemeanour she was taken back and thrashed with a rod then flung on the chancel floor, arms outstretched, to be kicked and trampled on by the congregation on its way to daily offices. She had been on bread and water so many times in the three months since her arrival that she had lost all excess flesh and Cousin Kit said she was like a skinny waif, a beggar's child, not a big juicy nun living high off the hog.

Without visits to her cousin she would have fallen deep into despair so it was worth any punishment just to hear the latest gossip: who was fined for fornication at the Longhall court sessions, who was carrying whose child, town gossip from the pedlars and journeymen, which was mostly about some terrible sickness in the southern shires where a man could break fast with his family in the morning and sup with his forefathers in the other world, such was its power to lay low. Agnes did not like the sound of this at all but they were strict in the Priory about letting in strangers from afar. It was the other night-time visitors to the dormitories no one ever bothered to report. Local men – the Reeve, the Steward, sometimes a friar or priest – often managed to pass a night under the Priory roof undetected, but they were not the type to bring in the pestilence.

Not that she was supposed to share any of these secrets. No one spoke to her if they could help it and she was all but invisible to the other novices, born as they had been in genteel manor houses. They had not had to endure a three-storey city tenement house in Baker's Lane with an open sewer running down the street, sharing the upstairs lodgings with her family and the apprentice bakers. The smell of warm bread still made her stomach heave, she hated it so much.

At least being ignored meant no one wanted to bed with her in her cubicle but neither was she allowed one of the boarders to warm her toes on at night. Agnes hated it when they whispered and tittered in front of her. Sometimes they left muck in her bed or dead mice or bloody rags and made her change it before them. Dame Iseult, niece of Dame Serena de Saulte, was the worst tease and seemed to take delight in sneering at her rough speech and homespun manners, calling her low-browed, coarse-skinned and freckled. The haughty nun in her silk veiling and fine linen had the power to wound or reward with a look or a smile. The other young nuns bleated after her like stupid sheep.

When no one was around Iseult would catch Agnes alone and spitefully pinch her breast or under her arm where the flesh was thin. Agnes would never flinch which only seemed to make matters worse.

After three months her resolve was weakening. She felt such a sick sadness wash over her that she envied the nuns lying under the turf warmed by the evening sun in the orchard cemetery; their life's struggle was over while hers was neverending. She would take herself off to the little cluster of graves close to the shrine of the venerable Ambrosine de Saultain, founder of the Priory, who had lived just to see the day when the church was consecrated before being buried close to the stone walls with many of her family. Only here did Agnes allow herself to break down and weep.

It just was not fair that she was made to be the chosen one given to God while her sister Margery got the dowry *and* Hamon the apprentice when he became a master baker. 'It should have been me!' How often she had cried herself to sleep with that thought. She hated the Priory, Dame Juliane and Dame Iseult – but not as much as she loathed her twin sister, Margery Bagshott. She could rot in hell and Agnes would never say a Mass for her relief. Never in this world.

There'd been twoers in the Bagshott family for generations, as far back as anyone could remember, certainly as far as Edric the Miller of Longhall and his seed corn. Some poor soul always got two for the price of one, an extra mouth to feed and two dowries to find, so it was nothing unusual when Agnes and Margery were born within minutes of each other.

As she scraped more dung from the stone floor, Agnes brooded on her own misfortune. Hamon had belonged to her, not to Margery. It was her at whom he first winked and smiled. The sight of his fair locks curling down his neck, broad shoulders and fine physique, made her swoon in anticipation of their coupling. She was the elder twin and, although they were almost as alike as two peas in a pod, the taller by a thumb measure. But crafty Margery sensed the way the wind was blowing, caught the scent of handfasting on the air. She guessed that as the youngest the nunnery would be her fate if she did not act quickly to escape.

Margery knew all about trickery, already having a string of faithful swains hanging around the market square hoping to catch a glimpse of her proud bearing, lustrous corn-gold braids and green eyes fringed with amber lashes. So it was easy to call herself Agnes, dress in her sister's gown, curl her finger at poor Hamon and ascend to the attic to prove her love for him, hooking him like worm on the bait. The stupid dolt didn't realise he'd been duped until the bun was in the oven and a betrothal must be announced. Agnes fled in tears from the celebrations and the hasty wedding. It was the oldest deception and so easy to accomplish. Neither needed a looking glass to see a reflection of herself but under the skin the sisters were very different. Margery was sly and lazy, mean-hearted and confident of her power. She was evil and Agnes hated her with every fibre of her being for this final treachery.

Now here she was, mucking out a dovecote in the darkness, weeding the physick garden, collecting herbs and drying them in bunches to be stored, like any yard woman. All the other plots were tended by women from the village. The food was prepared by cooks and the Prioress had her own servants. Yet where was the life of embroidery and needlework Agnes had been promised, the chance to learn to read and sing offices? Her hands were coarsened now by grit not flour, her brow darkened and freckled by the sunshine. No fine tunics of silk for her, only the Guild gift of a black woollen habit, and now she was forbidden to wear a shift underneath as another penance for sneaking through the garden gate out on to the mead banks by the stream and so missing Compline.

Few of the other nuns wore a habit. There was always fierce competition to see who was wearing the brightest coloured summer gown, the fanciest of embroidered girdles and purses, and who showed the palest forehead and the softest hair under their veils.

The new Prioress, Dame Serena, had set a much more elegant and light tone among the Priory's occupants.

The Prioress drifted in and out as she pleased, trailed by two little hounds and a pretty child of about five to whom she chattered in French, referring to her as her little protégée Amicia, or Amy for short. Amy looked like a fairy, dressed in fine flowing dresses with a cascade of blonde curls down to her waist. She wore a garland of fresh flowers round her hair, freshly picked from the Prioress's private garden every morning. She slept in the Prioress's chamber and did not mix with the other boarders, being a house guest. No one knew how she came to be living with Dame Serena and who but Dame Iseult was in a position to question her presence? She remained silent on the matter.

In the four months since her arrival, Agnes had seen the Prioress no more than six times in all. Dame Iseult let it be known that Dame Serena was far too busy entertaining guests of great importance to attend the humdrum daily routine of their offices and chapter meetings. She had her own chaplain and a private chapel in which to receive Mass when it fitted in with her plans. Dame Serena gave fine dinners and feasts and had a constant stream of visitors.

Aggie was sure any guest must get better food than was dished up to her. She longed for the trenchers of broth and boiled beef, the pies and stews, which Mother had prepared. Here she was always starving. In a few months she had descended to little more than a field peasant with nut brown arms and hollow cheeks. No one had bothered to visit her and had they bothered she would have been unrecognisable to them all, except perhaps Hamon. Soon he would be bringing his new bride to Longhall to set up a bakery and oven alongside his uncle in the village. That would wipe the smile off Mags's face, being sent up here out of the city smoke and bustle!

Agnes had gleaned as much news as she could from Kit on her stolen visits but lately she had her own fresh source of supply – Hamon himself! How she had missed their talks, and the way they had danced when the shop was shuttered. He'd always gone red in the face when she'd smiled at him and she'd known he still desired her despite being wed to her sister so it was no surprise when she caught a glimpse of him over the wall, peering up from the mill ponds where he called with his cart on a roundabout route to Longhall to visit his kin. Agnes had waved and whistled shamelessly and signalled a tryst down by the brook.

At first it was awkward, they hardly dared look at each other, but finally he held out his arms to her and she knew he loved her. It had been so easy just to let him do whatever he pleased with her there and then in the bushes with darkness as their cover. She lay with legs open like a harlot, waiting for the touch of flesh on flesh. His tongue was rough in her mouth but gentle on her breasts, arousing such a fever in her groin that she screamed out for him to end this torment. The explosion of pleasure she felt then had taken her out of her body and into a new world.

After this it was easy to repeat the trysts each week. Agnes knew of a track through the boundary hedge, well trodden for just such occasions, and they would meet by the stream to satisfy their mutual craving. But soon she began to resent how little time they could enjoy together, and when Margery arrived in Longhall it was not going to be so easy for him to escape at night. Hamon said his wife was in no hurry to leave Baker's Lane and that she was no longer with child. It was all a mistake, apparently.

What a surprise! I bet she never was, thought Agnes grimly.

Darkness was the best part of the day for her. It held no fears. She would put a bolster under the meagre counterpane to hide her absence, sneak down the staircase and run to the cloister gate which was always left ajar for the comings and goings of other night visitors. Then she would speed across the orchard field to the back gate, out along Frideswelle stream and down to Black Brook, hoping her lover would not be late.

Afterwards it was hard to raise herself for the two o'clock bell which started the day, and the patter of cold feet along the cloister walk, hardly opening her eyes. She knew the bags under them were as heavy as an apothecary's pouches. But Hamon's visits were the elixir of life to her.

If only they could escape together and start afresh, far away from this wretched place. But try as she might she could not believe that Hamon the baker was strong enough to leave the bakehouse and his new wife and face the shame of living tally. So for them there could only be the dangerous stolen meetings for which Agnes lived and breathed.

She prayed the wearisome high-born bunch would be far too busy enjoying themselves ever to notice one more adulteress in their midst, especially a sixteen-year-old charity case, low-born and coarse. 'Common as muck' she was called often enough, but dove muck was precious it seemed. She should be safe so long as she kept her hands on the wheelbarrow, eyes meekly on the path, and her thoughts a secret from everyone but God.

'In the name of the venerable Ambrosine de Saultain, first Prioress and founder of this House, who at the calling of the Lord went the way of all flesh and paid to the earth the debt of human kind in the year of Our Lord 1120, who being potent in so many virtues, shining with many graces, restraining herself from all movement of carnal lust, by Divine urging withdrawing herself and escaping the embraces of men to be honoured in perpetuity by the prayers of this House, I do solemnly greet the Dames of Saint Mary of the Frideswelle and hereby announce my intention to make visitation to the above House four weeks hence, where as is custom I will celebrate Divine office...'

'Botheration... Hell's teeth! A visitation and inspection of the accounts. That's all I need!' screamed Serena de Saulte as she flung the parchment across the chamber floor. The child darted nimbly under the oak table board to shelter from this outburst. The Prioress dipped her fingers in the finger bowl, wiped them down her gown and picked up the parchment, bending to bestow a smile on the frightened little girl who crawled out and crept on to her knee, sucking her thumb.

'Do that again, Amy, and I'll put wormwood on your fingers. You know it will spoil your teeth. Why does the naughty man always write to us in Latin when we *parlons français*... See, he seeks to shame me again, *ma petite*.'

Amy snuggled into her. '*Le jardin, Maman, toute 'suite*? We play with Frou Frou...'

'Not now, darling. When Maman has done her nasty work. Be patient. See, I have a comfit for you. Now sit quietly, there's a good girl.'

There was no one to overhear this conversation, thank goodness. The child was growing like grass in springtime and every day Serena thought her more like herself and her kin. It was hard not to indulge in the fancy that Amicia was her very own baby, not a foundling left at the door, wet nursed by Kit the Miller's wife and brought back to her chambers when Serena realised that all she needed to complete her happiness was a little damozel to dress up and play with like a toy. Brushing the child's flaxen hair, soft as silk, always soothed her troubled spirits, and sleeping beside that little warm body smelling of rose petals and lavender was bliss. Whoever her kin were, one at least was high-born, judging by the height of her brow, her swan's neck and proud bearing. She was no cottar's child – unless seeded by one of Serena's own kin perhaps.

Becoming Prioress was always the prerogative of the de Saulte women but no one had warned her about all the tiresome duties and obligations which went with the privilege, such as regular meetings with Robert the Steward, a dour-faced lump who was always giving her bad news and insisting she sell off bits of land here and there to pay their mounting debts. He would stand there reeling off how many of their tenants were overdue with their rents, their fines, their days of obligation to work in the fields. How the Miller was holding back grain for himself, blaming the poor yields on the weather, the blight, the storms. She was sick of him, bringing doom and gloom with his muddy boots, smelly hose and grubby tunic. Then there was the cleric who dealt with the church tithes, which were so much down from last year that she wondered if he was cheating her. He dealt with payments on the deaths of tenants, and burial fees and Masses afterwards. The Church's own land close by needed better tenants and tools, and repairs to a leaking thatch on the barn and the withy fences. There was always something to be spent, accounted for, paid out. It made her head spin for she barely understood it all. No wonder her account books were a shambles of crossings out and blotches.

Another headache were the fees and dowries for child boarders and novices. Their numbers were down again and that was not good news for the income of the Priory. Anxious parents entrusting their little ones needed reassurance that St Mary's was the best school in the district and worthy of their patronage. The last visitation in 1331 received no '*omnia bene*' but a list of recommendations and criticisms on every front. Her poor Aunt Sabillia had been quite embarrassed at the furore and promptly resigned. The Sub Prioress did her best but was never really up to the task, having no head for numbers or brain for Latin and French. So the revenues fell and now Serena de Saulte was faced with a peasant's dilemma: how to eat within her tether. And de Saultes were not trained to make do with what was on hand.

'*Maman... vite*! Play hide and seek with Frou Frou,' called Amy as they descended to the garden.

'In a minute. And please be careful, Amy. It's dirty in the garden, all these mucky plants to soil our clothes.'

'Can I paddle in the stream?'

'Only if you lift up your skirts and save your hem.'

And there was the blessed garden to see to. What a nuisance! And the yard girls were so stupid. As she walked down the wide path, her train brushing the stones, all around her was as near to perfection as Serena could make it. Gone were the straggly borders and drooping plantings of the old infirmary beds, the wanton peonies and dreary lilies. She found lilies so waxen and depressing, reminding her that death must come to all. Serena had ripped out every plant and started again, instructing the Hortolana and the yard girls to lift the soil into neat raised beds edged with stones and to cover the ground over with soft grass neatly shaved, with a tuffet of camomile placed on top to form a cool seat in the shade under a trellis arbour covered with *Rosa alba* and eglantine. She preferred only soft colours on the eye, nothing brash or bright to spoil the neat effect. No weed must poke its head out of the earth to shame their husbandry; no floppy gillyflowers or wandering plants were allowed to stray out of their allotted space in the kitchen yard. Her private pleasance was laced tightly, corseted, staked and controlled, and Serena would brook no thorn or prickle to harm the child as she played with her hoop and hobby horse there.

The flowers were past their best now, flopping and rotting, and the roses were covered in a powdery mildew. It must all be hacked down for it offended the eye and Serena must look only to the ivy-clad walls and winter evergreens to refresh the coming greyness.

It was always a relief to turn indoors away from the bare winter drabness. There was so much to do. Amy needed warmer gowns and she must take herself down to the city market and the cloth merchant to examine the latest fabrics. She would have to order bolts of russets, white veiling, kerseys, friezes, hollands, fur and ribbons to trim up the child's outfits. Dame Dorothea the Sacrist would fashion her some lovely garments.

It gave Serena such pleasure to see the little one twirling and skipping down the wide paths towards the woodland walk, close to the forest wall.

'Mind the water, Amy, the stew pond is hidden...'

She worried about the Bishop's visit. He would expect hospitality and bring a whole retinue of officials and scribes. Inspectors would interview every blessed nun and novice, write reports, consume their meat and expect extra dried fruit and nuts, good ale and sweetmeats, before they left. If only she could think of an excuse to put him off. She did not want strangers to visit, especially now that there were rumours of pestilence in the shire. She was glad that she had her own separate apartments at the end of the buildings where she had rearranged all the services to suit her need for privacy with a supply of fresh water from the well before it was diverted all over the Priory to ponds, latrines and the mill, though lately there was trouble even there.

Everyone knew that pestilence was spread by the foul air from the south, it was carried on the wind and the dust. That was why she liked to be clean and keep any filth from her hands. Dame Maud the Sub Prioress was very lax with the House, letting them eat with fingers undipped. Serena's fingers were raw with the number of times she dipped her hands in pure water tinctured with Hungary rose oil. She had fresh squares of linen to pat them dry.

Amy and Frou Frou were bathed and scrubbed every day. Minon was not so easy to catch. Her coat was too dusty to enter the chambers and soil the fresh strewn rushes. This compulsion to keep washing her hands was troublesome at times and cost her many hours during a week to see to that her ablutions were checked. It extended to her clothing and once a garment was specked or marked with dirt it must be changed at once or she felt deeply uneased. As a child they had laughed at her fussiness but there was always a servant to pull off the gown and find her another.

Now she changed her shift every day and the laundry maid washed every garment by hand. Serena loved the smell of sun bleached linen and the crispness of flat ironed garments hanging from the dressing pole. Her bedsheets were washed daily and sprigged with lavender and tansy. Only her velvets with fur trimmed edgings to her sleeves had to be sponged down and steamed with hot water, the pile brushed gently and the pads under her arms renewed to her satisfaction. Only when every part of her body was bathed in her special tub and sponged could she relax into the feather pillows and flock mattress to snuggle up to the little one and drift into slumber.

Most of her day fled by in these ablutions so it left little time to attend the singing of the offices or the Chapter meeting assembly. She left all the daily business to Dame Maud. Father John, her personal chaplain and priest to the parish came to the little antechamber, consecrated as a chapel to hear her confession, read her devotions, celebrate Mass and take the other offices in her stead. No one could say she was not meticulous in her devotions although Dame Juliane warned her that constant washing was bad for the health. 'A little dirt, Madame, protects the skin, a little oil gives a gloss and a shine to an animal's coat. Salt is good as a preservative and skin salt preserves cloth. Too much laundry weakens fibres and they lose their stiffness. Bathing like blood letting need be done only twice a year whether we need it or not.' Dame Juliane was an old fool and her physick was not what it was.

In the privacy of her own quarters Serena de Saulte could run her household just as she pleased as lady of the manor, worthy to receive curtseys and bows. The religious life did not over burden her. She would fast only on the high days and holy days as was the rule. Fortunately fish had escaped the curse of Adam and could be eaten without penance and there was plenty of variety, eel, salmon, trout, perch to eke out the fast days.

Fish had been caught with poor scales and rotting fins, sickly-looking specimens no one fancied eating. They were thrown into the stew pot and promptly gave off such a foul stench that the whole broth was thrown on the dung heap to rot down. The Cellaress had been most apologetic and sent for the fish warden who did not know why the fish failed to thrive. ''Tis not a good sign when the Frideswelle gives up dead fish. Something must be fouling the water.' Yet another trouble brought to Dame Serena's door. What did she know about such matters?

Suddenly the child stopped running ahead of her and stood pointing excitedly.

'*Vite! Maman... pauvre petite... une faune perdue... vite!*'

Serena lifted her train and swung it over her arm, rushing to see why the little one was fussing. There in the middle of the pond was a young stag, its antlers caught in an overhanging branch. Exhausted with the struggle to keep itself out of the water, it was barely alive. It had obviously jumped from the forest straight over the wall and into the pond. 'What shall we do, Maman? The poor deer will drown?' cried the child.

'Run and fetch the damosel from the kitchen. Tell her to bring as many strong yard girls as she can find... and some rope too. Quick!'

'*Merci à Dieu...* we shall save it!' smiled the child.

Oh, yes, Amicia, we shall save it. And hang it, and carve it up for the Bishop's feast. No one can be executed now for killing a deer from a Royal forest but once His Reverence has filled his belly full of stolen meat he'll have no choice but to pronounce the '*omnia bene*' on our little Priory. All may yet be well, she thought, skipping down the track. Yes, all would be well now.

The Michaelmas Market

❦

It's today! The maid rose from her straw mattress, on the earth floor, shook off the arms and legs of her sleeping sisters, scratched her sores, straightened her twisty leg. No one stirred as she lifted the flap of the doorway cover and stretched her aching bones in the coming light.

It was market day and she had permission to leave the village with Mistress Kit to visit the city of three spires. She, Mary Barnsley, 'Limpy Mary' to the inhabitants of the Miller's house where she worked, was the first in her family to leave Frideswelle for the whole day.

There was no rainwater in their one bucket to splash on her blotchy face. The rash round her mouth was on fire but she mustn't scratch or it would bleed again. Mistress Kit sometimes gave her hog's grease with dried elderflower leaves in it to soothe away the itch. Mary could hardly wait to pin a kerchief over the straggles of her black hair. The mistress always made her tie it away out of sight even though it was her crowning glory for she was always scratching her head when the lice bit her scalp. Today she would be early to her tasks so as to be ready and waiting when the mistress loaded the cart with market goods from neighbours and the Reeve. She was a tranter and had permission to exchange goods, sell herbs and take flour sacks to her kin in the city. Mary was bursting with excitement to be her assistant today.

She let herself into the Miller's houseplace, stoked up the fire with dry logs and set the pot to boil. Next she lecked the rushes with a sprinkling of water to dampen down the dust. She was careful to sweep the dirty rushes out of the room in a neat pile for the midden heap, sweeping them first away from the hearthstones so that no sparks might set fire to them and brushing them inwards so as not to let the good luck out of their home. Then she shook out the new woven rush mats with pride; no one else in Frideswelle but the Miller's wife could sport such finery or cover the open window hatches with oiled linen flap overs. As she bent to place them carefully by the oak stools and the chest, her hip was pierced with daggers of pain which no amount of grease rubs and comfrey poultices would soothe.

Simeon Miller was already at work, spending every daylight hour at his mill, watching over the yard boys and his assistants. The harvest was coming in and there was corn from all over the district to be ground by the big quernstones, so much for him to attend to that he was in no mood for market fairs and fol-de-rols. Mistress Kit said she needed to find preserving spices and vinegar, there were green herbs to barter and they were to visit her Aunt Annie Bagshott and daughter Margery, the highlight of the trip. Mistress Kit wanted to get in early to pitch outside the bakery before other farmers' wives got there before her. Her two sons could make themselves useful in the yard where Mary's own mother, Alice, would keep an eye on them in return for Kit taking young Mary down the track on her cart.

She worried that her mam would let the mistress down again and steal from her shelves while she was away, or else lie on her flock mattress in the solar upstairs, sullying the covers with her sour smell. Mother had little enough time to rest, looking after her noisesome brood. They lived from hand to mouth, one meal a day of pot herbs dunked with a bit of broiled bacon, which was usually rancid for lack of salt. No wonder all of them were chitty-faced with hollow cheeks and festering sores. Mary Barnsley was grateful for the chunks of goat's cheese and hunks of bread her kind mistress gave willingly to her kin to stave off hunger. It was a pity Mary's father, Jack Barnsley, was so fond of the ale bench and lashing his fists into Mam's face.

Nothing like that went unobserved in the little pinfold of houses and cottages set back from the entrance of the Priory. Bruises and black eyes were common enough, but no one interfered in case they ended up the worse for it. How Mary longed for the peace of that world behind the convent wall, one where no one went hungry or cold and women lived far from the rough beatings of brothers and fathers. She longed to be allowed to work inside there but knew it would never be.

The mill was the next best place to be employed. It was timber-framed with large ponds and a stream coursing through to turn the wheel at breast level, giving the best wheel power. The Miller's house stood proudly next door, lifted above the other dwellings by being larger and higher than the rest with a big yard and buttery shed for the cooking, gardens full of vegetables and an orchard too where Mary loved to walk and scrump apples. Across the green were the smaller houses and lastly the hovels of the three cottar families who had only a little patch of ground around them and a few tumbledown sheds with cows tethered inside. Here was where she must sleep at night.

All the men were in the fields doing service for Dame Serena de Saulte. Mistress Kit grumbled at how much they were expected to give to the church: tithes, funeral dues and death gifts. The families were allowed to worship at Longhall or occasionally in the Priory chapel so long as they were well to the back and kept quiet. This was nigh on impossible with two naughty lads so Mary sometimes went too to help keep them quiet. How she loved to sit in the cool of the chapel and stare at the beautiful pictures on the walls, the statues covered in gold, blue and red; so much colour and lovely singing to brighten the daily grind. If only she could live her life within these walls. But only gentry folk were allowed to be holy nuns.

She loved the way Father John intoned the service, the bells and smells of incense and candles. She could not wait to go to Heaven. Not that Mary understood a word that was spoken usually but last week Father John, priest to Frideswelle and Barnsley Common, read out a letter from the Lord Bishop himself, in English, warning the congregation to repent and pray for their sins in order to avoid the great pestilence descending over the land like a plague of locusts – whatever they were. There was a hushed murmuring and a shaking of heads at such terrible news but Mistress Kit said that she could not imagine anything disturbing the peace and quiet of this sleepy hamlet. The nearest double cart track was three miles away, closer to Longhall and the City of Spires.

Now, as they jiggled down the track in the cart laden with flour sacks and herbs in baskets, Mary was willing the journey to last forever. Mistress Kit had lent her one of her own smocks to cover up the grime of her skirt but none of her shoes would fit Mary's twisted foot. She sometimes had a strange knowing without words of the thoughts of others and knew that this good wife was counting her blessings to be wed to a kindly man, with two healthy boys and her stew pot always full.

'When we visit poor Annie Bagshott at the bakehouse don't speak about her troublesome daughters,' the mistress warned. 'Stay well back out of their wind and observe all I do.'

Mary knew all about Aggie Bagshott's woes. Every day she would sneak over the wall to bend Mistress Kit's ear about Dame Iseult and Dame Juliane. How her father must be told how ill his daughter was becoming, how she struggled to breathe in that place, like a fish out of water, dull-eyed and lonesome. 'I'll wilt and die if I don't get away!' she'd say.

Then there was Mistress Mags, her sister, who was all airs and graces, trying to pretend she was the Shire Reeve's wife not wed to a baker. Mistress Kit had whispered once that Margery led poor Hamon a merry dance with her flirtations and spending sprees. Her poor mother was quite worn out with her idleness too. Mistress Kit said she was glad she had no girls to worry over yet. Boys were simple; feed them, beat them, cuddle them, let them run wild like puppy dogs until they snuffed themselves out like candles each night. In Mary's family the boys were rough and coarse, kicking her and stealing her food, and she hated them all.

Her eyes were soon on stalks as she turned and twisted to get the best views as the countryside around became unfamiliar to her. This track was lined with thick high hedgerows, arching over in a canopy of golden leaves. The rustle of the wind through the branches, the scent of mist and fruit on the air, stirred Mary's feelings of excitement even more. Mistress Kit explained that the Michaelmas Fair was the best one of all, especially when the ripe fruits were displayed and the sweet scent of meadow rushes and herbs underfoot mingled with their scent. It lasted for four days sometimes.

Along the hedgerows the last of the summer flowers looked tired and grey but the rosehips were good and they decided to pick some for winter cough syrup on their way back. Soon they would enter the city through the north gate, entering darker alleys, clumped up together like a tangle of roots. There was little light or air in the city which was always wreathed in smoke.

Mary was disappointed by her first glimpses of the fearsome place. There were smelly channels running down the lanes; putrid carcasses were flung out of the butcher's on to the road to be snatched by beggars with boils and toothless grins. She found the rumble of carts and constant shouting a little frightening. The mistress said not to be afeared, she would soon get used to it. She also warned it would be noisier today as the fair stalls would spill out of the market place down the side streets. At least the market place itself was open and bright.

As the mistress steered the cart into the procession of travellers and handcarts, tumbrils and wagons, the line drew to a halt. The stall holders parked and waited. 'What's the hold up?'

'No strangers to be let in,' came word down the line, 'on account of the sickness coming into the city.'

'What sickness?'

'Haven't you heard? The fever has come to the district and they don't want it in their city. Turn back now or you'll be driven away by the constable,' a pedlar spat out.

'Saints in heaven preserve us! I'm here to deliver flour to my kin at the bakery. How many times have you seen me go through this gate? Hell's teeth, I live but three mile up the track! Mary, mind the cart.'

The mistress, in her best russet gown and kerchief, was in no mood to be gainsaid and jumped down, her back stiff from the jolting ride. She marched up to the gate, smiled at the constable's assistant, gave her maiden name of Bagshott, and their cart was waved through – much to the anger of some of the pedlars and chapmen hanging about hoping for entry to the fair.

Once inside the city, they made straight for Kit's usual pitch outside the bakery but the shop was shuttered and the streets quiet for a market day. There was tension in the air and the goodwives did not linger at the few stalls which were open in 'Women's Ceaping' but hurried on with their baskets clutched tight and their faces veiled. The street corners were quiet; no jugglers and fire-eaters, no dancing bears, no troubadours or travelling players. It was quiet as a fast day.

To the mistress's amazement, there was not a fresh herb or an ounce of spice to be bought anywhere, no fennel seeds or liquorice root, ginger pieces or treacle. Nothing medicinal left at all. Only rumour was in plentiful supply: how sickness was in Tamworth and the villages around, creeping ever closer; how once it came no one was safe; how the priests could do nothing but pray and would not even bury the dead; how whole families were wiped out in a day, in an hour even, as they tended their sick. Mary suddenly felt ill with fear and clung to the cart.

'Perhaps we should just make the one stop and go straight home?'

The sky was dark indeed, even the light seemed foul, and she no longer felt safe. But the mistress was battering on the bakehouse yard gate, shouting, 'Will! It's Kit, your sister's child! Let me in to deliver.'

A lad peered above the wall to check them. It was Hamon.

'It's only the flour, and Mistress Miller and her maid.'

The gate was opened gingerly and the cart quickly pulled in.

'You're mad to risk these streets today, Kit. Whatever possessed you to wander abroad? Have you not heard about the pestilence?' 'Poor Aunt Annie' emerged from the bakehouse, her flushed cheeks dusted with white. Margery followed at a distance, looking at them suspiciously.

'We didn't think it would reach here so soon, Aunt. The gossips on the stalls are full of it.'

'And so they might for it's battering down our doors even as we speak, I fear. Go home now, Kit, don't dawdle. Consider your bairns. It fills me with dread to think how God will punish us all! I cannot sleep for fear of it creeping through the casement to strangle us in our beds as we sleep. Many are fleeing to the hills. Dark times, Kit, I fear, dark times.'

'You've water at the Grey Friars gate piped fresh from the hills. I hear the pump is free to all. How does this fever spread? Who brings it to the door?'

'No one dare go to the well for fear it travels in their buckets from the pipes. Strangers with fever on their breath may drink from the tap. Touch no sore or body with the sickness unless your hands are soaked in vinegar, I've heard, and keep garlic by your side at all times. They say it will protect. That's all we know here.'

'Annie, I couldn't buy a clove of garlic. It's sold out.'

Mary listened closely, sweat pouring from her brow in the oven heat of the bakehouse, trying not to shame her mistress by scratching.

'Aye, you'll have to pay in gold for a single clove, such is the demand. There's not a gillyflower head or a jar of vinegar to be had within these walls. The herb seller is fled and his garden ransacked. Warn our Aggie to stick close to the physick garden and to store herbs for herself, then get on her knees to pray for her kin. I'm glad she's safe behind those walls. Nothing can harm a godly nun.'

Now was not the time for Mistress Kit to tell them the truth about Agnes's unhappiness there. It would have to wait for better days.

Margery could see their news was scaring the visitors.

'Stop it, Mother! You'll bother us all to death with this chatter. It's only talk, Kit. Have no fear. It hasn't come here or no one would be let in or out, not even you. You haven't come all this way to hear such tittle-tattle, take no notice. A few dead of fever in the back alleys… dogs and beggars. There's nothing new in that, is there? Now how's that bad back of yourn and your two young scallywags? And who's this ragamuffin by your side?'

But Mistress Kit did not alight from the cart after these friendly words. Instead she turned it around and bade them farewell. Margery darted out with her, glad to be in the weak midday sunshine. The streets of board stalls were so quiet and the streetmongers strangely silent as they swayed from alley to court with their baskets. Few had paid over their pence to set up a stall.

For once Margery kept her eyes from their ribbons and trims, making straight for the cloth merchant and the haberdasher's stall. She needed to cheer herself up. Goodwife Harwise's stall was always just round the corner in Women's Ceaping, tempting the local girls with second-hand garments. Goody would always keep back special items in her sack for one of her most regular customers.

What Hamon didn't know would do him no harm; how

she stole the odd coin from his leather purse belt, delivered more loaves than were ordered and kept the difference for her clothing allowance, overpriced and cheated customers when the opportunity arose, so that she was never without a few bits of silver to treat herself. Everyone admired Margery Bagshott for her genteel outfits, the way she harmonised colours and fabrics, wore different gowns to all the civic occasions and Guild parades. She wore dagged edgings to her sleeves and tunics, bought fresh ribbons and embroidered on them flowers and motifs like the finest Lady of the Manor. She won disapproving glances from the higher ranked wives for showing off and could see them wondering how she obtained such quality cloth and other finery. Well, it was the early bird that caught the worm and usually she shot out on market day to catch Goody's stall before the streets were thronged. But today there would be no hurry. No one would be buying anything but herbs and spices, such was the general fear. There would be bargains to be had.

Margery waited until a few browsers had moved on before she tapped the stallholder on the shoulder. 'Anything for me today?'

The dealer spun round, her face pink and sweaty, eyes tired.

'You startled me... no, I've nothing much.' She saw the look of disappointment on Margery's face and grinned mischievously. 'But just for you, there could be this beauty here...' Goody pulled out a sleeveless surcoat of the richest heavy wool, edged with fur and slashed to show any gown worn underneath. 'It belonged to a lady, that I do know, but she has no need of it now, poor soul.'

'Don't you go telling me she died of the fever?' Margery dropped the coat quickly.

'Now would I sell my best customer such a death robe?

No, I have it on the finest authority that the widow woman had no daughters to pass it on to in her will. I gave a good price for it.' Goody rummaged around her stall, not looking the girl in the eye.

'It's beautiful and so thick. Just what I need with winter coming on. How much?'

'For you, my dear, two silver pieces.'

'So much? I don't think…'

'Mistress Baker, look at the quality, feel it. You'll not see the like again for many a year.'

'The fur looks flea-bitten to me.' Margery was desperately trying to find a reason not to buy the garment.

'Only dust… it's travelled many a mile in its time and will grace your slender outline for many more. Think how you'll look in it on the arm of your handsome husband. He'll be admired for having such a worthy wife.' The dealer knew when to soothe and flatter away any indecision. For Margery this was the stuff of dreams.

'Go on, you've twisted my arm. I shall have to pay in bits, as I can. Here's all I have for now. Next week there'll be more. Save it for me.'

'Nay, lass, take it. I know where you live. If you don't pay up I can always knock on the bakehouse door. I'm sure you'd not want that, would you? My legs are weary today and my head aches so much the stalls spin around me… I'm in no mind to carry something away only to bring it back again. Keep it and enjoy the fortune it brings.'

Margery bundled the garment into her basket under the few loaves she had brought to disguise her purpose. No one must see her surcoat until she was ready to dazzle them with her bargain. It must be hidden in the sack with her other pur-chases, high on a shelf away from rats and mice. She would brush it and check it closely for any fleas but it was worth every penny. Wait until Aggie clapped eyes on her in it! It would be worth traipsing up to Frideswelle to visit her sister, just to see the green stalks of envy shooting from her eyes at the sight of Mags in her glory. What a lark that would be!

'Where shall we wander now, Mary? This has been a poor show for you today. Not at all what we expected. Would you like a honey cake or an apple? We can take the high road back by Overstowe towards the shrine, if that pleases you? We'll pass the swampy grounds where the King himself walked barefoot in pilgrimage to the shrine of the Blessed Chad by the well a few years back. What a day that was for our Prioress and her nuns, to process behind the King and his courtiers! Don't you remember how Father John feasted on every detail?'

Mary smiled wanly. Kit was doing her best to cheer them both up, to repair the day, but nothing was how she had dreamed it would be.

The maid did not like the foul-smelling streets, the noise and the dark passageways. Frideswelle was fairer by far and she longed to be back in the orchard, looking over the wall into the peaceful Priory.

'Come, child, that's a sad face… Let's go to the shrine ourselves and buy a blessing token for you.'

There was just one stall selling token badges and pilgrim biscuits, and a pardoner selling his indulgence scripts. Mary watched the pilgrims kneel by the well, which was little more than a puddle of water with a thatched roof over it. An old woman knelt for a sprinkling of holy water, praying for some cure. Perhaps the saint could cure Mary's leg of its twist, straighten it out so that she could be a lay sister across the lane? Why did God make her come out all twisted, pulled out backwards and bottom first? How many times had she been told it was His miracle she had lived? If only she could have been born healthy to a mother like Mistress Kit.

There was such a wistful look in her sad dark eyes that even the mistress felt tears welling up and shoved her hand into her purse to pay for a blessing on the girl. 'Here, you go and dip yourself in the holy well and buy a honey cake. But don't tell your mother. Then we'll go home the back way, through the pretty woods at Elmhurst, on to the Longhall cart road and down into Frideswelle.'

Mary knelt with difficulty, waiting for her miracle for a long moment, but nothing stirred. There was only the sound of a blackbird pinking. The best of the weak sunshine was fading and soon it would be dusk. The Michaelmas Fair had been a poor show indeed and news of the sickness had dampened their spirits but high up at Frideswelle they would be safe enough.

It was almost dark when they returned down the windy top road past the Priory gatehouse. In the twilight a little girl lurked in the shadows: the Prioress's little minx, Amicia, standing sucking her thumb as she always did when she sneaked out through the hedgehole for a kiss and a cuddle from her wet nurse.

Kit unbridled the mule wearily. 'Go inside, child. I'll see to this madam forthwith.' Mary paused, hearing the child whining, 'Want some titty…'

Every day she would cry for comfort and Mistress Kit always opened her shirt for the child to take from her teat. Mary knew it wasn't right and the Prioress, if she learned of it, would have them all punished. Amy had been at Kit's breast these past two years. The pretty poppet who had everything wanted only her wet nurse but this was their little secret. They huddled together under cover of darkness while Mary stood guard, not understanding any of it. She sniffed the air, which smelled sweet in her nostrils, and was glad to be home, safe from the vapours of the city in the valley below.

Two days later there was panic within the Priory and Dame Juliane was in a crotchety mood again, barking orders for jars of hog's fat and leek seeds. Her shed had been ransacked again and all her newly set lozenges stolen. The herbs in the physick garden had been scythed down and trampled so that the infirmary garden lay desolate and bare, tinged with silver in the first autumn frost.

'Who's doing this, child? Who's stupid enough to steal the herbs with no knowledge of their use? Some of the yard girls, fearing for their lives, have run away. See, they have taken poison berries and deadly roots… Without the right star signs to guide us our medicines are useless. Come on, Agnes, shape yourself. I want more clove gillyflowers. See if there are any creeping up the wall. They like that position best now that Dame Serena has torn them out of the old garden to make her fancy pleasance. She's sorry enough since her damozel fell sick yesterday.

'The poor little mite lies stricken but she cannot be moved now and the Prioress has fled to another chamber in the nuns' dorter so as not to catch the fever herself. The child is left alone with only the dogs, but she must be isolated for the safety of us all. Only Father John dares risk the sick room to say prayers for her recovery.'

Agnes was for once all ears, greedy for news of the outbreak of sickness in the village beyond the wall. It had started at the mill with Cousin Kit falling into a swoon and vomiting up blood, her skin all covered in blotches it was rumoured. Poor Kit, Agnes's only friend, had barred her children and husband from the room but Simeon broke down the door in his distress and now was sick himself. Their crippled maid was also ailing with tell-tale swellings under her armpits, the size of tiny apples, but she saw to them all until she was laid low in the apple loft. Her own kin across the green, afeared for their lives, barred her from their hovel to keep out the sickness. Simeon Miller had sent his boys to Longhall village, thinking someone would take them in, but they were met by his old childhood friends bearing staves, forcing the lads back down the track. Frideswelle village was now cut off even from the Priory, such was Dame Serena's determination to keep out the fever.

Agnes climbed on top of the wall to shout to Simeon but the mill wheel was silent for once and she feared the worst. Someone had repaired all the gaps in the wall with stones and thorny branches. The beggars and wanderers came sneaking out of the forest under cover of darkness to plead with the priest to bury their dead. Father John hid from them in the church. Hamon had not visited for weeks now and Agnes was going mad for want of his touch.

She reckoned that if there was sickness here then it must have come from the city. For the moment she was safer inside the wall than out. The Prioress now appeared every day at the chapter meeting and insisted every room be brushed and freshly strewn. She'd ordered all the nuns to be bled to improve their blood and now Dame Juliane issued leeches to gorge on each nun as close to the heart as possible.

Agnes hated blood letting for it drained her spirit and left her tired and foul-mouthed, but she had to admire the way Dame Juliane had braved the sickness to soothe the child,

Amy, with elecampane grease one morning. One look at the size of her swellings and a whiff of their foul stench had sent even her scurrying for safety, however. 'She's doomed, such horrors cannot be borne by a child for long,' she'd said sadly.

Later, feeling guilty for abandoning the girl, Dame Juliane took her novice to the door of Amy's bedchamber. Mercifully the child was dead, already covered by a shroud. Father John lifted her with gloves on his hands and buried her out of sight at the bottom of the orchard field with only the Prioress as witness. For three nights the Priory held its breath, waiting for the Angel of Death to pass over. Three nights of vigil and prayer. No other case of fever broke out.

Mary woke in the darkness. Her throat was on fire and her limbs ached too much for her even to turn on her side. Where was she? It did not smell of hearthsmoke here. The sickly sweet smell which had been in her nostrils was no longer there. Instead she could smell the ripeness of fruit and fresh hay. There was not a sound. Then she felt the swellings, once the size of apples and now the size of plums, which ran down her belly to the top of her itching legs. They were hard, sore, but unruptured. Her neck felt swollen and stiff, her ears throbbed with strange noises and her tongue was hanging out with thirst. By her side stood a pitcher of water but she could scarce move to lift it. Instead she bent forward painfully to lick the cool earthenware. Where was she? Not in the mill, not by the hearth but alone, covered with a thin shroud, somewhere in the darkness.

She heard the sound of mice scampering through the straw, a cock crow at a distance and with the approach of dawn came remembrance.

I must get up and see to the fire. I must set the pot a-boiling as I've always done... But a sickly weakness seeped into her limbs. She had been ill of the fever like her mistress and all her kin. Mistress Kit and her boys were gone now. In her heart Mary knew she was the only one left alive. The rest was a blur, she did not want to recall how they'd suffered, but how did she come to be here, safe from harm in a cool loft?

Then she heard the bell tolling. The sound was almost on top of her. Surely she was not within the Priory? Who had left the jug of fresh water close at hand? Someone must know she was here. She must wait to see who had come to her aid.

All Agnes could think of from Matins to Vespers was escaping from this place. The Priory had been frightened from its lax habits into strict observance of the rule again. Every nun was to wear her black habit, cover her head and wash her hands before offices were said. There was also a steady procession to the Frideswelle spring to drink the water, risky though this might seem, but the Prioress swore by the efficacy of holy water and they knew the Blessed Ambrosine had once seen the Virgin in the well.

It was Dame Juliane's theory that Amy had died for being too clean and protected from the foul air. How else could the child have sickened, being totally confined within the Priory walls? Agnes volunteered to wash down the Prioress's rooms so they might be used as a temporary infirmary should it be needed. She liked to sit there amongst the fine tapestry wall hangings and oak four poster bed with its rich drapes, admiring the view over the pleasance garden, cut off from all the turmoil. The bed was stripped and dismantled at the Prioress's order, to be stored out of sight. Dame Serena could not countenance any reminder of the little maid. The floor was freshly strewn with rose petals.

Sometimes Agnes was woken by the sound of a child crying out. The thought of such sufferings filled her with horror. If ever she was to catch the fever she would not endure such lingering agony. Oh, no! She'd want out of the suffering and knew enough now to ensure a hasty exit. That was the one good thing about being yoked to the infirmary, with access to lotions and potions, some much deadlier than others. Poppy syrup would make her drowsy enough to swallow anything to ease her discomfort and safely locked away there were tiny balls of dog's mercury, henbane, cowbane, hemlock and monkshood, any of which would hurry her on her way. She wasn't yet sure of the quantity but stole enough of each to make up three round lozenges which she wrapped in dock leaves and put in a leather pouch carried around her neck. She made up the remedy slowly and skilfully, remembering each prayer which the old nun usually mumbled, each charm uttered in the making. Agnes was learning fast out of necessity. Just carrying such deadly protection made her feel strong and calm and she noticed now that there was no bullying from the high-born nuns, from Iseult de Saulte or her favourites. In fact, just the opposite. Agnes was now an object of interest and respect. If they fell sick then they would be in her hands, for her to do with as she pleased. For the first time she knew what it was to wield power and the feeling was good.

Margery Bagshott pleaded with Hamon to send her to Longhall to live with his kin away from the terror in the streets around them. The air was heavy with the stench of death. Every night corpses were thrown like garbage into the drain. The night soil men lifted them for a fee but more often than not, if the corpses were far gone and uncovered, left them to stink for days so that flies and rats scavenged among the debris. The tide of fever had washed over the city in several waves since the Michaelmas Fair. It would recede for a few days only to return again to catch another street, another alley of houses. It was the lucky and the blessed who woke to see another dawn.

The bakery had remained shuttered and locked, no one going in or out. Will Bagshott fed his family on his reserves of flour and water from the deep underground well hidden from view. The dogs were set on strangers trying to break in for supplies. He sold the surplus at a high premium to members of the Guild, knowing that when all this was over many favours would be owed him. Margery sat by the upper casement, looking out over the city, like a prisoner in a condemned cell. The tolling of the church bells would drive her to madness if she did not escape. There was a common pit on the outskirts where the dead were thrown from carts in the night, and when the wind came from the west the stench of rotting flesh was overpowering.

She *must* escape. It could not be so bad in the villages and Aggie was the safest of all, she'd heard, walled up in her Priory. If only she had known the future Margery could have been there and it would be Agnes suffering here. Mags felt sick with fear.

She knew it was not the fever for it had gone on for many months. A child was kicking in her womb and she would bear no babe in this festering hell hole. Hamon knew her condition and was weakening in his resolve to keep them all together.

'Please, Hamon, let's go together, far away from this place,' she pleaded again.

'And be beaten to death by strangers? No, you must go to

my parents' cot or to your cousin's mill. Don't put our child at risk, my sweet.'

Hamon was thrilled that his seed was ripening in her belly at last and had so many plans for his son and heir. Margery hoped it wasn't another cursed double seed. If so she would smother one herself for she wanted no bairn of hers to be burdened with its own reflection in the looking glass, like she and Aggie.

'I'll go in the morning by first light, after the first batch of bread is baked. I can bribe the gate guards if I have to and take the field path through the long meadows and the streams up to Frideswelle. No one will see me,' she said eagerly.

'Then wrap up well against the wind and the vile humours abroad.'

Thinking of keeping warm reminded her of the secret in the flour sack. It would be a perfect way to cover her condition and keep them both snug and dry. She raced down the wooden stairs to the outer yard and felt for the sack on the shelf, shaking out the garment and seeing fleas jump out. In the corner the cat whimpered sickly and snarled at her, spitting out vile breath. She would be glad to be out of this place. It smelled of must and rottenness, damp yeasty sickly smells which turned her stomach. Mags wondered if it was right to wear such a fine cloak. Would someone rob her of it? The old cloth dealer had never returned for payment, but then no one much came into the city and the market was deserted while the fever raged.

The surcoat would dazzle Hamon's parents with the Bagshotts' standing in the city. Only wealthy traders could clothe their wives in such finery. She would freshen it up with the last of the vinegar rub and some rosewater. That should keep her safe from pestilent odours.

'You look mighty swish in your outer coat. Is this another of your bargains?' smiled Hamon indulgently, for he knew that when Margery was well dressed she was happy and compliant to all of his needs. Who else in the city had two such baker's buns to satisfy his hunger?

He opened the gate quietly, careful not to stir the rest of the household. She was right to get away to the forest, find a safe haven for the sake of their child. He kissed her on the cheek and patted her belly.

'Hurry, Mags, before you're missed. I'll explain. They'll understand. Fare thee well, and don't return until the fever has gone, no matter what.'

She hugged the simple loon with genuine affection. As husbands went she could have picked or stolen worse than Hamon the baker.

She waved until she turned the corner then decided to dodge the guard by taking a rat run down a very dark alley, carefully picking her way over the scattered bodies. It was a terrible sight and she chanted the charm against plague over and over again: 'Anazapta… ana… zapta.'

It was going to be a long dreary walk uphill. She would try Kit Miller at Frideswelle first and send a message to Aggie to meet her by the gate. She wanted to see the look on her sister's face when she saw Margery in her surcoat and the twisted gold loop set with a garnet given to her as a bridal morning after gift by Hamon. Then she would point to her swollen belly. That should really wipe the smile off a dowdy nun's face!

Face to Face

'What's this I hear? You've disobeyed my orders and brought that crippled maid into this house – she who brought the fever almost to our door. Father John, I can't believe you'd be so foolish!'

Dame Serena paced her chamber, beside herself at his boldness. The priest was a simpleton.

'Madam, please hear me out. In Christian charity I've done what I thought best for you all. Be it that Our Lady in her wisdom saw fit to reprieve this girl from the fever and she being the only one that I know of so far, her swellings shrunken and her recovery complete, I saw fit to let her rest in the loft of my lodgings awhile to observe this miracle of grace. Think, madam, we now have amongst us one who will not succumb again. She has no kin alive to shelter her, is alone and unprotected. We have no lay sisters left to serve us for they've all fled into the forest away from gatherings of folk. Would it not be wise to let her abide within these walls as helpmate to us all?'

What use is a cripple?'

'Our Lord in his wisdom blessed such many a time. She told me she took a blessing at the shrine of Chad and I believe it is he who saved her for this purpose. She wears his token around her neck. I believe, such is his power, he prevented her swellings from bursting as a sign that the humble can be blessed in the sight of God. She should be used to give hope and encouragement. Who knows when we may need her here? She can come with me to bury the poor souls. Perhaps she will protect me in my work too.'

'Keep her well cleansed and tidy and out of my sight, then. I don't wish to be reminded of how perfection is mocked. Why could not my little maid be saved, not some limping wretch? It is not just.'

'The Lord sees us from afar. Perhaps he does not see imperfections, only what is in the heart. Mary is simple and rough, as you say, but pure of heart. We should be kind to her.'

'Very well, on your own head be it, Father John. Now, leave me. All this talk of death wearies me.' The Prioress waved him away and stood staring out of the window. She was as cold within as the scene beyond the shutters, the icy clutch of winter tightening around her heart. The last blooms of the flower beds and arbours were withered and shrivelled by frost. A white veil of rime silvered the cloister grass, froze the stew ponds. The fish lay hidden deep under water. Would they all die like the summer flies, one by one, within these walls? When the first fall of snow covered the cemetery, would the perfect whiteness conceal more untimely deaths?

At least there was to be no visitation for the Bishop's men were falling sick and he had no mind to wander abroad in such times as these, fleeing instead to his winter house deep in the forest. They could eat their stolen venison undisturbed but Serena de Saulte had little appetite for celebration now. Dearest Amy... you are cold and I was too afraid to stay at your side. Can you forgive Maman? There was no solace in her daily offices but she must stick to her tasks if they were all to survive. Perhaps the priest was right to bring the girl inside. They had been sorely punished for their lax ways. Suffering must stiffen their sinews. Only prayer and fasting would keep the enemy from the gate. And perhaps some other precautions, too.

She peered towards the dovecote. The birds must be slaughtered, and the cats too, but not her dogs. It was rumoured that animals could carry disease.

In the heart of the cloister and out across the far fields the soil lay tinged with silver, freshly harrowed and waiting for the spring. Who among them would be spared to see those fresh green shoots?

'There's someone at the gate for Miss Agnes. Beg pardon, Dame Juliane, but she's not for turning back.' Mary Barnsley hobbled into the physick garden short of breath.

'No one comes in or out... you know the rules, child,' snapped Dame Juliane as she pounded crushed leaves in her mortar. 'Send her away.'

'Oh, please! It may be my mother with tidings... Is it bad news?' Agnes shook the girl's shoulders. 'Tell me!'

Mary hung her head, not wanting to tell her it was only the sister she hated.

'I know not. She wouldn't say but kept on asking for you.'

Agnes shot a worried glance at her superior, asking for compassion.

'Oh, go and see who it is but be quick about it. No loitering at the gate – and cover your face, just in case. Speak through the port hole and, remember, if there is sickness we allow no one inside, not even the Bishop himself.'

Agnes's heart was thumping. What if it was bad news from home, about Mother or Hamon? She scurried to the wooden gate, peering eagerly through the hatch and catching sight of a huddled figure in a cloak with a half veil over her mouth; a face she knew only too well. 'Oh, it's you, Mags. What do you want after all this time? Is it Mother?'

'No, they were all well enough when I left them this morning. I'm so puffed out! I had hoped to sup some ale with Cousin Kit but all is deserted there. Have they the sickness?'

'They're all dead but the maid, gone within a week of Michaelmas.'

'Mercy on us! Kit came to visit us then. And Sim and the boys too?' The visitor's voice trailed away and she crossed herself. What a narrow escape for the Bagshotts after Kit had been inside the bakery. Thank the Lord she had left Baker's Lane. 'Let us in, Aggie. I'm done in with circling round from Longhall. The de Saultes have barred the way and no one goes in or out there. I was going to stay with Hamon's kin but got no further than the crossroads. Unbar the gate and let us in, sis.'

'Can't do that, Mags. Orders are orders and this is a closed house. You're a fool to yourself to be wandering abroad. What was Hamon thinking of, letting you roam about? Or does he want you to catch the sickness? Has he tired of your spending yet?' Agnes gave a twisted smile, not able to resist the barb.

'Who're you fooling? It were his idea right enough. On account of this...' Margery lifted her cloak to reveal her swollen belly and patted it proudly. 'See, another little baker's bun in the oven. And this time swelling like a loaf.'

'So I see. And how many moons are you then?' Agnes's voice was steel-edged.

'Six nearly… it dances inside like a carol. Round and round it quickens. Aren't I the clever girl?'

Agnes felt sick with rage. Hamon had been promising her the moon and swearing his love when all the time he was still ploughing and harvesting his wife. For one moment she felt dizzy with the shock.

'Fetch us a drink, for the love of Mary, I'm that parched in the throat and faint,' whined her sister. 'Aren't you glad you're safe here and not stuck in the city? I'm so afeared of catching this pestilence I go to church every day to pray to St Chad himself… What do you think of my new surcoat, eh? Best woollen cloth. Only the finest for Mags. Don't you think it suits my colour, this plum shade? So rich and warm, isn't it? And I made these net coils for my braids round the ears in the high-born style.' Margery twirled around to give her twin the full effect. 'Come on, get me a drink. Where's your charity for your poor sister?'

'You can get water from Frideswelle stream, it's pure enough, higher up the lane.' Agnes was in no mood to pander to her rival.

'I'm not going another inch, Aggie. My tongue's swollen and my head is spinning. For pity's sake, show some mercy.'

Aggie felt the thoughts whirl inside her head like spinning tops. Why should I pity her plight when she stole what was mine? Hamon and I were handfast, pledged in secret, but she made sure she got herself handfast to him before witnesses. Why should I help her now?

Then a terrible idea coursed like a hare through her head, a blazingly obvious idea which left her feeling giddy. A bird in the hand… or 'Carpe diem, seize the moment as the priest said in his sermon. Now is the time and the hour. Only now matters…

'You go and rest yourself by the stream on yon meadow bank outside the wall. But speak to no one. I'm not supposed to leave here but I know a place to slip out and I'll come to you anon.'

Margery's face slackened with relief. 'I'm sorry to be a bother, but I knew my sister wouldn't let me down – not when she's safe and sound in her little nunnery. And that's all down to me, isn't it? Blood's thicker than water any time.'

Agnes smiled. 'It is indeed down to you, Mags.' She closed the hatch and walked slowly back to the hut in the physick garden struggling with her demons. One look at her troubled face and Dame Juliane bit back a rebuke at her lateness.

'What ails you? Is it bad tidings?'

'Sort of. I had to tell my sister of the death of our cousin Kit and all her kin. She feels unwell, tired from walking. Now she must return to the city before dusk and take the bad news to our mother. She has no fever but is of poor health. What drink can I give her to soothe her sadness and put vigour in her bones?'

'Make her a cordial of elderberry and honey, and infuse it with leaves of camomile and lemon balm. That should soothe and refresh. You know how to do it by yourself. Not even you can spoil such an infusion! But hurry up, there's so much to do about the garden. You must dig over the beds, and it's time to mulch and prepare the ground for winter.'

Dame Juliane waddled off to sweep away some leaves herself, cross that there were now no yard girls to help.

Agnes found her hands shaking as she reached the crock of honey and pots of dried leaves from the shelves. She found a small pitcher and filled it with cordial, warming the spring water over the fire for the infusion. When all was prepared she took the narrow ginnel from the garden path, edged with the last stiff lavender spikes and low roses, along the edge of the buildings and through to the Prioress's quarters. Only the sad, neglected Frou Frou followed her meekly, wagging her stubby tail, eager to be out for a romp in the woods.

'I'm just letting the dog out... I'll keep an eye on her,' she called and crossed over the stone slabs set across the Frides-welle spring whose banks were overgrown with icy weeds. There was no one around to hear her ploy so she opened the snicket gate into the woodland and darted out, carefully keeping the jug from spilling over. In her tunic pocket she carried a wooden mug.

She shooed the dog from her as they passed the stew pond, lying hidden under the trees. She stopped to check that no one was following then wound her way through the shaded glen to the outer wall beyond. The path was damp with rotting leaves and blackberry thorns tore at her robe as if to hold her back but she ploughed on. Now was the time. Now was the hour.

Margery huddled in her cloak by the bank of the swollen stream. She was glad of its warmth and snugness though she fancied it smelled now of foetid breath and stale sweat. She watched the ploughmen in the distance turning over the red-brown soil. How strange that despite the sickness and the barriers on the roads, the death carts and tolling bells, men still went about their age old tasks. The mill wheel was now turned by lay brothers from the Friary in the city. She had feared the worst on first spying strangers at the mill. Poor Kit, the kindest of hearts, and her little boys. Margery shuddered at the thought of such a terrible death.

As she lay back on her elbows she felt a strange sense of relief. If she worked hard on her sister then it might be possible to make her come up with a safe hideout where Margery could rest up away from the fever. Aggie could fetch her food and as a reward she would be allowed to hold the babe or make him a fine embroidered robe to swank around in. Yes, it was definitely a he... How proud Hamon would be of his son! He must have a strong name, a regal one. Edward, Henry or Richard, perhaps.

She turned with relief to see her sister coming down the slope, carrying a jug. Good old Aggie! Margery had always been able to rely on her.

A Mystery

The Priory was settling down for the night, supper was over after the usual grumblings about the meagre fare. The nuns glided back to their quarters and Dame Juliane searched again for her troublesome novice. She'd get the sharp edge of the broom for hiding away, or had she perhaps followed her sister back to the city? Soon it would be time for Compline and she would have to report to the Prioress that there had been a breach of regulations. Just when she'd thought Agnes was shaping up and taking a proper interest. A loud banging on the shed door broke her concentration.

'Are you in there, Dame Juliane? Come quickly! Something terrible has happened outside... there's a sister, one of ours, I fear, lying in the field by the stream.'

The agitated voice belonged to Dame Iseult who had taken a garbled message from the porter and, accompanied by Limpy Mary, was searching for the Prioress who was not in her quarters. The old nun opened the door in alarm.

'Calm yourself, Dame Iseult. What nonsense is this so late at night?'

''Tis true, madam. The old ploughman on his way back

from the fields found her lying by the meadow bank and came to raise the hue and cry in case he be accused of some villainy. If you climb on the mount you can just see where she lies.'

'Is it the sickness? Who is it? What was the silly nun doing outside the wall? Haven't they all been warned?' puffed Dame Juliane as she followed them by torchlight.

'The ploughman was afraid to go near in case it was the pestilence, but he says there are no sores on her face. We have sent for Father John but he has gone to bury the dead at Barnsley Common. Two more families are gone there.'

'She'll have to be brought inside. It's not right for her to lie unshriven all night. We can send Sister Mary to examine the corpse as she's safe from any contagion,' panted the older nun, out of breath from trying to talk and keep up. 'But can we trust her not to speak of this and spread fear among the ladies?'

'She'll get boxed ears from me if she does,' said Iseult shakily. 'Trust Aunt Serena to be unavailable at a time like this. She goes home to Longhall Manor whenever she feels like it, storming through the barricades like a warrior Queen on her chariot.'

'Enough, Dame, do not dishonour our worthy Prioress before menials. It must be Agnes... I haven't seen her since this afternoon when she went to take a drink to her sister. I wonder if she's been up to her old tricks again...'

'But this nun is dead, not run away. I can't believe it's Sister Aggie Bagshott.' Iseult was both fearful and curious to see whose body lay under cover of darkness. 'Where's that maid? She's never here when you want her.'

Mary was found gathering leaves for the Cellaress's rotting pile and brought to the outer gate into the meadow. Dame

Iseult produced her own key which Dame Juliane thought disgraceful. These de Saultes used this house as if it were a private residence, she thought to herself, then instructed the girl: 'You go and see who it is... be sharp about it and check if it was the fever. You know what to look for by now.'

Mary edged her way carefully down the slope, trying not to slip on the frosty turf. The night air was chilly and her breath trailed behind her like smoke. She could not get used to having cloth wraps around her feet with hard leather soles, such luxury to have no chilblains, and a warm skirt around her legs. How could she possibly deserve such riches?

The body lay spreadeagled and stiff. It was as they'd thought, poor Sister Agnes in her black habit. Her eyes were wide open, startled looking as they stared up at the stars. She had no sores, there was no blood or any sign of a swelling. But such a strange position in which to lie. Mary was sure there was no fever. She clambered slowly and painfully back to the nuns gathered by the gate, shaking her head sadly.

'Please, Mam, 'tis who you feared, Sister Agnes. But there's no blackness or swollen lumps on her.'

'That'll do, Mary. Leave us – and mark what I say. Not a word about this until the Prioress returns. Silence on this matter or else! I wish Father John were here to guide us but I fear he's delayed. We shall have to bring the corpse inside in secret. It'll not look good for us if she is found by others.'

Dame Juliane returned to her garden for the wheelbarrow and trundled it down to the outer gate into the field. Between them she and Iseult slithered down the bank and half dragged the stiffened corpse on to the barrow to push it slowly back to the infirmary where it could be examined.

Dame Juliane was puzzled by the strange appearance of the novice. 'Her face has swollen up but it definitely is her.

She's quite unmarked but such a strange colour. There are no obvious buboes under her armpits and in the groin... nothing but a swollen belly.' She lifted up the tunic to reveal the source of the mound. Dame Iseult gasped when she saw the size of it. She had seen her mother blown up in this manner many times and had no doubts as to the cause.

'That's not the buboes but some other shame! Our novice was hiding a secret. Some fleshly lapse, I fear. *Enceinte* these many months by the looks of her.'

'But why is she dead if not by the fever or miscarried? She looked pale earlier and made that sister of hers a drink, or so she said. Mary came to fetch her to her visitor. What if it was no sister but a lover in disguise and he murdered her?' whispered Juliane, hand to her mouth, her eyes rolling with shock. 'Let me see, I told her what ingredients to put in the draught – the usual cordials, just camomile and elderberry. But, look, her eyes are staring as if she suffered pain and the pupils are strangely wide. Her colour, too. Her body is so cold but her face looks hot. I don't understand.'

'Ah, hah! See, around her neck she has a pouch... some amulet or witchcraft, the silly vixen.' Iseult bent forward and tore off the pouch, opening it. Inside were two lozenges.

'Look at these. You must know what they are?'

Dame Juliane took them to the candle in the hut and examined them closely, sniffing and prising out the herbs one by one. 'This smells to me of poison. I'll heat it and see what happens. But perhaps the stupid girl has merely taken some emetic to clear herself of her burden and, being the ignoramus we knew her to be, took too much.'

'You are most charitable, Dame Juliane. It looks to me as if she tried to end her shame by taking her own life. That's what I think at least.' Dame Iseult felt a sneaking admiration for this common girl who was brave enough to commit a mortal sin.

'You have the most likely explanation there… a disgraced vowess, paid for by the charity of the Guild. She would be expelled and condemned to eternal damnation. Now she shames us all by this foul deed.'

'But no one knows. We could say she died of fever?' Iseult felt her cheeks flushing. 'No, on second thoughts that would throw Aunt Serena into a fit of apoplexy. She'd seal us all off completely for fear of its spreading. No, there must be another way.'

'But look, there are tiny swellings under her armpits. Perhaps she has caught something after all. She must be buried quickly, don't you think?'

Dame Iseult nodded.

'But she's not going in the churchyard with all my ancestors if she's committed a mortal sin. There can be no office read over her. We'll have to do it ourselves and quickly, somewhere outside, else plop her in the mill pond to be found drowned by accident. No, that won't do. What if she floats up and then there'll be even more questions asked and Aunt Serena will have to know.'

Iseult was searching for a solution, her heart beating fast at the thought of such deception. She wanted it all kept quiet. One day the Prioress's lodgings would be hers by right as the next eldest daughter of the de Saultes. She wanted no scandal attached to her claim.

'Leave her with me, Dame Iseult. I know just where she can be useful for once. Agnes Bagshott was never a worthy wight. Now she can do us some good,' pronounced Dame Juliane.

'Whatever you say, reverend sister. Where shall we bury her?'

'By this wall here, a few feet from the fig tree. It's been

looking a bit lanky, needs a good pruning and some root nourishment. She'll be useful here, I reckon, for a good few years to come and no one but us will know where she lies.' Both fell silent at the thought of this deceit.

'Shall I strip her?' said the younger nun.

'No, the wool will rot down well enough. Leave nothing as evidence of her return. The pouch and that ring on her finger must stay where they are. I'll tell the Prioress in the morning that Agnes Bagshot has run away again. It will be no surprise to her.'

'But what about the maid?'

'Limpy Mary knows only of the first half of our discovery, not the second. She'll hold her tongue. Who else will give a bed to a cripple with lumps on her neck? Leave her to me. I'll tell her Father John took the body away. She can take Agnes's place in the garden. Mary works hard for all her misshapen gait.

'Come now, let's find the spades and finish the task. All will soon be well.'

The figure darted downstream under the creeping shadows of dusk, gathering pace as it sped southwards, surcoat unclasped and flying behind like wings outstretched, etched against the orange skyline and the black ribs of trees from which the last of the summer leaves dripped dolefully. Seeing the three spires of the Minster down in the hollow below, the solitary figure began to skip with excitement.

'You did it! By God's blood, you took your chance of freedom. No more rules and regulations, no more black habit and measly morsels to eat. You're free, Aggie Bagshott.'

For love of Hamon she had accomplished the impossible,

secured her freedom from the tyranny of Frideswelle Priory and unyoked herself from her terrible sister forever.

Now together she and her man would make a new life. It would be easy enough to convince everyone that Mags had died at the Priory gate of the fever and was buried hastily with Kit and Sim in the common grave. Come to console them in their loss, her vows not yet taken, Agnes would be free to return to her rightful place at their side.

Mags had been so thirsty. Like a fool she'd gulped down the draught like a grateful ploughman swallowing water from the well, not for a minute imagining it would be laced with poison. It was easy enough to crush seeds and roots from beautiful plants into devilish potions if you knew how. All those months under Dame Juliane had not been wasted and now Agnes was revenged on all of them.

Mags did not suffer much.

Agnes had lain by her side to see if her breath had stopped, stripping away each of her garments carefully, exchanging them for one of her own garb; wimple for netted head-dress, bare feet for shoes, tunic for gown and surcoat. She was thorough. Only the ring would not budge from Mags's swollen finger, the lozenge pouch like a necklace was the final touch. That would give them something to think about when they found the body of a fallen nun great with child. No wonder the poor soul took her own life.

Agnes felt strangely numb and calm, as if floating in mid-air. She had not flinched once from her plan for fear of immortal death. The God of Mercy was killing poor men and women like Kit and Sim and their babes by the thousand. He would not bother about one more. It was time to claim what was rightfully hers, time to return to the City of Spires.

She slipped the watch and the curfew, creeping through

the back alleys and banging on the bakehouse gate, making enough racket to wake the dead. No one answered so she beat upon the shutters with a stick.

'Go away!' shouted a voice from within. Was she a fool to return to Baker's Lane to tell them she was safe? 'Open at once! 'Tis Aggie come to visit you.'

Through a chink of an opening her mother's worried face peered out into the darkness. 'Is that you, Mags?' Mother must be so distressed she was mistaking her for her sister. 'Thank St Anthony and all the martyrs you are returned to us! We were so worried. Hamon has not been well since you left. Go see to him yourself. Upstairs, quickly, out of sight!'

'But it's me, Aggie… Poor Mags died of the fever yesterday by the Priory gate.' Aggie's tale was well rehearsed but seemed unconvincing when she was wearing her sister's apparel.

'So you say, but your wits are addled by too much walking. Rest and give your man some water. You must see to him now.' Mother was pushing her up the rickety stairs, scarce looking to see who she was guiding.

'I've come to take him away with me…'

'Yes, dear, that's right. Up the stairs to the top.'

Mother was taking no notice of her so Agnes turned to go back but found the stout door slammed in her face and the iron key turned, barring her escape. 'Mother! Open the door!' she heard herself scream.

'It's for the best, Margery. You've been abroad and may have the plague on you… see to your husband and we'll see to the bakery. Your father knows what's best. I'll bring you broth and bread in a while, have no fear.'

'Mother! It's Aggie, not Mags. You should know the difference. Aggie from the Priory come by special leave to help you. I have no sickness on me. See for yourself!'

'That's right, you rest up. Hamon needs you by his side.'

Only then did Agnes turn to see his terrible sores, blackened face and swollen tongue. Only then did she see the destruction of all her dreams. She had exchanged one prison for another far worse from which there was no escape. She could hear the curses of her dead sister in her ears. Agnes grasped for the pouch around her neck. It was gone. She had been too clever by half and now she must pay. Oh, God, no! *Mea culpa, mea culpa... mea maxima culpa...*

Mary Barnsley sat on the high chair, her long dark hair bedecked by a wreath of ivy leaves, mistletoe and berries. The Chapter House was garlanded with holly boughs, bright candles glimmered in the darkness and for once the hearth fire burned brightly, flames darting and flickering, the smell of the Yule log warm and welcoming. Was she dreaming? Was it really she who was picked to be the Mistress of Misrule, Prioress for a whole day, to play tricks and games, make merry and lord it over all the nuns? How could such riches be hers? She had ordered the cook to bring pittances of nuts and sweetmeats, played tricks on Dame Juliane, danced a carol as best she could with all of the nuns while the minstrel fiddler played a jingle. The inhabitants of the Priory were spared from the fever, all but Amy and poor Father John whose kindness had saved Mary's life.

Now here she was, dressed in the finest kersey with a skirt which hid her deformity from sight, leather boots on her feet, braids shining and free from the itch thanks to many dippings in Dame Juliane's pungent bowl. Her sores were all but disappeared and her face clear. Only the solid lumps on her neck reminded her of the reason for her arrival here and of poor Mistress Kit. Mary must wear these tokens forever as a sign of the mercies of God and St Chad in cruel times. Why she had been so favoured she never could fathom out.

Now she spent her days in the heart of the Priory, weeding and clearing, planting and pruning, to the older nun's instructions. Sometimes she was sent to the laundry or up into the forest to chop down ferns, burning them to ashes for the making of the special lye. She loved to roam free over the bracken paths and gulp down the fresh cold air. Her chest was growing, her body filling out with good food. One day some lad would look on her face and forget her limp. No one called her Limpy Mary now and sometimes even the Prioress glanced in her direction with smiles instead of scorn. Mary could always tell for she had the knowing without words. It was a useful gift.

Each time she reached the wall of oak trees and the Porteress's gate which boundered their convent, she could not wait to be inside these walls. Of her own kin she never thought.

The winter would be long and cold and the feast of St Stephen would soon make way for Lent and fasting, but for now there was only feasting and warmth. When the snow flowers opened she would take a bunch to the burial pit to remember all those not so fortunate as herself.

The ways of the Lord were mighty strange but every day of her life henceforth she would thank the saints in their glory for her sweet life within these walls.

In The Rose Garden

Iris

❦

The sun has dipped over the hill now, the moon climbs high. On the brick boundary wall a Little Owl shrieks and flaps into the nearest tree. Iris moves quickly away from the sad spirits of the herb garden, along the shale pathway edged with tubs of white tobacco plants wafting a fragrance like pot pourri into her face. On now to the back of the house where mullioned windows look out on the oval floribunda beds under which froths of yellow *Alchemilla mollis* are billowing like Grandmother's petticoats on to the close-shaven grass. Time to inspect the roses for blight and aphids, but first she steps back to admire the buff-coloured 'Gloire de Dijon' and the last of the 'Mai Gold' climbing the brick wall.

There's a companionable feeling to the way those two roses twine with creamy honeysuckle up the chimney gable of salmon stone and red brick, climbing up to a russet-tiled roof; a later addition to the older side of the house, a buttress of warm stone against the iron hand of winter.

Iris sits on the wooden bench looking down on the beds. This was always her mother's favourite spot. She liked her flowers sunshine yellow. The tea rose garden has a feel of her to it; a backs straight, no-nonsense, best china on the lawn and Sunday manners atmosphere. Perhaps it's the formal layout, prim and straight-edged, teamed with such an optimistic colour. Only the sundial, its focal point, always scared Iris as a child with its warning note: *Smoke and shadows are we.*

She examines the sundial for more cracks on its grey stone, weathered by centuries of winters, the lichens and moss crusting its northern side. This was always a lady's bower not a child's hideaway or man's refuge. Neat, polite and uncluttered. In memory of Mother it has been kept just so.

Come next springtime will I still be here to see my annual show? Iris wonders. Have I dug like a navvy to shove hundreds of bulbs into this claggy soil on my knees, bidding the blighters to go forth and multiply, all for someone else's benefit? That's garden magic. You toil and sweat and finally, months later, up they pop in a pageant of colour. First the snowdrops and sunny aconites, then crocuses, purple, white and yellow, followed by daffodil trumpeters and narcissi, clumps of gaudy polyanthus, frilly auriculas like china plates and sweet-scented wallflowers. And finally a display of scarlet tulips to give the grand finale to the spring parade.

Well, they'll all have to do for themselves now. I've no puff to slave over them like an anxious mother around her brood. The days of outdoor housework are over for me. George in the village does the heavy stuff so why am I worrying about this place?

The sight of 'Golden Showers' cascading down the wall stirs sadness deep inside. Would Mother be pleased to see she had kept it shipshape for so many years, even though Iris herself loathes the acid yellow blooms?

Rules are rules and the Gospel applies to roses too. They should give value for money, look good, smell good, and give more than one performance.

I've been seduced by too many fly by nights who bloom for one day and drip their petals the next. Boring old 'Golden Showers' gets two out of ten for persistence. With hardly any perfume to mitigate its harsh colour, it's there under sufferance!

She touches the arched trellis with white roses cascading over it like creamy froth. This on the other hand belongs in the garden: *Rosa alba pleniflora*, a wanton hussy draping herself around the *Clematis montana* 'Elizabeth' with no shame! A visitor once got excited about this stock, said it was a very old variety and could possibly have been here before the chimney itself went up.

Iris wonders if anything could possibly survive all that time in one place. If so, someone had the sense even in those days to recognise a good thing when she saw it. It had to be a woman. Women and roses were made for each other so who exactly should she thank for such a gift?

PART FOUR

THE NEW HOUSE

1565

'Who soweth in rain, he shall reap it with tears
Who soweth in harm, he is ever in fears
Who soweth ill seed or defrauds his land
Hath eye sore abroad, with a coresie at hand'
—*The Country Housewife's Garden*,
William Lawson 1618

'The Rose
What a pother have authors made with Roses!
What a racket they have kept! I shall add, red Roses
are under Jupiter, Damask under Venus,
White under the Moon, and Provence
under the King of France'

Staying On

The Barn Owl swooped noiselessly across the ruined garden like a white-faced ghost, its night eyes in search of mice and voles. Circling higher over the broken wall into the copse which lay north of the Priory, the bird alighted on a thick branch of one of the mighty century oaks which had stood sentinel at the crossing of the tracks since time began. Here it paused as if surveying the buildings which crumbled like jagged teeth in a rotten mouth. Only the tithe barn stood foursquare in the cobbled yard close by the Porteress's gatehouse. The ancient church lurched precariously, its roof in desperate need of repair. The rest of the Priory lay robbed of stone and beams, red bricks scattered amongst the piles of rubble; a rough landscape of ladders, barrows, hods and scaffolding.

Here and there in the moonlight the outline of the old garden could be picked out in evergreen hedges of holly and yew, ivy-clad walls, an outer circle of shrubs, shadowy shapes of orchards and meadow hedges. And through it all the winding ribbon of the stream, curling and looping down towards the wider brook and the mill ponds beyond the cloister wall. Here thatched huts and cottages marked the living from their dead in the old churchyard. The scent of humans abroad kept the owl perched on its branch, wary and watchful.

The night woman was on her rounds, wandering over the rubble, careless and mazed, with another human following anxiously behind her calling softly, 'Dame Felice! Wake up… 'tis far too cold to be abroad in naught but your shift… Prithee stir thyself and come inside. Why do you search so among the ruins?'

Leah Barnsley shivered in her hempen shift with just a rough woollen shawl to ward off the frost. Each night she was woken by stumblings on the stair and a draught in the passageway as the old woman stalked in her sleep all unaware, puddled and confused by the new building works, tripping over planks and boards. It was a mercy she had done herself no injury.

Baggy's tools lay scattered. He must not fear any theft but her cousin could be slipshod and careless. Leah would not trust him to make a pig sty when he was full of ale. He cut corners here and there. His wood was never hardened enough, he scrimped on nails and left rough edges. How he had ever made himself builder in charge of the new house she could only guess; some tom foolery, dubious dealings with Squire Salte to keep the costs low, perhaps.

The house was taking shape slowly, built from the nunnery and chapter hall, the old buildings razed to ground level, only the solid oak beams standing firm like the ribs of an ox. There was to be a new chimney piece and bricked stack, a leaded glass window instead of shutters or so it was rumoured, but now was not the time to be roaming over the site to check the truth of such gossip.

'Come on, madam, it's ever so late and soon the cock will crow. Mistress Salte will be vexed if I'm late to her washing.

You know how she likes me to prepare the wash bucket and see to her linens.'

Leah drew closer to the shrunken figure and stretched out her hand to guide the sleepwalker back towards the Prioress's lodging house which stood alone at the end of the old buildings, the last remnant of the nunnery with its sloping roof intact. The old woman made no protest. Her grey eyes were filmy and glazed, her shoulders humped and sloping, jaw drooping open for she had few teeth.

'That's right, Dame Felice, back to bed… 'Tis all gone now, the nuns and the choir. No night offices for you to sing. Is that why you rise so early? Do you still hear the bell and make for the cloister? Nothing's left but a heap of bricks for your nephew's new house. He wastes nothing, all will be changed around into a fine dwelling for you to live in warm and snug. Prithee, come with me back to the lodging. You must to your rest and I to my tasks or I'll be getting my ears boxed again from Mistress Sarah, if I'm late.'

Leah Barnsley sighed as she led the frail figure back down the little garden path to the open door then up the ten stairs to the old woman's bed. The lodging was little more than a humble cottage now, all the tapestries and wainscots ripped out and put in store for Mistress Sarah's new rooms; even the ancient carved chests had been carried off. There was nothing left but the four poster bed on which generations of Salte Prioresses had lain. Indeed this new wife would have whipped that away given half a chance. Her hawk eyes missed nothing of value. How could these pennypinching Saltes so humble an old woman who once held high rank in the Frideswell district; neglect their own aunt who was over seventy years in the world and forty years released from her vows?

Dame Felice had overseen the closure of her Priory with

dignity and humility, so Leah's grandmother had told her many years ago. Barnsley folk had always been in service to the Priory, ever since the terrible pestilence when one of their kin had saved the nuns from the fever or some such tale, and the century oaks were but saplings. But soon even the lodging house would be razed and the old Prioress would be without any place to call her own. It was not right or proper. It turned the order of things upside down.

Sarah Salte was not a woman to be gainsaid, least of all by her servant and menial. The mistress was a stranger to the district, all for the strict new religion and for tearing down the fair statues and carvings in their church. The poor Parson did not know which way to turn. He was quite grey with all the turmoil. First King Hal's changes and his son's, then back again in Queen Mary's terrible times of burnings and Popery when he'd had to hide his new wife away for fear of harm. Squire Timon appeared to turn a deaf ear to it all, especially his wife's barkings, so the chapel lay untouched. The villagers were agog to see how she ruled him but sad that he failed to honour one of his own family. Leah was utterly powerless to change any of it, being a mere tenant with use of the lodging house only for as long as Dame Felice drew breath.

As she opened the solid oak door, polished to the colour of peat, the old nun seemed at last to recognise where she was and sank with relief on to the feather mattress. She curled into a ball like an infant and Leah gently covered her with the quilted counterpane and drew the fine damask curtains around the bed to seal out the early-morning dampness.

Soon the morning chores would begin but first she warmed the milk in the pan. The fire in the inglenook still had heat enough. Joseph, her new husband, snored on their straw mattress humped under a flock-filled counterpane, their only wedding gift, made by her mother and sisters. Soon he would join the Bagshott brothers in the building works, sawing beams and timber, fixing posts and joists. Bagshotts and Barnsleys were always to be found somewhere in the Frideswell district and the city in the valley where once they were bakers and now were brickmakers. Still bakers of sorts, respectable citizens much in demand with the spate of new buildings springing up from the ruins of old monasteries. How proud she was of Joseph who could turn his hand to any task on the estate. They had been wed for a year now when she had left her mistress's direct service to look after the old nun.

Leah was expected to keep all the Salte laundry fresh and clean among this building site, for she was considered the best laundress from here to Longhall. Her linens were the whitest and softest, and she could bleach out stains, freshen lacework, frill up caps and ruffs to starched perfection. The secret of her success lay in a special receipt handed down from Bagshott and Barnsley women: instructions for the making of a lye which would soak away stains swiftly and gently from linens when they were tied and laid expertly in the wash barrel. Mistress Sarah had often tried to prise the secret from her but Leah was not going to part with it; not for a bag of downy feathers or a jug of best ale. Not even a new cap. One day she would tell her daughter just how to get the washing white but Leah and Joseph hoped for a son first.

She took the posset of milk up to her charge but found her fast asleep, straggly white hair on the pillow, her night bonnet loosened. She knows not that she wanders abroad, thought Leah. Poor lady, she knows not what year it is or that we have a Queen on the throne. She thinks she is still the Prioress, I fear, and is no longer with us. When I'm old, I hope I'm not abandoned by my children or pushed into some corner to rot.

The girl trailed back down the narrow stairs to the warmth of her man with relief. When a woman did not marry she was left alone, ignored, parcelled around among her kin. Poor Dame Felice was faring little better than the Priory; both of them half-forgotten relics of times past, brought low by neglect.

In the warmth of the feather bed Dame Felice Salte was dreaming of grassy cloister paths and the sound of nuns singing like a dawn chorus. Her nest of singing birds, all gone now. There were only six of them at the end, sharing the peace, embroidering altar cloths and vestments with two live-ins to serve their meals and wash their clothes.

The sun always seemed to shine in the Prioress's pleasance garden with its rows of pale roses, lilies and lavender beds, gillyflowers and bright marigolds flopping over the path's edge. The neatly clipped yew archways linked one part of the convent to the other like green doorways; herbarium, cellarium, cloister walk, and the steps up to the holy spring of Our Lady of Frideswell... all destroyed now because of her silly mistake.

Was it not she who'd heard that Cardinal Wolsey's team of inquisitors were on their way to close the convent? Bad news always travels fastest. Felice had told them to scatter into the forest, then it would appear that the nuns were already departed and no inventory taking would be necessary. So the sisters all hid like robbers, waiting until the visitors passed by. How she prayed to Saint Edith of Polesworth that the strangers would lose their way in the Chase and find themselves another route and another House of Prayer to close.

In her dream Felice cried out: I was too hasty! I thought they were gone. Rejoicing, I rushed to the chapel tower to ring the hammer bell... a sign for all my sisters to return home. But *they* were the cunning ones, waiting with smiles on their faces, smiling for this was an old trick, smiling for we were now at their mercy... Oh, foolish woman! Lists of tenants and rented land, lists of buildings and endowments, lists of vestments and artifacts. Nothing of any great value to them but our lives lay in ruins. How we wept as we sang the last services. No one wanted to say farewell or leave our chapel. Dame Muriel was sent back to her kin in Newcastle, Dame Elinor to Warwick, Dame Philippa to Brewood. She pleaded to stay with me but her brother insisted, for she was young and of marriageable age. And here I am still, the last Prioress, my own brother, Richard of Longhall, insisting I stay on to guard the site like some Porteress at the gate. He harkened not to my plea to be sent to another order, some quiet cloister, and where after all could I go when there were none left in the land?

Yet in her dreams still she savoured the tastes and scents of youth. The familiar smells of candles and beeswax, fresh fowl roasting with apples. Sometimes she could see young Leah polishing, polishing, as her mother and grandmother had before her. Nothing remains forever. The heart of her Priory was ripped out, the peaceful places despoiled, when these two young Saltes came with their schemes. There was no calm remaining for prayer and contemplation, not with that dreadful Sarah ruling the roost like a puffed up hen, shouting her orders like a fishwife. They would soon have everything stripped but would not lay hands on her secret: the great Seal of the Priory which was never returned to the Bishop. It was thought lost but Felice knew just where it was hidden, safe from the plunderers. Now it would stay here at Frideswell forever. Sometimes she removed it from its leather wrappings to finger the carved effigy of Our Lady with the Holy Child, honour the vision of Dame Ambrosine, her forebear and founder of the Priory.

But then she would awake feeling guilty as she struggled to recall where it lay. Secure in the closet – or had she put it outside somewhere? Her memory was playing its usual tricks again, befuddling her vision. Dame Felice could no longer remember where the seal now lay. She rang the bell by her bedside. She must rise at once and find it.

When she was dressed and fed she would take a stick and slowly pick her way around the building works to the quiet of the holy chapel and the choir stalls of carved oak where she had once sat with her sisters. The walls were damp and stained, the colourful murals already half erased by whitewash. Even the alcoves for the statues of the saints lay bare, for this new mistress insisted there be no effigies to pollute her place of worship with idols. Felice could make nothing of all this fuss. Like a stranger in a foreign country the services were unintelligible to her, being in common English and from a strange Prayer Book not a Missal. The Parson had a wife and children now and consorted with the village as a squire not a humble priest. How could a nun accept such changes? And where had she put the blessed package?

Perhaps if she sat in her stall, adorned with her carved initials, Felice Salte might recall better. How she longed to join Dame Muriel, Dame Elinor, Dame Philippa who had long since gone the way of all flesh. Why would her body not yield up its stubborn spirit but keep clinging on to breath? She could always refuse food, that would surely hasten her end, but her stomach rumbled and protested each morn as she wolfed down her porridge with satisfaction and not a little shame. Food and warmth were her only comforts now, but she must remember just where the great seal was hidden or else it would be lost forever.

*

Cramped upstairs in the old guest hall by the Priory gate, hemmed in by heavy oak furniture and bed hangings, Sarah Salte, new Mistress of Frideswell, poked and stabbed her husband awake.

'Hurry! It's past cock crow but still dark... I can't sleep. Wake up, good Timon, I need to talk.' The man grunted and snorted, turning his back from this rude awakening. She dug her elbow into him. Wake up! My feet are cold and there are urgent matters to discuss.'

Timon Salte opened one bleary sleep-encrusted eye. At thirty he was still in the full flush of manhood, plump-faced with sandy hair the texture of straw, his features squared off by a fine auburn beard. His cheeks matched the scarlet hue of his nightcap, but being partial to best malmsey wine his tongue always tasted like rough matting and his head was befuddled by such a rude awakening. 'What now, Mistress Salte?'

'I can't put up with it another day!'

'Put up with what, prithee?'

'That woman still living in the lodging... It's time the place came down.'

'We've been through this before. She *is* my aunt. The place is her home, and it's solid enough to build alongside. The foundations are sound...'

'It will spoil the effect to have a higgledy piece stuck on our new house like some lean-to byre.'

'Don't be ridiculous. It's a perfectly good building. Why pull it down? It makes no sense.'

'She'll have to go then. And soon, sire.'

'Go where? This has been her dwelling for nigh on fifty years, since she went into the nunnery in... let me think...'

'When our new house is complete, I don't want that old dodderer wandering about, off to sing Matins with her nonexistent nuns. She still does it. I've seen her wandering like a will o' the wisp at two of a morning.'

'Go back to sleep, woman. She must have rooms here. Where else can she go?'

Timon was feeling thoroughly annoyed by the thought of his aunt being thrown out into the village. Sarah was new to the family and did not yet understand how much the Priory had meant to them all. How closely their wealth had been tied to its success or failure. How lucky they were now to be able to seize the property and claim the right to rebuild a dwelling house.

'She can go to Longhall Manor and retire there, out of my way.'

'And just where can they house her? With the servants? They're full of children, jumping like fleas from a dog, hither and thither, out of each other's way. Talk sense or shut up!'

'But you promised my father to build me a house befitting my station in life.'

'Come on! Your ideas are way *above* our station, dear heart. More befitting the seat of a nobleman than a country squire's farmhouse…'

'We are Saltes and can hold our heads up with any in the shire, especially those dreadful Pagets who seem to be taking over half the county to extend their property.'

'He has made a fortune while my coffers are almost empty, what with the bad harvest and losing rents and tenants to pay for all this extravagance. The estate is smaller than it was.'

'And we all know whose fault that was! Which one of your illustrious ancestors was it who chose to sport the wrong colour of rose and nearly beggared you all?' Sarah knew that the Saltes had taken up the cause of the red rose of Lancaster and lived to regret it.

'Don't exaggerate, mistress mine. Be content with all our present plans and generous to those less fortunate.'

'If I want a sermon, I'll speak to the Parson. If I can ever find him at home. Felice needs putting away quietly out of sight. She shames us with her wanderings...'

'She does no harm. She's old but still has most of her wits.'

'Oh, aye, wit enough to live no better than her servant wench, digging the garden and picking herbs like a witch. All those animals and other familiars she has make the place smell like a farm yard. She looks like something from a bygone age. Tom laughs at her. Children do at oddities.'

'If ever I catch him at it, I'll beat him sore. She's a good woman, a little lost in these times, but no child of mine will berate her for being old-fashioned.'

Timon could feel his ire rising. Sarah spoiled their only son, doted on him too much, making a sissy out of him. In truth Timon sometimes wondered how he had ever been ensnared into marriage with such a scold and shrew. Her tongue was always lashing out at someone. She could not bear to be thwarted and it was often hard to keep her under control. Her extravagant schemes would ruin them all one day. In truth he did not always know how to rein in her unruliness. He feared it would come to a beating in the end.

'She's still a Papist and a heretic. What an example to the village, that we should harbour recusants! When she's dead her body should be pickled in a barrel as a warning.'

'Stop your ranting! Aunt Felice knows no better. Even your parents were Papists in their time, before King Hal took the church for himself. We should protect her, not shame her.'

'You're too soft and lily-livered. You always put your family before my needs.' Sarah was trying a different tack now.

'I'll hear no more of this. Goodnight!'

'Timon, sweetheart, let me comfort you... the special way. I know you like my fingers here...' He could feel her searching out his body under the bedclothes, feeling under his buttocks.

'Not now. Go to sleep. You're becoming a scold and a tease, Sarah Salte.'

'Then it's time for my ducking, time for me to be punished and chastened. Subjected to your will.' The witch knew exactly how to torment him and arouse his senses. That was why he'd married her. For all her pious outward show she could be a wanton. Timon groaned, weakening.

'Dearest heart,' she wheedled, 'don't you want us to take advantage of the south slope to build me a pretty little knot garden, a green park for our children to frolic in? If we pulled down the hedges and opened the enclosed garden... there, do you like what I'm doing to you?' Timon moaned again. How did she manage to find such a sensitive spot? Like a strumpet up to her well-practised tricks.

'We can't trample down Aunt Felice's bower, her herbary and rose arbour. It's lain untouched since the Blessed Ambrosine was found asleep there... Salte women have always loved their gardens.'

'It's little more than a vegetable patch with a few paltry flowers and roses left. It's badly in need of a good trim and some shaping. I hate to see them spreading linen on sticks over the yew hedges like peasant folk. Leah Barnsley has got above herself and will not tell me what lye she uses, the minx! It's a disgrace. We can grub up the ground around this lodging at the gate and they can move here. See, I've found a solution. Come, let's make love and forget about your wretched relatives. If she were my aunt...'

'God help her,' Timon muttered under his breath.

'What did you say, sweetlove?'

'Be content then.'

'How can I be content when she ruins my scheme, my garden works? The lodging is in the wrong place. It will have to go.'

'Then wait a few years, 'til she passes away. It can't be far off. She's over seventy. Then we can do what we please with her garden, my pretty dove.'

'Don't you lovey, dovey me, cold heart! Take your hands off me! You had your chance. I'll not wait until Doomsday to please her. Oaks will grow quicker than my garden will. I want it now, while we're young and have children to raise. I want a terrace on the slope, full of rose hedges and fine herbs. A walkway of stones, to make a feature of our yew arches, and a pretty arbour with a mazey hedge. Can't you see it, Timon?' Sarah turned to him excitedly, her chin firm and fixed, eyes brilliant and sharp as flint. 'Timon?' But he was fast asleep.

The girl turned over in disgust, pulling all the bed clothes with her, wide awake now. There was indeed more to marriage than four bare legs in a bed. Where had she heard that marriage was like licking honey off thorns? Felice Salte was the thorn in her side. She would have to go.

'Baggy' Bagshott was feeling on top of the job as he jolted his cart down from Longhall, along the winding track towards Frideswell Priory. He had a good feeling about this crisp bright morning. There was no breeze to unsettle the ladders, no rain to soak him through, and the sun was burning through the mist strongly enough to promise plenty of autumn daylight. If only they would decide where the chimney would be stacked or whether the lodging house must be pulled down. For days

Squire Timon had hedged and dithered. Time and the seasons were moving on apace. Far be it from him to influence his betters but if they wanted to pull the Yule log into their new house and welcome 1566 into their hearth, he needed to know now.

Nowt as fussy as folk of quality. You had to understand from the start that they must have the last word, and believe that all decisions they made were the right ones and all mistakes entirely the fault of the jobbing builder who did not do as he was told. That was the rule and the Saltes, being almost gentry, would be no exception to it. Not that he personally thought it right to turf an old nun out of her home for the sake of a few years' wait. But as long as he was paid for his work and gave satisfaction he must not quibble. All things considered, life was looking up for this humble member of the Bagshott clan.

Baggy liked to think of himself as a man of the world. Had he not travelled some twenty miles, from Longhall to Stafford? Did he not know every ale stop on the tracks through the Chase? Had he not seen the new iron forges and charcoal burners at work, the coal mines springing up all over the forest, the logging of the oak forests by timber merchants? Had he not stood on the ancient hilltops to see the vast plains of the Trent valley cleared of woodland into open fields and parklands?

There was not a ruin in the deep forest from which he had not managed to salvage stones, bricks or timber, surveying them by day and collecting his spoils by night, avoiding the forest wardens, muffling the horses' hooves to cart back his loot to the yard and barn by his cottage. All in a day's work. Did not his wife have the best of everything: a coverlet of downy feathers, three buckets, willow baskets and a pewter jug, a candlestick and buffet stool, even bed hangings and more pots than there were days in the week. He missed nothing on his travels. It was a pity that the Saltes had installed themselves on this site so promptly or there would not be so much stone left up standing for them to play around with at Frideswell, that was for sure.

Ned Bagshott hoped that a wagonload of success was about to tip in his direction. Already he was gathering all the trappings of respect: a fine beast to pull his sturdy wagon, a soft leather jerkin and apron which covered his barrel belly, brown wool breeches cross-bound with straps and thick hose under his leather boots. On cold days he had a short cloak and leather fingerless mittens to hide his warts, a warm cap and thick wolsey shirt. His wife could fill her wash bucket with just his shirts alone. She kept him filled with meat and broth, ale and thick bread. What more could a man of forty want from life? He had two strong sons and enough wenches to help tend his fields and do the dairy work on their smallholding.

Bagshotts came either red-haired with fair skin or dark and swarthy; a strange mix when two came at the same time, like Jem and Eddy, his sons. Ned himself was stocky and one of the black heads, now tinged with grey. His brown eyes bulged enough to lend a permanently startled look to his expression. His beard was still thick and rough like a hedgehog's back, his shoulders were broad and strong and thighs sturdy. Altogether he was pleased with the effect. His girth bestowed confidence, for who could trust the expertise of a builder who was as thin as a lathe with no flesh on his bones and no weight to his elbow? He judged by appearances himself when he sat at the Court sessions before the jury men.

He knew the importance of looking a fellow straight in the eye when he paid his fines for tipping his cess pit into Longhall stream after eight of the clock in the morning, for building a wall on the public highway, for extending his own hedge or failing to clear out his bit of the ditch. What a fuss they made about nothing! He still shook hands on deals in the church porch but managed to avoid stepping inside whenever he could. He left that sort of thing to the wife who was no slither pudding but a comely matron with callouses on her hands and elbows as plump as a goose from all her honest endeavours.

The young squire, Timon Salte, was a sound master, fair and square. 'Twas a pity he was saddled with such a loud-mouthed mistress who trumpeted her boasts all over the district that this would be the finest manor house ever made from the stones of Popery. If they would just make up their minds where he was to start! He had stripped everything down, sorted the stone and bricks, measured up, hired his help, agreed a price. He did not want to pull down the lodging for whoever had put it up was on top of their job and he didn't like to waste a perfectly good bit of building. It went against his craftsman's sense of fair play.

As he drew closer to Frideswell he looked around with pleasure at the way the village was shaping up around the mill and the green at the bottom, the land sloping gently into the sunshine; a fine prospect for a house. Perhaps it was one of his own forebears who had helped build the Priory and church in the first place. Bagshotts had been rooted into the soil around these parts since Adam was a lad or so his father had told him.

It was all about putting up and putting down, shoving in or shoving out. His distant kin in the city were as stiff and starchy as their ruffs, being strict on religion nowadays and miserable for all their success. His Uncle Reuben Bagshott always wore a black fustian doublet and hose, a tall hat and pointy beard. He drank small beer, his calves were spindly, and his wife wore a sourdough expression above her plain gowns. They seldom mixed with their rough country kin, being too grand or too mean to entertain them or make progresses out of the city, but Uncle Reuben was much respected for all he was a ranter and raver, hating all things Popish.

Give him his rightful due, he had helped the city fathers secure all the land from the Church which allowed lead pipe to be laid from the high springs in the forest to the water taps in the city streets. Miles of pipes were to be laid and he made sure that young Ned got his chance to dig and delve with the best of them. It was digging these pipes which gave him his chance to learn about building works and the ruined monasteries waiting to be quarried. He watched and learned from the tricks of others: how to measure short and estimate generously to keep one's own purse well lined; how to lay bricks meanly and stone sparingly; to set casements into the wall, pitch a fine roof, hire skilled men for the special jobs who would take the blame if summat went wrong. Observing the mistakes of others was a good way to learn. Ned would always be grateful to old Reuben for seeing that his distant cousin's son got a slice of the pie.

He wondered how the Barnsleys were coping with the battle for the lodging house. Joseph and Leah were too humble to bemoan their lot, being only servants paid to look after the old woman. Leah Barnsley was a fine lass, one of the fairest in the district, yet modest with it. She had the fair skin of some of the forest folk, a milkmaid's complexion unmarked by any pox. How Jo had managed to secure her affections was a mystery for he was a bit of a worryguts and a fusspot. Baggy's own son, Jem, had been cut up when their banns were read in the church for he had always looked in Leah's direction, without success. He was shy and had a bit of a stutter at times, held himself back too much, while his twin brother, Eddy, was just the opposite, wild and skittish and full of jokes and mischief though settled now with his Mary. Sometimes Meg worried about Jem, spending his time alone, brooding or walking down to hear the wandering preachers in the market place and eat at Uncle Reuben's table. Baggy hoped he would not become a sobersides. Still once the job began properly Jem would be too busy on top of a ladder to mull over sermons.

As he turned into the gate he could hear the racket coming from the Porteress's hall where the master and mistress were having a right set to. Squire Timon resembled an urn in his high boots and full breeches, his hands on his hips looking like handles.

'It stays!'

'It does not!'

Mistress Salte peered up at her husband, red in the face and poking him in the chest with a candlestick.

'Hold your tongue, hussy, or I'll have you put in a scold's bridle!'

'But you promised…' she whimpered.

'I said no such thing. Gold doesn't grow on trees for us to throw away. The lodging stays where it is and Aunt Felice within it undisturbed. We shall make our chimney breast against it, with chambers above and below. The warmth in the bricks will benefit all of us then. Be content for this is my final word on it. Prithee see to thy busyness and I will see to mine.

'Here comes Master Bagshott. He's waited long enough on our indecision. Good morrow, time for us to make a start. We need not disrupt the lodging house until we are ready to break through. Prepare the outer walls by the corner. Save as much of the fig as you can for it likes that sunny wall. I want no undue wastage.'

'Huh!' Mistress Sarah, dismissed, picked up her kirtle's skirts and made for indoors.

'A wise decision, sire. Although may I be so bold as to point out that the lodging house roof is somewhat in need of repair...'

This stopped the lady in her tracks and she turned around quickly with a smirk on her face, a look of pure triumph.

'Then what you save on the demolishments you can put into the making of a fine roof! If all is tiled in the same hue 'twill make it more of a piece, a grander effect in the new style.'

The master looked at his wife, taken aback at her sharpness. Baggy recognised one of those moments of compromise between a strong man and his awkward wife. It was time for the olive branch to be held aloft. The man smiled.

'You do well to point out that one roof will make for unity. I trust it will do so in more ways than one, my dear. And you shall have your garden, too; a fine little terrace for the ladies to take the air and show off their gowns, no doubt.'

The woman's smile burst through her sullen mask like a moulding from plaster. She was such a plain creature for one gentry born. The strongest feature was her firm jaw which jutted out like a wedge. Her pale blue eyes were cold, small and too close together, giving her a slight squint, but they darted quickly enough, missing nothing.

She eyed the quality of Bagshott's jacket and the edges of his linen which began each morning spotless for Meg was a stickler for crisp clean edges, knowing the secret of good laundering. The woman showed a line of yellow teeth, sure sign of a sweetmeat lover as she gazed from him to the empty space which would soon be occupied by her new house. Ned Bagshott was only the instrument of their will and of no more consequence to her. How could any man have found this scion of the Sapcotes' appealing enough to marry? Perhaps Squire Timon had taken the old advice. When he fixed his eye with love, he made sure he fixed it prudently on a gentleman's daughter.

Mistress Salte would hover over Ned's men like a hawk, stiff and starchy like the ruff around her scrawny neck; the slightest error, deviation, delay, and she would descend upon them, trying to insert extra fol-de-rols as her right at no extra cost. Winning the lodging house battle was going to prove expensive for Timon Salte but that was none of Baggy's concern, thank God. His hired hands would build the house. The other poor sod must live in it with her!

Ned Bagshott spent the day going over the site, assigning each man his task, then took a spade to clear the overgrown pathways around the old lodging house, testing the stones to see if they were firm and the wooden cross beams were free from rot. The pathways were choked with tough weeds and thick roots and needed a good hacking back. Jo and Leah set about the task with vim and vigour, relieved that their mistress lay undisturbed within. He'd warned them that once they began the great chimney breast the noise would be deafening for days.

As Baggy gazed up at the old walls, covered in briar roses and honeysuckle, plants sprouting out of the holes in the plasterwork and ivy rampant almost to the rooftops, he knew that they must prune everything back to ground level and start afresh. The fig nestled in the corner, warm and sheltered in the last of the autumn sunshine, its broad leaves a hand's width.

He thought of Adam and Eve sheltering from the wrath of God and covering their shame with a leaf. Yes, they could just about get away with it by his reckoning from the size of those glossy specimens but there were few figs to be gathered now, only brown-splattered rotten splodges under the foliage. The master was right to want to save such a fine tree but its stem was woody and hard. It too would need cutting back and a good feed. He would have to loosen some of the tangled growth below the surface and dig out the bushes which had once grown alongside. What a mess! He looked for Jem to assist him but he was on another task out of sight.

Ned smiled to himself. If you want a tricky job a-doing you does it yerself. That was his dad's good advice so he went in search of his spade, a pick axe and sturdy barrow, and bent to the task. He felt the shadow flit over him and turned to see the old lady holding out a yew branch before her to tickle his arm.

'Dame Felice.' He raised his cap and bowed. 'I bid thee good day. I trust I'm not disturbing you?' Would she remember how once she ran after him with a stick when she caught him scrumping apples from the Priory orchard? How could this little woman, so grey and silent, be the firebrand he remembered from his youth? One look into those vacant eyes persuaded him that she remembered little of those times.

'They say a branch of yew carried to the fore will search out all things lost so why it lingers here I do not know. You are not lost.' She wandered away on her mission, not waiting for his reply. He smiled to himself and pointed her out to Leah Barnsley who nodded and began to follow in her footsteps.

Baggy turned back to his digging and sifting, hacking out the dead wood and loosening the soil. He would carry on until the low sun slid away from the house then call it a day for this task. It was going to be a slow job to fettle this corner cleanly.

He was quite deep down into a trench when he saw what

looked like bones wrapped in bits of cloth. He was always coming across the remains of cats and dogs, sheep jaws and cow horns in his job. Nothing like that bothered him. If you couldn't melt them down they were best buried to feed the soil.

He pulled one or two bones aside. Some crumbled to dust at his touch but others were preserved, longer bits, some leather too. And then he saw the skull. Ned Bagshott jumped back.

'God's blood!' He crossed himself and made to blart out the hue and cry then stopped to see if anyone had witnessed his discovery. Not a soul within a cockstride of him. His heart was beating in his chest like a hammer, cheeks flushed, hands shaking. Someone had been buried under here out of sight after some foul deed. These bones must have lain undisturbed for years and trust him to find the secret burial. Now what was he to do? Raise the alarm and fetch the constable of the watch, inform Squire Timon and his mistress, or put the soil back quickly so no one would know? His instinct for the moment was to earth over this grim find, lay stones to mark the spot and let sleeping bones lie a while longer. There was nothing he could do for the poor soul, whoever it was. The last thing anyone wanted was a delay at this stage.

But did it matter that the body had no decent burial? Did its spirit wander abroad like the grey nun in search of her missing treasure? Had the yew branch known it was there too? These were far too many questions for his mind to fathom out at the end of a long day's digging. He must chew it over until the morrow, sleep on it but not tell a living soul of his grim discovery.

Bagshott the builder stowed his tools neatly onto his wagon and gathered the others from the hired men. He returned uphill along the high track to Longhall, silent and thoughtful, for he was a man with a burden heavier than any stone. Had he disturbed a malicious spirit or opened the place to boggarts and mischief? Being by nature wary of the other world and careful always to observe old customs – laying talismans for good fortune, placing objects into walls and roofs, sticking green men carvings where they could bless a building – he needed to preserve his own good luck or else he might chance on some mishap or bad weather to blight his progress. What on earth should he do now to right such a wrong as this?

The Knot Plot

'Just what on earth are you doing there?' shouted the mistress, waving a broom. 'I told you to dig me a knot *path*!'

'Yes, ma'am, and that I am doing.' Baggy pointed to his effort to trace out a curve. Sarah Salte sniffed in disgust. 'What mean you by this shape? 'Tis twined like a hempen rope.'

'Aye, so it is. Crossed over like the Shire knot, tried and tested, made to endure.' Baggy was pleased with his twisting pathway.

'You stupid man! I want a proper knot for my box plant-ings – a diamond shape, not a hangman's noose! My roses are to be enclosed in a boxed hedge shaped like a rose itself. See, winding round like this…' The woman swayed around in a fancy circle. 'See to it that the width of the path around it is befitting the span of a lady's gown, not a gardener's wheelbarrow.' Her wide skirt billowed as she paraded down her imaginary walkway and Baggy smirked behind her back.

'Put back the turf and I'll mark it out for you, step by step. Here are the petals, looped so… here the next row of petals. It must be edged with box and the edges lined with smooth stones to show up the shape overall. It will all gather into the centre... *comme ça*. Be quick about it, Bagshott!'

'Yes, Mistress Salte.' Baggy muttered foul oaths under his breath, clenching his fists. How she got up his nostrils with her haughty manners and prissy little voice! He was sick of all the 'can you just get on with this or that now', all at the same time! They were employed to put up the chimney stack and the roof, breaking through into the lodging, not to dig her garden, level her terrace and pave it over. That was a job for others more experienced than themselves. A knot garden indeed! How was he to know what it was? It was a gardener's job, not one for a bricklayer, carpenter and plasterer. Yet he was pleased with the way they had dovetailed the new house neatly into the old place. The joists were laid in the upper chambers, sturdy floorboards in place, the stack almost completed, the staircase carved with wooden scrolls and embellishments. Bagshotts were indoor workers not outdoor. Each to his task. But the Saltes would squeeze every ounce of work out of them to save costs.

The weather was merciful and had caused no delays. All had been going well until now. He still wondered if he should shift those bones from their hidden grave and felt uneasy that he had told no one of them yet. Perhaps they were better left in the ground.

Squire Timon left all the household decisions to his quarrelsome wife, which went against the grain for his craftsmen. What a to do when things were left to a woman! Surely she should know nothing of such matters? And how she drove them with her constant demands. 'Hurry up! It must be done by the feast of Christemasse... I'm not spending another minute in that guest hall by the Porteress's gate. If my father, Sir Sidney Sapcote, could see my distress... to live in such a manner like peasants in a hovel... poor little Tom!'

'Poor little Master Thomas' was in fact a boil on the bum, constantly scampering over the site, pulling faces, climbing ropes and throwing bricks around. If it had been his Jem or Eddy misbehaving so, Baggy would have leathered his backside a long time ago. The spoilt brat seemed impervious of any danger to himself or others. Jem had already rescued him from the roof, the scaffold and the stew pond. And as if *he* wasn't enough, there was the old dame, forever tripping over mounds and ditches with Leah following behind to pick her up and Jem blushing like a lovesick loon every time he caught sight of the lass. It was like bedlam at times but they kept on working through all the distractions and Baggy was proud of the way his sons had helped.

Now they must dig up all of this blessed plot, lifting bushes and briars when the ground was fair nailed down with frost. They must tear up the old Prioress's walkway and her privy garden and herbarium. It didn't seem right to him to pull up ancient yew, even though the garden was overgrown and neglected, just to please her ladyship's fancy whim. He would leave that task to last and perhaps then the snow would have fallen and someone else could dig it up in the spring. Let the winter tame this wilderness and strip the branches. There was enough to do just digging all this over. Ned Bagshott could do with a few more willing hands to wield spade and shovel. Perhaps a ploughman or one of the village louts but there was no extra to pay them and Sire Timon would not spare them from the fields in daylight hours. He was never around to discuss these matters anyway but spent most of his time at Longhall with his brother, Sire Richard.

Baggy leant on his spade. It was one of them mornings when the sky was icy blue and the rooks, cawing in forest branches, shone like sea coal in the sunlight. His breath steamed and he hoped Meg was making a fine crust pie for his supper. In the distance drifted the slender outline of the old dame as she went about her daily wanderings, first to the porch, then thrice around the church itself, poking into the walls. Next she made for the old fish stews and paced along the banks, down the orchard path to the field and back up into the cemetery, finally following the stream to sit by her spring for a while. Why was she so restless?

A short while later she stumbled past him, smiling sweetly to herself with vacant eyes. As usual he doffed his cap but was not sure she could even see him. 'Good morrow, Dame Prioress. Is there ought amiss for you to walk so many miles in search of something? I've seen you with the yew branch these past weeks. Can your humble servant help in any way?'

The old woman paused, startled out of a dream by this address. Who was this strange man? It took a few seconds to snap her wits back to the present. Dame Felice shook her head sadly, shielding her eyes from the bright day. 'I've lost a treasure, young man, one of great value to the Priory. I have perchance mislaid it somewhere. Every day I retrace my steps in circles but so far I mind not where I placed it for safety. Such are the infirmities of old age. Beware old age... it swallows up too much of your time.'

'Tell me what to look for and I will get my sons to help you find this treasure. What does it look like, this object?'

'It was given to my forebears at the founding of the Priory. The Blessed Ambrosine received it of the Lord Bishop – a jewel of great price to set seal on this House of Prayer. Now it befalls me to lose not only the Priory but the treasure also. Woe is me, young man!'

Treasure? Real treasure! How the word danced in his head. Somewhere was hidden a pearl of great price, with no doubt a reward for its recovery from the grateful Saltes. His mind was racing with possibilities. 'And you have no notion as to where this treasure lies, Madam Prioress?'

'It is mislaid but not in the church or the lodging. Leah and I have turned over every nook and cranny there. Perhaps it is lost in the garden. I know not for my memory is not what it was.' Her face was ashen and her eyes empty.

'Then leave it with me, my lady. Don't be a werrit. We'll turn over the sod and seek it out.'

Baggy beamed, his bushy eyebrows bristling. Lost treasure in the garden? Surely word of that would get the village folk off the ale bench in search of their spades, digging and delving under every piece of turf in search of a lost jewel? Just the scheme he needed to finish her ladyship's knot!

Baggy's Prediction came true. How they all dug at the thought of hidden treasure, delving deep into the ground with spades and hoes, axes and picks. The Frideswell lads and lasses dug in shifts at dusk and dawn. Out came all the hedges and the scrub, the bushes and the stones. Up came the old narrow paths around the kitchen patch. Spurred on by the thought of a reward they dug and dug but found nothing. Soon the formerly sloping garden lay turned, level and ready for planting. After such an effort the roses would come up a treat, thought the canny workman with a smile. My Lady Muck descended to dust over her design with powder and the plantings were laid to her satisfaction, edged with spears of box hedging. Baggy was a happy man at last.

Two nights later he was roused from deep slumbers, dreaming

of a cask of gold coins buried under the fig tree. Meg was tugging at his shirt with alarm.

'Wake up! Harken to that racket outside. 'Tis the devil and his homy hordes come to snatch us from our beds. Who else would come at this hour of the night?'

There was a cacophony of clankings and bangings as metal struck metal, cymbals chiming and horns blowing, the rough music of pots and buckets and a jabber of angry voices. The disgruntled village folk had gathered outside to shame him in the time-honoured way.

He rose from his mattress and wrapped his cloak around him for the night air was chilly and his bones stiff. He opened the wooden shutter to make his bow. The music grew louder and Jem dashed in, fearing for his life. Baggy raised his hands in salute with a sheepish grin on his bleary face.

'Aye, lads, 'tis well deserved... disappointing not to find anything, but the old dame did say there was treasure in the ground – I swear it on the Holy Book. May God be my witness, 'twas so; "a jewel of great price", her very words, from the Lord Bishop of olden times. So there's nothing found? That's not to say there's nothing there yet.

'I'm sorry for your wasted efforts. I made no promises as I recall but I will make you one now, lads. If I find so much as a groat or a farthing, a coin of the realm, it'll all be shared out, I promise. Would Edward Bagshott cheat his friends and neighbours?'

There was a jeer of derision. How many times had this man been up at court for a fine, a bit of land here, an extra inch or two there? 'Tell that to the Shire Reeve at the next sessions!' There was laughter and the music stopped. It was Jem who came to his rescue, serious dark-eyed Jem who loved a sermon on Sundays.

'Go home, friends, and rest up. We cheated no one for we promised nothing, 'twere yer own greed what made you take up yer spades. Next time me dad sees you at the sign of the Plough, I shall make sure he dips in his purse and buys you all a tankard of ale for your troubles or God'll strike him down dead where he stands. Back home to yer beds now or the night will run away with us. You've had yer say.'

He closed the shutters, shrugged his shoulders at the expression on his mother's face. It was the longest speech she had ever heard her taciturn son make. She was fired up with curiosity now.

'What's all this in aid of? What've you been up to now, Baggy? No good, I'll be bound, for our poor kinfolk to leave their beds of a frosty night to teach you a lesson. I hope you've not been shaming me again. How can I stand square at the well afore the gossips? I can't trust you out of my sight for one minute…'

'Give us a hug, you hussy. Come warm me bones. Now would I ever try to get summat for nowt? Would I?'

They hugged each other tightly and he laughed away her fears.

The Century Oak

※※※

There was something not quite pleasing about the view. As she assessed the overall effect of her new garden, Sarah was disappointed. What was it... the outer wall further down the slope or the church peeping through the trees? No, it was that tree to the far left. It was blocking the total vista, spoiling the sweep of the slope down to the stream and the meadow pastures beyond, the view dipping down to the valley then rising up to a line of trees. Those oaks were shading out this part of her design. Come the spring there would be dense shade and then at the fall of leaves a bare outline, displeasing to the eye.

'Look, sire, that line of trees... the one at the end must be felled. 'Tis a good thing I spotted it now when a remedy is at hand.'

'But those are the century oaks, planted in honour of the King's visit to the city many years ago. They're still fine trees with centuries of life in them yet.'

'Wood is always useful to us, especially with so much repair work to be done on the barns. Once dried and hardened you will find a hundred places to use it. Oh, Timon, won't it all be perfect? The rosebeds opening out like petals, the pretty low hedges cut into diamond shapes to please the eye, the new plantings of lavender. All that is missing is some fine statue or fountain at the centre. I shall speak to my father and take his advice on the matter. He'll know how best to adorn it with a flourish.' Timon nodded with a sigh.

'You've done well, dear heart, I grant you that, and poor Master Bagshott is quite downtrodden by your commands. See how he stoops and rubs his back. We are all quite exhausted with your alterations. How you keep so upright with your stomacher swollen with child. I do not know.'

'That's why we must be settled before Christemasse comes upon us. There's still much to straighten and clean. I've told Leah to leave her mistress and keep only by my side.'

'But Felice is unwell and keeps to her chamber these past days. We must send for the apothecary if she continues so. Do not disturb her routine with more thumpings and bangings.'

'Then the sooner she is moved to the chamber in the guest hall, the sooner we will all recover. The rooms there are sufficient for all her needs.'

'I'm not sure it's right at this time of winter to move a woman of her years. 'Twill unsettle her so. The roof leaks a little and the hearth will not be so warm as our new chimney stack.'

'Pish and twaddle, Timon! You're worse than an old wifie yourself to futtle so. She's strong enough and Joseph will carry her over the mud. I'll not be thwarted before my confinement. Have I not troubles of my own to attend to? Fair exchange is no robbery, now is it?'

Sarah was not going to listen to more fussing from her husband when there was so much to admire about her new home. Her rooms would be spacious and filled with the finest oak tables, chests and stools. The old panelling from the Priory was in place on the walls; the fireplace stood proud in the main hall. The staircase had their initials carved for all to see and admire. The roof was almost complete. Once the old nun was removed out of sight then her former lodging would make a fine food hall and buttery with a chamber above for Sarah's own private use.

'My lady's garden will be the talk of Longhall. No mere country hussif's patch. Felice's old privy garden will make a laundry yard and I'll supervise Leah's laundry – see how that minx manages to lay the bucket with linen and get it all so clean.'

Sarah smiled. Everything was working to her will. Next would come the lying in.

Every night she prayed hard that she would be saved, for was it not a fact that a pregnant woman had one foot in the grave, however high-born she was? Sarah had kept so busy to keep her own fears to the back of her mind, taking comfort from her new knot garden to cheer away gloomy thoughts. Perhaps a trellis with musk roses would form the central feature, or a yew arch carved from the old hedge? No. It needed something more spectacular, more in keeping with these modern times, a timepiece or a sundial... Of course! Why had she not thought of it before? They were sprouting up in all of the Queen's palaces, she had heard tell. How clever that the sun could cast a shadow that gave the precise time of day. If it were raised on a pedestal of stone with an outer circle of box hedging, why, it would complete her own palace of dreams.

The new house would be magnificent, the envy of the district and of the Longhall Saltes who would come to stay and admire their taste... her taste. Thomas and the babe would play with their cousins as equals not mere offspring of the second son. She could pretend that they were as rich but not so common as the Pagets. They would still be screened from the village by the older oaks at the Porteress's gate. They might as well stay put but the century oak had to come down. Bagshott must see to it immediately. Nothing was going to spoil the view from 'my lady's garden'.

'She can't cut down the century oak! Why, it's been a-standing there since my grandsires fought with old Sire Richard Salte's father at Bosworth field… It's doing no harm where it is,' muttered Joseph as he kicked open the lodging house door, bringing in the logs for the new fire. He stopped up the heavy wooden door with the door stopper while Baggy and Jem looked on. 'If she wants to lop off some branches, tell 'er to cut 'em off them by the Porteress's gate. They're older and far too tall. No one would miss them. You can't just cut down a tree 'cos it's in the wrong place, can you?'

Baggy shrugged his shoulders. He was saying nothing. If this mistress said jump, you jumped. That was the way of things in the new household. What a carry on when a woman wore the breeches! Still with one on the throne of England and in Scotland too, it seemed it was the way of things today. In his opinion it wasn't natural for the daughters of Eve to have opinions, let alone give orders, unless they were in a nunnery maybe and now all them had been scrapped.

Perhaps some of they bossy spirits of the place clung on within these walls. He would be glad when they were away from this strange place. Winter was gripping fast now and there were just a few details to finish in the roof. It would soon be time to put the talisman in there, close to the chimney where the evil spirits were most likely to sneak in while the household was fast asleep. Some small token, a few choice objects, would ward off the evil eye from making mischief.

He looked up at their handiwork with satisfaction and pride, recalling the way Jem had laid the bricks in neat patterns and quoted, '"If the Lord build not the house, the workman laboureth in vain".' He was good with Bible words, Jem, and could read a few now that Uncle Reuben was taking him under his wing. Reuben preached a lot about both plain and fancy folk being on the road to hellfire. The Saltes looked more and more like fancy folk to Jem and he said young Leah and her husband needed protection.

Baggy must give them a strong talisman, something to keep them safe. There was nothing better than a dead man's hand… or bones perhaps? The bones under the fig had not buried themselves, some foul deed had happened there. He must find the shoes if he could for a murdered man would haunt the place if he were buried shod. But perhaps the bones themselves might protect all within. Baggy must go at once and see to the matter.

He waited until dusk to follow the path by the fig tree. Leah was watching him and he pretended to be fixing the stonework until she closed the door behind her. He uncovered the bones but the dampness and recent airing had crumbled most to dust. What was left he lifted into a meal sack and took up the outside ladder into the eaves, to the point where the new and old buildings were joined together.

The wind was whipping the last of the leaves into flurries. As he rose higher up the ladder he could see the outline of the knot bed, the newly laid paths, then over the boundary wall to the line of oaks and the glistening mill pond. In the springtime all would be green and covered, the wilderness tamed once more according to her ladyship's commands. He did not see much in these gardens, himself. It was a waste of good growing space for food and fodder, in his opinion. Only fancy folk could afford such fripperies. Jem was right. There were plain folk and fancy folk here.

Baggy hoisted the sack and pushed it neatly into a crevice, distributing the bones evenly and then filling up the hole in the tiles carefully with a silent prayer. This was being done for the best and no one would ever know of it. The bones could sleep quietly here, undisturbed by wind or rain, guarding his handiwork. He hoped the poor soul understood this change of residence and wished it peace. The few bits of leather shoe he had found he was going to destroy. There must be nothing left to haunt the house's inhabitants.

The December gales lashed through the forest, great trees bending to their force, yielding branches in submission to a superior power. Thatch flew from any roof which was not weighted down with stones and rope. No one slept in the valley for thunder and lightning crashed overhead, rending the sky with streaks of silver and gold. Rats fled from the open fields to the shelter of houses and barns. Falling branches closed the cart tracks with debris, blocking village from village, families from friends, and many stones were loosened from the steeples and towers of the old ruins.

The century oak lay prostrate before it was hacked and butchered into joints. The mistress had given the order to fell it before the storm and it was obeyed. She now lay in the upstairs soller, propped up against feather pillows, her new daughter lying swaddled in the wooden cradle and given the name Elizabeth in honour of their great sovereign.

The Queen of the new house lay contented for once in all her triumph, oblivious at first of the storm roaring overhead.

Everything was perfect: the house, their garden, the removal of the old aunt, all done with scarce a murmur from Timon who snored by her side. If only this racket would die down, it spoiled her peace. At times she feared the new roof was going to lift off and they would be whirled away. The wind moaned down the new chimney breast like a soul in torment but they were warm and dry and safe in their own dwelling, thanks to her endeavours.

Sarah's eyelids drooped in blameless sleep as the old oaks groaned, keeling over into each other like skittles, crashing one by one down on to the Porteress's gate house.

Man that is born of a woman hath but a short time to live; and is full of misery. He cometh up and is cut down, like a flower; he flee-eth as it were a shadow, and never continueth in one stay...

'For as much as it hath pleased Almighty God of his great mercy to take unto himself the souls of our reverend sister, Felice, late Prioress of St Mary's Frideswell, and her servants, Joseph and Leah, here departed...'

Timon Salte bent his head, more in shame than sorrow. Because he could not withstand the onslaught of his wife's demands this terrible accident had happened. Those trees were old and rotten and should have been felled long ago, while the healthy century oak was felled purely on a whim.

What have I done? he berated himself. Overspent on every item in this cursed house and not a coin in the coffers to pay Bagshott his due. And now this fresh shame: the needless slaughter of his aunt. Suddenly he felt the sap of youth drain from his limbs and the sparkle fade from his eyes. He peered into the burial vault with sadness and regret.

I must learn to stand up to Sarah or we are doomed, he realised. Please God, give me strength to be a man, though beggared now for the sake of a garden and more shamed than any cuckold.

There would be only scrimping and scraping for them this harsh winter. Furniture and hangings must be sold, rents raised and dues collected from all his tenants, however poor, if they were to survive.

Lord be praised! It could have been us struck down in our beds, my innocent babes crushed by tree trunks! Sarah Salte gripped her son's shoulders to steady herself. We have been spared and others sacrificed. That was the will of God in His Wisdom. Her instinct to get out of that cursed lodge before Christemasse, before the birth of the child, had been a miracle of grace and no mistake. It was an honour to be so preserved. For the others 'twas a pity, she conceded, but Felice was old and the servants had no off shoots. None of them would have known a thing about it. How could she be blamed for their deaths?

Timon brushed past her roughly, not deigning to look into her face. There was never any meeting of minds with him nowadays. She could sense he blamed her for all of it and this was not how it was meant to be. This tragedy had spoiled all her joy in her new home. Sarah was seen as a murderess by his family, a cruel killer of their kin. Now Timon was ripping her new tapestries from the wall and the brocades from her bed, telling her they must be sold. How could he shame her so? Not once would he walk in the winter garden to admire the stone sundial and her knot garden, only talk of ruin and shame. Pish and twaddle, they would survive! Saltes had lived above all others around these parts for centuries past. Things would turn around for the new house. They must, for the sake of Sarah's heirs.

Baggy stood silently with the stunned villagers of Frideswell, with the men who had scrambled to rescue the poor trapped victims under the mighty oaks, with Jem who had crawled to his beloved Leah, cradling her lifeless form in his arms while screaming with rage. They had pulled out the bodies and demolished the gate house, leaving only a pile of stones as evidence of this terrible night. Had he brought this storm about by meddling with the spirits? Had he helped turn the world upside down?

No, surely not, 'For it is the wrath of God who thunders where he wills,' said the Parson to his troubled soul. He could scarce look upon that Salte woman without wanting to clap her in irons and duck her in the fish pond. The master was tardy with his payments and did not hold his gaze. A Bagshott had trusted the word of a Salte, a risky business as he had been warned by Reuben, and now it was turning his hair white with worry. It would go hard for them if payment were delayed. He had neglected his own fields and harvest to secure the Saltes' comfort while all he was given so far was a share in the century oak for his pains. What use was green oak which would take a year to harden? If all else failed they would be reduced to burning it in his cold hearth.

This blessed house would ruin them all, one by one. He feared he had built a greedy monster from the ruins of the Priory. One that had fed on his ambitions to better the Bagshotts in this new world where opportunities for wealth and fortune lay open to those brave enough to take risks.

Now he wished he could climb the ladder and snatch back those bones and fling them on a pyre. They brought down a curse on all who touched them, of that he was certain. Had he disturbed a malevolent sprite with spiteful power and influence over this cursed place? For once in his life he had no ready answer for himself, only the satisfying thought that if he had the Saltes were doomed for certain. As he lifted his weary eyes over the cemetery field he thought he saw the grey lady on her rounds again, searching for her lost treasure. Baggy blinked. It was just the light playing tricks. When he looked again towards the churchyard wall she was gone.

Jeremiah Bagshott stood by his father's side, towering over him, hands clutching his wide-brimmed black hat. His dark face was set grim and stern. He would shed no more tears for Leah, his love lost twice to him, once on her betrothal to Joseph and then by this cruel misfortune.

'Vanity, vanity… all is vanity saith the Lord.' Enjoy yourself now, my lady, for you Saltes will pay for your vanity. Not now perhaps but one day, in the fullness of time. In the Lord's time.

His heart was ice cold as he looked up at the new house with its fine chimney and tiled roof, fancy windows and gracious doorway built by the Bagshotts with craftsmen's skills. It looked so spruce and strong but like the century oak could be felled by the hand of the Lord at any time. The vanity of that witch Sarah had accomplished all this, the curse of Eve made manifest in her. The temptress would surely be humbled.

'My lady's garden has cost us all dear. A curse on her and all who tread therein from henceforth.'

They must be punished for this wickedness against his love heart, Leah, whose humble beauty far outstripped the witch's charms.

Strangely her death had brought with it a sense of release and peace, a new purpose free from the bonds of passion which had kept him by her side. He would shake the dust of Frideswell from his boots and make his way to the City of Spires in the hollow. There he would work his way up to Reuben's side, make something of himself, harden his heart and his children's against the vanity of the Saltes. One day this place would be laid low.

Jem scattered the sod into the grave pit with grim satisfaction. 'The Lord giveth and the Lord taketh away... Blessed be the name of the Lord.'

Down The Path

Iris

⸎

The path meanders round the house under a pergola heavy with the fragrance of *Rosa* 'Zéphirine Drouhin'. Iris Bagshott dead heads as she goes along, carefully inspecting for tell-tale signs. There's always some plague of Egypt waiting to erupt here when her back's turned: rust, mould, blight. Ah, hah, the dreaded black spot!

Who will see to you lot when I'm gone? she muses. Autumn is when you'll see my true colours, this Fridwell slasher who gives you all the chop for your own good. So behave!

> Gather ye rosebuds while ye may,
> Old time is a-flying.
> And this same flower that smiles today,
> Tomorrow will be dying.

Do they still learn poems by rote in schools? I bet they don't have to recite them with a cane hovering over their heads. It certainly sharpened my memory for things past. As for the present, I forget from one minute to the next without my note pad.

Iris is not satisfied with the effect, the rose parlour lacks warmth. It needs more arches and trellis work to soften the stiffness, arches dripping with blood red bourbons, blushing damasks and pale musk roses.

That's the trouble with this garden, I'm never satisfied but haven't the stomach or energy now to tear it all up and start afresh. Perhaps the roses do need a younger, more romantic set of green fingers, to fiddle and twirl, drape and design? I've seen too many of life's nasty tricks to believe in romance as the panacea for all ills but a sweet-scented rose arbour would make a lovely hideaway.

Iris stands back, looking towards the flat end of the L-shaped house. The spirit of the place talks loudly here and now it's telling her to watch that variegated ivy clambering over the roof at the end of the house which is sliced off like a cut loaf. It needs a firm haircut, and soon. Out comes the note pad again.

She remembers when the Local Studies Group came to walk over her bit of the monastic site, tracing the outline of the old buildings, tithe barns and ponds. They pointed to her stonework and the Tudor brick addition which was out of proportion with the rest of the house. They cleared the boggy pond at the bottom of the slope, close to the one remaining stone arched gate into the churchyard, telling her it must be the nuns' fish stew.

One weekend a group of them drained it carefully but found no treasure, only some broken crocks and a few brown bottles of Father's stout. Iris showed them her granny's tiny ring of twisted gold wire with a stone missing, unearthed whilst mulching the wisteria by the wall in the vain hope that it might break out in blossom. The fingers of ancient ladies were certainly small and she wondered if some poor lass had searched and searched for her precious jewel.

Then came the visit from members of the Sealed Knot Society who were going to re-enact the skirmish of Barnsley Bridge for the Gala Day. They said a small garrison was billeted on Fridwell during the Civil War. Was it the soldiers who chopped off the house with cannons? she'd asked, but the group didn't know.

I can't move in this garden without treading in the footsteps of the forebears who made me what I am. I live with these blessed ghosts always trooping behind me, whispering in my ear. They don't bother me much except one: a troubled soul who lives on the old stairs. There's always a chill when she does her rounds. There I go again, making assumptions, but a chime hour child can't be witched. I have 'the knowing without words', as Granny used to say, and it's been quite a burden to me at times.

PART FIVE

FRIDEWELL GARRISON

1646

'When Gardens only had their Towrs,
And all the garrisons were Flowrs,
When Roses only Arms might bear,
And Men did rosie Garlands wear...
But War all this doth overgrow:
We Ord'nance Plant and Powder sow'
—'Upon Appleton House',
Andrew Marvell

'Rosemary
The chymical oil drawn from the leaves and
flowers is a sovereign help... one drop,
two or three, as the case requires
for the inward griefs'

Arrivals

❦

The standard fluttered like a tattered sail in the warm breeze. It had seen much action and the banner motto and ribbons, 'In God We Trust', were faded from sunset orange to a weak sunrise apricot.

The trooper waved it triumphantly as they rode out of the cool shade of the oak forest on to the high ridgeway where the breeze tore at its ragged edges. There was no one to see their coming, not even the welcome of birdsong, for the heat was sending all creatures in search of shade under roof, branch and hollow, out of the sun and bracken dust of the August afternoon.

The Captain of the troop held up his hand and they circled around, scuffing red dust into eyes and faces. The horses flicked their tails to scatter away a plague of black flies which descended upon the party the second they stopped to recce their position.

'Halt! We're nearer the city than I first reckoned, not a league from the Malignant garrison. See down there, the spires are still standing – more to our shame. Yonder village is Fridewell and Barnsley Green lies to the west. This bodes well for us for I've many kinfolk in these parts. We shall feast from those fields ere long. Take heart.'

Micah Bagshott, Captain of Horse in Sir Thomas Fairfax's New Model Army, veteran of Edgehill and Naseby and many a recent bloody skirmish, late of the city below, smiled with satisfaction at their good luck. He was on familiar territory, almost home ground, near enough to receive a cautious welcome and respect fom the lowlier peasants and journeymen who recognised his illustrious name. If anyone were to stop the siege of the Royalist garrison by secret supply convoys, creeping out of the forest at dead of night, then he knew all the rat runs, crossing paths and streams down to the walled fortress below. If they waited here little would get past their patrol or the others of his Company scattered over the thick forest. It was not so wild and dense a forest now as to be unmapped and cleared for miles around the main routes north and south. He wiped the dust from his eyes which settled in the grooves of his sunlined face and smiled a roguish smile, his lips stretched into a thin line, his black eyes flashing with glee.

He was on Salt land now, he could see the blue smoke curling eastwards from the chimney stack, the tiled roof of the Newhouse and the layout of its fancy gardens like a map drawn out before him. This was the place built on the broken backs of Bagshott men in the time of old Reuben and Jeremiah the preacher; his grandsire who told of humble beginnings and his father, Ned the builder, whose penury at the hands of those cheating Salts, sent him to an early grave. The name, Salt, had lain like a curse on Bagshott lips since that time. Micah had no reason to wish any of the Salts well for they were for the King not Parliament as was most of the City.

Micah had been driven out of the city after the first fateful seige and the death of his hero, Lord Brooke, following with the horse and troopers to find quarter where he could. Revenge for parading such humiliation before his neighbours would be sweet one day but best savoured and eaten cold.

There were recusants hiding in the forest, he could sniff them on the wind, Papists and mercenaries. Some had escaped from custody and were on the run making south for their garrisons. They must be dealt with swiftly and without mercy. He took no prisoners. The Company was split into groups to patrol over the Chase. The Captain was delighted now to be in reach of this village with its supply of fresh water, flour mill, barns, stables and harvest almost gathered in. Fridewell would suit his men well. He would see to the Salts personally. He would enjoy sleeping on their feather beds, sipping from their cellar and feasting on their meat store. But he would mind his manners for he was an educated man who knew how to use a pronged fork. His education had been thorough and now thanks to three years in the army he had acquired a taste for the niceties of genteel living acquired from raiding parties on the tearful gentry who watched their houses burn to ashes and scattered in the wind.

The army had given him another education, though, a steel-edged rough awakening into the rigours of warfare. The cruel blade slicing into flesh, the spurting of blood as a man hovered 'twixt life and death. The cries of men pleading for a merciful end to suffering; comrades torn limb from limb, or crushed to mangled guts and bones. He was growing inured to the sight of such horrors and ever more confident in his power of leadership, demanding respect and obedience as his due. He was respected for his ruthlessness, the way he instantly dispensed harsh justice for any infringement of discipline. Captain Bagshott did not hesitate to flog or execute in order to enforce his will. He demanded the utmost loyalty from his troop for they were his family now, a tie forged through blood and necessity. All that was foraged he shared fairly among them.

If Micah felt relief or sadness to be so close to home he would not be showing it before his men. He feared to reveal any weakness, had seen it betray other men into folly and death. Those who lingered over their actions or examined their motives too deeply soon came to grief. It was as if they were fighting the battle from both sides and exhausted themselves with the effort to remain humane and generous. Such emotions did not sit well beneath a helmet.

There were no gun carts to hold back their progress in the rutted lanes but the heat was getting to all the men in their thick buff coats and black breast plates which roasted them in such a heat. Micah could feel his own shift crawling with lice. They had been living from the saddle for a week, sleeping rough in tinder-dry bracken beds, searching out water from the trickles in the stream beds. It was little things like this that discomfited him most for he was a fastidious man by nature and longed to dunk himself in the fish pond below, feel the cool water washing away his weariness and filth.

It had been hard at first to leave a soft bed and lodge upon the cold earth, to give up choice meats for a little coarse bread and hard cheese, with only brackish water to drink and a foul pipe of tobacco to suck on. It was hard to leave Mother to her constant worrying, his childhood friends and the scholars in exchange for the whistle of bullets and bodies dropping dead at his feet. He was sick of that music. Given time one got used to being lousy and hungry, saddle sore and unwelcome. Yet, oh, to be so close to home! This would be a temptation but in such a summer of plague and sickness, he could not risk his men by moving further in towards the dirty streets and filth of a town. Let the Malignants suffer such for their sins. He would keep cool and clean up here at Fridewell.

He slitted his eyes to get a better view of the village nestled against the side of the slope. They would put up no resistance, not with kinfolk to protect. There would be no one of any consequence down there to co-ordinate an insurrection. There'd be an old widow no doubt, for both the Salt brothers were slain at Edgehill. He had seen their bodies laid out with all the other Midland men and marked their standard in the bunch of ragged colours captured on that day. No, there would be no resistance, but just in case it would give him great satisfaction to soften them up; a little scaremongering, a little throwing of Bagshott weight about the place should do the trick.

The Captain stabbed his finger down towards the red brick house which stood proudly on its own, set apart from the other village dwellings, bordered with green turf and knot beds, shrubs and sturdy outbuildings, upright and prosperous-looking in the glinting sunshine.

'Shift yourselves down there. Turn it over... search for any silver, arms, treasure. And leave no stone unturned. I do not trust these folk. Search the usual places – ponds, gardens – and see where the soil is fresh turned over. Rose beds have yielded many a fine piece of silver plate. Go to it but do not sack the house. We shall rest up there in comfort, lads, guarding the lanes from the enemy abroad. Yes, we shall let Fridewell's golden fields feed us and our horses for a while.

'Now, hurry about your business! It'll give me great pleasure to see the Salt riches spilled o'er the ground.'

A woman in a black gown trimmed with a collar of white lace paced anxiously over the terrace, back and forth, back and forth. She stopped to examine the rose bushes. The leaves were sparse, dappled yellow and brown, the foliage thin, and the June show long past. If she had dead headed more carefully there would have been a second flush to admire. But who was there to see?

The earth was parched. Even the weeds were wilting in the fierce glare of sunlight. She had never cared much for the knot beds with their stiff plantings dotted here and there between the box. The formal patterns had long been neglected and stray meadow flowers were creeping back from the fields beyond to reclaim the space. If only she had the heart to see to the garden chores, but her spirit was too downtrodden by the war to make any effort with 'my lady's garden'.

It was too hot to be wearing black, too hot for thick petti-coats and ruffles, but she had no mind for colour. These sickly blooms were colour enough, only their scent soothed the ache in her soul. Why did you go? Oh, Beavis... leaving us alone and unprotected. How can I forgive you for being so strong-willed, choosing to leave this blessed plot and your heart's home and abandon us to the mercy of fortune? For three summers I waited for your return. How can you be dead when I never saw your body? Oh, Beavis, how will I survive this affliction? It is not to be borne.

Nazareth Salt felt the hot tears sting her cheeks. She looked once again at her husband's garden. Once she had come here as a young bride, full of hope, dressed in pale blue silk bro-cade edged with fine lace in the latest fashion, a bridal gift from her mother. How slender was her waist then and how full her bosom, her hair lovingly glossed with a tincture of rosemary. She had none of the usual Sapcote plainness, being only distant kin to them. Not like her own poor child, Lucilla. A perfect English rose she had been once, now a blasted bloom with her widow's weeds and suntanned complexion. She could scarce be bothered to wear a cap.

Benjamin and Elizabeth Salt had nodded with approval at their son's choice but the stern old ancient in her ninetieth year, Old Sarah, had prodded the girl Nazareth with her stick like a sapling oak under inspection. 'My lady's garden' was Old Sarah's joy and none of Nazareth's choosing. Beavis had taken such pride in the house and it was not hard to love its sturdy brick walls and tranquil air. Yet she was never able to take to the formal terrace. It was a showplace, too formal, too redolent of Old Sarah's presence, turned as it was southward and westward to catch the slope of the land, showing off the knot beds and roses. Hidden beside the older part of the house was a walled hedge and a quiet patch, much neglected, close to the spring from which the house took its name. It was a sorry sight now, partially blocked with fallen masonry, weeds choking the banks of the stream. This source and fount of their very lives lay neglected, ignored in favour of a fancy sundial and a regimented row of rose bushes.

It was to here that Nazareth turned, directing her efforts to restoring the wellspring and old hedged garden. Here she felt peacefully secluded, safe at the heart of things. To her surprise she found she had a way with plantings, a softness of touch, a feel for the red earth and the heart of the soil, instinctively knowing when to sow and when to wait. Patience was a gift with which she was well endowed. For three summers, while she was waiting for Beavis to return home, this part of the garden had become her refuge when sleep would not come. Now her patience, like the stream, was drying up.

Nazareth yearned for someone strong to take the burden of responsibility from her shoulders. She was sick of making decisions, dealing with the estate and the field men. Her own kin were far away and it was dangerous to travel. Blewart's widow, Letty, had her own troubles and young children to raise at Longhall. She had remarried a kind soldier with one arm and was soon to bear another child to him. A new life was beginning for her. Letty did not have a daughter who refused to accept that her father would not be coming home but nursed forlorn hope like a lantern in a dark night.

If only Lucilla would be her mother's little companion and share the joys of the hidden garden. Why would she not chase the butterflies and bash down the bushes like the children at Longhall Manor, who raced around the gardens like playful puppies when they came to visit? Lucie stayed indoors instead and sewed, looking down with disapproval at their antics.

The child was watching now through the mullioned windows at the top of the stair. Nothing was missed, not the glint of metal flashing on the ridge or the line of soldiers with their banner flying high. Their sashes were bright orange not pink. Strangers in the village again, soldiers of the other side, not attired like Father in lace cuffs and feathers. She could still see him in his thigh boots, bright breast plate and shining helmet. She had raced eagerly to the gate to wave him on his way, so small in stature then that she'd had to look up into the sky when he was on horseback. Now she took no interest in horses or armour. Only when Father returned would she step outside the door to jump into his arms.

Lucilla watched her mother pacing about as usual in the rose bed like a witch in her black garb. Why did she wear widow's weeds when she knew Father would come home at the end of the war, returning to watch over them again? The child hated to see her in that hideous flat cap with her ringlets tossing about like a milkmaid's. Indeed, Mother no longer behaved like a lady. Father would be displeased that she had let herself go so thoroughly. Everything was topsy-turvy since he'd left them. Lucilla could not fathom out the reasoning of her elders. You were for King or Parliament, pink or orange, Protestant or Papist, rebel or recusant. She knew all the words by rote but what did they mean? Could they not sit down and talk together or hold their hands up and say 'barley', making a truce? Why did they have to end up quarrelling and fighting like her stupid cousins, Richard and Tobias?

Lucie liked to sit at the top of the stairs and watch life going on through the window. It was well placed between the old dark chamber and the new house. Here she was safe and cool with no wasps to sting her or creepy crawlies under her skirts. This was Lucilla's Kingdom and she was the Queen of the stairs; no one could pass by inside or out but she had knowledge of it. No one bothered how she amused herself as long as she had something in her hands, a Bible pamphlet or chap book, a piece of sewing, her pretty wooden doll. Mother scarce noticed her as she went hither and thither like a servant about her tasks. Martha carried up the clean linen into the press and she loved to sniff within the dry place where lavender balls and tansy were strewn.

Soon it would be her favourite hour when the sunlight shafted through the leaden window panes like a golden fan onto the dark oak staircase with their initials carved deeply into the wood. The beams fell on the portait of 'Old Sarah' who rebuilt the New House and 'My lady's garden', always to be said in one breath. Old Sarah went with the house like the bricks and mortar, Mother would sneer. Martha Barnsley said the dame was a fearsome woman and strong willed and that Miss Lucilla had that same cleft chin and steel eye for detail.

The child wondered what Old Sarah would make of all this terrible turnabout. Perhaps she would have taken up a pike or cudgel and beat these strangers out of the village with her bare hands.

There had been letters from Mother's kin, brought on horseback from the city, which had made her cry. She had retreated into the garden to savour their news, reading the sheets over and over again until they were worn thin. The news for the King's Cause was never good.

Lucie would stand in the doorway, pulling the door stop back and forth until she had once noticed that it bore a faint picture engraved into the surface: a lady with a child on her knee and some inscription too worn by the years to decipher. Martha the maid could make nothing of it but Mother, puzzled and intrigued by its weight and shape, took it upon herself to show it to Reverend Masterson, who got all flushed in the cheeks, saying it was an old seal, perhaps the lost seal of Saint Mary's Priory, founded centuries ago by one of their forebears. It was he who suggested that it was the Virgin and Holy Child depicted, and advised that such an effigy was best hidden away in these troublesome times. But he'd fingered it lovingly for all that. Mother said it must be kept safe from view or they would be taken for Papists, and found another weight for the old door.

Lucilla was vexed at such a fuss and pleaded to hide it in her own chamber in her treasure box, inlaid with mother-of-pearl initials. Finders should be keepers, she argued, and for once Mother had agreed.

It was so heavy it fell to the bottom of the wooden box along with the precious letter, the only reminder of Father she had left to herself. Lucie knew every word of his note by heart: 'Greetings to Lucilla, my own trew Little Light. Be good to your dear mother and keep her safe until I return.' She also had a piece of fancy ribbon from his best jacket and the little phial of Hungary water which was passed down to all the ladies in the family as a relic or something like that. There was a feather fan too which Father said was made from the wings of fairies. With such a box of treasures, and such delights therein, who needed to go out of doors?

Lucilla glanced upwards again to the top of the lane. The soldiers on horseback were riding fast, galloping down in the direction of the house. Lucie knew they were not the King's men. They wore strange helmets like masks and their ripped banner streamed in the breeze as they stormed through the gate and into the cobbled entrance yard.

The child fled to her chamber, hiding under the counterpane, clutching her treasures tightly to her chest. Perhaps if she lay quiet they would all go away.

At the sound of clattering hooves the mistress and her servants made for the courtyard. Nazareth tried to stay calm as she undid the knot of her apron, smoothed her hair back from her sticky face and beckoned to Martha and Gideon to walk behind her.

'For King or Parliament?' shouted a Sergeant roughly.

'We are for ourselves… as you see, there is only a boy to defend us here.' Nazareth stood as tall and straight as she could, looking the man straight in the eye.

'Those who are not for us are agin us, mistress.'

'Whatever you say, sire, but there is nothing here to take your interest. No arms, horses or cattle left. The last visitors saw to that.'

'Then we must check there was no oversight. Stand aside! See to the usual places, men, and search it well. Necessity makes liars of ladies and beggars alike.' He laughed down at her, pushing past to dismount and order the troopers into the store barn and then the garden. Nazareth followed quickly behind, running to keep up with their progress. 'This is my house, sire!'

'Then hinder us not and 'twill come to no harm. Impede us further and it will be torched. That's right... search the garden!' He waved his arms in the direction of the rose knot.

'What could be hidden in a bunch of rose bushes?' Nazareth screamed after him.

'Ah, madam, you would be surprised what Popish trinkets find their way into such roots.' He was laughing at her help-lessness. She watched them push over the sundial. It splintered and fell in pieces. They hacked at the roses, scooped up the soil, shaking their heads with disappointment. 'Oh, sire, I beseech you, this is an ancient and holy dwelling. See, the church has already been ransacked. Not a window is saved and the bell tower has fallen. Tell us what you require and we will see to it.'

She was pleading now, afraid of the glint in the Sergeant's eye which was cruel and cold. He cared not a jot for her feelings. His men were busily pulling out all the tools from the barn, the wheelbarrow and forks, the bales of straw, tossing them around the yard. The Sergeant was angry at this and sent them to search down the well.

'There's no well here, only an everlasting spring to the rear... you are welcome to share our fresh water for your horses look tired.'

Nazareth was ignored as they stormed towards the buttery door where the last of the ham was hanging and the jars of fruits. 'This is more to our liking.' A trooper lifted a crock and smashed it on the stone flags. 'Oh, dearie me!'

Nazareth felt such a blaze of anger rise within her that it overwhelmed all other fears. 'How dare you spoil precious food when we have all fasted like nuns for weeks to preserve this for winter? Sergeant, keep your men under control... they are like ravening wolves! I demand to speak to your commander. This indignity is not to be borne. It is not a Christian act...'

'No more! Halt. Harken to the lady's bidding,' the Captain ordered as he rode slowly into the yard. He held up his hand in salute. 'That's enough, Sergeant. Don't destroy what must support us.'

Nazareth recognised the orange sash of an officer of the Cavalry. She could not see his face for the sun was in her eyes, merely a broad and towering presence casting a long shadow. She shaded her eyes to see what manner of man greeted her but all she could make out behind the visor was the face of a dark man, dusty and lined.

'Why have your men seen fit to raze my garden and raid my stores? Asked civilly we would have shared what little we have left. You see, we live like peasants. I have but a maid and boy to serve us. This is not the act of gentlemen, sire.' Her voice trembled with rage but her legs quivered.

'Madam, I apologise if they have been overzealous in their industry. I see but a few upturned roses and will have them replanted forthwith.'

'Save your breath, sire. I care not for those beds nor ever have. Let them continue with their rout so that I may plant a better crop of flowers and herbs. But the sundial is smashed. It was a particular favourite of my dear late husband and goes back many generations.'

'Aye, to old Sarah Salte who built this house, if I am not mistaken?'

'How come you have knowledge of us, sire? We are but farmers whose fortunes are now laid low for all to see.'

'I am Captain Micah Bagshott of the Company of Cavalry, late of the city. I know full well the fortunes of this house and how its vanity brought great misfortune on my own kin in these parts.'

'This was none of my doing, being related by marriage only and lately widowed. I know nothing of such stories but your name is familiar to me.'

'So it should be! Bagshotts were ever at the tender mercies of Saltes in times past. Now Almighty God is redressing the balance at long last.'

He was laughing as he dismounted and took off his helmet, shaking free a mop of greasy curls which reached his shoulders. He towered over her like a huge black bear, broad-shouldered, rough-hewn. His dusty thigh boots reached almost level with her waist. His face was lean and strong, clean-shaven, and his confident manner was disarming in its simplicity. If he were indeed a true Bagshott then he was much improved in station and speech on the peasants who lived scattered around Longhall. He was almost a gentleman. Nazareth drank him in with grim satisfaction. Would he be gentleman enough to protect her honour from pillage and shame?

'I suppose you require quartering? You're not the first to demand such. There are few other hovels in this village which are not o'erspilling with children. Your men can lie in the barns and sleep on the straw in the cattle stalls...'

'And no doubt you will invite myself and my lieutenant to bide within these walls and guard your virtue? Such is the usual custom. But first send your maid with water so that I may wash away the grime. I stink of the forest and must make myself worthy of the elegant company which shines before me in the sunshine.'

'You mock me, sire, and it is unworthy of you. I am but a poor widow with a child to protect. I have little appetite for elegance, having eaten only vegetables and stew pot fare these past months. Take what you must but I can offer no indulgences here. I have a child who is sickly and needs to eat. Permit me to go to her at once for she will be afeared by your presence.'

'Do not let me delay you, Mistress Salt. Far be it from me to tear a child from its mother. Let us dine in harmony this evening so that you may see we mean no damage to your property. As for arms and silver, pots and fodder – an army on the march must fill its belly.'

'How long do you stay?'

'As long as the garrison besieged in the cathedral holds out against the Committee of Two Kingdoms. It is only a matter of time with hunger and sickness, this heat and little water. The King may claim to have the best cause but Parliament has the better army, do you not agree?'

'I care not either way. This war has robbed me of the only treasure I prized, the love of a good and honest husband.'

'Squire Beavis Salt, am I right?'

'You know of him? He fell at Edgehill but my Lucilla still prays that he will be returned to us unharmed.' Nazareth searched his face in the vain hope he might offer a shred of comfort.

A muscle twitched on his right cheek as if he held himself in check. He looked away and shook his head.

'I thought as much... but there was always hope since his body was never returned to us.'

'Sadly, madam, 'twas the fate of men on both sides to lie

together in death though they fought opposite in life. Warfare is a fickle partner. It takes from us more than it gives back. Who can say he is the winner after losses such as we have all seen?'

The widow nodded as she brushed past him to go inside. With a few words he had extinguished forever the feeble glimmer of Lucie's lantern of hope but now was not the time to break such news.

'Have they gone, Mother?' Lucilla peered up at her from under the counterpane, hopeful grey eyes fringed with thick dark lashes. She was tucked up snugly with her doll and the dog, her box and fan.

'No, little one, they must needs lodge here awhile. I'm afraid you'll have to bear with the enemy like a brave soldier as you did before.'

'Will they search the house again and find the secret room?'

'I'm sure they'll go through it with a nit comb, tapping panels and checking all the presses, though the Captain seems a gentleman. He wishes to use some rooms as a lodging. He will dine with us this evening.' Lucie sat up.

'I'm not hungry…'

'I know, I know. But, Lucie, we must be courteous to him. He holds the key to our safety and the well-being of the village. Try to be polite.'

'Father would not want us to sit with the enemy.'

'Father knows not what we do.'

'But when he comes home…'

'How many times have I told you? When you live in Heaven with the angels you cannot come home again to live on earth.'

'No, that's not true! He's busy on the King's secret service, a spy behind enemy lines... You'll see, one day he will come home to us and then he'll want to know all our doings. He will be very vexed to hear that you fed the enemy.'

'Oh, child! If I do not then we are utterly ruined and they will sack the house. We could be slaughtered like cattle. Do be sensible.'

'I am not going to speak to any of them. Ever.'

'The Captain is a Bagshott, he knows our district well.'

'Then he should know better than to meddle with a Salt. We are above them... Bagshotts are peasants, bracken gatherers and jobbing men. Martha has told me about them.'

'Lucilla, silence! In God's sight we are all equal. We do not choose to whom we are born but He in His wisdom places us where He wills to fulfil His destiny. He makes some high and some low, as he makes some flowers beautiful and long-lasting, others little more than grass. Try to understand you must not say such things. Speak when you are spoken to and do not anger the Captain, please, I beg you.'

'If you say so, but only for Father's sake. Will we dine around the kitchen board or are we to eat civilised?'

'Tonight for a change we will eat civilised like ladies around the table made from the century oak. Well have a lace cloth and a posy of fallen roses to grace our meal. You will tidy your hair and put on your sprigged muslin and a clean cap.'

Lucie jumped out of the bed and pointed to the closet. 'Then you must go to the attic and pull out your best blue, not those black weeds. There's no need to wear mourning when Father is not dead. Loosen your ringlets and powder your face. It's freckled with the sun like a maid's. Let's pretend we dine with Father and not a cruel soldier.'

Nazareth nodded, relieved that she had humoured the child enough to make her compliant. It would do no harm to put on fresh garments, to rinse her hair in rosemary oil and lace her bodice. Lucie was right, she had worn sombre black for too long.

The four of them sat around the table whilst Martha dished out the soupy broth, a mixture of summer greens and meat flakes, trying not to tremble and spill the liquid. Lucie kept her eyes on the tablecloth, watching to see if the soldiers spilled on it. Peto the dog nestled on her lap in eager anticipation.

'Pardon the broth, you'll have to send in a search party to find any chicken within... the bread is thick enough. I did not jest when I said we lived on hard cheese and plums.'

The men smiled politely but the child bent her head in shame at her mother's apologetic words. The plums came gently poached and softened with the last of the skimmed cream from their one milk cow. They were bitter and sorely in need of a drizzle of honey but the bees had swarmed into the forest and the honey was poor.

The soldiers sat stiffly at first, sipping the broth and the goblets of small beer. Micah had washed himself down in the trickle of the spring, searched in his saddle bag for a clean collar. There was none so he tried to turn the grubby one inside out, to no better effect. He had combed the lugs out of his hair as best he could but the effect was erratic and it hung stiffly with grease and grime.

'This is an excellent meal, sister, considering your short-ages. And you, little maid, do you help your mother with her chores? You look a bright button to me.' He was not used to child talk, having nieces and nephews enough but no time for conversation with them.

The girl stared at him fiercely, jutting her chin like the

woman in the portrait on the stairwell. She looked right through him as if he were invisible, sensing his awkwardness, then turned back to her pottage bowl.

'Forgive Lucilla, she is a shy child not used to company. She will come to, given time. Ignoring her is the best way to engage her curiosity, I find.'

There was an air of tension in the room, a thunderous heat which stifled the chamber. No one spoke much, listening instead to the drone of insects, the slurping of soup, the clink of spoon on bowl, the patter of the restless dog as it scoured the wooden floor, in search of scraps.

The sky was darkening for a storm. There was a light wind, a few spits and spots of rain and the rumble of thunder in the distance. Nothing more. They waited at the window for cooling showers but none came.

The Captain could scarce take his eyes from the widow's face; the way her cheeks flushed when she spoke, the shiny coils of golden curls with no trace of silver threads, the blueness of her eyes which exactly matched the bright blue sheen of her brocade gown, the heave of her bosom beneath. This was not the feeble old woman he had expected. Nazareth Salt was beautiful to behold, wearied by suffering but fresh still and courageous to live so unprotected.

His plans to destroy her garden had withered before the frost of her total disinterest, nay relief that the deed was begun! In every manner she had outwitted him unknowingly, robbed him of his petty revenge on the Salts, made him feel mean and small in his own eyes. There was no fear or contempt in her gaze, only a mild interest and an obvious admiration of his physique which had conquered most of the women he had dallied with. She liked the way he bowed to no man but his Maker.

The shock of her presence this evening as she came down the stairs in the blue gown, with lace ruffling around her like mist and the scent of rosewater in her hair, had taken him off guard, arousing his senses shamefully. A Bagshott dining with a Salt – who would ever have thought such a thing possible? She was at his mercy. One command and all this could be destroyed. But while she made such efforts to please him he could be generous and accommodating.

Nazareth could not sleep. She paced across the floor, covered only in a sheet. The heat was unbearable, the itch of the summer bugs a torment. How could she sleep when she was surrounded by alien strangers… and him. Oh, yes! He'd known she was watching him; the way he tilted his head to one side intently when she spoke, the flash and sparkle of his dark eyes. His teeth were yellow and his mouth stank of baccy but there was another smell to him, a pungent smell of youth and vigour, sensuality and the carnal; a dangerous smell on one so close to one so lonely and starved of affection. It had been too long… Nazareth had been safe as a lonely widow, undisturbed, but in one day all was changed. The twinkling of an eye, a crash of thunder, and her peace was disturbed.

Nazareth had never looked at any man other than Beavis until now. Soldiers and priests, schoolmasters and gentry had passed this way but not once had she taken a second glance. To look with lust on an enemy agent, one of the killers of her own sweet husband perhaps, to assess his broad shoulders and slim hips, the thickness of his thighs. What would it feel like to be crushed between them, overpowered by his embrace, taken by storm? Harlot! she chided herself. Was he not a mere Bagshott, a merchant's son, a scholar perhaps but of no rank worth noting? He had little finesse and was rough-spoken. How could she contemplate such a betrayal?

It had been madness to wear the brocade, to display herself for all to see, flaunting her breasts. His eyes had lingered there. She could have covered up rather than revealed herself. He had caught her gaze, holding it overlong, and she like a strumpet had boldly stared him out.

He was roused by her, she could sniff it like smoke on the breeze, and it pleased and terrified her equally. This power betwixt a man and a woman... there should be a statute against it in the courts. A man and a woman sending smoke signals like spies in the forest.

Lucie searched in her bureau for some parchment scraps left over from the estate bills, some empty space upon which to scribble letters and practise her script. She had tutoring with her cousins from Vicar Masterson occasionally, could write her name and some Latin phrases. At last she found a tiny scrap of clear space and dipped the quill into the dye to scratch her words. She must write to Father at once. He must come home. There was a new danger in this place, a strange smell of change and something she did not understand. It had begun when Mother came down the stairs and the men stared and stared at her.

'Venite, Pater, Venite ad Fridewell. Lucilla Salt, 1645.'

It would have to do. Those were all the words she knew. Where should she send it? To Aunt Letty at Longhall? She might pass it on. Mother would be no help at all. But how to get it there? Letters had no wings.

Under Sufferance

※

The pulse of the village beat slowly in the fierce heat of late summer. The sun hung like a brass ball in the sky and the field workers struggled to keep their rhythm, pausing to take breath and wipe the sweat from their brows. Cart wheels crackled over stubble and the gleaners bent to their task, feeling the dust and grit on tongue and teeth.

The garrison at the Newhouse went on their daily patrols like huntsmen to the chase; the first enthusiasm for digging up, raking and sifting ponds in search of silver, sawing off palings and hedgerows for firewood, thankfully waned in favour of fisticuffs between each other or any locals foolish enough to cross their path. Fridewell's initial panic changed to resignation and then sullen resentment. Had not Barnswells and Bagshotts, Millers and Hoptons, rallied to Parliament at the first clarion call to arms? Had they not refused to pay the Lord of the Manor any silver for the King's cause? Now they were sick of this conflict and invasion; sick of bugles and drum beats and horsemen who stabled their beasts in their church and ambushed sheep for supper, chasing them round the green like knights in a tiltyard. Some silly lasses hankered after a shiny uniform and a strong arm until the night when drunken troopers chased a maid into the forest and mowed her down like a roe deer in a stag hunt. Mistress Salt took up the grievance for her weeping parents and made a complaint.

Only then did Captain Bagshott accept that his men were shaming his command. He took one of the accused and had him strung up on the oak tree by the green as an example to all. Here the body swayed until rooks pecked out the eyes and the bloated and blackened sight sickened the miller enough for him to cut it down and bury it out of sight on the high track. There was little trouble after that and the Bagshott kin were satisfied that Captain Micah knew where his loyalties lay.

In the Newhouse Martha and Gideon went about their tasks cautiously whilst their mistress saw to the drying of the herbs – lavender, tansy, rue, mint, fennel, borage, comfrey and pennyroyal – gathering them into bunches to hang in the dark press. It was time too to dry the peas and beans, store the apples and pears, but few were left after the troopers' raids.

Everyone searched the skies for some sign of rain. The hard earth was solid as red brick and it was difficult to set to the rebuilding of the rose bed though some of the men were shamed into taking picks to loosen the soil.

Nazareth, wearing a wide-brimmed straw hat to hide her face from the sun, strode out determined to reclaim my lady's garden for herself, leaving only Old Sarah's path around the house where the fig tree still yielded more hard wood than fruit. She would make a wheel of green herbs, with spokes to separate out the different plantings. One or two roses would be entwined around the restored sundial at the centre. Perhaps she would leave the rest to grass over. She'd cajoled two men to piece together the bits of stone and re-erect the pedestal. They huffed and puffed but she smiled sweetly and tossed her curls, trying to lift the thing herself until they were shamed into doing the job. All this took her fevered mind from the oppressive heat and the constant tramp of men and horses over her land. But most of all from the intimidating presence of the Captain within her household.

They were circling around each other politely as if performing some courtly dance, a *bourrée* where the partners never touched or moved together but were ever in sight of one another. Then came the blessed relief of three days when all the patrol disappeared on manoeuvres; three days of peace and quiet, a chance to wash privately and stroll uninterrupted, to see to the household duties and for a message to be sent to Letty at Longhall, announcing the troop's arrival and telling all the news. They were but a league from each other but Letty was near to her time. Then Nazareth decided to carry the news herself. To bide with another gentlewoman for a day or two, to win some relief from Lucilla's stubbornness and incessant questions. There was no way that the child would be allowed to stay on those blessed stairs, staring out of the window, this time. She must be bribed, cajoled, beaten into the mule cart to play with her cousins.

To Nazareth's great surprise the little minx sweetly accepted the prospect of a journey, packed her doll in her basket, tied a ribbon on Peto and prepared to board the cart. Just as they were about to set off, a patrol of cavalry galloped into the yard, blocking their exit.

'On whose orders do you leave this place?' asked the Sergeant with the cold blue eyes and sneering mouth.

''Tis time to visit our kin. We need no permission,' Nazareth retorted, cursing their ill luck in not departing sooner.

'The Salts of Longhall? Papists and notorious Malignants. You go to give them knowledge of our whereabouts, no doubt?

To espy on these men, giving such information as might be to our disadvantage. Get thee down, mistress, and retire. You go nowhere.'

'How dare you? I will not be ordered into my own dwelling as if to a prison!' Nazareth made to stand her ground.

'That's for our Captain to decide, dame. No one is to be let in or out of this village without his say so.'

Nazareth felt a surge of impotent rage. She pulled her daughter down from the cart. Lucie was in tears. This was to be their first outing in months and now it was thwarted by this jumped up peasant in uniform. How dare he behave in this manner?

'Come, child, let's go to see to our new garden,' her mother suggested.

'I want to go inside. I hate your silly garden. Martha will find me some wool to card and brush...'

Lucie dashed back towards the front door and her mother shook her head with frustration. The Sergeant smiled, pleased that he had stopped her little game. He did not trust the witch. He had seen the effect she was having on the Captain's manner, making him as soft and yielding as a ball of dough.

It was later that afternoon when Micah and his escort arrived back at Newhouse. He had made a detour to the city to check on his family, Martha gleaned from the gossip. The plague still raged among its streets but his mother was safe and well. The siege of the Cathedral was continuing and it could only be weeks before they would yield.

Nazareth prayed for the poor men and their wives trapped in such cramped conditions in this heat. It made her own discomfort easier to bear but still she confronted the Captain about the embarrassment earlier in the day.

'The Sergeant was right, Mistress Salt. Without my

permission no one enters or leaves our garrison here. It is a fortress against infiltrators and spies. We're surrounded by enemies, hiding in trees and mine shafts or secret rooms in mansions. We know all their tricks. Where better to hide than right under our noses, within our own fortress, under your protection? Such an act would be treason, of course, and all involved would be dealt with severely, man or woman. You understand my concern. I would not want you to put your child at risk or any other kin. You will stay put though your cousin may visit us if she so desires.'

'How can she travel abroad when she is great with child and close to her time? And besides, Lucilla needs the companionship of her cousins.'

'Send for the village children to amuse her. Children play the same games whatever their condition. Or had you not noticed?' When he sneered he was quite ugly, his mouth hardening into a thin mean line. He kept himself on a tight rein. Nazareth would not like to see this man drunk and out of control.

'Don't be ridiculous! She is a Salt.'

'Miss Lucilla is still a child though a mighty peculiar one… such a sour stare on her face it would curdle the milk.' He laughed at his own wit.

'What gives you the right to talk of my child in such a manner?'

'See how the tigress protects her cub, Lieutenant?' The other soldier turned away, distancing himself from this spat. 'Women – there's no pleasing them.'

'I care not one groat if I am pleased by you!' she snapped.

'Oh, I think you might be surprised by the pleasuring I could give you, Madam.'

Nazareth walked quickly up the path, stumbling in her

haste to get away from this outspokenness. The Lieutenant walked away, embarrassed.

'Tarry, mistress! I see I have o'erstepped the mark once more. Pardon me. 'Tis the heat and a surfeit of city sack – a fine vintage of which I have commandeered a few jars for your pleasure. Please stay. I have brought something else for you from my sojourn. Do not flee from me before I have a chance to make amends. It is a token of reparation for our upheavals here. See...'

Nazareth halted on the stairs and turned around to see him lifting the flaps of his saddlebag, searching for a package which he held out towards her with first a penitent expression and then a sheepish grin on his face.

'Sire, I need no reminder of your presence here and will tolerate no more coarse remarks. It does your cause no honour to shame me so before your officer.'

'I know, but see... what do you think?' He produced dozens of delicate creamy white bulbs for her to inspect. 'Tulip bulbs for you to plant in your wheel. They'll stand tall and bright among your greenery. And here, this is a sprig of rosemary from my mother's herbary. She is a fine plantswoman and tends all her cuttings well so they spring up from the old. I've not seen it growing in your patch. Take this cutting and place it well and soon there'll be a bush for you to use as you wish.'

Nazareth was taken aback at this unexpected thoughtfulness. This uncouth man had taken the trouble to think about her garden; the very garden he had first tried to destroy. How strange! She knew how precious real tulip bulbs were and how the mania for them had spread through the country like fire years ago. These fancy bulbs had ruined many a Holland merchant in their quest for the perfect shape and colour. To own some of them which would yield their own harvest each year was a pleasurable shock. It had been so long since any man had given her a present, let alone such an apt one.

'I can't accept such a gift from you. It's a worthy thought but 'tis impossible for me to receive such valuables...'

'Tush, lady! You are too scrupulous. It is the least I can offer for the discomfort our presence affords you. It's a gift to your garden not to your person. Who can take offence at such a gesture of remorse?'

'I suppose not, but I'm surprised you take a keen interest in a mild occupation such as gardening?'

'Mild, you call it? Why, it's a battlefield in itself – all that hacking and pruning, harrowing, digging and burying, burning and scattering. A very violent occupation is more like it. Not for the faint-hearted. What envy, pillage, stealth and destruction is there not in the heart of a true gardener? Did not these very tulips once wreak havoc in the Lowlands?

'Come, walk with me to the wheel and let's see where they might best be put for shelter when autumn comes. This rosemary can grow anywhere so long as it is sunkissed and sheltered from winter's frost. My mother heard tell that the rosemary bush, being a sacred herb, will grow only to the height of Christ. She says it makes a good lotion for the hair and the soul, but I know not of such matters.' And Micah laughed, relieved that the bad feeling between them was gone.

'Your mother speaks the truth. It's a herb with many uses and its oil soothes those who are low in spirits. I shall treasure this cutting.' They walked in silence down the slope to the outline of the wheel in the bare soil.

'See how you might follow that circle when planting the bulbs. They will be red, I am told... a circle of flame to cheer a cold spring. We shall be long gone by then and this dispute with the King over. These will be a reminder of our enforced visit. If I stay much longer, I fear I shall feel like the Barnsley Green Bagshotts – rooted to the spot.'

His eyes stared dully and she looked upon him with sudden pity. This man belonged nowhere, blown this way and that by the fortunes of war. The urge to touch his sleeve, gaze into his face to savour his countenance, was overpowering. This was a mighty oak with few roots to sustain it, easily crushed by a storm.

'It will seem quiet when you all depart.'

'How can that be when our very presence is obviously grievous to you?'

'Aye, true enough, but while you bide we are safe enough and the noise and busyness of the troopers is strangely welcome after so many sad years of silence. There's little enough to feast on here.'

'Do you celebrate harvest home?'

'Sometimes, when there is food and ale to spare, a fiddle for a few dances. Why ask you?'

'Perhaps 'tis time for my men to help gather in the last of the corn and then let us all celebrate the ending of our visit and the siege in the city, for they will not survive the rigours of winter.'

'I thought all you Puritans were against dancing and feasts? They are to be banned, I hear.'

'Do I act like a Puritan or sobersides in black hat and sourdough face? I am a mere soldier of fortune. A feast will put some heart in my men before the winter bites our boots and fingers. A little singing and dancing will do no harm and help lighten our spirits.'

The moon rose high in the gathering dusk, the Little Owl on its branch hooted its approval. Nazareth shivered with fear or excitement, she could no longer tell. Lucie watched them both from her window perch as they stood together over the stupid circle with scarce a chink of daylight between them; beauty and the beast from the old tale. Together they had destroyed Old Sarah's garden. She must be the ears and the eyes of Father, protecting the Newhouse until his return, keeping them ever in her sight.

Harvest Home

❧

The preparations for the harvest home took many days of plucking and drawing, skinning and boiling of fowls. Hares were snared for the pies and stiff pastes made to cover them in the brick oven. There were apple tarts to finish off the modest meal, cheese, honey cakes and bowls of crisp cabbage salad.

It was hard for Nazareth to summon up any joy in this annual task. Harvest home was usually the crowning feast of the season's calendar of hard toil but this year there was little to spare and she must hold back on generosity to the villagers for fear of shortages to come in another harsh winter.

Everyone who could be spared was out in the fields while the glorious weather held, stacking corn into stooks, threshing, storing the straw and delivering the corn to the mill. The Captain made his men put their backs into the tasks but they were derided for their efforts. They were town boys at heart and had no feeling for the job.

After a mere six weeks in residence, how could they be other than alien soldiers garrisoned for convenience upon the village, tolerated but only with suspicion? It was going to be an awkward gathering for a harvest home.

Martha, on the other hand, intended to let nothing spoil the dancing. There was little enough fun for young folk in the village, and if the war was lost and there would soon be edicts banning Christmas and feasting she wanted to make sure this one was a night to remember. She was determined to dance with every single man, soldier or no, and to wear her best kerchief around her plump neck. Miss Lucilla was being a trial as usual, not wanting to help with the chores or rise to the day's busyness but lying abed looking pale and fevered. Sometimes she thought the child could turn on the heat and shivers at will but then, she was of a particular nature, not like any other bairn in the district. Martha knew how to humour the girl with promises and set her to plaiting the last sheaves of corn for a corn dolly. That would shut her up for a few hours.

They were going to set up the board planks across the yard and the older folk would take cover from the night air in the barn. Cloths would be stretched over and garnished with green ivy and bunches of wheat in the usual way. The harvest sheaves would take pride of place and afterwards would stand all year in the fields to protect next year's crop. Special loaves of wheat, rye and barley would be buried in the four corners. It was something they'd always done here since Adam was a lad. Mother said something about giving back what was taken out, but how could soil eat up bread? Martha thought it was a waste of good loaves but you must never tempt the hobgoblins to mischief so she would do as she was bid.

It was going to be another sticky night. The moon was full in the dark sky and if she was lucky she might wish on a shooting star. The midges would be biting, the moths fluttering around the torches. She could not wait for the feasting to begin.

At seven of the clock the fiddler arrived and the villagers drifted in, bagging the stools in the yard when they saw the soldiers lodged in the barn. It was going to be a stiff start, two opposing groups staring suspiciously at one another in the dusk. The food was placed upon the tables and folk munched warm pasties and chunks of bread, sipping mugs of ale and cider, stretching out to make sure they got their share before anyone else. The children darted under the boards, stuffing themselves from handouts like ravenous dogs.

Nazareth could not bear to look at the gap at the end of the table where Beavis had once carved the roast beef and the haunch of venison. All was so utterly changed, it was useless to torment herself, but when she glanced up she saw Captain Micah sharing out baccy and clay pipes amongst the strangers and her heart jumped for a second at the sight of his handsome profile, his broad shoulders and courteous manner. How could she have borne this garrison without his presence to hold his men's excesses in check? The pies, the beer and cider were beginning to loosen tongues and the tables were cleared. The children raced up and down but Lucilla stayed indoors, peering from the staircase with Peto jumping up and down at the window.

'She'll melt that pane of glass away with her breath,' said Martha as she glanced up with a smile. 'Shall I bring her down here, mistress?'

'No, leave her be. Go to it and set the fiddler to a tune. It's time for the dancing to begin.' The fiddler tuned up his strings and from the shadows women glided forward to find their partners for the jig, promenading around the yard in an ever-changing pattern of lines and circles. Nazareth found her feet tapping and her hips swaying as she watched from the open door.

In such a half light it was easy to imagine there was no warfare, no widows, no siege, no danger. As the cider and fruit wines rose to her head, loosening her resolve, it was easy to be guided into the circle by the Captain's firm hand, to turn this way and that, sway and swerve, bend and bow, dip and dive. Her full skirt swished and swirled in his half embrace, soft supple fabric slipping from his touch. She felt his fingers caress hers; the touch of them in her palm sent shivers of tension and promise through her. This was madness but a little harvest dancing would do no harm, cementing peace in the camp.

Oh, Nazareth! Who do you fool but yourself? Where will this madness end as end it must? She sipped more primrose wine to cool her brow but the heat of the night burned within her and as the harvest songs were sung and the old men got up to recite their ghostly stories to an eager audience, smoking pipes and steaming from the dancing, she drifted away down the path behind the house up to her hidden garden by the well. Away from the noise and the crush she could collect her thoughts. She kicked off her shoes and dangled her feet in the water to cool her fevered spirits.

You are lonely and lust for the touch of any man who might soothe away this aching... Be strong. How long will this feeling last?

I don't want to test it. When he is not present in the company there's no colour, only black emptiness. Micah has brought back the bluebell and the pink and the crimson of roses by his attentions. How could I have forgotten how deeply I need to feel desired? He is a strong man and I am weak. He will be strong for both of us, my shield and protection.

'Oh, Micah.' The name drifted from her like a sigh. She heard a rustle of leaves and footsteps but dared not turn round. 'Micah Bagshott, is that you?'

'Yes, I am here, Nazareth, by your side... What is your will of me?' Her heart leapt that he had followed her across the hidden garden at a safe distance, like a moth scenting out the night stocks in the darkness.

'Come with me.' She drew him by the hand further down the bank into the darkness by the water's edge. He needed no second bidding.

Later, as he lay sated with lovemaking, looking up towards the canopy of stars and the hedgerows which curtained this bed, he felt panic begin to rise; panic that he was caught in a luxurious bed of roses with thorns like daggers to stick into his flesh.

You fool! This changes everything. You have succumbed to her witchcraft, now she has you bound to do her bidding.

A dance, a dalliance perhaps, but not this overwhelming, crushing need of her. They were lost now in a dangerous labyrinth of secret trysts, cover ups and deception. How could he have forgotten himself so far as to fall into her perfumed trap? How many times had he spilled his seed over her body that night?

Later still he crept to her room and whispered in her ear, 'A garden enclosed is my sister, my spouse.'

In the dim light he could scarce make out where she ended and he began. Some dark flame hidden in their hearts had guided them both to this place and he was afraid. For so long he had kept himself safe, aloof from life, and now by her side in this bed there was at last something he felt a part of. Was this what was meant by the union of man and woman? There had been many couplings before, flesh with flesh, bargains sealed usually with a coin. This was so different in its power and intensity. He had never realised a woman could expose herself so openly to pleasure and pain.

Now she slept while thunder rolled over them and lightning flashed in the night sky, Nazareth lay like a baby with arms outstretched and he felt such tenderness towards her, and such fear. She was so strong and he was made weak by her power. He wanted to shake her awake and tell her all these foolish thoughts but the moment passed. He heard the creak of the chamber door. He was unarmed and naked, instantly alert to danger.

'Mother... I don't like it when God plays bowls in the sky above. I can't sleep, let me in...'

A tiny figure in a nightgown and cap fumbled at the draperies and slid on to the bed. She was shaking her mother when she felt another body on the other side of the bed, saw him smiling back at her.

'Why is that man in your bed? Go away! Mother, are you ill?'

Nazareth awoke to the dawn light, trying to comprehend all the fuss. 'Shush! Climb in, Lucie, and let me go back to sleep.'

'How can I when there's a bad man in Father's bed?'

Nazareth turned with shock to see Micah's smiling face. 'No, Lucie, shush! Father would not mind now.'

But the child would not be pacified and pulled back all the curtains, tearing at the rings and hitting Micah on the arm. 'Go away! You are a traitor to the King! Mother, how can you bed with such?'

'Lucilla, be calm! You don't understand these matters. Go to your room and I shall come and comfort you and explain.'

'I'll tell Aunt Letty Salt and you'll be denounced as a formycator from the pulpit! I know what that means. Cousin Richard does it in the barn with the maid and Tobias watches to learn how to put that thing inside her and shake it all about. They told me and I said that I never, ever, ever will let someone do that to me. Bawd! Harlot! That's what they say about maids who do that. I shall tell on you. You're wicked!'

'Your mother's not wicked, child. She's lonely and I am lonely and so we comfort each other. We mean you no harm. It is privy to ourselves what we do here. None of your business.'

'But it is! You do harm. You stop my father coming back to us. Go away!'

Lucie beat on the bed with her fists and started to cry. Nazareth sat up, holding the counterpane before her to cover her breasts.

'Lucie, dear, you don't understand about your father.'

'He stops my father… the soldiers of the enemy stop my father coming home to us.' Tears rolled down the little girl's pink cheeks.

Micah did not know how to put right this mess. The girl was in some mummer's play, pretending Saint George would rise from the dead to slay the dragon. 'How can your father come home when he is six foot under the sod at Edgehill field?'

''Tis not so!'

'Yes, it is. I saw him lying slain on the ground with his brother. He will never come home again with limbs all smashed and his head stove in.' The hard words were out plain enough but cruel in their sharpness.

'Shush, Micah, please!' Even in the first light Nazareth could see her child turn wild-eyed with shock. She was white, jaw dropping open as the words hit home. A whirlwind roared over her, lifting her from the scene. Within the eye of the storm she could see the lovers under the counterpane, their faces filled with pity and concern. Their voices faded as the whirlwind carried her away to the corner of the room where she huddled to ward off the picture of her poor father's broken body.

Lucie curled into a ball and began to shiver, not uttering a word. Her mother leapt out of bed, not caring that she was naked, cradling the child in her arms.

'You have to believe what the Captain says. We are all alone now, unprotected in this wicked world. I have tried to protect us both but Father is gone from this place forever. Do you believe me?'

The child nodded feebly from her far off land.

'I hate him... I hate that wicked man. Make him go away from us.'

Nazareth looked up in desperation. Micah was already at the door with his clothes half on. She pleaded with him with her eyes to stay and help her deal with this distress. 'Oh, please, wait! She will understand one day...'

'But I cannot wait around to see it, ma'am. I shall trouble you no further.'

The door was shut and he was gone from them. Nazareth was doing battle on both sides and had lost. Sick, shamed, tired and confused as she was, she knew she must protect her child. None of this turmoil was of her daughter's choosing.

'Come to bed with me, Lucie. The thunder is silent now and the storm is over.'

She could hear the patter of the rain lashing on the window pane. It would be cooler and calmer tomorrow. Time then to sort out the misunderstanding and clear her head. But what was to become of them all after this?

In the nights following their passion Micah got so drunk he could scarce stand. Each morning aft his head throbbed and beat like a muster drum. His recollections of the harvest home, the dancing and their coming together, were hazy but he could remember every detail of Nazareth's beauty; how one pale breast was larger than the other, the curve of her hips, the blue veins on the inside of her thighs and the rivers of silver marks across her stomach, the yeasty, salty smell of her passion. Then the coming of the child and his shame like a dousing under cold water – that stupid, stubborn child and her accusations. Surely he did right to dampen her self-righteousness, destroy her foolish hope? It was cruel and hard for all of them. He had only himself to blame for his weakness. How could he let his emotions rule, making a fool of himself before his men with the wife of an enemy?

Micah was bitterly ashamed of these yearnings for her but the stubborn streak which had kept him alive for so long against the odds in this Civil War told him he must escape from this witchy place soon and the charms therein if he were to survive. Here be danger indeed!

Bitter Seeds

The Mistress of Fridewell House rose early to prepare a basket of alms for the families of woodsmen living by the miners' camp. Taking Gideon as her escort out on to the Chase, they went from hut to hut, giving out cheese and fruit, hog fat and honey comb. It was November and the mists from the valley drifted through the trees like ghosts swathed in grey shrouds. Nazareth shivered in the gloom, glad not to be alone on such an eerie dank path where bare branches reached out to grab at her cloak like desperate beggars in the market place and the last of the leaves hung like carrion from the treetops.

In her hand she clutched the potion from the cunning woman who lived close to the charcoal burners' camp, consulted and feared by all in the forest. 'Moll i' th' wood' had remedies and spellings for ailments no lady should know about. She could stiffen the limp, dampen the ardent, empty the belly of all unwanted contents for the price of a silver coin or some hens, dry wood cut to size or a crock of the woodland hooch. Under the guise of charity Nazareth had visited her alone and confessed that her maid was in trouble and needed help.

The crone stared in disbelief at her story, sucked on her pipe and scratched her whiskers as she peered into the smoking fire. Then she reached on to her dusty shelf for a phial of penny-royal and wormwood juice.

With hardly a word or a glance the transaction with the Devil was made, thought Nazareth as they walked slowly back along the track. Only cunning folk had that special knowledge of herbs and incantations, the mystical powers to prevent such a public shaming if she delivered a bastard. It was over two months since her courses had stopped suddenly just after the harvest home. She needed no conjuror to tell her that in the excitement of passion she had released seed to the man. At first she put such an absence down to the upset of Lucilla's tantrums and the silence between herself and the Captain, but there were other warnings: a tenderness in her breasts, a dizziness and fatigue. She had trodden this path before and knew the signposts.

Since the night of the storm she'd scarce looked in his direction and he had avoided being alone with her. Captain Bagshott now preferred to lodge with his men, patrolling the outskirts of the city both day and night.

Nazareth felt humiliated to have such a sickness in her belly; to be with child by a common soldier; to be a fornicator not fit to bring up a child and now a bastard.

Oh, Beavis! How have I besmirched your memory. What deceptions must I practise now to secure your name. It was lust and loneliness not the love we shared together. Please forgive me for what I must now do but I will not shame your name any more than I already have. If I die then so be it. It will be God's punishment for my weakness and wickedness.

If this potion works its effect then no one will ever know of this shame and I will spend the rest of my life in penitence and prayer. I will visit the sick and the poor, restore the church of your forebears to its former glory and teach Lucilla to be a God-fearing woman. Never again will I walk abroad on feast days nor waste time in dancing or dallying in the garden unescorted. The lure of the roses, the scent of the lavender, was my undoing. All shall be ripped up and burnt. You shall find me an example, nay, an exhortation to all widows in my piety and soberness. I will be purer than any Puritan in black plain garments. Oh, God, hear my plea! Forgive this foolish woman but it must be done to protect others and for the sake of my child...

She pulled out the rag stopper and gulped down the liquid with a grimace, out of view of Gideon who was walking ahead. The juice burned down her throat. If it was so painful then its bitterness must surely do some good. Whatever suffering followed this act of contrition she would bear it alone.

Where's the mistress, Miss Lucilla?'

Lucie was mixing a bowl of pot pourri in the still room. She loved to sift the dry crinkly petals and sniff the scents of summer, preferring them better in the chamber than out in the wet garden. She had counted all the different shapes and colours; bay leaves and calamint, meadow sweet which smelt of honey, delicious spearmint, sweet briar and sweet Cicely, tansy and rose petals, all the colours of the rainbow. Mother always said that dry roses put to the nose would comfort the brain and the heart, carrying sad spirits back to Heaven. She wondered if Father could smell roses in Heaven too; if so she would make up a special bowl of them for her own chamber and he would see that she still remembered him.

Since that terrible event she had slept with Mother every night. Lucilla was afraid to leave her alone in case the evil man came creeping back to her bed. But she sensed that his power had waned and they were safe again. He did not sup with them and the garrison force hardly camped in Fridewell any longer.

'Lucilla! Is your mother still in her bed chamber at this hour?' Martha was interrupting her dreaming.

'Aye, she said her stomach pains were cramping her too much to rise early. She slept badly.'

'Then hurry along, child, see if she needs some physick. It's not like the mistress to be a lie abed when there's the linen to be soaked in the bucket.'

Lucie bounded up the stairs with Peto following at her heels. Since the Captain's departure she spent more time in the kitchen with Martha and less sitting on the stairs waiting for her father's return. She was still the Guardian of the Kingdom, though. Once an ugly beast had crossed over these portals to steal the faerie queen but now he was repelled, just as the King's men were still holding off the siege in the Cathedral close, so all was well.

There was a hump in the bed. Mother peered out and groaned, beads of sweat dripping from her brow. 'Go away, child. I'm just a little unwell today.'

'Shall I fetch Martha?' asked Lucie, seeing how pale and pinched were her cheeks.

'No, no… One day you'll understand. 'Tis a woman's curse to bear this ailment, the price of bearing children. Tell Martha to see to it all and you take my place at her side.'

'I will, but she asked if you needed some physick.'

'Go… please let me rest. I have all the physick I need. I shall be well enough ere long but fetch me the close stool just in case.' The child dragged the heavy chair with its lid across the room. Nazareth summoned all her strength to sit up, forcing a false smile of reassurance as if what ailed her was a mere trifle. 'Go to your duties, hurry!'

All day the pain ebbed and flowed like the tide on a beach she'd once visited many years ago; the place where the river flowed out to the sea. She had watched enraptured as the waves lapped over her satin shoes and then was beaten soundly for her silliness. Now she tried to ride the waves of pain as they crashed within her bowels, sending spurts of bloody matter on to the cloths. Moll i' th' Wood had told her to rest and wait for the purgings to begin, to catch all the matter in a bowl and burn it at midnight or cast it out over running water to take away all stain. She had not expected such pain but it must be endured. She could not bear to look within the bowl or on the cloths. Thankfully she had prepared a tisane of poppy juice, camomile water and vervain and she sipped it from a goblet to soothe her head.

As the meagre November light faded into darkness she felt the pains ease and their intensity weaken. Soon it would all be over. The Lord in His Mercy would understand. Her penitence would begin the minute she rose from this bed; all those fevered promises made on the journey back from the forest would be honoured.

Later, when it was dark, she crept down with a candle jar to the still room and buttery to help herself to a chunk of cheese and a cool glass of cider to quench the dust in her throat. At first her legs wobbled like a blancmange but slowly, as she shuffled on the stone-flagged floor, the strength seeped back into them. All the soiled cloths she stuffed into a ball and then saw that the fire was still ablaze and burned her sinning bit by bit. The terrible smell made her feel sick but soon enough the charred remains of the cloths were nothing but ashes.

The bowl from the close stool she had covered with a napkin.

This she took out into the garden, taking care to open the latch of the old Priory door carefully so as not to disturb Martha in her cubby hole across the corridor. There was only one place to take the bowl and she walked carefully over the frosted grass, glinting in the moonlight, which torched her path to the wellspring. The recent rains had swollen the spring which flowed like a torrent downstream. Nazareth stood over the running water and emptied the pot.

'I cast my sins upon the water. Flow, secret shame, flow away to the everlasting sea. Have mercy on me, Lord.'

The spring would tell no tales for it was a holy well and heathen spirits must surely have departed long ago. In this shady bower had the seeds of her enemy been sown, now it was right to be destroying that shameful harvest here. Nazareth bowed her head in gratitude that such madness was over. Had she not seen the bloody evidence with her own eyes?

By Christmas she was so swollen in the belly and ankles as to fear she had some dreadful disease. Her courses never returned as she'd hoped but that was only to be expected after such a purging. She had little fluid to spare now. Her back ached and her limbs swelled, her hair lost its lustre and her stomacher would not lace up properly, but it was the tiredness which overwhelmed her, making her search out a stool whenever she stood to a task.

Christmas was a meagre affair: a little greenery and extra candles, a visit to Longhall for the mistress had forsworn any feasting and drinking now that she was a sober matron. Whatever ailed her caused her to throw up food at the slightest sniff of spice. Martha thought it some strange green sickness and bade her mistress rest. The garrison had gone from the house but roamed abroad in the forest, tracking down the supply routes to the besieged fort in the Cathedral. The weather hardened and the snow fell in the New Year but the thaw came quickly after and the forest was alight with alarms and rumours of battles and raids. Nazareth turned her ears from the gossip. It was none of their business now. They would need all their strength to survive the onslaught of winter.

One morning Martha rushed in from the yard. 'Come quickly, mistress. There are wounded soldiers in the yard... in a bad way though I know not whose side they are on.'

'Does it matter? They are all sons and husbands, I will not turn a sick man from my door. If some kind soul had taken pity on Beavis then perhaps we would not be so unprotected now. See to it. I'm coming. It's no morning to be abroad with wounds.' The men lay scattered about the barn and she recognised some familiar buff coats from the old patrol. Like wounded animals they had come back to a safe lair to die. Some were gashed about the face and arms; others were merely exhausted, and blue-lipped with cold.

'What happened?' she asked as she tried to see who was alive or dead in the crumpled heap.

'What a rout! We was ambushed in a narrow lane and the horses at the rear panicked and bolted into the troops at the front, trampling them like straw. "Away! Away! Shift for your life. We's all dead meat here!" The wagons were overturned and the poor horses trapped so we cut their harness and they bolted. They was firing at the troopers on horseback from the bushes. What a bloody mess! The spoil of the horses left a trail of blood which froze upon the snow... a terrible sight, ma'am. I never want to see the like.' The soldier drifted into a faint and Nazareth tried to stem the gushing of blood from his neck.

'Bring him out into the cold, mistress. It will freeze his wound and stem the flow. This frost will save many a life.'

She turned around and there he was, the man she'd hoped

never to see again. Captain Bagshott, propped up by two foot soldiers, half dragging him across the couryard. This was no time for debate, only action.

'Take him upstairs to his old quarters. He will show you where.' She tried to stay calm and composed but her heart was racing with concern for him and for their own danger. Were there other forces following in hot pursuit? Would they all be slaughtered as harbourers of the enemy? Whichever side you aided in this cursed war you were a turncoat and traitor. She was sick of this slaughter in her own land. Better one side was finally victorious than all this mayhem in country lanes.

Martha brought the bags of healing herbs from the men's pouches. Thankfully most soldiers carried their own supplies, lovingly sealed in embroidered bags by mothers and sweet-hearts for their protection. Now that loving care would be put to the test. Some had only dried herbs for cooling teas; others had stuff for poultices and presses. They would have to do their best with what she had stored from the garden for their own physick.

First she dipped her hands in the lye bucket. She often did this although it burned her chapped fingers, but if it purged the dirt from linen then it would purge the dirt from her own hands and purge the muck of the soldiers as well. It made sense to her to touch each with clean hands though why that was impor-tant she did not know. It was just one of those things you did.

Only when all the other survivors were comfortable did she tread heavily up the stairs to see the Captain. He lay on the bed in his filth, face white and his dark pain-filled eyes sunk in their sockets.

His wound was close to the groin on his inner thigh and she made Martha cut away the cloth of his breeches so that she could examine it closely. A sword had cut through cloth and skin to the muscle, a clean cut like a slice from a joint. It would have to be sewn together and dressed with a poultice. She found a needle but her hands shook when she got close to that flesh and the smell of his filth made her retch and leave the room. When she returned Martha whispered that he had sewn it up himself with not a squeak and what a brave man this Micah Bagshott was. Nazareth felt ashamed of her own weakness and made sure that she saw to his dressing daily, but it was a stubborn wound and at first would not heal.

Lucie took to her vigils on the stairs again and otherwise never left her mother's side, peering through the door at the soldier, stabbing dagger looks of venom in his direction. They found leeches from the pond and placed those on his leg to suck away the rottenness. Gideon gathered the moist spaghnum moss to dress the soldiers' wounds and Martha said that a mouldy bread poultice would help any injury of the flesh, with a spider's web in it for good luck. Captain Micah jeered and said her poultice was so strong it should be stuck on the walls of the Cathedral, its force would surely bring the ramparts down! In desperation all remedies were tried at once and the gash turned from purple-black to pink but the leg was weak and would not bend.

Captain Micah was not the easiest of patients but would read any book put before him. The old chest in the roof space was opened to find any printed material left in the house after their first raiders had torn out pages to smoke in their pipes.

Outside the wind blew from the north-east across the Trent valley, driving swathes of snow into hillocks and drifts, trapping the men in the barn and setting the whole village shivering under sheepskins and flock mattresses. The fireplace blazed with the last of the fuel and all sat round its warmth, Nazareth dressed in black with a white cap once more and blanketed in a thick woollen piece of tapestry cloth she had found in the chest to keep her warm.

'You look more upholstered than my sisters in the Holy Brethren, Mistress Salt. Just like a preacher's wife. Why such plainness?' Nazareth looked up, shocked at his comments.

'Do you not forget that I am a widow and a mother? Have I not an example to set, sire?' That should put him in his place.

'But you are not yet thirty, madam. Surely there are years ahead for another life to begin?'

'No! Not after that episode of shameful weakness. I have to take care of my reputation. It's all I have left.'

'Then have no fear from me. The watch dog child who guards your door and bed will see you remain unsullied...' There was a silence so awkward that neither of them looked up again. Words of apology floated like a mist upon the air.

'You look so burdened, woman, so down at heel since last we met. What ails you?' The Captain leant forward to touch her hand and Nazareth jumped back on her stool.

'I know not. Some women's troubles. Come the spring, the warmer weather and sunshine, I will be renewed.' She could never tell him what she had done but his obvious concern touched some rawness within her and she found herself weeping.

'Oh, Mistress Nazareth, how I would love to take you in my arms and kiss that troubled brow... Do not look so afeared. I have neither the stamina nor the inclination, being so crippled in the leg. What was so wrong with our union that it was conducted only by stealth on midnight stairs? Did you not find my wooing to your satisfaction?' Micah's eyes pierced into her very soul.

'I beg you, sire, no more of this talk. I have forsworn your bed and company. It is not fitting for a widow...'

''Tis not befitting for a proud Salt, however stripped of lands and fancy titles, to be courted by a humble Bagshott, however successful be their ventures! My great-grandfather built this place which now shelters us all and now Bagshotts could buy and sell it many times over but you see gentility only in a name, not a deed. Is that why we are enemies still?

'Give me but a chance and I will lay siege to your cold Royalist heart and batter down your cruel resolve like this stinking poultice sears my poor leg.'

'And I shall repel all your salvoes and grenados until the last trump!'

'You are heartless, mistress.' Micah bowed in mock salute.

'And you, sire, are a wicked master to ill treat me so...'

Nazareth saw how ridiculous were these mutual threats and verbal fencings, point on point. How could she too not laugh at this dalliance, dangerous as it was? While he was wounded he was safe enough, but once restored to full vigour... in truth she knew not how she would withstand his attacks again. Her heart was not in the matter. Yet the memory of her terrible crime should stiffen her defences against temptation.

Then after a week of convalescence he was gone, scarce able to ride his horse but commanded back to the Cathedral city to support the final onslaught on the garrison. Against all the odds the King's men had held out thus far. Guns roared across the valley and from the high ridge they could see smoke rising as the beleaguered city walls crumbled. Humans there were reduced to skeletons eating vermin or buried in their hundreds under courtyards. The poor horses had been released to the enemy to save them further suffering. The great spire of the Cathedral had crashed down into the nave, crushing those still sheltering inside.

Terrible tales of suffering and endurance made Nazareth

face her own worries with humility and resignation. She had watched the Captain's departure with a heavy heart. He'd promised to return with new plantings for her garden wheel which was growing well.

They had stood side by side, watching the spears of green poking up out of the red earth. Soon there would be a circle of tulips, a circle of flame to admire. She could have told him then what she had known for months. Soon she would give birth to a child and it was far too late for any second remedy. She had seen the evidence in the bowl so how could a second child now grow in her womb if not by witchcraft or the Will of God? The potion she had swallowed was some foul substance of false trickery, cheating her senses, lulling her fears until it was far too late to change the course of events.

How could she have fooled herself into believing her prayers had been answered at the well? God was not mocked. Oh, no! He would have the final judgement in this matter. But what of Lucilla? How would she cope with such treachery? She must be sent to Letty on some pretext of contagion and danger in the village. Lucie would protest and scream but the little madam could now walk and run when it suited her, constantly following the Captain into the shadows. Nazareth knew her daughter would never accept Micah in Beavis's place, at his hearth or in his bed.

She looked up at the tall stranger who had stolen her heart. Poor rootless man, ever obedient to the commands of others. Thank God he knew nothing of her condition. He would wish to make their union public then – or perhaps not. She would never give him the choice.

There would be no midwife at this bastard's birth. What happened must happen in secret with the help of a chit of a girl. Martha must be sworn to secrecy and be prepared to help in the lying in. Nazareth would be making all the preparations in her own chamber, even her last will and testament, writing to Letty and doing all that was possible to secure some future for this coming child. But not yet... First she must wave goodbye to the soldiers and carry off this awful pretence.

The Circle of Flame

❦

'Mistress! Please, mistress… bear down no more. Let me send for Goodwife Tipley. She will know what to do next. Help yourself a little, hold back. I know not what to do!'

Martha scurried about the bed in the flickering candlelight. She had seen few birthings but this one was too quick and violent to be normal.

'Just wash the babe, clean him up. Does he breathe?'

'Aye, listen. See, he's gone from purple to pink – a bonny lad. He seems well enough.' She held up the plump child to the mother, sagging on the pillows, who turned her face from the sight of him.

'Bathe him and tip the water outside in the night air, not on the fire ashes. We want this boychild to roam abroad as a man should. I have the swaddling bands in the chest, see, to keep his limbs straight and firm… The room is so cold and then so hot… Put him in the cradle and another log on the fire.'

'I must see to your bed linen. 'Tis so blood-sodden I scarce can mop it up. There's no after birthings still?'

'No, not yet. Press on my belly, see if you can shift it. It must be there somewhere…'

But hard as she pressed no after birthings were drawn forth and the mistress grew weary, feverish and flushed with pain. The babe wailed and wailed and young Martha Barnsley was so desperate that she called Gideon to her side. He had hovered outside the door, in awe of the happenings within. Martha shivered with fear and concern. This was no ordinary birthing, being so unexpected and secret with none of the ladies who usually camped in the chamber to see to the lying in and the ceremonies.

How could her mistress bring forth a child so long after the death of Squire Beavis unless there had been some mischief with the handsome Captain of the Horse? Could the soldiers' ribald jests in the barn about the couple being secret lovers have been right enough? Her lady had sired a son from a Bagshott soldier, son of a city black hat? Surely not!

Martha turned to look again at her sweet mistress who was so fair and had only boxed her maid's ears thrice. She who had saved the house from ruin by her charm and hospitality. Surely not? But there in the cradle screamed the truth of it all, a darkling child with a fiercesome wail. No runt of the litter but a plump babe who feared he would be left alone in the world as a bastard. Never! One look into those screwed up eyes and tiny mouth and Martha was his slave forever. He must be protected... hidden from view.

'Gideon,' she ordered, 'go to Longhall and batter down the door until someone wakes. Tell them the mistress is ill and close to death, but nothing of the babe yet. Fetch Mistress Letty... at once.'

It would take hours for him to walk the three miles. All their mules had been requisitioned by the Captain's men. This would give her time to hide the child in the old quarters, conceal him from prying eyes and gossip. She would have to hide the mess and the blood, all the evidence of a birth as well. Tired as she was she must clear the room and prepare for visitors. The babe could wail unheard through the thick stone wall in the old Priory lodging house but it would not survive long without a nurse to feed it. Who did she know in the village who had given birth these past weeks? Who would keep this terrible secret?

'Martha! My babe, bring him to me, let me suckle him... Martha!' Nazareth had hardly the strength to whisper the words, drifting in and out of a deep peace, carried along a gentle river of sleep out towards the estuary and the deep water towards the golden light and Beavis... She was floating above the chamber bobbing as light as a leaf. Only the distant cry of her newborn, a tiny whine of sound, pulled her back down to the bed. 'My babe... where's my babe?'

'Rest, mistress. Hush, he's safe enough. I have sent for Lucilla and Mistress Letty... you need to rest. Is there ought else I must do?'

'Micah, send for Micah... He will take care of things.'

'No, mistress, 'twould not be right. Captain Micah is departed to the city.'

Nazareth grabbed her arm. 'His mother will take care of... she gave me rosemary... in remembrance. A flower for my wheel.'

'What mother? Who is Rosemary?' The poor lady was now so befuddled as to make no sense, weakened by the loss of all that blood.

'Not Lucie... no, not here. Keep away!'

'Have no fear, the child will not see the babe here. He's safe with me. Have you a name chosen for his baptism, Mistress Nazareth, a name for your son?'

'God have mercy on us... mercy and penitence. See to him. Have mercy and penitence...'

Nazareth could not withstand the tide's pull, drifting into sleep again, floating along the river towards the open sea, waves of peace lapping over her head, her face, her lips.

Martha bent her head and wept, crossing herself slowly. The mistress was so deep asleep no mortal would wake her this side of Heaven. There was nothing to do now but clear away the evidence, wait, and then open the casement to let her spirit roam free. It would be morning before the party from Longhall heard the dreadful tidings. What would become of the Newhouse, of Lucilla and little Penitence, for that surely was his given name?

As Captain Bagshott rode out of the city on a fine May morning, up the winding narrow lane to Fridewell, he felt light with relief. The siege was over at last, the walls of the close battered to rubble. The feeble garrison had walked out with dignity intact under the white ensign and now the whole of the city was in their hands. He had had enough of warfare and the saddle to last him a lifetime. Now was not the time for burning bridges but for repairing them. He sniffed the blossom on the air, noted the petals strewing a path before him in the dust. He thought of a bridal path and white garlands. Yes, he would leave the army and marry his widow. Make an honest woman of her.

Trotting slowly at first, he began to quicken the pace as he drew nearer to his destination, past the mill and the green and the cottagers going about their chores in the sunlight. He had taken off his armour and was dressed in high boots and fancy breeches, a fine jacket with plain collar, his hair combed and cut shorter, cheeks scraped raw with the knife to make his skin appear smooth. It was a time for celebration.

For the first time in his life he felt a lurch of pleasure to see the old garrison barn, the cobbled yard and L-shaped house. No longer was he burdened with envy and contempt for the Salts. He knew he possessed a little of her heart. It would be enough to start their journey together. Her daughter would have to tag along, sulking and silent, but he would win her over in the end if he gave her enough time and shared her with her mother.

He drew into the yard and dismounted. It was as he'd left it last in March. There was no sign of life about the place, no smoke from the chimney stack, just a cart standing outside the front steps. He turned towards the garden slope to look for the wheel and the circle of tulips. The leaves stood like spears, stiff and upright, but there was no circle of flame, just green tops. Every red tulip head lay on the ground, neatly severed like a head on the execution block. He did not understand and looked back at the house. The face of that wretched child stared back at him then was gone. Who would cut off flower heads before they were over? Who but a sullen, spiteful child? She deserved a beating.

He marched to the foot of the stairs and called loudly, 'Mistress Nazareth, are you within?'

Footsteps came running down the hallway and a shocked Martha looked at him sadly. 'Oh, Captain, you are come at last! You have heard our sad news…'

'What news is this? Where is your mistress?'

Martha bobbed a curtsey. 'Come inside to the parlour and sit thee down. I fear I have grave tidings for such a lovely day. Come inside and shut the door.'

Lucilla sat on the stairs trying to eavesdrop on the whispering below. The ugly beast had returned once again but now there was no faerie queen for him to snatch away. Mother lay in the churchyard under the earth with a garland of yew and rosemary, holly and rue, about her head. Mother would not be coming to live at Longhall. She had fallen sick of the plague and died and now Lucie must pack all her chests and leave her kingdom forever.

Aunt Letty was kind and let her hold their new babe, Arthur, but she'd pleaded to stay at the Newhouse with Martha and Gideon. Longhall was not her home and she hated her cousins, those rough boys. She did not want to pack up and live there.

And now the enemy was back again. What if the Captain was going to steal the Newhouse, to live in it himself as he did before, sleeping with her mother like a common doxy? How dare he come back to haunt them, to gloat over their misery? She would show him who ruled this kingdom. She was still Queen of the stairs.

The Captain sat stunned, head bent as the tears fell. Martha had never seen a grown man cry before, real tears of sorrow and shock. The poor man could hardly believe a word of the lies she was telling him, the same ones she had told the others.

The babe was cradled safely in the lodging, kept out of sight of all but Gideon and her. It had been a struggle at first to feed him but they milked the goat and soaked a rag in its milk and she nursed him so that he sucked on the rag as a teat. Gideon shaped a funnel from a piece of soft calfskin with a hole at the top. The babby soon learned to suck vigorously for its milk. Sometimes she made sloppy sops with honey and soft bread mixed with milk. The bairn supped eagerly. He would thrive and she loved him as her own.

It was a terrible sin to deny his birth but what else could she do? Could she trust this Captain not to shame her mistress? And Miss Lucilla would not understand any of it. The sooner that mardy child was packed up and away from this place, the sooner her sad little heart would be mended. The house was to be tenanted by strangers until such time as the girl grew old enough to claim her inheritance, poor little mite.

Sometimes Martha wondered about the spirits in this house. Were they kindly or evil for there'd been nothing but misery for the Salts since the left wing had been built in Old Sarah's time.

Micah made his way to the churchyard, to the new mound of earth by the east side of the ruined church. Pigeons flapped around the tower and the first of the swallows swooped high above his head.

Oh, Nazareth, this was not how I planned to honour you. Now all I can do is plant these wretched cuttings on top of you in memory of what might have been between us. There's nothing left but a few beheaded bulbs and these offshoots. How could you fall so ill and die when you battled so hard to keep your home and protect your child? Nazareth, I should have come sooner if I had known…

He stood and bowed his head. Once more he must journey alone, just when he'd thought of joining her life here. He walked slowly back and stood one last time to examine Nazareth's house. To one side were the old stone walls of the Priory, to the other the long brick and wood extension.

Black smoke was rising not out of the chimney but the doorway, flames leaping up as far as the top of the stairs. He saw the frightened face of the child peering out from the blackened glass. Martha was screaming, 'Fire!' and running for the bucket, Gideon racing down to ring the old warning bell which might summon help from the village.

'Oh, sire, Miss Lucilla… she's set fire to the stairs with her boxes. The wood is dry and the drapes have caught the blaze… Lucie… the casement!'

Micah needed no second bidding. 'Fetch the bucket and go to the pond. Get a chain of buckets from there to here. Throw that one over my head first.' He tore off his jacket and soaked it in the water, running towards the screaming child.

'Shift away from the smoke, Lucie!'

'Peto is here… and the cradle.' The girl lifted the dog.

'Oh, God, no! She has the baby! Oh, sire, quick! There's a bairn in the cradle… you must rescue them!' screamed Martha.

He peered up. They were trapped by the stairwell, black smoke swirling round. If he could get to them another way… Micah shouted for ladders but none could be found for the soldiers had stolen them on their last forage. Then he saw the fig tree, its wood hard and rung like. If he stretched, he might just be able to do something.

Lucilla was choking on the smoke. She fled to her chamber, shutting the door, but it was dark and scary there so she moved further towards the old house and the connecting door by the linen cupboard. It was locked. She was trapped in her kingdom and did not like it one bit.

Peto was shaking and she clutched him. This was all her doing, the lighting of that circle of fire around all her toys to stop the ugly giant from stealing them. It was silly to play with fire. Had that not been beaten into her many times at the hearth? The candles had spilled on to the rushes and they had caught alight. Now she was trapped and there was no one to rescue her, no one but a frightened maid. Then she saw the face at the casement and drew back.

'Open it!'

She could see the beast at the window, clawing to get in. She shook her head and saw him punch his fist through the glass.

'For God's sake! Unlock the window and let me carry you out...' Micah tried to look less fierce. 'Come, there's danger and Martha waits below. Hurry!'

For a second the girl hesitated but the smoke was seeping under the door and the corridor was ablaze. She could hear the flames crackling. Poor Old Sarah was melting in her picture frame. She pushed the little dog into his arms and he lowered it down gently to the other rescuers below.

'Come, please, Lucilla. I mean you no harm. I loved your mother with all of my heart as you did. We're all bereft.'

He lifted her gently. Her slender frame slid easily under his arm and like a bundle of thatching straw he lowered her to safety.

'The cradle? Where's the cradle, child? Have you taken the babe?' Martha was screeching like a woman possessed.

'There's no babe, only my dolly in her cradle. I fear she's all burned up too.'

Martha sank to the ground in despair. Was the child telling the truth? Had she snatched the baby from the upper chamber and thrown it in the fire? If so she was deranged and must be punished.

'I don't believe you. I left the young master in the chamber...'

'And here he is, safe and sound, fusspot.' Gideon was holding the swaddled child in his arms. ''Twas the first thing I did when you shouted fire. He's been asleep on the straw safe out of the smoke.'

The crowd stood round the babe looking not a little surprised. Martha and Gideon were mighty young to be fathering childer. Catching their unspoken thoughts she yelled, 'You needn't look like that, 'tis not mine... is it, Gideon?'

'Then whose be this foundling?' The Captain examined the bundle.

'Funny you should ask that, sire. Would you step this way and we will explain.'

'It can wait... the house is still on fire!' he said and ran to organise the chain of water buckets. If they concentrated on the old building they might just stop the roaring flames from devouring the lot.

Micah stood with the child in the dusk as a welcome downpour of rain finished off what the men had started. It was worse than he'd first feared. Sarah Salt's extension lay in ruins, nothing but the old Priory end lay intact. The men had made a barrier to stop the fire in its tracks but it was Bagshott's fine bricks which had stayed firm, protecting the stone walls. To one side were the ruins of Old Sarah's vanity, to the other the ancient stonework, holding its ground. All was not lost but it was in a sorry state. He felt a fleeting sadness for Nazareth's child whose own silliness and stubbornness had robbed her of her home. Now she was safely placed at Longhall out of harm's way and as they'd parted she'd smiled at him for one brief second before she turned her head away.

He could make no sense at first of what Martha told him as he prepared to mount his horse and leave the ruined house.

'Not so fast, Captain Bagshott. Haven't you forgotten something in all this smoke and debris?' She came towards him, carrying a bundle, and pushed it into his arms.

'What's this?'

'Someone I should have told you about long ago. I was not sure if you would accept it.'

'Accept what… this babe?'

'Aye, your son, born on the fifteenth of April. She died giving birth to your son. I was there and Gideon. Only we three know of this and so it shall remain.'

'You've looked after him as your own?'

'But mine he is not. One day the Good Lord will give me a child to suckle but this one is surely yours. See for yourself.' Micah gazed into the pink face – those dark eyes, his very own, staring back at him. He kissed the child's forehead. 'Did she know?'

'His name is Penitence. 'Twas whispered with her very last breath. I did wrong to hide him. She called for your mother too. I know she wanted him to be brought up a…'

'A Bagshott not a Salt. Had she lived we could both have shared the task but now it is mine alone. With your help, if you're willing. Like Miriam in the bulrushes, is it not?'

'Something of that ilk, sire. My mistress will sleep easier, knowing her son has a father to protect him in this wicked world. Will you ride down to the city with him?'

'No, tonight we'll rest in the Priory lodging. Tomorrow my mother will be getting a big surprise. I think 'twill be better if she has a good night's rest first, don't you?'

Micah lifted the roaring babe out of his wooden crib in the old lodging house and wrapped him tight against the air. The night was balmy, stars twinkling in the midnight sky.

'Hush, little howler. Come, let's go round the place one last time to see what is left of it all.'

The garden at Fridewell lay smouldering under smoking timbers and rubble, my lady's fancy knotbeds crushed by charred furniture. A stench of woodsmoke and burning metal hung on the air. All the old fripperies were gone. Which was how it should be, thought Micah grimly, though not this way. He peered at the face of his child. Poor motherless bairn!

Something in the night air drew him through the yew arch up the steps to the hidden bower, some wayward spirit urging him onwards to the very place where his heart had been stirred. Moths fluttered on the night-scented stocks for the air was purer here. White flower heads waved like ghosts.

'Come and see the spring... this was your mother's favourite hiding place. I feel her spirit here with us.' Micah stretched out his arms to lift the child high over the water towards the moon.

'Spirit of this cursed place... bless my bairn. May he bring mercy and forgiveness with his name. Let Bagshotts and Salts wage war no more but rest in peace with one another. That which was wrought unfairly between us is now forgiven... Oh, Nazareth, if you can hear me, my tears mingle with the water. Pray for us and the seed we planted, let him flourish and grow strong. Pen will be safe with me, our secret secure, but why did you have to leave us now?'

The Tipsy Hedge

Iris

❦

This summer is holding up well and yet every year I get lazier about gardening chores when there's a thousand jobs waiting to be done. Now I won't have to worry any more.

From the far end of the house Miss Bagshott looks down the slope towards the orchard field and the meadow croft beyond. It is getting harder to keep the natives from scaling the fences; squirrels and rabbits, mice and voles, the occasional roe deer. Bindweed twines around the hawthorn hedge; overgrown grasses are full of thistles, docks and nettles, much to the delight of the butterflies. In daylight goldfinches feed on fluffy seed heads; buttercups, campion and oxe eye daisies struggle for air and the strong prickly arms of the blackberries sprout pinky-white blossoms. Here fruits will ripen in due season without any help.

As she walks down to the picket gate through an arch of overgrown rhododendron and azalea bushes the gloom deepens and she thinks once again of smoke and shadows. This spot is farthest away from the home end, a wilder place where the air is cooler and the light spectral. The woodland full of whispering oaks is only branches away from the boundary wall. It would not take much for the forest to reach out and reclaim its own.

Once there were black banties scratting in the orchard meadow, a white goat tethered by the hedge to keep down the grass, and a dusty donkey in the croft who earned his keep on Palm Sunday, brought out of retirement to carry a Sunday School Jesus in the old days when village church and school were the centre of this community.

However much the orchard is neglected, the apples will bend the branches with their weight and the magpies will have their fill. The cherries have been filched by scavenging birds and the damson blossom was caught by a spring frost. The bark of the pear trees is rotten.

'Plant walnuts and pears for your heirs.' Who will fall heir to this place when I've sold up? What if they don't like the orchard and rip it apart? If the bulldozers come this wilderness will be gone forever.

Tears well up and Iris struggles to hold them back.

Am I doing the right thing? Trees grow old just like humans. I should be replacing them for the future. A garden needs a bit of wilderness. What if the new owners are fusspots who'll strim away every inch of my undergrowth? Then where can the mice and the voles hide or the hedgehogs hibernate? Life itself is never neat and tidy, but this mess... Would there be time to scythe a path through for the visitors on Saturday afternoon?

Perhaps it will rain and no one will come? Anyway, who will take offence at a few scruffy bits? Now the sign is up there'll be a steady trickle of viewers, some critical, others not, and some here on a secret recce of Friddy's Piece, not interested in the garden at all. Saturday is Judgement Day for us all. Will it be easier for me to sell up if everything looks run down and neglected?

Time was when I'd have been up those ladders, tar washing, coppicing, lopping off branches, carrying baskets of apples to the cider press, gathering blackberries, sloes, elderberries from my tipsy hedgerows for the winter booze. But those days are gone, Iris. Let George do some more mowing if it bothers you.

Who said a sense of the past is the best sauce for an unpalatable present? What, after all, have I got to look forward to but bath chairs and bedpans? Stop that! You're not doing the tour to depress yourself. Come on, it's not that bad. Some might call this orchard corner quaint and there's much of interest to the well-tempered eye; the quince straddling the wall, and the mulberry tree, even an ancient medlar with its grey bark, crooked trunk and unexpected leaves, large and downy to the touch.

The note pad comes to the rescue once more. In the dusk her eyes alight on the old apple tree with a rope swing dangling down temptingly. She eases herself cautiously on to the wooden seat. It holds and she pushes gently back and forth as she did as a child.

I'd better just check the ropes. Some little toe rag will climb on it on Saturday, I'm sure.

There's always been a swing in the orchard and Iris wonders who was the first to hang one here?

PART SIX

THE SCHOOL

1770

'If the meek flower of bashful dye
Attract not thy incurious eye;
If the soft murmring rill to rest
encharm not thy tumultuous brest
Go, where ambition lures the vain,
or avaunce barters peace for pain'

—Dr Erasmus Darwin

'The Medlar Tree
The fruit is old Saturn's and sure a better medicine
he hardly hath to strengthen the retentive faculty,
therefore it stays women's longings. The good
old man cannot endure women's minds
should run a-gadding'

Secrets

The patchwork kite soared upwards, gliding on the wind, its tail rippling above the open fields beyond the orchards of Fridwell House, over the jigsaw of field shapes and hedges where men shielded their eyes to glimpse its progress, above the new brick church tower of St Mary Virgin, then the Parson's farm, the mill and the ponds and the line of cottages strung along the road to Longhall.

Down below a string of boys chased after the kite master begging their turn, tugging at his shirt. For a second there was dispute and fisticuffs. In the struggle the kite was freed from all constraint, flying like a bird out of their grasp, escaping towards the valley of the Trent where workmen on the turnpike road leant on their spades to watch the strange bird passing overhead. Its flight was marked with a smile until the gaffer bawled them out for time wasting.

The kite floated onwards over the grey ribbon of stone road going north to south through the Chase. Then the breeze softened and the kite dropped out of the air like a shot pheasant, tumbling down into the brook and floating far away from Fridwell village.

A small boy in brown breeches, loose shirt and waistcoat, stared up at the empty sky in disbelief and turned on his companions. 'It's... all y... ye... your f... fault.'

'Oh, ye... ye... yes, says who?' mimicked a lad with his hands planted defiantly on his hips. 'Going to tell yer precious m... mam, are you? Tell-tale tit, your tongue is split! Spit it out, Barnswell, if you can. We've not got all day.'

Ephraim Barnswell bowed his head in frustration. Why did his words not spill out like everyone else's in the school? Why was he so slow and clumsy? Now he had lost the patchwork kite Mother had made for them all. Why did these stupid louts have to come into his orchard anyway, to pick the fruit and disturb him, swinging on his rope and sitting on his swing, breaking the branches with their weight? Why did she make him share his playing ground with a bunch of village bully boys who knew nothing but stone picking, weeding, and scrumping apples? He hated the school being in his house. Why did Mother keep on with it? Was it not bad enough to have to live with Iron Man, who called him 'stupid', 'runt' and 'the bastard'. Never once did Ephraim hear his real name.

I'm not stupid. Just because I can't utter words at one go. In my head they're perfectly formed, it's just my teeth and tongue chitter when I speak aloud and then Iron Man roars with derision, making it worse.

When Ephraim was alone with his mother there was little problem but they were hardly ever alone with this bunch of dullards and dunces always interrupting.

The boy looked in vain for his kite. His hands trembled. Another of his precious toys gone. Why should he have to share his chap books, board games, hoops, hobby horse and soldiers? In no time they were all battered and torn, ripped and ruined. It wasn't fair!

There were ten children in the Dame school: the miller's sons, the farmers' daughters, the wheelwright's child, even cottar children brought learning pence now and again. Mother turned no one away. She said they needed money for 'the fund'. Ephraim thought that Iron Man had sufficient coppers in his leather purse, from digging and draining ditches, supplying labour for the turnpike road building.

Anyone could see that his mother was a lady in disguise. Had she not a fine-spoken accent? Did she not play a spinet? Was she not one of the Salts of Longhall Manor, a name once revered in the district? Could she not read, write and draw fine flower pictures, knowing every name in the Latin like a scholar? If he lived to be a hundred Ephraim would never understand how she'd come to marry such a drunken swine as Abel Barnswell, his father.

How he feared the lifting of the iron latch, the thud of Abel's boots on the flagstone floor, the smell of the farmyard and the tavern on his breath, the stench of his clothes and the iron of his fists. Sometimes if his meal were not on a plate in the kitchen, piping hot, the table laid in his honour, Iron Man would fling Mother across the room in a rage and kick her with his boot. Ephraim knew better than to go to her aid. The punishment would only be repeated. Instead he would slide out of sight and curl up in a corner, trembling at his own weakness until he heard the chair scrape, the chink of a knife on a platter.

With luck the brute would burp and belch and brush his way past them to go out again to the tavern. They were the good nights when Ephraim would wipe away the blood and mop his mother's tears. She would bank up the fire then go to the secret trunk kept hidden and locked under the stairs to bring out the parchment and pens. She would show him her botanical drawings and together they would dissect a flower on the table and draw each petal, sepal, stamen and leaf. By rushlight she would read to him from old leather-bound books found in a chest in the attic, her face raw and blotched but her grey eyes shining with interest.

On a bad night Iron Man would stay indoors, snoring by the fire. They would creep about on tip-toe so that he was not disturbed. While there was moonlight enough they could sneak off into the garden, to get as far away from him as they could. Mother would flap her arms like broken wings or sit on the swing, arms curved around the ropes, rocking back and forth, weeping. He would sit on top of the gate which looked out over the meadow fields, listening to the dusk calls of foxes and owls in the copse, wondering why they must endure this awful prison.

He hated Iron Man with the white heat of rage but his own puny hands were useless, powerless against the bully's blows. One day, Ephraim promised himself, he would grow tall and strong and then Iron Man's rule would be over. He could not wait for that day to come.

The old Parson knew about the drawings and the beatings. He always called during daylight when Iron Man was about his business. Sometimes he took Ephraim to one side and whispered, 'Be patient. The Lord sees all… Look after your mother. Her burden is great and unjust, I fear. If ever she needs help, you know where I am.'

Ephraim saw there were tears in the Parson's blue eyes and his hands trembled as he spoke. He often slipped a coin into the boy's hand as he took his leave. 'For the fund… child… for the fund.' Sometimes the old man stopped to admire the plantings with Mother and they would whisper out of ear-shot. Sometimes Parson Thomas took her drawings away with a sigh, rolling them carefully under his cloak away from prying eyes. Then Mother blushed with pride and pleasure for there would be more coins for the fund. She would pace the terrace garden, muttering to herself, wrapping her long shawl across her chest.

Why did they have to live so secluded from her kin? Why did no carriage ever come to their door, no letters in the post boy's saddle bag? No one but the Parson ever crossed their threshold except the stupid pupils of Mother's little school. What had they done to deserve such shunning, such misery with Iron Man? Hetty Barnswell could not wait for her pupils to depart. The girls had been doing the laundry with her maid, Nance, learning how to prepare lye balls from burnt fern ashes sifted, dried and mixed with grease. They stirred up the cleansing, pummelled the clothes with the dolly posser, agitating the fibres and loosening the dirt. It was good training for the older girls with many town houses in the city looking for country girls as servants.

Now Hetty was busy with the evening meal, a stand pie filled with meat scraps and vegetables and new fangled potatoes from their vegetable plot. How she wished she could be at her drawings or planting out the cuttings from Parson Thomas's own collection of specimens, instead of herding away a gaggle of noisy children before the master's return. If he saw them there would be trouble.

She could see Ephraim walking slowly up the path. The kite had flown past and she knew the boy would be upset at its loss. He hated her having a Dame school, hated sharing his private world with such rough children, but their pennies were needed for the escape fund and for extras which the meanness of the master would never provide. How else could they walk to the city with sacks of green herbs to sell or purchase ribbon for her bonnets, paper for their drawings, treats to make this existence bearable? No one in the city recognised her as Mehetebel Salt, only as Goody Barnswell, herb hawker, in her scarlet hood and cloak. Her beauty was faded now as the dark bruises faded to yellow on her cheeks, her once glorious mane of red-gold hair paled to a bleached straw under her black chip hat.

Abel laughed on market days to see her trussed up like a peasant. If he knew she tucked paints and pens, paper and drawings in her herb basket on her return, he would have ripped them off her and torn them to shreds. She was his rightful possession, sold to him on condition there were no heirs to make demands. He found this part of the old bargain hard to keep as he speared her with his lust, rolling his heavy body on top of hers, spilling his seed over her in contempt.

'No issue, Hetty Salt, or I don't get the rest of my inheritance. I've waited ten years for those bottom fields to be mine. If you spawn a brat out of me... I'll rip your guts apart with my own bare hands and tear it out of you!'

His foul breath stank of ale and baccy, his trousers of piss and stale wind. He used her body then flung her aside. There was no reasoning with him when the strong brew addled his brain.

He looked upon his son with scorn and loathing, kicking him like a puppy, but Ephraim would never cry out. Sometimes Hetty thought they would be better dead and freed from this tyranny but somehow death would be Abel's ultimate triumph over her. The Salts would be rid of their nuisance forever. She would never give them that satisfaction until the escape fund was big enough to support their flight and feed them while she found work far away. Until then she must go on saving and scrimping and hoarding under his roof – under her own family roof for Fridwell House was always a Salt residence, once belonging to Great-aunt Lucilla, burned down in the Troubles and left to rot for years.

Sometimes in church she could feel village women staring at her with curiosity, wondering how Squire Richard and his lady, Drusilla, could allow their daughter to be wed to a humble ditch drainer and jobbing farmer with scarce a few fields to his name and no traceable connections. Hetty would smile politely, knowing she needed the village matrons to support her school. It had taken all her resources to repair the parlour roof and stairs and clear away the debris of years to make a small room with benches, limewashed walls and a stout table. She was not allowed to light a fire until the master came home.

Childhood was short enough in these parts and her few lessons of instruction in letters, scripture, a little finger work, stitchery and baking for the girls, garden work for the boys, was as much as any of them wanted. The only luxury was the inlaid walnut spinet which she had been allowed to bring to Fridwell on her marriage. Sometimes Hetty sang and played to them as a treat for her voice was still clear and true. At midday she ladled out broth, bread and cheese. The pupils had to learn to sit still and say Grace, use a knife and be quiet before their elders, especially if the master was within earshot.

Sometimes Hetty wondered what she had done that was so wicked as to keep her in this miserable state. At eighteen she had danced at the Assembly Balls with the best in the county, attended Miss Smith's Academy for young ladies, worn silks and brocades, paraded around the race course in the season to catch the eye of some suitable young gentleman. This achieved she was courted and wooed ardently by John Stamford, an ambitious young lawyer in a city practice, an Oxford scholar who met with much approval from her mother and aunts for she was the youngest of three sisters and of little importance.

The couple walked in the gardens of Longhall, carefully chaperoned yet managing to hold intimate conversations out of earshot. Her greatest mistake was to trust Mr Stamford's word when he persuaded her to sneak away alone and meet him secretly in the summerhouse bower where his kisses took on an urgency which shocked her. He imposed himself strangely and caused her much pain and discomfort but she told no one until it was obvious that something was awry. She informed her mother, not understanding the true nature of her condition or its consequences, such was her innocence of such matters. It was after all only a matter of time before they would be wed.

John Stamford was summoned and denied any knowledge of such intimacy, calling her dreadful words: 'a wanton trollop, baggage, drab and a liar'. He said he wanted no scandal to ruin his career and so would not seek further satisfaction on this slur to his honour. He removed himself to London and made an advantageous marriage there. Hetty was kept locked in her room and spoke to no one.

One morning she was led down the curved stairs of Longhall Manor into a side room where a rough man in dark country tweeds stood cap in hand, not looking at her. He was introduced as Abel Barnswell, farmer of Fridwell, who would escort her to church forthwith and marry her on condition she withdraw all claim on the family. This whole unfortunate matter was never to be spoken of again.

Her trunk was packed, her dowry written up as a piece of Fridwell House and field, meadow and orchard, and if no further issue were forthcoming, Farmer Barnswell would receive three more enclosed fields: Banky Piece, Far Orchard Field and Meadow Pleck.

In such a manner was Hetty dismissed and her former life destroyed, reputation sullied forever, parents estranged. She was to be disposed of quickly in the church porch by the new Parson who asked few questions.

Hetty arrived at Fridwell House to a damp musty reception of mice and mould. The Salt Estate had mended the property just well enough to suit the needs of a small farmer's wife. In due course the babe came, rumoured to have been born early; he was red-faced like a skinned rabbit and from the minute she held him Hetty felt a fierce love for him. She found no difficulty in feeding him herself.

Abel took one look at him and sneered, 'That bastard is as ugly as the sin that begot him.' He rode down to the ale house at Barnsley Green to get roaring drunk and stayed away for a week or more, leaving his wife to fend for herself. Hetty knew then that she would always be alone.

For ten years she nurtured the boy, the house and the garden. The Dame school became her life line to sanity. It filled the hours when she could not garden, sew or draw. With Ephraim tied in a shawl around her chest, she had hacked and dug, weeded and planted, brought the neglected garden back to life. In summer she took her parchments and pens down to the orchard to record all the trees. Hetty had an eye for the smallest detail of leaf, stem or flower, and a fine delicate touch with a brush. She could capture the way the poppies danced in the breeze, the delicate shape of goat's beard. She cleared the old kitchen bed to grow green herbs and strewing herbs to sell in the market. On wet days she would bring out her dried plants and take pleasure in drawing their distinctive features.

It was the repetitions of patterns and shapes which fascinated her. How the old village field strips had given way now to a patchwork of fields enclosed in hedges like picture frames.

The pattern of bricks on the new tower above the larger stones of the old parish church walls. Wherever she looked there was pattern and shape. She liked to plant out in order, one colour followed by another, tall and short, thick and thin.

The old garden was a hotch-potch of shapes and curves and borders; some she straightened out, others were let be.

By the light of the one candle she was allowed in the evening she shaped fabrics from her scrap box into circles and triangles, fan shapes and squares, to make Ephraim a quilted counterpane for the cold nights. She looked at these pieces and saw the scraps of her life laid out before her on the table; a pitiable sight. There were muslins sprigged with rosebuds in palest pink from childhood, a piece of blue-gold brocade which reminded her of summer fields and blue skies, a scrap of lilac taffeta from her first ball gown – not the one worn the night she met her seducer. That she had burnt in disgust. There were scraps of her sombre wedding gown, its russet brown a reminder of that first terrible night with her husband, and a few high and mighty bits of curtain fabric from her other life. From now on her lot was cheap off cuts, plain sturdy weaves, sludgy earth shades to hide the mud. These filled in the quilt blocks, together with shirting and sheeting, coveralls and aprons. It would be a hotch-potch of colours, mostly drab and with little gaiety like her life now, but she would make something beautiful for Ephraim or die in the attempt.

Sometimes when he was a babe she would creep up to his tiny chamber and watch him sleep so peacefully. He had the Salt fair skin, sandy hair and grey eyes. Refined features which only drew attention to the jowly dark face of his 'father'. Sometimes she feared for his future for she believed that a child was Nature's fresh picture, drawn newly in oil, and much mishandling and violence would dim or deface him if she did not take care. His soul was yet a blank sheet of paper but in this terrible place his freshness could be marred and spoiled forever.

Yet Fridwell House was good for them; hidden away so no one observed her grief or her bruises, the garden her solace and task master. It had drawn her into the world of plants and botanical science. Hetty even managed to beg a store house for her tools and dried herbs which quickly became her refuge and studio.

Only Parson Thomas knew the truth of her endeavours and his lips were sealed. Through him she was learning about the science of botany, the art of seed propagation, hybridisation and the newly formed Botanical Society in the city, under the guidance of no less a figure than Dr Erasmus Darwin himself. This was her greatest but secret triumph. The good doctor was impressed with her drawings and was commissioning her to illustrate his own collection of exotics. How could she bear to contain her excitement? Hetty sometimes feared it would burst forth everywhere like dandelions in the spring.

The Water Gardens

❧

At Parson's Farm the Reverend Thomas woke with a start. 'Have I shut the glasshouse door? Is there a frost outside?' Once awake he donned his night cap and padded coat, shuffled for his slippers and a candle, leaving the warmth of his bed for the chilly stairs and the back door. All this fuss for a few hot house plants when it was others in need he should really be worrying about.

Outside the night sky was bright with stars and misty swirls of cloud. The glasshouse door was fast and he felt a twinge of guilt to be nursing his new shoots like babes. Across the village there was hardship and suffering with the loss of the common lands and strip fields. Men were losing their livelihoods. But one woman and her child needed his support in a different way.

Why was a woman of obvious virtue and piety so cruelly shunned for just one lapse of the flesh? His spirit was troubled by the sight of those scars on her face, her tight-lipped silence and loyalty to that bully Barnswell. The Parson himself would not like to face that drunken hulk on a dark night. Something ought to be done.

In his opinion Mistress Hetty did not disgrace the Salts like the other painted Jezebels in the family, displaying a shrubbery of foliage on their high headdresses, fluttering fans the size of windmills, trailing flounces and frills, their faces painted white and rouged like harlots in a stew house. How could Drusilla Salt sleep in her bed knowing her abandoned child and grandchild were so ground down in misery?

But why was he laying all the blame with the Salts when it was he who had agreed to marry the couple, to his eternal shame? Yoking a race horse to a mule went against the order of Nature. It made him uneasy to consider the consequences of such a union.

What could you have done, Benjamin? he told himself. Be honest, you were in no position to give orders or refuse your patron's demand. You were new in your post, disgraced for being a follower of the Reverend Wesley and his band of enthusiasts. You were grateful to old Salt for giving you a living, but there's always a price for favours. Squire Salt knew you had connections in the district, that your grandfather, Penitence, son of Micah Bagshott, was a Dissenter and his daughter, Kitty, married to another Dissenting clergyman. How many times does Richard Salt spit in your face that the old rebel who rescued his great-aunt from certain death as a child was 'a Captain amongst those seditious varlets who went against Church and King, to their Eternal shame. A fine pedigree for a Vicar indeed!'

Benjamin Samuel Thomas never intended to take holy orders but at Oxford had come under the influence of the 'Holy Club', following the progress of the famous field preachers, George Whitefield and the Wesley brothers. His mother had named him Benjamin in the hope that the Almighty would spare the last of her brood of twelve and then he would be dedicated to the service of the Lord. There was never any choice in the matter for him: Oxford, a curacy, marriage and the birth of twin sons, and always the lure of scientific study eluded his grasp. The nearest he could get to study was a little amateur dabbling in astronomy, botany and zoology, and this glasshouse under the stars linked to the end of the old farmhouse off the village green. Here he nurtured his blossoms, swapped seeds, pollinated his prized auriculas with the frilled edges, envied those who could afford the fee of ten pounds per annum to subscribe to botanical expeditions and seed catalogues.

These plants were his family now that Mary, his wife, had departed to her higher calling and his two sons served as missionaries overseas. Yet there was an emptiness at the core of his being which churned his stomach like a hunger pang.

Had he sinned against the Holy Spirit, the one unforgivable sin? Was he denying the inward witness of that spirit, the knowledge of his personal salvation? He had followed the field preachers from afar, watched them rouse the rabble from riot to reverence, facing danger head on without so much as a sign of outward fear. How could he sit safe in this backwater tending his blooms, when the world should be his parish, as Wesley so often said?

The old man put him to shame, touring the country on horseback in all weathers, preaching the Gospel of scriptural holiness throughout the land. What had happened to his own vocation? Sometimes Ben felt it had been his mother's, not his own, foisted on him like a heavy mantle weighing him down.

I am weak, Lord. I should have examined that couple more closely before I wed them. But I did my patron's bidding and turned my face from her suffering. What little I do now is to salve my own conscience, that's all, though I am half in love with her beauty. When I see her bent at her painting or at peace in her garden I am reminded of the lovely lines:

> There is a garden in her face
> Where roses and white lilies grow...

Stop this! Who do you fool? You've hidden in this backwater out of fear and laziness, your sermons are as flat as kippers, your heart is heavy. Where's that burning spirit which John Wesley gave to you on the night your 'own heart was strangely warmed' by the certainty of salvation? It has cooled like any burning ember cools when fallen from the fire. You fled at the first whisper of criticism from your Bishop when he called the Methodists 'Hypocrites, Jacobites and mere Enthusiasts'. The cold blast of derision soon dulled your ardour for revival!

Sometimes when he stared down from the pulpit of St Mary's with its meagre congregation in boxed pews and benches he tried to imagine his sermons whisking up a fervour of revival in the village; joyous singing, good works spring-ing up like fountains, eager students of the scriptures poring over the Bible. How might it be if they all burst with the joy of personal salvation instead of sleeping through his words, bored and fidgety?

But Ben Thomas knew he deserved this fate for he had disobeyed the heavenly vision, as Saint Paul so rightly put it. He was lukewarm, preferring plants to preaching, his own comforts to life on the open road. Was he not nearing sixty and his knees puffy and sore, not with kneeling in prayer but planting bulbs? He would see his life out in this dreary place, keep his head down, write up the minutes of the local Botanical Society and do what he could to support Mistress Barnswell.

It was not as if he did nothing in his parish like so many lazy vicars who rode to hounds and dined with the gentry. There was his catechism class, and the jobs he did personally to ease the work of his two maids and yard boy on the farm. He visited the sick and searched the scriptures for consolation for them.

But only in the privacy of his glasshouse did he lose all sense of time and allow his troubled spirit to be eased.

'Where are you gadding to now, woman?' snapped Abel Barnswell, watching his wife fussing over baskets and posset bowls, handing them out to the assembled line of children.

'Just out roving for a few blackberries and the like. The weather will hold. The Parson knows of a new patch far out and we must collect them before the devil kisses them with frost and they rot on the briars.' She smiled weakly, hoping this would satisfy his nosiness. For one who cared so little about her welfare he was mighty curious as to her daily doings, resentful if he thought she took any pleasurable respite from her household duties.

'The runt can come with me then. Time he earned an honest penny instead of clinging to your apron strings. Berry picking is women's work...' Ephraim hid behind her in fear.

'No, Mister Barnswell, the Parson comes to give them all instruction while they're picking mushrooms, hips, haws, sloes. I'll make fine hedgerow wines and we can sell the surplus at market. Many hands will get the job done. Why not leave your digging and delving and join us?' Hetty offered, sick with the fear he might take up this invitation.

'Nah, I've better things to do than trail after skirts. 'Tis pity the Parson don't roll up his shirt sleeves more often and get out in the fields like a man instead of a milksop. You want to watch the likes of him in the bushes!' Abel roared at the lewdness of his suggestion.

'He's an old gentle man... a man of the cloth, sir. He likes to instruct the children in the ways of Nature.'

'Oh, aye, does he now? I bet he's shown his maids a bit of instruction in his time...' It was turning out to be the longest conversation they had had in weeks and Hetty was sick of it.

'Come on, everyone, time to be on our way. We shall be going over the stile and up the ridge into the next valley south-wards.' She drew her cloak around herself like a shield as she passed her husband and tried not to shiver as he towered over them with a suspicious look on his scowling face. 'Where's me snap?'

'Wrapped in the cloth where it always is.'

She did not look back as he yelled: 'Don't be late home. I want my dinner when the clock chimes, mind on.'

Shut up, go away, don't spoil the day before it begins, thought Hetty. He always wanted the last word, to hold the power of a beating over her head, to break her spirit as well as her body. I'm too strong-willed for him and he knows it. He's the weak one. Sometimes she felt a kind of pity for this lumbering, ignorant farmer who hated her as much as she loathed the family which had yoked them together.

They met up with Parson Thomas and his maid at the lane end stile, crossed over the meadows where sheep grazed in the green shoots rising in the stubble. Up the ridge they trailed towards the Barnsley footpath then downwards into a dip where the thickets were laden with berries, blackthorn, acorns and hazel nuts. The sun was high and warm and the children set to picking like demons. Flies hovered over the riper fruits, birds darted for cover, the last of the butterflies descended on the thistles which scratched bare feet and legs. There would be enough fruit for pies and wine, cordial syrup and preserves. Soon Ephraim had purple lips and fingers and leapt from bush to bush, trying to catch the richest branches which were always too high for his reach. The Parson's maid filled a basket in no time and went to the aid of the younger children who were acting silly and chasing around. It was generally agreed that a walk to Dr Floyer's nearby water gardens would dampen their high spirits.

'If we come at the site from the north we should not intrude on the works there. There is a law of trespass now which forbids you to cross lands without permission, children. Hark at what I say for there are men who would set traps for their own kind to stop you in your tracks and charge you with trespass. I have seen woodsmen crippled by iron gin traps and hanged as poachers. We have leave to be here today but don't interrupt the women at their garden work. We are just going to take a peep.'

The party walked a mile downhill to open parkland past gracious houses set amongst trees with gravel driveways curving around through the fields. Then the track narrowed and became shady in a gorge of overhanging rock covered with green mosses. Holly trees arched over them and they wound their way into another park where the bushes were thick with strange leaves. Here the brook was being diverted into small lakes fed by a stream with banks of shrubs shielding the spa from public view.

There was much debate about cold bathing and Hetty remembered as a child how her father had consulted the famous physician, Sir John Floyer, on some health matter and undergone the prescribed treatment, sitting alone under the roof, bathing in the icy waters of Unitt's well. Whatever the cure it did his temper no good and he took to his bed afterwards, proclaiming the man to be a charlatan and quack. Somehow she'd imagined this new temple grove would have an arched dome, a fine aspect, lend a Grecian air to the scene. It was just a little brick hut over a spring, not much to trample over hill and dale to see. The children wanted to race down the slope and splash in the water but they were shooed away by the gardeners and told to depart.

Hetty did not understand why the good doctor wanted to improve such a simple rustic scene, divert streams, make islands of shrubbery. She thought of the open parkland at Longhall. The trees were cut down now to open the views and the sheep fenced off. The garden was trussed up, enclosed and fussed over as if it were some overdressed lady in need of a stiff corset. What was wrong with simplicity? A beautiful face needed no painting. She watched Parson Thomas disappear into the bushes. To steal cuttings, no doubt. It was kind of him to want to cheer up her spirits but seeing the parkland only reminded her of her fall in life, the hopelessness of her position, being neither fish nor fowl in the village, and the misery of life in her marital prison.

'Come... come. It's time to get on with our picking before that black cloud catches up with us. Let's race it!'

As she spoke she could feel droplets of rain drizzling down on her face. There was a nip in the wind and soon the heavens would open and soak them to the skin. None of them was clad for bad weather. The barefoot children were the best shod for the journey back to their hoard of berries. Their baskets were sodden and the berries soggy and squashy to touch. Some creature had knocked over the bowls, leaving the fruit trampled and useless. It was a bedraggled party of adults and children who climbed wearily back over the stiles to Fridwell. Their harvest was ruined and they were late. With a sinking feeling in the pit of her stomach Hetty sensed trouble and made sure that all the children and the Parson were safely home.

Abel Barnswell was waiting for them on the door step and strode out into the yard to greet them with a grim smirk on his face and a glint of steel in his eye.

Ephraim knew there would be trouble. Iron Man's mouth was set in a thin line, his cheeks were flushed. The boy sensed his mother stiffen as they moved nearer and slow her pace. Why had she let the Parson go back down to the village with the others? He alone could have excused their delay, explained the poor harvest of fruits, delayed the inevitable onslaught if only for a few minutes. Ephraim was so cold and wet and tired and hungry. Their blackberry pickings would not satisfy Iron Man but the boy would offer to go back there again himself and collect more for his mother. There were other bushes to pick from nearby.

'Well, what time do you call this to be out whorin' with yer fancy friend?' Silence reigned as Mother prepared a gentle reply to his challenge.

'Come, Mister Barnswell. You see the weather, our condition... soaked to the skin. It took us longer than expected. We brought plenty home, see?'

Iron Man snatched her basket and flung it across the yard. 'Do you call this soggy mess a day's work? While I break my back, you gad off into the fields like some shepherdess pretending you're still Miss Hetty bloody Salt, Lady of the Manor... not the whore I was paid to take off their hands for carrying a bastard!'

'No, Abel, please... the boy! Not here...'

'He might as well know that he's a bastard, given my name to spare the blushes of your high 'n' mighty family. Just a mangy whelp, born from a harlot's belly… that's my boy Ephraim. He should know he's no flesh of mine and will get nothing from me but my name in this life.'

'Pr… pr… praise b… be to G… God I am none of yourn!'

The words flowed out of Ephraim in rage. Iron Man strode over and lifted him like a rag doll, flinging him against the stable door which gave way. He fell not on to the cobbles but unharmed on the soft straw. 'Useless little runt! Get out of my sight!'

'No, Abel! Not the boy. Don't touch him… it's not his fault… not the child!' screamed Hetty as Abel's hard eyes turned to her. She rushed towards him like a tigress defending her cub, battering his chest, her puny efforts making him roar with laughter. Then his face hardened as he loosened his belt. He was going to strap her to the floor again.

'No, please God! Not in front of the boy…'

Then a strange look of surprise flooded his dark face. He flung up his arms in a gesture of surrender as he staggered forward and fell twitching at her feet.

Parson Thomas was woken from his fireside nap by the loud ringing of the bell at the front porch and the dogs barking. He was sitting with his feet in a bowl of hot mustard, a shawl around his neck for the afternoon soaking had chilled him to the marrow. He had been shivering all evening and the mustardy fumes were making him sneeze.

'See to it, Mollie.'

The maid returned promptly. ''Tis Mistress Barns well in a right old lather, sir. Shall I bring her in?'

'Of course. What on earth is she doing abroad on such a foul night?'

The woman was dripping with water, her face half hidden beneath her hood in the flickering candlelight. She hovered at the door.

'Come quickly, sire… to my house. There's been a terrible accident. Hurry, you are sorely needed there.'

Not used to such a disturbance at this late hour, the Parson dried his feet, saw to his hose and leather boots, put on his bad weather cape and black tricorn hat.

'What's all the fuss? Why such secrecy?'

He was puzzled by her demeanour, the way she rushed him across the green to the snicket gate through the churchyard path, out to the stream bridge and into the orchard. He caught his arm on the swing and jumped back as if he had been assaulted. They hurried to the courtyard where a torch was burning with a smell of tar. He saw Abel Barnswell prostrate, face down on the cobbles with a hedge cleaver stuck between his shoulders. Ephraim sat curled up by the stable door, weeping.

'Dear God! Who did this?' The Parson knelt down to see if the man was still breathing but his spirit had long departed from the sturdy body which lay stiff on the ground.

'We do not know… do we, Ephraim? He must have been here when we returned from the outing. We went straight into the kitchen to prepare his meal for we were late. I was too busy to come out into the yard. Ephraim saw to the fire and was with me so it was not until it grew dark that we became anxious and went to look for him. Is that not so, Ephraim? We found the master with that… thing in his back. I did not know what to do.'

'You should have raised the hue and cry and called for the constable or church warden to verify your findings.'

'I came to you, sir. I could not think straight. Who would do such a terrible deed? Parson Thomas, I beseech you, help us… What do we do next? What's to become of us?' A look of pure terror passed over her face.

'You must go straightway to the Parsonage. Borrow some dry clothing and Mollie will make up a bed for you somewhere. A warm drink… some medicinal brandy to warm you. Go, take the boy. Tell them I sent you and will call the constable myself. Go, child, God speed!'

He watched Hetty drag the silent boy into the house. They emerged shortly afterwards with a bundle on a pole, setting off through the rain down to the green.

Oh, God in Heaven, she lies! Every word has the ring of careful fabrication about it. The day has come… *dies irae, dies illa*… I knew it would come to this ere long. Now what am I to do? Denounce her and let them both hang on the gallows for that worthless piece of shite? Worthy no doubt in thine eyes, oh Lord, but not in mine.

Ben Thomas knew the moment he saw the body that this was foul murder and he need look no further than one of the pair for the culprit. Hetty Barnswell's control was remarkable, that firm fixed stare, not a tear, no flinching at the sight of the wound gaping and the blood oozing from the back of her husband's waistcoat. Which of them had struck him? Could a child have such strength? Did it matter? They would both surely be found guilty and she would shield her child from the wrath to come as he surely must shield her…

He knew when he saw the blackberries strewn like rubies in the torchlight across the yard, mingling with the dark blood.

He knew there must have been a vicious argument and one violent act too many. Control had snapped, unleashing years of pent up fury, lending strength and accuracy to the hand on this sharp weapon.

He knew for he had the Bagshott knowing without words. He knew mother and child would both hang unless he could think of some way to save them... Perhaps she could plead insanity but who would testify to this, knowing her to be the calmest and most rational of creatures, born of gentry and of careful manners at all times? Perhaps she could claim to be witli child but the team of matrons who would examine her carefully would find her barren and it would go even harder on her. Perhaps she could flee the district at once but then suspicion would fall immediately upon them both and they would be hunted as outlaws, vagrants living on the mercy of poor law charity. Her funds would not last long.

Oh, Hetty! What must be done to rescue you? The Reverend Benjamin Thomas knew he must perjure his soul and lie.

Ephraim watched his mother searching for seed heads in the flower garden, fussing with arrangements in a jug for her painting. He watched her tongue darting in and out of her mouth like a snake when she concentrated on her brush work. They sat by the stream watching the water rush over the stones. She was free now to conduct her household as she pleased and he saw some colour in her pale face. She was free from Iron Man, now bound fast in a wooden box under the soil.

Ephraim could still feel the fury inside him, the fury which had made him grab the nearest heavy tool with which to beat Iron Man as hard as he could. He had done a terrible thing but Mother said nothing to him about it and the Parson told lies. Sometimes he wanted to blurt out the awful truth but his voice was silenced since that hour. Not one word had he uttered such was the shock of it.

Mother said they were going far away to forget this place and must take only basic necessities for the journey. The fund would stretch to pay for their sea passage. The journey would be hard and they would never return. Ephraim was glad in his heart. No more school, no more gossip and whispering, no more beatings, no more fear. He scribbled his questions on scraps of paper.

'Will Parson Thomas be coming with us to the new country?'

His mother shook her head. 'I asked him to escort us but he says he must obey other orders.'

'Who will look after us?'

'We must look out for each other now and the Lord above will guide our path.'

The child frowned. Would He who saw everything protect a murderer from due punishment? So far there had been no thunderbolts of swift justice, only a deafening silence around the village and an avoidance of their company.

'There's just one journey we must make before we leave, child. One long overdue.'

On the first fine day of October 1770 they set out to walk the three uphill miles to Longhall, past the field men who doffed their hats and turned to their tasks, past the carter, past the wheelwright and his apprentice who waved. They walked through the gateway to Longhall Park where the cattle grazed in open fields beside the gravel drive. In the entrance porch his mother rang the bell. A young maid, seeing the shabbiness of their clothing, shooed them round to the back yard and the kitchen block.

They waited for the servants to answer the door and were ushered into the kitchen hall. Ephraim stood in awe of the place: the roaring fire, the roast on the turning spit with the little dog at the treadwheel going round and round. He had never seen so many pots and pans, busy people scurrying back and forth. The noisy bustle was suddenly hushed by their presence and the servants stood staring and staring at his mother. An old manservant beckoned them aside, shaking his head regretfully.

'I'm sorry, Miss Mehetebel… she will not receive you today. Perhaps if you were to call some other time? I am sorry.'

'Think nothing of it, Bailey. It was just on the off chance as I go abroad soon and do not intend to return. I thought perhaps they might wish to glance once at my son here… but please give them these.'

The boy watched her withdraw a scroll of drawings – roses and field sketches, some of her finest flower work.

'If you would be kind enough to give the Squire and his wife these. I would not like them to think I had wasted a lady's education…'

Her voice broke. She grabbed her son's arm. Slowly they turned towards the outer door. All clattering of pots and murmured conversation ceased and a hushed, embarrassed silence fell. Only Ephraim saw her tears.

In the years that followed the terrible event, Parson Thomas could never ride past a blackberry bush without breaking into a sweat. He crossed himself and prayed that whatever good had come from his lies would glorify God in due course. As he wandered the highways and turnpikes of his new parish, stopping to feed his old nag, preaching in barns and market crosses, begging his supper from the lowly congregations who supported Methody itinerant preachers, he often spoke of sacrifice in the Lord's service. The world was truly his parish now and his spirit rose above his aching joints, chapped fingers and tissicky cough. He'd left behind the comforts of a regular living for life on the open road. There had been little choice when the scandal broke.

It was his testimony, and his maid's silence, which saved Hetty. He swore that he had escorted the widow safe to her door and seen for himself the body after it was abandoned by thieves. No one had dared to query the testimony of a man of the cloth, but there had been plenty of gossip and not a little scandal. He allowed rumour at the village pump to suggest the Parson would soon marry the widow. But much as he loved her Ben knew that a union with an old man, grey-haired, stooped and shabby, would never be of Hetty's choosing but would be done from gratitude only.

How she had begged him to accompany them across the world, to serve on the mission field in the colonies somewhere, but he knew the price he must pay. There was much to be repaired in his lazy life. It was time to return to the field preachers, to the comfort of scripture instead of a fireside. He must devote the rest of what was left of his earthly life to saving souls.

Once on one of his journeys he turned off the turnpike to Stafford and climbed again the steep hill up to Fridwell. He was so bent and worn and aged that no one recognised the figure walking in the churchyard and pausing at the hump in the grass where Abel Barnswell lay. Through the thicket he could see the orchard and Ephraim's swing but no child now rocked back and forth or scampered around the trees.

For old times' sake he took the path up the slope from the churchyard, pausing on the bank of the stream which was full of marsh marigolds and dog violets. There was no smoke coming from the chimney stack, the grassy mounds were overgrown with meadow grasses, sheep were grazing in the orchard. Nothing of Hetty's presence remained; only a few straggly roses, a wilderness of chickweed and couch grass in her herb beds, no sign of life. He turned away with tears in his eyes for it was a good building now gone to ruin. He knew the village folk feared that a spirit of violent death still roamed the garden. What a waste of a sturdy roof! If no one was inside he would avail himself of a free night's lodging, share his scraps with the mice. If he searched he might find stray berries and fruit, and there would be fresh water from the spring to wash away the dust.

There was a sad smell to the dwelling. Upstairs a flock mattress lay plucked for nesting on the bare boards. It felt like a lifetime since he had seen those exiles who now lived on the other side of the world. He sat on the stairwell and fingered the one precious letter she had sent on her arrival which had been delivered by a sea-faring man a year after it was written. He carried it around with him always and knew every word by heart:

Dear Benjamin Thomas, Brother in Christ,
I greet you as a grateful daughter, for in this life you have been of all men the most loyal and faithful in my troubles. Without your aid we would have been lost and my child would not have the wonderful life he now enjoys here in the New World.

It is hard to believe we are but an ocean away from the tears and sadness of life at Fridwell. Yet I bear the place no grudge for the few times of peace and tranquillity there with you often come to mind. Without your letters of introduction to this Christian community here, and the gracious kindness of General Oglethorpe, my life would have been little better than those who are transported against their will and yearn to return once more to England.

In the eyes of God's law I am no better than they and our crimes are grievous indeed but I think again of the verse which once I knew as truth:

How wretched is a woman's fate
No happy change her fortune knows
Subject to man in every state
How can she then be free from woes?

By His Mercies I am transported indeed into another state, another country, where opportunities can take hold here in the smallest patch of earth and thrive without tending. Ephraim speaks again and works hard as a scholar, training also as a militia man for there is much unrest and division in the Colony as to whether we be better off independent from His Majesty's government or no.

We have settled in the garrison town of Frederica, close to the coast by the Savannah river, a site of much beauty with its gracious parks and squares. Our journey here was long and not without danger. Ephraim was sick in the storms but my stomach was cast in iron. There is much to do yet to make our lives comfortable and safe amongst the convicts. I spend many hours with the wretched women newly released from bondage, teaching them the basics of stitchery, and we cut out patterns from paper and transpose them on to cloth for them to make dresses of their own. The scraps I gathered in England you will be pleased to hear are never wasted for we gather in groups at nightfall to praise God and pass around the pieces, sewing them together to make quilts.

There's little time now for painting or drawing. Besides, they remind me too much of my other lives.

I grow a few of their strange vegetables. There is no space for flowers in my yard patch but be not sad for now I grow gardens in my quilts and shape the patterns into flowers of all hues, piecing up scraps into the flowers of my memory: roses, tulips, scrolls of leaves. It gives me pleasure that the gardens I grow in cloth provide far more warmth and comfort than ever did my Fridwell piece of ground.

I have placed a packet of wild flower seeds within these pages as a token of our gratitude. You are often in our prayers. May God, who looks into the heart and sees our deeds, have mercy on us all.

Your dear friend in Christ, Mehetebel (Hetty) Thomas

PS: As you see we have shed that cursed name and chosen your surname for ourselves, to honour all your kindness to us both, the name which Ephraim, God willing, will make us all proud to own in due course.

Benjamin Thomas sighed as he fingered the fading letter, folding it carefully. He peered out of the dusty window on to the wilderness below. Once he had hoped to see new life blossoming in this beautiful garden, and to have lived out his own span in the comfort of the Parsonage. His plants he'd shared out far and wide amongst gardeners in the district before he left. Nothing was lost. His off shoots would flourish but he could not stay here amid the colour and scents, the red earth and the bird song. Sacrifices were made for the best. He snoozed until dawn and walked again down to the medlar tree which Hetty once sketched for him. He thought he saw her crouched over her pad but it was just a trick of the light and his fevered brain.

This was too lovely a spot to lie unloved and untended. He knelt by the bank to pray for forgiveness once more. Did the soul of Abel Barnswell wander here in torment? If so he must lay the ghost to rest and pray for its repose. Would the Lord of all mercies look down favourably and restore His peace once more?

He rose painfully from the cold earth, leaning on his stick. He must not idle about here but make for the sign of the Red Lion and the route north. His heart seemed lighter for this detour, the words of the Hebrew scriptures springing from his lips as he marched onwards:

Praise, for the earth restored to goodness;
Praise, for men and women restored to themselves;
Praise, for life fulfilled in sacred celebration.

The Shed Garden

Iris

⌘

The church clock chimes nine and it's still light. Miss Bagshott watches Lady sniffing the trail of a hedgehog under
the bushes. She lifts one paw, not sure of her prey. At the
orchard gate Iris leans out over the silent meadows and sees
the twinkling lights already lit in the camper van which is
parked for the night further downstream in Mill House field.

She hopes the young couple have had another good day in
the Archive Office tracing their ancestors, a friendly earnest
pair of Americans all the way from Phoenix, Arizona, spending their honeymoon vacation tracing the bride's relatives in
the parish registers and rolls, searching among the ancient
tombstones for Barnsleys, Bagshotts, Baileys, Salts, her forebears; not, they assured Iris, in the hope of finding themselves
akin to nobility but to ensure those past souls would not
miss out on their eternal inheritance within the Church of the
Latter Day Saints who baptise their forefathers and hold the
world's largest genealogical archive.

Aileen and Barney had knocked on her door and asked
if they might park their van and Iris invited them in for tea,

telling them all she could remember about the history of the village. In truth village history was not her strong point but she could remember some basic facts from her classroom talk on 'Our Village'. The couple declined her Earl Grey in favour of orange juice and clung to her every word with gasps of, 'Ahh! Yeah?' Iris sighs at the thought of such a worthy quest.

Perhaps someone some day might include me in the blessings of an afterlife. I suppose I ought to have an opinion on the matter and this garden teaches me I'm mortal enough every time I bend down to push the wheelbarrow. So many generations have tended this land and passed away but the garden's life just goes on. What is this soil but bits of other people's dust, chalky bones, generations of plants and animals; the compost of many lives?

Have I clung to this place all these years in some pathetic attempt to root myself deep, leave my mark in an everchanging world? Did all the gardeners before me hope to leave something of themselves behind in it, some object, tree or bush, ornament or flower? Is this what our immortality is all about? What will I be leaving behind here: a hotch-potch of plantings, no grand design for sure. But I've put my heart and soul into the place, repairing, restocking, changing bits. Isn't that enough?

If I sell up and move away, will I float rootless once I'm detached from this special corner of the world which has both smiled and spat on me... the place where I was spawned? Is that what I dread most of all?

There's a definite nip in the air. Time to move back to the warmer end of the house, up the shrub path again and around the side to the working end which fronts on to the lane. This is where Bagshotts have shown their workaday face to the world, a no-nonsense, no frills wooden gate opening into a cobbled courtyard-cum-driveway for Landrovers and carts.

The old oak front door is never opened except for strangers yet Iris softens the bareness of the steps up to it with a display of terracotta pots of 'Raspberry Ripple' pelargoniums, like sentries on escort duty, and on the wall a wrought iron manger is festooned with trailing begonias alongside some old drainpipe funnels planted up with silver foliage and scarlet verbenas. She is quite proud of this continental effect, hoping it will take the eye away from the shambolic scene around the corner.

Here there are sheds to be locked up, tools to be collected. The hen run lies empty now. Iris finished selling eggs years ago when that salmonella scare brought in too many regulations. The tithe barn stands silhouetted against the night sky, holding firm against the rigours of wind, storm and dry rot. It has served many purposes in its lifetime: grain store, stable, garrison and garage. Perhaps this is the only bit of the property she should sell. Arthur Devey says it has commercial value and there would be grants. It's self-contained and close to the road, but an ancient building going back to the old Priory would be plastered with preservation orders.

The edges of stone and brick, cobbles and rubble, are thankfully softened by her strays, bless them! Orange mountain poppies and pink chiffons again, feverfew and more *Alchemilla mollis*, verbascums and a thistly clump of 'Miss Wilmot's Ghost' have mysteriously appeared among the workshops, lean-tos, the greenhouse with more broken panes than whole, a whole collection of distressed outbuildings which have seen better days, like fading gentlefolk in dire need of charity.

This was the scene she could see from her attic bedroom window as a child, the end of the garden which grew sheds and washing, spare parts and old engines; a garden of remembrance. How could she possibly think of selling all this?

PART SEVEN

THE SHED GARDEN

1918

'For where the old thick laurels grow, along the thin red wall,
You find the tool and potting sheds which are the heart of all;
The cold frames and the hot houses, the dungpits and the tanks,
The rollers, carts and drainpipes, with the barrows
and the planks'

—'The Glory of the Garden',
Rudyard Kipling

'The Poppy

*The wild poppy or corn rose is plentiful enough and
many times too much so in corn fields of all counties
in this land... The herb is lunar; and of the juice of
it is made opium; only for lucre they cheat you
and tell you it is a kind of tear or some such
thing that drops from poppies
when they weep'*

A Chime Hour Child

❦

T he Sopwith Camel rose up from the aerodrome in the valley, circling high over the shrinking woodland of the Chase, levelling out to circle over Fridwell like a huge bird with ice-cream wafer wings. Every creature below stopped to hear the pish and stutter of the engine as it looped and circled overhead; the deer in the outer forest froze at the strange noise, the dogs barked, the birds scattered back under cover. In the open fields the sheep raised their heads from the grass; the hedge trimmers looked up, scratching their heads in wonder that man could defy the elements and fly like birds.

Women hanging washing from the posts on Fridwell Green thanked God their own sons were safe on the ground even if they were in trenches in some foreign land. They hoped this poor mother's son would get himself safely down again in yon contraption, glad it was not one of them Zeppelins come to drop bombs on the Midshire's factories, striking terror in every heart at the sight of its huge bulk breathing fire like a dragon.

The pilot, in goggles and flying scarf, leant out to wave as he saw the crocodile of school children walking along the lane up towards the heathland, pointing excitedly.

'It's one of ours!' yelled Iris Bagshott.

''Course it's one of ours, yer daft bugger!' laughed Dippy Devey, shoving his nose into her face with a sneer.

'Well, I'm going to be a flyer when I grow up,' she piped up, undeterred.

'Girls can't be flyers… yer too fat! It'd never get off the ground with you in it, Baggypants.'

'I'm not fat, I'm bonny, and my gran says I can be anything I want, so there!' Iris punched him in the back.

'It wouldn't be lady-like to go up in a machine, Iris,' interrupted Agatha Salt, smoothing down her starched smock and shaking it so that it stuck out like cake icing, crisp and white. 'Ladies don't drive machines.'

'Your mam does, I've seen her at the wheel of yourn.'

'That's different, there's a war on and she drives parcels and comforts for the Red Cross.'

'No more talking at the back!' Old Dog Barker, the headmaster, was on the warpath and Miss Weston was gathering up her infant stragglers at the back. 'Get a move on, we've not got all day to do our bit.' The little red brick school which stood out on a limb by the crossroads lay far behind them now. It was time for all the Fridwell contingent to serve King and Country and help their brothers who were serving with the Midshires regiment somewhere on the Western Front.

Iris was puzzled as to where this front was. It seemed to move backwards and forwards very slowly and the Hun kept shoving up against it like a scrum in the school play yard. For four years, nearly all the life she could remember at school, she'd been praying for the Western Front. That was where her big brother Nat was, and the mantelpiece at home was lined with his postcards. Mam had put a special card in their front window which said: SOMEONE IN THIS HOUSE

HAS ANSWERED THE CALL OF DUTY AND IS SERVING WITH HIS MAJESTY'S FORCES.

Nat was nineteen and doing his bit kicking the Kaiser up the arse, Granny Bailey said as they sat by the oil lamp knitting scarves and balaclavas so that his other bits would stay warm and dry. Now the school was doing its bit too. Dippy Devey's brothers were up the front and Iris wished he was old enough to join them. She hated the snot-faced bully for always teasing and jumping out at her from the holly bushes in the lane, scaring her witless by pretending to be the grey lady who haunted the churchyard by night.

Aggie Salt's brother was doing his bit too but he was an officer and Aggie swanked that his bit was better than the other village men's because he was more important.

Today, the headmaster announced they were all going on the hills to collect spaghnum moss for the soldiers. He had shown them a piece of the damp green squidgy stuff which they were to search out and put in baskets for the Red Cross.

'What's it for?' asked Iris to her crocodile partner.

'It's to patch up the wounded soldiers, silly. Don't you know anything?' Aggie sneered, rolling her steel grey eyes fringed with the blackest lashes.

'You don't patch up soldiers, do you? Granny patches up Granddad's trousers and his shirts at the elbows. Dad's always patching up your dad's tyres for him. Do they sew it on then?'

'It's for the wounds, stupid, to heal the gaps. At the Red Cross meeting they pack up the moss and send it to hospitals with the bandages they roll. I know because my mother told me.'

Why did Aggie Salt switch between being her best and worstest friend every time she opened her gob? She was the biggest knowall in the school but would only be staying there until it was time for her to go to a private school in the city. The Salts lived in the grandest, newest brick house in the village, down by the old water mill, with their own pond and lawns with gardeners. Iris was never allowed in the house of course but sometimes played with Aggie in the stables.

The Salts were the first to buy a motor car, which seemed to spend most of its time in the Bagshotts' barn where Dad got under the bonnet, stripping down the engine and buffing up the brasses. Aggie's brother, Henry, was a friend of Nat's until he went away to school. He was the big hero of the village: in the cricket team, a popular member of the Hunt. Aggie was always crowing about him. Iris wished it was Nat in the aeroplane doing his fancy stunts above their heads. That would take the shine off Aggie's apple, to see Iris's brother up in the air above them all. Everyone knew that Air Force pilots were the bravest of all those doing their bit.

The school party straggled across the heathland, gathering moss into the laundry baskets. Out of sight of their teachers the children raced and hid, fought and scampered in the bracken, getting filthy. All except Aggie who stood aside from any rough play, preferring to gather wild flowers. Soon Iris's legs ached and her feet were rubbing against her boots which were too tight. She kept sprouting like rhubarb and Mam had to keep letting down her hems and widening her waistband.

'You're going to be a big lass for a Bagshott. That must be the Bailey side of you. But you've got the dark eyes and shaggy brows, and hair the colour of conkers, just like all of yer dad's kin. And the cheek as well. No one can talk down a Bagshott when they're well oiled. Stand up straight or you'll get a curved back.'

As they walked slowly down the hill back to the village, tired and hungry, Iris could see the smoke rising from Fridwell, washing fluttering in the breeze and the two cottages where all her family lived together, cheek by jowl, Granddad and Granny in the stubby bit they called Friddy Piece and Mam and Dad in the longer half of the stone cottage with its tiled roof.

Gran said in the olden days it was once all of a piece but had lain empty for many years until it was turned into two cottages for farm workers. It lay snuggled against the church and the lane but the back was Iris's special place and she couldn't wait to be home to see how her tadpoles had grown in the old pond. Why couldn't they gather moss every day instead of being shut in the dark classroom? Aggie raced her down the lane, waving as she sped off towards the lower village and the big house. Iris skipped to the gate. For once there were no clanking sounds coming from the barn or hammering from Granddad's many workshops. She was starving and could eat a horse. She tore up the cobbled yard, in through the open door and down the passageway to the kitchen.

The grown ups were sitting around the deal table in silence, Mam, Dad and her grandparents. There was a hush she didn't like, food on the table but no one was eating and Mam's face was the colour of an ash bucket, all silvery grey. She was twisting her apron into a tight knot. Dad stood up awkwardly, his dark brows knitted together in a frown. Iris stood in the doorway, suddenly afraid. 'What's up?'

Mam wafted a piece of paper. 'Bad news, our Nat's gone missing…'

'Missing from where? Can they find him again?'

There was a terrible silence in the room and Dad handed her the note. 'I regret to inform you that a report has been received from the War Office to the effect that Private Nathaniel Bagshott was posted missing on 29 April 1918…'

Iris did not understand.

'He's just missing, not… not gone, is he? Gone to heaven like Tommy Arnold's brother and Susan's and Albert Machin's.'

Granny sniffed into her hanky.

'Shush, don't upset yer mum. He might be a prisoner somewhere. We must just hope and pray.'

Dad was tinkering at the slopstone, trying to fill the kettle. He was never in the kitchen unless for a meal; he looked out of place and smaller with a kettle in his hand.

'Here, I'll do it.' Iris lifted it out of his hands and slung it on the range. Mother said nothing but sat with her head bent. Iris could see the grey strands sprouting like silver wool in her hair.

'It's such a shock for our Rose. To have gone two years and now this, just when things have taken a turn for the better. Still, it's not for the likes of us to understand the will of the Almighty.' Granddad sat dabbing his eyes, tears glistening on his walrus moustache. 'And such a grand lad. Summat to be proud of, a lad like that.'

Iris looked out of the window to the blue sky and the spring green of the leaves. Somewhere out there Nat was lying still like a dead rabbit in a trap. Were his eyes open? Did the flies buzz over him? He was gone. She knew it deep in her belly. Now she would have to wear a black arm band and the poster in the window would be taken down and changed to one with a big black border around it. She would be important at school until the next telegram came along. I'm never going to see Nat again, she thought, and shivered. All they would have of him would be that serious-faced soldier in uniform in the picture on the mantelpiece and that wasn't Nat at all.

'I'm going out… I'm not hungry now, Mam.' Iris fled from the kitchen as fast as she could. There was only one place to hide.

She hid by the little stream at the bottom of the garden. She loved to watch the water trickling over the stones and search for little fish, all the time clutching Nella, her wooden-faced doll, trying to remember not to get her clothes wet. Nella was very old with pretty petticoats and a muslin top dress stitched with ribbon. She had once belonged to Granny Bailey's granny and should not by rights be outside but everything was changed now and nobody had the heart for Sunday rules.

After worship at Barnsley Green Primitive Methodist Chapel where Granddad was a pulpit preacher it was usually straight home for quiet Bible stories. There had been many condolences, prayers and pats on the arm, as word got about. There were boys lost similarly all over the nearby villages for the Midshires were in some 'push' again. It was rumoured that Captain Henry Salt was also wounded and Dad had driven his family to the city station to catch the London train for he was not expected to live, apparently.

Today Iris lay back on the damp grass, not bothering to search for fairy rings and toadstools or wade through the flag irises chasing frogs. She could not be bothered to run through the ghost walk at the bottom of the garden between the church and the orchard where the grey lady often drifted like mist. It was a spooky overgrown path where the tangled bushes grabbed at your arm, nettles stung your legs and the rooks swooped and cackled overhead in the churchyard beyond the old brick wall and the gate with the creaking hinges. She never ventured through the gate to Saint Mary's. That was the road to hellfire, Granddad said for: 'Wide is the gate that leads to perdition!' The archway over it was of fancy stone pillars carved with squiggly figures; part of the old broken monastery wall which encircled most of their land.

When she went to take the spring bunches to old Granny Bagshott's grave she was careful to go the long way round by the path along the stream, the narrow way. The primrose path, she called it, with its pale lemony flowers on the bank, buttercups and purple violets. Today she did not feel like going anywhere.

They had joined a new club now, not the Mutual and Friendly where you paid sixpence a week for sick relief but a silent club with only one rule. As a sign that you belonged there was a black-rimmed poster in your window which said FOR KING AND COUNTRY, and people spoke in hushed voices when you passed and stared pityingly. A club where everyone wore black and was 'in morning' and there was never any afternoon. Visitors called to express their sadness, saying what a clever lad Nat was, going to the grammar school and getting an education. It had cost them dear to send him for Dad worked at this and that but mostly mending machinery and cars while Granddad laboured on the nearby farms.

No one bothered with this end of the garden; the wild bit where Iris could play undisturbed in her own magic land. Here no Devey boys bullied her or mother chivvied her to feed the hens, see to the stick collecting, gather some greens for the caged rabbits. No Aggie Salt to pull faces and call her names. No bloody Kaiser pushing up and down like a yo yo, and no ghostly picture of Nat staring out from its black drapery.

There were only wild things to play with and they didn't know about any of that. She could escape here. Dad could burst his chest yelling but she couldn't hear his orders or Mother's sighs and Granny's tears. Here she was Queen of the country and she made the rules. Here Nella and Muffy, the old dog, obeyed her orders. No one else knew about the kingdom and she could do as she pleased so long as she didn't get too dirty and came in for meals on time with hands rinsed clean at the pump.

Iris knew she possessed this part of their garden with a certainty beyond her eight years. Friddy's Piece belonged to her: the orchard, the bog pond, the stream, but most of all, the Ghost Walk and Stinging Nettle Lane which led into the heart of her kingdom.

Everything here obeyed her command and she needed answers. Iris looked at the dandelion clocks which always told the time or if your sweetheart was true. Perhaps they could tell her whether Nat was still alive. She picked off a clock gently and sat down. One puff for yes, the next for no... puff, puff. Today not one of them would tell the truth for they all gave different answers. She tried to conjure up a memory of Nat on his last furlough.

He'd looked so grown up in his khaki, his puttees and black glossy boots and peaked cap; a proper soldier, with a wispy moustache on top of his lip which made Mam weep with pride. Where was he now? Puff... puff like the fluffy seeds blown away into the air? She knew Dad would go down to the far orchard field and tell the bees in the hive that one of the family was missing. Why did everything go on the same, the sun come up and go down, the moon rise each clear night?

I don't want a postcard picture. I want my brother to come home. I want the telegram to be wrong, all rubbed out with an India rubber, all of it dusted off like chalk on the blackboard.

It was lunchtime and she was ashamed that her tummy was rumbling. Queen as she was she could not hold back time or banish the Sunday ritual, but she would go on puffing at the clocks until she got a comforting reply.

'Here, let me help you with that luggage, Captain Salt,' said Jim Bagshott, rushing forward to help the young man struggling with his case and stick while coming out of the city station. 'Do you want to drive her? She's the best yet.' He pointed to the car with its biscuit-coloured folding hood and gleaming leather upholstery.

'No... perhaps later when I've got rid of this damned stick.' The young man took little interest in his father's latest automobile.

'Bit of a surprise, you coming home so soon. Your mother will be pleased.' The chauffeur sighed, thinking that since that final telegram of confirmation his own son would never be able to fling his cap round the door and give his mother a hug.

'I'm terribly sorry about Nat, a fine soldier... one of the best.' Young Captain Salt could not look at his driver.

'We did hope, sir, just for a bit. But then we heard the truth of it. Still it's grand to see you back. You've made a quick recovery, considering...'

The young man fell silent, his dull eyes averted. As he'd suspected, his injuries were the subject of some speculation. He sat in the back of the open-topped Model T Ford, already searching out the familiar landmarks; the three spires of the Cathedral, the tall rings of the gas works, the rise towards the ridgeway, the green hills of home. Another world, away from the mud, the shelling, the hospital tents, pain, numbness and the pitiful remnants of his Midshires regiment. He felt ashamed to be alive while Jim's son and his pals were cut to pieces by shrapnel in some bomb crater, crucified on wires, rotting in the quagmire.

Stop it! No more such thoughts. You're going home, no more looking back. No one in Fridwell wants to know the truth of it all. Don't talk about it and you'll be safe.

Mother had sat with him and Father coughed and wept, looking away in embarrassment when the nurses came to dress Henry's wounds. He had seen the tears. 'Just a cold, old chap.' Reginald Salt was not one to show much emotion, leaving that sort of thing to the ladies. Their visits had been awkward, painful, and the silences uncomfortable. His father didn't know what to say about such unspeakable injuries. Henry could see him trying to imagine his son's sorry fate.

The reconstruction had been done cleanly and promptly. It was adequate enough for passing water, a bit lopsided, painful when peeing at first but at least he had a bit of a stub. Some had nothing much left. Many took one brave look at what was left of their manhood, turned their faces to the wall and died.

As he was joggled on the back seat he could feel the twinges in his side growing worse and bent double with the pain. His driver turned round and saw his green face. He stopped the car with a jerk.

'It's all right, Bagshott, drive on… early days. Stitches, you know.'

Jim Bagshott didn't know but he could guess the poor bugger was in agony down below. He'd heard the rumours that Captain Salt got a blighty in the worst place of all.

Henry thought of the family at The Grange, wanting to embrace him and touch him, mollycoddle him as their hero returned against the odds. His war was over now, finished by a blighty in the goolies. There was no place for a eunuch in the trenches – a bloody eunuch, fit only for a desk job or a Sultan's harem! Why was I not killed with the others, with men like Nat Bagshott, one second charging over the trench wall, the next blown to smithereens? But at least a good clean death, not a lingering one like Charlie Machin, hanging on until his leg swelled into a balloon and turned black. Now only Henry was left to tell of their passing but never to grandchildren of his own.

Outwardly he knew he looked like any other officer returning from the face of Hell: ashen and baggy under the eyes, vague in his manner, as if he couldn't really see ordinary folk going about their daily grind. His thoughts were constantly slipping back to his friends who were mostly dead now.

'Stop!' he told Bagshott. 'Stop here, thanks, this'll do. Take the bags on up. I need a bit of fresh air. Tell them I won't be long. I'll walk from here up by the brook. If I'm not home by dark, send out a search party.' He tried to smile but was shaking with fear.

Henry lit a cigarette and dragged in deeply to steady his nerves. He needed to control the homecoming, accustom himself to public exposure slowly, savour his own thoughts before the onslaught of good wishes and curiosity. Besides Aggie would be a fusspot and a pain. She was too young to understand.

He paused by the brook, standing on the stone culvert bridge for a moment and walking slowly past the willows which hung their branches into the water. He could smell the fresh clean-rinsed scents of summer. He would follow the stream up towards the square church tower, he decided. In the distance he could see the outline of The Grange, its tall chimneys and fancy brickwork. Over the wall would be shaven lawns and edged pathways, neat borders full of Mother's favourite flowers, tea on the lawn. Nothing had changed much there. But he walked on towards the village and the cottages by the church.

His heart was pounding from the exertion. He was unfit, out of breath, and still not sure if he wanted to go on living in this clean, neat English world. He was a stranger now for he came from a foreign country the likes of which he hoped none of them would ever have to see. He stopped and took in big draughts of air to steady himself and saw the child watching him.

The girl was sitting by the stream, dangling her feet in the water, picking watercress. It was Jim's girl who played with Aggie sometimes, a sharp-faced creature with big staring eyes and a mop of dark hair tied up with a ribbon on top of her head. She stood up, shading her eyes in disbelief to see his uniform. She waved frantically. 'Is that you, Nat? Nat... Mam! Mam! He's come home!' She turned to run up the slope towards the cottage.

'Stop! Stop – Iris, isn't it? It's only Aggie's brother, come for a walk. Captain Salt!'

She turned back and glared at him fiercely.

'I thought you were sent to hospital?'

'I'm home now for a while, just walking up the stream to see if it's all still there, like the old days.'

'Did you see our Nat?'

'Yes, I saw him, Iris.'

'He's gone missing and we had a letter. Is he with Jesus in Heaven?' The girl was looking up at him, expecting a reply.

'I expect so, along with his pals.' That should soothe her, he thought silently.

'I don't think so. He's still in the ground. They never found him. Aggie says he's all in pieces somewhere.'

'Little Miss Knowall isn't always right. He'll be buried properly,' Henry lied. How could you tell a child or a mother that a body could lie for days before being collected or was scattered to the four winds with the next shell? 'Are you two still falling out?'

'Yes, and I don't care, she's not my best friend anymore. I don't have friends, but I have this garden all to myself and it doesn't argue like she does. It doesn't tell tales or take sides. Look, this's my patch.' Iris pointed to the tumble down wild den where she had fixed up a tepee of sticks and cloth.

'You are lucky. I'm surprised it's not turned over to potatoes by now, with all the shortages.'

'They shan't! I won't let them. Everywhere else is fruit and veg but not this. Would you like to walk around it?'

'Not now, Iris,' Henry humoured her. 'I must be making tracks. You look after your garden. I know… knew a man who made a garden in the trenches…' He stopped himself. He suddenly could not bear to think of Percy Allport's rock garden. ''Bye, young lady.'

He turned back along the stream and walked through the church gate into the cemetery where so many of his fore-bears were buried, generations of ancient Salts going back to Domesday. His branch of the line would end here up a siding for no seed would ever grow from him. Henry felt dead inside but the charade must be performed, duties rendered, visits paid. It was time to face the reception party, see the pity in his parents' eyes. Time to die again.

Iris walked back up the slope to tell the others she had seen the Captain. She stopped by the orchard to tell the bees but the hens clucked round her feet, wanting to be fed, so she ignored them, searching among the sheds for someone to tell all her news to.

Granddad Bailey was a man of many sheds, tools and opinions. He collected sheds like Granny collected bits for her button box. First was the hen hut with a wire run to cage in the birds from the fox who feasted around the village at night. Then she lingered by the pig sty where the fat Tamworth snorted in the mud with a grunt. She never could look the poor pig in the eye for she knew just where he would be hanging before Christmas. Meat was tightly rationed now. Next along the line was the smelly hut made out of all sorts of coloured bricks to shelter the manure. What a pong! Pig muck and horse dung from the lane, chicken droppings, anything that would rot down. A cloud of flies was buzzing all over it and she held her nose in disgust as she passed.

He was not in the woodshed chopping up logs. This was where she shoved the bunches of kindling sticks and furze which it was her chore to gather after school. She peered through the panes of glass to his greenhouse where the tomatoes grew on long stalks. It had been carried in pieces all the way from Parsonage Farm where it had lain rotting for years. Granddad put it together like a jigsaw and it leant against the old wall with relief, facing southwards. Here the cat stretched lazily on one of the benches, raising its head to greet her.

The next shed was his usual hiding place and Iris loved to sit on the stool watching him pricking out his seedlings into little clay pots. The smell was sweet and sickly, a mixture of fish and bonemeal which he sometimes gave her in a bucket to spread on Mother's roses. There was an earthy mouldy smell too and Iris loved to finger the tiny packets of seeds which he kept in a tin box with a scratched picture of the King and Queen's coronation on top. On the high bench which came up to her nose he stored his pots, string and ropes. A line of garden tools, oiled and rust-free, were neatly tied with loops on to hooks. It was like a shop full of spades and shovels, hoes, rakes, sickles, forks and brushes. There were Oxo tins of nails which rattled and shook like music and she fingered them. It also smelled of creosote and tar, which got up her nostrils, linseed oil and baccy, which Granny didn't approve of as a Methodist so Granddad sucked strong peppermints to scent his breath. There was always a little box of them hidden here. Iris liked rooting in this shed the best of all.

She would find him perhaps in his Sunday best shed, painted black and boarded neatly. This was where he wrote his sermons for the men's class on Wednesday nights. The local men came for a chat. It kept them teetotal and out of the Plough and Red Lion, Granny said.

Dad never went to the men's class but they all stopped off to chat with him and examine his latest machine lying stripped in the barn. Sometimes it was just a piece of farm machinery but lately he'd had some interesting automobiles, a Prince Henry Vauxhall and, of course, Mr Salt's new Model T Ford in for a decoke or a service. Mam said he ought to go and sleep in the barn, he spent so much time there.

One day Nat would have had the garage, Bagshott & Son, but not now. Since the war began no one was allowed to use their car much. The farm machines kept Dad busy enough and he 'chuffered' people to and from the station. Most of the village folk had to use Shanks's pony and walk, or beg a lift in a dog cart.

When she looked out of her bedroom window in the attic Iris liked to see the barn door open and hear all the familiar noises stirring the place to life. But since the news that Nat was gone it was strangely silent in there and Dad's face often had a grim look on it. He didn't whistle any more.

She would sink back under the bedclothes, looking up at the way the walls were curved with thick beams. She could bang her head at either end. Iris liked being high and lifted up above them all in her nest. There were lots of night people up here too: a girl with a sad face and a very old lady with a smile. Sometimes the wispy grey lady joined them along the passageway which linked the rooms. Mother had painted the walls and put up lovely flower drawings which she'd found in an old trunk under the stairs. Dad had framed them in polished wood and some were kept downstairs in the parlour on show.

The night people ignored Iris and went about their business. She never told anyone of her visitors. They kept her company when the wind howled over the roof and the moon was hidden and her candle blew out. She knew they meant her no harm for they belonged here as much as she did. Sometimes there was a warm smell of rose petals and smoke wafting through the walls but lately the cottage had been sad and silent. Everything had changed since the bad news came.

Percy's Patch

Iris caught glimpses of Captain Henry on his walks around the edge of the village. He walked alone at the quiet ends of the day or sometimes drove the Salt horseless carriage with Aggie sitting waving in the back seat. Iris was cross that her friend had a brother to crow about now that there were so many telegrams in the village and the list of fallen heroes grew ever longer; farmers' sons and the blacksmith's grandson, even Old Dog Barker's eldest was now a prisoner-of-war. The honour of having a black-edged poster in your window had lost its swank value at school.

The first week after they were officially notified that Nat was dead, Mother shut herself away. She scrubbed the passage-way, scoured and pounded all the spring bedding, bottomed the house thoroughly. She cut up Nat's school uniform to start a peg rug and Iris never saw her weep. She just screwed up her face tightly and clenched her fists whenever anyone spoke to her about him.

Granddad suggested a memorial service at the Chapel for there was no body to bury, but Mother would hear none of it. She would wait until the war was ended and only then, if he did not come home, would there be a memorial. Inside her there was still a flicker of hope which never quite went out and drove Dad to distraction. Mother muttered to herself a lot nowadays and wore a dirty pinny. She never brought flowers into the house and couldn't be bothered with her rose bushes.

There were queues for every item on their shopping list; the horse and cart farmer measured the milk and butter ration; even bread was portioned out. The grocer's cart never had any treacle and Dad said it was time to sort out the garden again to grow more stuff for themselves.

Then came the terrible afternoon when Iris came home from school to find all the men in the bottom garden with a mechanical plough, turning over her patch, grubbing up Stinging Nettle Lane and the Ghost Walk and even through to Fairy Glen.

'What're you doing?' she screamed as she watched all the wild patch churned over. The bushes ripped, her tepee destroyed. All that was left was bare soil. It was no use yelling at them to stop for it was all destroyed. 'But it's my garden,' she wept.

'It's no use being mardy, our Iris. There's a war on and we need food in our bellies this winter. This'll do well for tatties and roots... Think of all the soups your mam can fill us with. Food doesn't grow on trees, you know.'

'Yes, it does. Apples, pears, cherries...'

'Don't be cheeky with me! You've had your playing with it, now it has to earn its keep. You can look after the patch, if you like. You can be Dad's little helper.'

'But I don't *want* soup... I want my garden. The veg have stolen my kingdom. It's not fair!' She had gone to school Queen of the realm and come home robbed of it all. How could her own dad be so hard?

'Iris Bagshott... come back here or I'll clip your ear.'

'Leave her, Jim. Leave her be. We all have to make sacrifices but she's too young to understand. It was her play den. Come on, child. It's not that bad. You can have it back when the war's over.'

'Why can't the King fight his own battles instead of Nat doing all the work?'

'We have to do what's right and fair. We're lucky enough to have all this ground to grow food. And it won't be forever.'

'But it won't be the same, will it?'

'Nothing will be the same after this war, we have to accept that,' Mam sighed. Iris turned away, sniffing back tears, and ran off to the banks of Primrose Way. If her kingdom was lost for now, perhaps forever, she would never look in that direction again. She was the banished Queen of the fairy stories but one day she would return and never leave this place again.

It was raining. Iris sat in the kitchen at Granny Bailey's with all the contents of the button box spilled over the oilskin cloth of the kitchen table.

'Tell me again about the chime hour child?' She loved to hear the story of her birthing. It made her feel important and only Granny Bailey could tell it properly, with all the gory details and the relish of one who had actually been there on such a momentous occasion.

'You were born just as the parish clock struck the half-past or was it the quarter hour... a real chime hour child, born with special powers, never to be bewitched in life. Your mam and dad waited many years for your coming after Nat.'

'That's the story of the rosebuds, isn't it? The little rosebuds under the bushes. Mother's little roses, too small to flower...'

Iris could never pass the rose beds without thinking of all the could-have-been brothers and sisters buried there.

'Yes, she kept losing her rosebuds and Granddad and I put them away nice and close by so they would make her flowers grow. That's why she loves her rose bed. But when you were born... Ah, well! I didn't need to look out a burial gown or a box to put you in. I took one look and knew you were going to be staying around. There was something in the way you gripped my pinky, minutes after you were shed.' Granny grabbed hold of her little finger and squeezed it tight. 'Just like this.' Iris did the same.

'And she called me Iris.'

'We called your mother Rose, and she called all her girl babes after flowers... Lily, Daisy, Lavender, and then you, Iris Rose, the last. Your mam's a brave lady and now she's having to be very brave.'

'She never cries, Gran, just scrubs and cleans all day and won't sit down. Dad gets cross with her.'

'I know that's how it takes some but he's no better under the bonnet of some carriage or locked in his barn all hours. It's hard to lose a son.'

'But they've still got me?'

'It's not the same for a man. He had great plans for his worksheds. The Bagshotts have come a long way fast, from the town slums back to field work and engines. A man likes to think there's a son to keep his name going.'

'Can't girls keep it too?'

'They get wed and change their names.'

'I'm never going to change my name then. I shall be Iris Rose Bagshott all my life.'

'Oh, you'll change your tune soon enough.'

'It's not fair! Aggie Salt's dad got his son and his name back.'

'Aye, but at a price, lovey, at a price. His name'll not be going on if what I hear is correct,' Granny said in hushed tones.

'Why?' Iris did not understand.

'You're far too young to be told of such matters. Captain Salt will not be getting wed, now nor ever, take it from me.'

'He can marry me and then we'll both keep our names. I like him, he listens when I talk…'

'Don't you go pestering him with questions. He's an officer and a gentleman. He'd be far too polite to tell you to push off.'

Iris was fingering all Granny's collection of postcards and picked up the pretty tinted ones from Nat. 'Shall we put these in your box along with the other bits?'

'Of course, all of his cards must go in my box. But he'll live in our hearts as well. We don't need bits of paper to remember him by.'

'Tell me again about all the bits and bobs?' Iris was examining each item spread out before her. It was raining outside and she loved having her Granny Bailey all to herself.

'Surely you know them by heart by now? You tell me where they came from, so you'll always know about your kin.'

'This is the button from Billy Bailey's soldier's coat who fought at the Battle of Waterloo, yes?'

Granny nodded her approval and Iris picked up a piece of faded creamy lace.

'This is from the gown of a lady at Longhall Manor who once lived in this house, given to your great-granny who was her maid.'

'Her name was Susan and the lady's name was Hittybel, I think.' Iris always laughed at the sound of that name.

'This is a sea shell from the Coral Islands off Wales which was brought back by a preacher to the Chapel to show the Sunday School there is a real sea?' Granny smiled and nodded.

'Here's the pretty ring you found in the garden patch with no stone in it but made of gold, and the cart wheel penny you found by the barn door that's got a King's head on it. This's the bit of flower off your mam's wedding bonnet, who worked at Longhall in the dairy.'

'And this here's your Great-granny Alice Barnswell, in the photograph on the mantelpiece. Isn't she a fine looker, like your mam?'

Iris knew which piece to keep 'til last: a little length of striped orange and blue crinkly ribbon. 'Here's your sister Nora's ribbon, the one who was taken by Jesus just before her wedding day.'

'Don't forget the tin badge we bought off them ladies who called on the village in a horse and cart and stood on Fridwell Green and asked us women if we wanted the vote. Your mother felt sorry for them so she bought the badge. She's all in favour of it. I just liked the colours so she gave me it for my box. See, green for hope, white for purity and purple for sacrifice. Nothing changes, does it? That just about sums up these times.'

Granny Bailey sighed. 'Come on, enough chattermongering, you're holding up the works. Go and fetch me some potatoes from up the garden shed and take these bits of paper to the privy while you're at it. These tatties have gone manky. It's a good job they're on with planting the late crop. We shall be needing them come winter.'

'I hate vegetables!' Iris puckered her face into a pout.

'Think of the starving children in poor little Belgium.'

'They can have mine, if you like?'

'That's enough lip. Off and do your chores.'

★

As spring became summer, Henry Salt kept to his room, finding the atmosphere at home stifling. His mother fussed incessantly, overfeeding him and wanting him to tell her all about his injury. He could give her only the sanitised version and was thankful that his memory of the worst bits was beginning to fade.

Sometimes he woke and it was as if he was back there in the trenches again... explosions thudding through the soles of his feet as he was edging forward on a push; pain which shoved him flat on his face as the shell cut into his left thigh. Something had gone right through his chest and when he came to again he was lying in the mud, thanking his lucky stars it would soon be nightfall and the stretcher bearers might risk coming up and over to collect him. In his dreams he would relive the stench and the filth and the fear of rats gnawing at his open wounds. He would call out and no one came to rescue him. He could see the faces of dead men, their limbs crawling with maggots. Soon they would come to get him... He would cry out, waking in a sweat, feeling the pain in his balls which were no longer there.

By some miracle he was found and taken to a dressing station where a doctor saved his life by treating his wounds promptly but shook his head at their severity and put him in the moribund tent. Henry lay with the dying ones, listening to their gasps and cries of: 'Mam... I want my mammy!' It was always the last name on men's lips as they died.

The nurses were surprised to see him still alive in the morning and shunted him down the line in an ambulance, bumping over the ruts, the first of many agonies. Then a field hospital and afterwards he was laid by some railway track in the Red Cross tents where an angel in white fed him tea through a spout before he was shipped off to the port.

Henry lay on a stretcher for five days in his own filth,

listening to the groans of other ruined men. At some point he was taken to another hospital and cleaned up again, examined and patched together for the journey home. Hours and hours of being carried like a lump of meat, the pain of jolting movement and the harshness of plaster on his raw flesh and the horror of the maggots which sucked off his pus, keeping him alive. How could he ever tell of the humiliation of seeing his private parts picked over and examined, heads being shaken and commiserating looks directed at him?

Now the first flush of visitors had dwindled to the local Vicar and his wife who hovered meaningfully, as if about to give him a blessing. Henry never wanted any of that stuff again, not after he'd seen how some Padres ducked and dived away from danger. Only the Catholic priests stayed all the way with their men, kneeling in the mud and throwing back grenades to protect their injured. As the weeks went on it grew harder for him to rise from bed in the morning. He had no energy even to think about the future, to shave or wash or eat. His thigh ached with every movement, but it was toughening, the stitches held.

Henry could feel a strange void in his trousers, a movement of air. Sometimes he could swear all his tackle was in place, could feel it, but when he looked he saw the empty space again. He did not want to think about it.

He would go for a walk up into the Chase and shoot some rabbits. At least he could still shoot a gun straight. His hands might tremble but his aim was sure enough.

He had forgotten just how beautiful the woods were, coppiced spruce, larch and beech beneath the oaks, with the peppery sweetness of fir cones floating in the air for good measure.

A carpet of bluebells lay as far as the eye could see, dappled light streaming down on to shades of purple, lilac and the bluest of blues. The scent of the flowers brought back memories of those walks up to the front in springtime, before the French woods were destroyed by shell bursts, but this was the wood of his childhood, a place of magic and promise, fairy tales and dreams.

How many times in the trenches had he tried to lose himself in scenes of home, to stiffen his courage and resolve to stay alive? For this he had fought, this piece of England, this blessed plot, this Midland heartland. And it was still safe from the enemy. When all around him had been blackened stumps, craters swimming in blood, when all that grew fat were rats tussling for the limbs and bowels of his own men, it was thoughts of this beauty which had kept him sane. Now he was here, alive, home at last, Henry felt nothing but a terrible aching sadness.

What was the point of his endurance? He might as well be dead if he could not feel anything. Here was as good a place as any to end it all. If he could not return to active service, he might as well be dead. What use was a man who could give no heir nor service any woman? Better to end his humiliation privately with this shot gun, now.

But he had seen so many botched jobs in the trenches, the guns swerving from their target, maiming instead of killing outright. He had watched one poor soul take three hours to die with half his brains stuck to his helmet but enough left to let him suffer agonies of remorse for the impulse to end his suffering. Perhaps he should go deeper into the forest and find a sturdy trunk to sit by. He remembered his first Sergeant's words: 'When I does a job, I thinks about it three times, measures it up twice and does it once properly.' He must do the same. He would take off his boot and sock and put his gun so… placing the barrel carefully in his mouth. Then he could stretch his foot and fire the trigger. Henry fingered the stock, feeling the polished smoothness of the wood. He checked his bullets. One would be enough if he did the job well. There was a steel-edged calmness to his actions. He had all the time in the world to do the deed.

He checked in his pocket for his wallet and an envelope. Thank goodness he had a pencil tucked into the leather binding. He must leave no loose ends, no questions as to the balance of his mind. Never had he felt more certain, more sure, more excited. Why had he not thought of this before? He would say his farewells and try to explain why he cared nothing for the future.

Then he saw the girl, dark-haired, roughly dressed, yanking up the bluebells by armfuls and staring at him.

He jumped up, furious at her wanton waste of flowers. 'Here, you! Stop that at once, you vandal… they've just as much right to live as you. They'll be dead before you can get them home to a vase.

'Oh, it's you, Miss Bagshott. We meet again. Hasn't your own garden any flowers?'

'Not any more, Captain. It's all been dug over for tatties.' She was looking down at his bare foot but was too embarrassed to say anything.

'I'm sorry. You liked your garden.'

'How do you know? You never saw it. Aggie did, though.'

'Still, when someone likes a garden they can make one anywhere.'

'Like the man who made the garden in a trench?' Those black eyes looked up at him questioningly, expecting an explanation. They sat down and she cradled the bluebells in her arms.

Fancy the girl remembering that, strange child. He would have to amuse her... damn it, she was distracting him from his purpose, Henry mused.

'Last summer, when it was a bit quiet before a push, a group of men decided to dig out a garden. There was this lad, Percy Allport, who at home was a gardener in a big place near Walsall. He set to and built a rock garden. There was no shortage of white stones and boulders to place around it and he collected all the coke cinders and clinker to make a path edged with stones. He found many wild flowers in clumps, poppies and broom and wild geraniums, and dotted them about his patch. Set quite a fashion for a while. Talk about green fingers! He got lads bringing in seeds and cuttings to sprout. There, in all that mud, he made this lovely garden.

'Then they had a competition to find the best blossom garden in "no man's land". Really and truly. I can't explain how but it got them fired up. One group created a funny garden out of shrapnel and tin hats and statues made from broken bits of machinery. I liked Percy's flower garden best, though. It was the first and the best.'

'I suppose flowers don't know there's a war on, do they?' said Iris. 'Did he miss his own garden back at home?'

'Yes, he missed his bit of turf so he made another where he was. There were so many poppies... fields of red poppies. How they grow on the battle field! Percy said they liked freshly turned soil, and there was plenty to feed them.' He stopped, hearing the quaver in his own voice.

'Is it still there then?' Iris leaned forward, fascinated by his clean white toes and the bumps on top of his foot.

'No. When the shell fire came back the garden disappeared but Percy kept on making them wherever he was until he...'

'Until he went home or went west,' Iris prompted. She knew

about going west. It meant more black armbands and wreaths on the door.

'I expect so, but *you* mustn't give up. You could make a rock garden anywhere like Percy Allport did. It makes one think.'

'How would I get the rocks?'

'Some boulders out of Fridwell brook would do the trick. You find another spot and we'll see what we can do, eh?'

Iris nodded solemnly. What a strange thing, for the Captain to be standing here with one shoe on and one shoe off. Didn't he realise?

'Will you help me?' she asked.

He smiled at her.

'Yes, I think I can manage that. Or at least give you a start.' He could see her looking down at his bare foot and wondering.

'I think you'd better wear both your shoes, if you do.'

He turned back for the boot and his gun, feeling both foolish and grateful at the same time.

Captain Henry was true to his word. The following week he called in at the garage-cum-barn to discuss the purchase of a touring roadster, a four-seater Chevrolet, with her dad. Iris hovered by the door, listening to all the guff about double declutching, horse powers and miles per hour which seemed to get them all excited. She wandered back to the kitchen, bored by this grown-up talk. Mam peered out of the window, watching the tall young man and her husband as they pored over a mechanical diagram.

'Just what yer dad needs to get his mind off things. What is it about those carriages that has them jumping about like dogs with fleas... nasty stinking things!

'Poor Captain Salt. He's hanging about like a knotless thread most of the time. Can't stick at anything, they say. Too much money and time on his hands, *I* say... still all the stuffing's been knocked out of him.'

Mam darted back, seeing the young man coming towards the kitchen door. Iris went to greet him shyly and ushered him inside. 'I've come to borrow your daughter,' he said. 'We're going to build a special garden, aren't we?'

Mam looked puzzled. 'Has she been bothering you?'

'Not in the least. But I promised, and a promise is a promise. So where shall we start, young lady?'

During the weeks that followed, Iris paced over Friddy's field to decide just where to put her new garden and plumped on the corner by the old fish pond which was choked with bulrushes and green weeds. There were plenty of old stones and the Captain marked out her patch with twine. She wanted to make it in the shape of a heart, edged with stones. Captain Salt nodded and began to dig out the turf, pausing to draw breath every so often as if the task was draining his strength. Once the ground was cleared it was redug and sieved and extra soil added to make a mound in the centre.

'What did Percy Allport have in his garden?'

'Only wild flowers, I told you.'

'Then we can have a clump of soldiers and sailors. They're red and blue mixed up, like an army.' Iris pointed up their garden path to the straggly clump of spotted pulmonarias lying under the old hedge.

'I suppose they might do, but why not have something which will stay green all the year round?'

'Like what?'

'A bit of lucky heather for winter days. I like heather. It reminds me of Scotland and the hills.'

'I don't know it,' she sniffed. 'I want poppies, bright red ones, dancing...'

'I'll see but it's a bit late to plant them now. We can sow seeds for next year perhaps. 'Til then I'll scrounge what I can from the gardeners at The Grange.'

Henry felt like a child again, poking about the formal borders, annoying the old gardener who liked to keep a strict eye on what went in and out of his garden. He was one of the old school and much preferred the Squire to let him get on with it unquestioned. Mr Reginald never followed behind him like a ghost while this young man did and actually had the cheek to dig up a clump right before his very eyes for some silly patch he was growing. The war must have addled his brains for him to be concerning himself with things which were not in his realm at all. It made the gardener nervous. Whatever next? People like the Salts might start digging their own gardens and what would become of him then?

Henry took to reading up on all the plants which took his fancy. It was funny how he had never noticed how tall the monkey puzzle tree was growing, the way the pampas grass waved in the breeze, the file of red pelargoniums lining the driveway like an escort of Guards.

Sometimes when Iris was at school he would dig up more earth and extend her patch further, slipping in extra boulders for effect. Jim Bagshott got used to seeing him pushing the wheelbarrow off down to the field though Granny Bailey thought it mighty peculiar for a toff to be down the bottom of their land, thrashing about like a navvy.

To Henry it felt good to be lifting, sorting, digging. Pulling out the weeds from the pond became almost an obsession.

He had planted a mixture of bedding plants to give bright colour, some evergreens, anything which took his fancy. The next Saturday morning Iris went down to Percy's Patch and didn't recognise it any more. It was one huge flower bed with red salvias stuck next to French marigolds and snap dragons. To her eye it looked a bit of a mess.

'Did you do this?' she said to Captain Henry accusingly, dark brows furrowing into a deep frown, her lip curled.

'Don't you like it?' Henry stood back, admiring his handi-work.

'It's not Percy's Patch any more, is it? It's like the flowerbeds in the Valley Park. Why did you change it? I thought we were going to make it red, white and blue and put flags in?'

'And I thought you would be pleased.' Henry felt deflated by her obvious disappointment.

'Is this what Percy Allport's garden was like in the trench then?'

'Well, no, his was smaller and there was a lot more earth, I've told you before.' He could see every detail of that pathetic bunch of weeds with its paper flags and stones tracing out the Staffordshire knot. A special garden, never to be reproduced anywhere except the trenches. 'I wanted to make ours a bit more cheerful.'

Iris put her hands on her hips.

'But it's not cheerful, is it? It doesn't fit in this field, does it? I wanted everything jumbled up...' She was nearly in tears.

'I thought you'd be pleased but you're a fuss pot like all the rest,' he snapped impatiently.

'I know what I wanted and now you've spoilt it.'

'I see! Thank you very much, young lady.' What a cheek, criticising his artistic endeavours. He thought he'd captured the spirit of Percy Allport's garden, embellished it even, but the girl was right, damn her. It did look out of place in this field.

There he goes, spoiling it all, thought Iris. Why did grown ups have to interfere, take over and ruin her dreams? First her fairy kingdom with its dainty plants and hedgerow pickings, pixie stops and magic circles. That had gone under the plough, and now this silly garden wasn't at all the way she'd thought it would be.

Captain Salt had been her hero, someone who had bothered to give her his time. Now he was just like all the rest: dim, dull and deaf to her dreams. Once again Iris felt very alone in this topsy-turvy world. She would never understand the rules.

She was fed up with silly gardens and broken promises and things she didn't understand. From now on Iris would stick to playing with Nella and Muffy among the sheds, teasing Aggie Salt and getting under Granny Bailey's feet.

Henry whistled as he lurched his way down the winding lane from the Red Lion at Longhall. He was drunk enough to feel merry and mellow at the same time. If his CO could have seen him, building a garden to the orders of a nine-year-old girl and then taking the huff at her displeasure! What did he know about gardens anyway and what did he care? Why had he even bothered to humour the child?

Because it amused me and because it kept me alive, giving me something to get up for each morning. The stare of that fiercesome child stopped me from using my gun, ending it all in the forest, and I've never dared go out shooting alone since.

But you're still alive, old boy. Nat and the other village lads weren't so lucky. You have choices, the dead have none. Time to stop farting about, dear fellow, and find yourself something useful to do with the rest of your life.

I can carry on feeling sorry for myself and give up. Shoot myself. Or I can get on with the life I've been given back, move on, find some new interest to absorb me fully...

The more Henry thought about it, the more he felt that perhaps his future lay with motor vehicles, bikes and transport. There was definitely a business to be made there. He was never happier than when racing around the country lanes at speed. The excitement and danger got the sap rising again. Just because he was crippled in one place didn't mean he was useless everywhere.

Jim Bagshott was a sound chap. Henry would need a good motor mechanic with ideas whatever he did. Perhaps they could rent some premises in the city, hire out vehicles for outings or run a fleet of charabancs. The ideas were flowing fast.

They could invest in the future, maybe get the old Pater to cough up some dosh to fund the business. When all the soldiers returned there would be a new demand for transport using engines not horses.

For the first time in months Henry Salt was thinking forward not living in the past and that challenging prospect no longer terrified him.

On the morning of 11 November 1918 there was a frost and a sharp bite in the air. Iris was sitting at the wheel of the latest vehicle in for a decoke, pretending to be Lady Oftenbroke. Dad was cranking up the starting handle, yanking it round, his breath hanging in the cold air. Nothing happened so he tried again.

'It's frozen. Usual rigmarole, our Iris. Get the kettles going.'

He found the enamel basin and began to drain the radiator. Iris dashed into the kitchen.

'Kettle drill, Mam. Hot water treatment.'

They all knew the routine. First the kettles had to be boiled on the range, then in came the sparking plugs for a clean and warm up. If all else failed they would be doused in petrol. 'I'll give your dad hot water! Coming in with all that grease and them smelly fumes on him. Don't you get dirty before you've even got to school.'

'Do I have to go?' moaned Iris, for the news of the Armistice was far too exciting for her to be thinking of school. Mam waved her towards the door.

'Take our flag and join the parade. It's only right to honour the day. But don't ask me to join in any of it.'

'Do as your mam says and get out of her hair,' said Grandad Bailey, who was composing a celebratory verse for his Armistice sermon.

Soon the kettles had boiled and were poured into the radiator, the warmed up sparking plugs were put back in the engine, Dad and Grandad took turns to start up the engine and, wonders of wonders, it pished and spluttered into action. The best treat of all was to be driven up the lane like a princess alongside Dad who was taking the car back to its owner in Longhall. All the boys stopped to admire it when Iris got out.

No one could concentrate on lessons that day, not even Old Dog Barker who was quite pink in the cheeks and smiley for he knew his son would be coming home from the prisoner-of-war camp at last. Iris couldn't get her tongue around the word 'Armistice'. Was it something to do with arms being stiff after all that saluting? Agnes said she was a dumb cluck and everyone knew that an Armistice was a piece of paper which was signed to say there wouldn't be any more fighting ever again. So Iris kicked her and made her cry and then gave her her own snot rag and said she was calling an Armistice in the playground. Aggie ran off and went to play with some of the other flower girls, Ivy and Vi. Iris joined the crocodile of boys as they wound down the school lane into the village and in and out of cottage gardens, singing and dancing. No one seemed to mind the noise.

The village was awash with coloured bunting, flags, red flannel petticoats hanging out of windows. Even those who were sick with this new Spanish 'flu managed to get themselves to their window to join in the celebrations. From the Cathedral to Barnsley Green Chapel and Longhall the bells rang out, filling the air with their glad news. Only then did Granny Bailey actually believe that this terrible war was over. Mother brought out some of her hidden rations and baked some buns to hand around on the green. Everyone stood chatting out of doors, wanting to stay close to each other. The war widows and bereaved mothers in black made their own special huddle, weeping gently into their shawls, and for the first time Rose Bagshott shed healing tears for her son. Iris was too busy playing tag to notice any of this. Someone brought out jugs of ale but the Bagshotts drank only sweetened tea.

'The cup that cheers but does not inebriate,' intoned Grandad.

Henry Salt heard the news and walked alone along the banks of Fridwell brook, cursing and weeping and thinking of the dead. He passed the church gate and the bottom of Friddy's Piece field where Percy's Patch lay forgotten like an overgrown grave, the flowers wilted and the stones silted with mud. A few clumps of greenery limped on sadly but its brief hour of glory was past.

As far as the eye could see the Bagshott plot was thronged with vegetables like a market garden. Yet here, in this ramshackle corner, he had found the path back to life. Henry could not take his eyes from the stream as it rushed past.

'Time like an ever rolling tide bears all its sons away.' He remembered that hymn. Iris was right. Theirs would never have been a proper trench garden. It was too green, too full of hope. There would be other memorials and statues to come, all clean, white and unreal. No garden of remembrance could ever bring the dead back to Fridwell or tell the true horror of war. But thousands would return, a silent army of walking wounded who had visited the borders of Hell and now could not speak of it.

Yet Henry sat by the water full of gratitude. What contrary spirit had moved across this piece of earth and saved him from himself?

In the Heart of the Garden

Iris

◆━━━━━◆

Iris surveys the lofty barn roof with its crack beams swathed in cobwebs, sniffing the lingering odours of her childhood; oily rags, petrol, rubber, polished leather upholstery and exhaust fumes. In this old barn were the humble beginnings of S & B Motors. Out of it grew the Fridwell Garage and petrol station, the charabanc tours, taxi and car hire services, which saw both Salts and Bagshotts through the inter-war years and into new premises on the main road. Their modest prosperity enabled the Bagshotts to buy the freehold of Friddy's Piece and to knock the cottages back into one when Granny Bailey finally passed on.

Now the barn houses only her ancient Sunbeam Talbot which sees Iris safely into the city for the weekly shop and back; the sum total of her driving these days. Each year she threatens to give up her licence but each year conveniently forgets her vow.

Iris shuts the barn door and closes the gate, hovering by the 'For Sale' sign. Should it be there at all? The goodbye gate was always left open to let in cars for repair; the gate through which she bade farewell to Nat, and to her own childhood when she went off to teacher training college the year Granddad Enoch made his last journey to Barnsley Green Chapel.

So many goodbyes at that gate when another war threatened; goodbye to the fly-by-night soldiers and airmen from nearby camps in the forest who came to strip down their motor bikes in the barn and never returned to collect their spare parts; goodbye to so many wartime pashes and friendships; goodbye to the evacuees whom Mam welcomed as long-lost sons, billeted on her briefly during the worst of the raids in Birmingham. There were so many memories attached to the garden of many sheds.

Time now to turn back towards the cottage for that last and dearest bit of the tour, around the side of the house and up the slope of friendship's garden to where my heart lies buried. Through another arch of evergreen honeysuckle and laburnum, a path edged with many shrub cuttings to remind her of friends: golden forsythia in the spring; white Japanese anemones shining in the moonlight in autumn; orange Chinese lanterns tucked by the low wall together with purple euphorbias and silver *Eucalyptus gunnii*; the tassels on the *Garrya Elliptica* already forming nicely. So many joys to look forward to from gifts representing a wealth of past friendships.

How could I have hated gardening so much? For a time Friddy's Piece lay neglected like my cold heart after the Dig for Victory efforts were over. Then just when I was growing old and bitter, when I thought romance had passed this sleeping princess by, the magic garden kissed my frozen heart alive.

PART EIGHT

FRIDDY'S PIECE

1956

'To be happy for a day – get drunk.
To be happy for six months – kill a pig.
To be happy for a year – find a wife.
To be happy for a lifetime – make a garden'

—Chinese proverb

'Mistletoe

This rises up from the branch or arm of the tree whereon it grows with woody stem putting itself into sundry branches... it hath no roots of its own. Some have so highly esteemed it for its virtues thereof that they have called it... Wood of the Holy Cross.'

'Lore

Large bunches are hung up in houses at Christmas. All who meet beneath its branches should kiss as a sign of friendship, peace and goodwill'

Arrivals

The heron circled the frozen fish pool, alighting at the edge to stand like a grey statue, upright, alert to morning movement. In the silver field a rabbit sniffed the air; a fox slunk into the shadows of the woody copse. On Friddy's barn roof a blackbird pinked, watching the tortoiseshell cat pad its way sleekly across a thick bough overhanging the gate, curling itself, waiting to pounce for its breakfast. The blackbird screeched the alarm and flew higher out of reach. December was the blackest, cruellest of months for birds and beasts as they scavenged for the last of the food, huddled together for warmth.

In the winter garden at Friddy Piece Cottage all above ground was frozen and dormant, crusted and nailed hard by frost, but far below there was a flurry of movement. Moles were mining a tunnel to the surface, turfing up a fine tilth, and worms turned again, sifting and reburying all the hidden treasures though the snowdrops were fast spearing upwards for their brief January show.

In the cottage the loo handle cranked but nothing happened. Iris turned on the brass tap in the bathroom. Just a splutter of brown water dribbled out. She sat on the wooden seat and howled with frustration. 'It's freezing and damp and now there's no water. What a welcome home! Thanks very much!' She stormed out of the bathroom, kicking the black banister rail and stubbing her toe. 'It's not fair, not bloody fair!'

A hot tear of self-pity rolled down her nose and acid rose in her throat. It was no fun to be starting one's forty-sixth year alone, with Christmas approaching, without even a single invitation on the mantelpiece.

I should never have agreed to come back now the house is empty and Mother gone. I can cry about a frozen pipe but not about all the other things.

Iris perched on the sill of the mullioned window, halfway up the stairwell. Funny how it was the place she'd always thought of as hers in the house; a snug hideaway out of sight of the grown ups.

What am I doing here? she thought, scraping the frost ferns from the inside of the pane and licking the ice from her fingers.

For months now she had shed no tears. There was just this frenzy of grief; sadness and fury were like two tethered horses trying to gallop in opposite directions, tugging the guts out of her. How could she have been so naive as to think Gerry would ever leave his teaching post and his wife for her? How could she have clung on to their stolen moments, burying herself in after school activities, prolonging the moment when she must leave to face her empty flat? Now the whole world had gone topsy-turvy, with hostilities breaking out in Europe and Suez. She didn't know what to think of it all.

Mother had managed well enough on her own. S & B Motors was run by Henry Salt when Dad died. She tended the garden throughout the war, filling the house with evacuees, doing her bit and never complaining that she was out of breath and bone weary, until the afternoon when she came into the kitchen and fell asleep by the fireside.

You and I never got to say goodbye or make our peace, thought Iris. A senseless argument over her affair had led to a serious quarrel which festered for years in stubborn silence.

Now I can't make any of it right. You wanted what was best for me and I was blind to your love until now. I don't deserve to be living here. How could anyone be so blind, so stupid, as to ruin their career over a love affair?

In wartime there were passionate encounters all around her but Iris had stayed unscathed. Then, once it was ended, Gerry Parker arrived fresh from his emergency teacher training course with wife and child. Iris found herself drawn into a passionate friendship and then a clandestine affair which had lasted ten years before one day she bumped into Gerry's wife, six months pregnant, radiant and full of news, gabbling on about them moving down south to a new Headship. So much for his 'not sleeping with the wife for years' routine, and all those wasted years of Iris's life.

Now she was marooned among frosted fields with over two acres of jungle, ramshackle outbuildings and stables; hemmed in by narrow lanes with familiar hedges. She had struggled up the ungritted winding lane in Gertie, her neat blue Standard, slithering on patches of black ice treacherous beneath her bald tyres. It looked like a scene on a Christmas card but that tunnel of a lane on to the hilly ridge was dark. The wooden gate stuck fast against her on the gravel. Not a promising start. Not one friendly light to guide her in the gloom of a December dog day. The wooden sign was half hanging off the gate, its plastic letters announcing FRIDDY'S PIECE.

'Home at last!' she muttered, fumbling to find the key in her bag and sort out which door it would fit. Despite the alterations it was still a higgledy-piggledy sort of building with windows all over the place and no symmetry. Inside the air was cold, and smelled of Izal and disuse.

She hoped she might feel more kindly disposed to her old home after she had lit the fire. Disappointment stuck in her throat like a fish bone. I've stayed away too long and now dampness has invaded the place, she thought. The rosebud wallpaper was peeling off the wall. The oak beams were painted gloss black and ominously pitted with holes overhead. Here and there were white bare patches where pictures had once hung.

Friddy's Piece would have to stay as it was, unloved and unwelcoming, for a few months until she could get her confidence back enough to apply for some menial job. She had given in her notice and fled back to the Midlands, using her mother's death as an excuse to get away from Gerry's embarrassed avoidance in the staff room.

The tortoiseshell cat stirred with disdain at Iris's entrance, curling back on to the chair close to the fire which was almost out. Someone must have been feeding her for she looked smug and plumped up. There was just enough coke in the sack for her to stoke the fire back to life. After that she would have to do a Cinderella and collect twigs and ferret in the outhouse sheds for any dry wood. What a pantomime that would be!

She switched on the kettle which did at least have some water in it from the night before. Nothing. She tested the light switch. Not a flicker. No wireless either. The power was off. A rush of panic flooded through her as she paced back and forth on the sticky lino which curled up at the edges.

I don't believe it! No water, no power. What am I expected

to do… die of thirst or freeze to death or both! The metal tips of her shoes banged down the stone passageway to the door into the cobbled courtyard leading up to the kitchen patch. She was looking for the water butt to flush the loo. Banging her arms across her chest like Magwitch in *Great Expectations*, she stormed down the garden path, snagging the sleeve of her thick cardy on the over hanging rose thorns.

From the top of the garden she could see the rooftops of the ribbon of cottages strung out along the high road to Barnsley Green. There were no lights anywhere in bedrooms or kitchens.

The crow of a cockerel startled her for a second. Sometimes she could still hear the roar of city traffic and buzz of cafe chatter, the overhead drone of aeroplanes and clink of milk floats. How quickly she had forgotten the sounds of country living, especially the cawing of the rooks from their churchyard roosts, the rumble of a distant tractor, a dog barking in response. Now the silence was broken only by a trickling, gushing sound.

She pushed her way through the undergrowth like a pioneer to find the source. There at her feet, running from under a mossy stone culvert, was the old spring which tumbled into the brook, half iced over with frozen weeds curling at the edges. The water looked clear as crystal and Iris stooped down, scooping her hands to taste. Metallic, sharp but drinkable. Buckets and pans would do the trick. She smiled with satisfaction, remembering her Girl Guide days of campfires and tents. Now sticks could be gathered for the fire, candles from the cupboard under the stairs and pans filled. All was not lost. Iris Bagshott would survive.

As she marched purposefully back to the cottage she surveyed her domain. Her eyes glanced up at the lead-paned window seat and she thought for a moment she saw the face of a child peering down at her. Iris blinked in disbelief and looked again. There was nothing. Chime hour child or no, now you've really flipped over the edge, girl, she chided herself. Wake up, this is no dream.

Where did she start first? Iris looked around the kitchen with dismay. This would be a Herculean task. The larder shelves were sprinkled with mice droppings, the cupboards swimming in silverfish. She wanted to shove everything into the bin and start fresh but there was no time to nip back into the city for her trunk would soon arrive from the station. The first task was to fetch up water from the stream and light the old range. At least with some hot water she would feel civilised again. There was still no power and snow was beginning to fall on top of the ice outside.

She swept out the kitchen dust and stood back, leaning on the brush to picture once again all the family gathered around the table, smelling the roast meat and steamy fug of a childhood winter. Home was always safe and warm before the fallings out and arguments about the garage and the Salts and the premises.

Henry Salt was ruled by his head and Jim Bagshott by his heart. It was inevitable that they went their separate ways in the business. The Captain ran the show and Jim ran the motors about, gathering and depositing people around the district. By the time of the Second World War Henry was an officer in the Home Guard and Dad tagged along with the rest of the Fridwell gang to the local Drill Hall.

Then Henry Salt made an unexpected marriage to a young slip of a war widow whose husband had died in a Jap prison camp, a lively lady with a small son to support. Flora

Bowman and her boy James brought new purpose to his life and put the sparkle back into his eyes. Iris liked the woman but she was everything that Iris was not: smart, energetic, pretty with her snub nose and bright green eyes, indefatigable at WI meetings. Mother had said her heart was in the right place but never worn on her sleeve.

When the child went off to boarding school Henry and Flora took holidays abroad in Jersey and the South of France. Iris caught glimpses of the glamorous woman in her mannish slacks, driving a jeep at top speed. Daunted by her air of enthusiasm she tried to avoid Flora Salt on her infrequent visits home. Yet at Mother's funeral Iris had been touched by her kindness and frequent visits though still determined to keep the lady of The Grange at arm's length.

As the crow flew Flora was her nearest neighbour now that the cottages down the lane were derelict and the farms dispersed. Fridwell had shrunk to little more than a hamlet; all the shops had moved to Barnsley Green and the school scarcely supported itself. The water mill was disused and empty and Parsonage Farm was turned back into a house. The quietness of the place would suit her fine, Iris thought as she scrubbed on her hands and knees, back and forth across the grimy floor with the old brush, worn away in the middle from all her mother's efforts. It was oddly satisfying to be so violently busy.

Then she heard the rat-tat of the front door knob. Iris's first instinct was to duck down and ignore the visitor but a voice called through the letter box, 'Iris! Iris, is that you? Only me come to feed the cat. Saw the car…'

It was Flora Salt, standing in her winter glory covered in snowflakes, a trim fur hat and thick pre-war sheepskin jacket worn with tweed trews and wellingtons. Her cheeks were flushed and pink as she shook off flakes on to the clean floor.

'Whoops! Hard at it, I see... That's the ticket. And just in time, eh?' She beamed and Iris stood up, knowing she looked like a stoker's mate.

'Mrs Salt, how kind of you to call.'

'Tosh! Call me Flora... if you'd told me when you were coming, I'd have sent Mrs Barnswell down to lay a fire and dust a bit. No water? It's frozen solid again right up the lane. I shall have to get on to the Council to lay the pipes down lower. The power line's playing up again too. No peace for the wicked, eh? Still, not as bad as some, eh?

'The rush is on, Iris. All hands to the pumps now the refugees are arriving. Can I count on you? They've rustled up some sort of transit camp for them out of the old barracks in the forest. You know the sort of thing – for medical checks and rehousing. Not exactly Butlin's but the best we can do at such short notice. So much to do and only three weeks to Christmas. James will be home from school soon and poor old Henry's tied up with the garage. If you're at a loose end, I could find a ton of jobs for you.'

'But I've only just arrived and there's so much to do here!'

'I know, I know. Just like the poor blighters stuck out in the woods in this weather, with only the clothes they stand up in, no families or comforts and so far from home. Doesn't it make you weep? I feel so sorry for them, don't you?'

How could Iris admit that the current upheavals in the world had slipped her by unheeded in the midst of her own misery and isolation?

'What exactly happened to them?'

'Iris dear, have you been living on another planet? It's been in all the newspapers though squashed out by the Suez crisis, of course. These poor people tried to hold back the Soviet tanks for days as they rolled through their cities, and died in their thousands in the attempt. Didn't you hear that terrible broadcast, "The light is going out in Hungary. Help! Help!" I'm surprised at you, not knowing that.'

Flora stood four-square, her fair hair gently waved and caught in a clip at the side, nails polished pink, fingers stained with nicotine.

'Come on, Iris, where's your Christian compassion?'

'A bit thin at the moment. How can I possibly entertain people here? I'd hardly be good company for them. But when I'm sorted, I'll think about it.'

'Tosh! They won't notice a bit of damp! I'll pick you up tomorrow and you can see it all for yourself. It's awfully bleak up in the forest, and there are children too.'

'Do you want some coffee, I've only got Camp…'

'No thanks, I ought to be getting along. Just wanted to see that old Topsy was OK. We've been feeding her, hope you don't mind?'

'If it wasn't for you the poor old thing would be dead. She looks contented enough. Thanks again.' Flora stood in the doorway, watching the feathers of snow settling on the path.

'At least it'll cover up the jungle out there. Your poor mother would have a fit if she could see it now. Shall I send Grumpy Greggs to see to it for you?'

Iris smiled to think that the old gardener who had shooed Aggie and her out of his domain was still at work.

'He must be ninety! No, please, it'll have to wait. I may sell up and move on, then someone else can have the pleasure.'

'Nonsense, you can't sell the family home! How proud Rosie was to own her own place. Give it some time. We don't want to lose you just when you've returned. You're far too valuable an asset to the village. I was only recently telling the ladies of the WI how you saved poor Henry's life.'

'I did what?'

'You heard. When you were a little girl and he was so badly wounded in the war. It all got too much for him and he went into the woods to end it all. Then up you popped from the bluebells, making him feel very foolish. You and your little garden helped him stay around.'

'I never knew all that.' Iris was taken aback by such frankness. She stared out at the whiteness covering the ground.

'How could you? You were only a child, and a stroppy little madam by all accounts,' laughed Flora. 'Never underestimate your own strength. Whatever has brought you home to us, you've arrived just in the nick of time. Welcome back. It's good to have you on board.'

'Wait a few weeks before you say that!'

For a brief second she wondered if she might tell Flora all about Gerry but then drew back. 'Give me time and I'll help you out.'

'Good show. See you tomorrow then.'

The women struggled up the twisting dirt path through the oak woods to the barracks, bouncing over the snow-lined track in Flora's army surplus jeep. It was a slow bumpy ride and the windscreen was soon splattered with dirt.

In front of them, looming out of the mist, a man limped his way back towards the camp; his shoulders were slumped under a gabardine mac several sizes too big for him. He wore a black beret and carried a string bag. Flora shoved on the brakes and jerked to a halt, almost flinging Iris into the windscreen. 'Let's give him a lift.'

The young man jumped back, startled by the noise of the engine. He whipped off his beret, revealing dark hair slicked back. His shabby clothes were obviously straight from one of Flora's salvage boxes.

'Lift?' Flora smiled but the man stepped back, unsure. 'You, camp?' She pointed far into the distance and then to Iris and herself in an exaggerated gesture. 'We... go... *à la* camp?' She turned to Iris appealing for back up.

'*Parlez-vous français?*' Iris leaned across the dashboard to make eye contact. The man shook his head.

She waved to the back of the vehicle. 'Here, in the jeep, hop in?'

He saluted them with his hand and made for the back of the jeep, opening the flap to climb in amongst the boxes piled high with clothes and groceries gathered in the Hungarian Relief Collections in the city. He turned his back on them, dangling his legs over the edge until they reached the check post at the gate of the old barracks. The refugee jumped down, bowed to them both and limped away without uttering a sound. The women watched the lone figure in silence for a moment.

Iris looked around in dismay at the depressing sight before her. It had always been the windiest and bleakest of places, beautiful in full leaf and in autumn but the forest here always dark and forbidding. In this secluded camp the military had carried out secret manoeuvres.

'This is grim, Flora. Just rows and rows of battered huts in the snow. What a place to escape to.'

There were groups of men and women lounging about in doorways, smoking and watching the new arrivals.

Flora waved at them. 'It's better than prison, torture or execution back home. The interpreters are all telling the same grim tales. They've chosen to come westward in search of a better life but of course new arrivals must be vetted and checked over. Wouldn't put it past the Russkies to slip a few spies through the Iron Curtain, posing as genuine refugees.'

'If that's the case then they'll soon be wishing themselves back home, far away from this bleak spot in the middle of nowhere!'

Iris was trying to imagine what they must be thinking of their new abode. 'Whoever they are, they've had to leave wives and girlfriends, mothers and children behind. Freedom will cost them dear. Anything worthwhile usually does. How do they pass the time? It's miles from the nearest town.'

'Living like POWs mostly. Playing cards, reading old newspapers, mending their clothes and waiting for the next mealtime. They've rigged up a cinema and there's the old gymnasium. It's not that long since there were National Servicemen here... surely you remember them? They're trying to put on a few lessons but it's been hard to find interpreters and English teachers.'

It needed little imagination to see how quickly boredom would set in, stuck in this foreign land with no money and no means of communication. 'Someone ought be organising crash courses in Common English to help them settle in. Take their minds off what they've had to leave behind. Keep them busy over Christmas, don't you think?'

'Right on the button as usual, Iris, so what are you waiting for?' challenged Flora. 'You're a teacher, you live close by, you've no work on...'

'Hang on a minute! I've never taught English as a foreign language before. I wouldn't know where to start.'

'Start with all the words a stranger would need to know and read to get themselves from A to B. Then words to do with food, asking for directions, greetings. Lots of practice at speaking and writing. Most of them are young and bright with spunk enough to have got themselves to safety here away from the tanks and the tyranny. They'll pick up English soon enough, given direction. Let me put out a few feelers to see if we could start a group.'

'Don't go treading on any toes, Flora. They may have it all set up already and I'd only be a nuisance.' Iris could feel her pulse racing at the thought of such a commitment.

'Rubbish! There are hundreds of them here. They'll be grateful for any help they can get. Don't you worry. Leave it all to me.'

'Bulldozer!' Iris slammed the jeep door with a smile.

'Come on, where's your Dunkirk spirit? Give me a hand with these boxes and I'll show you round the camp.'

Iris looked around the bleached landscape. Not much of a place to be spending Christmas. She tried to imagine herself in their predicament. If the Germans had driven their tanks up the Trent valley would she have thrown herself before them in protest? Or would she have fled across the sea to Ireland, America or Timbuctoo in search of a better life?

She saw again the dark eyes of the man by the roadside, his gratitude and effort to understand. How could she ignore people in such a plight? Flora was right. Never ignore the impulse of your heart. The hour was chiming loudly.

'Give it a try, Iris. You can only do your best,' she told herself.

What have I done? thought Ferenc Hordas, lying exhausted on his bunk. The long walk uphill had strained his tendon again and he could feel the dull ache of his weak calves and poor circulation. He mustn't lose his muscle tone or he would never play football again. Coaching it was so much a part of his life that he had hoped to get a few games going here, but no one had the energy. He was weaker than he'd thought and his chest hurt but he rubbed warmth back into his legs with the ease of long practice. Yet his heart was cold, ice cold.

The two women with smiling eyes had briefly touched it with their spark of kindness in giving him a lift back. There had been sympathy and warmth but his soul was frozen by the knowledge of what he had done. Those crazy ten days of hope erupting into the hell of 4 November. On Radio Kossuth he heard details of the invasion. Comrades who had escaped from Buda had seen tanks lumbering along Stalin Avenue, dragging the bodies of Hungarians behind them as a warning. '*Ruszkik Haza!*' the crowds had shouted from the barricades, fired into acts of heroism by the righteousness of their cause. But words could not destroy tanks and bullets could not hold back the waves of Soviet reinforcements.

The nightmare of his escape still haunted him. His voice was hoarse with shouting and his eyes dried up with weeping for Ilona, his woman. What would become of Ili, who had refused to leave her country and her family; of all those other brave souls who were staying on to nurse the dying and patch up the wounded, or pump petrol into the veins of police spies as punishment for their betrayal? He had escaped over the border while others were still fighting or already dead. He had decided that if he was to have any future he had no choice but to run away.

Now he sipped the last of his *palinka*. The bitter juice of the fruit brandy reminded him of the sunshine of home, the orchards, the lakes and lush vineyards. Never would he see them again. He was doomed to this exile amongst strangers with only the bitter spirit of defeat burning in his throat. Soon his comrades here would be scattered to the four winds and he would be alone. The English priests gave their blessings, the nurses and the camp staff were doing their best to cheer them up, but he was locked in the silence of despair.

English Lessons

The officer sat smoking a pipe in front of a portrait of the young Queen Elizabeth, bedecked with faded paper chains. The mess had made a brave effort to look festive with paper bells and bits of tired tinsel strewn haphazardly around the windows. Iris, who had been summoned for an interview, sat nervously wondering what orders she would be given.

'Miss Bagshott, your students will come and go. This is a transit camp. Three weeks at most and then they'll be off to another hostel and hopefully a job. We don't expect you to work miracles but we're bulging at the seams and most of our intake will be staying over Christmas now. A smattering of the lingo would help them get resettled. Damn' shame it's so near to the holidays, don't you think? Our chaps in Suez and these poor sods... it gets to them all, being away from home and all that.' He sucked on his pipe and sighed.

'Would it help if they worked in my house? It's not far from the camp. I could familiarise them with some of our ways of doing things and teach them vocabulary at the same time. I have a car of sorts.'

'It'll do them good to walk, and you don't want to be

using up your petrol coupons, do you? I'm afraid we couldn't allocate you extra ones and fresh air might cheer them up a bit. Bit of an imposition on you, having strangers and all that...'

Iris shook her head. It would suit her far better to work with a group in her own home. It might settle her nerves and reduce the panic she felt about failing them. What if they came away without learning anything? What if she was useless with adults instead of children? It would make her get off her backside and clear out the guddle of boxes and books, clothes and belongings, which lay scattered around the cottage.

When Flora heard the news she was round like a flash with bags of kindling and sent Grumps the Gardener with coal and logs. She tried to chivvy her friend into some festive decorations too but Iris stood firm.

'First you get me into this and then you try to make me into Mother Christmas! First things first. Just let me get them started. I'm shaking at the very thought of trying to teach them our language. What if I scare them away?'

'Nonsense! You'll be fine, just be yourself. Henry says you're a natural. And don't forget, it's open house on Christmas Day... you're coming to us, and all your students too, of course. We dine after the Queen's speech. Give them some turkey and all the trimmings. Cheer 'em up with plenty of booze, eh?'

Iris nodded meekly. She was in no mood to stop the bulldozer and it would save her making an effort. Food was the last thing on her list of priorities.

Iris frittered away the morning of her first class in a frenzy of anxious cleaning and polishing, as if they were sanitary inspectors not students. The cold snap was back and the paths were like mirrors so she set to clearing away the ice and laid salt and cinders in a sooty trail to the goodbye gate. At least the water was trickling through the pipes and the power flickered only now and then.

She banked up the fire in the old parlour. Shabby as it was, the flickering firelight added an extra warmth to the room, setting her newly polished brass fender and coal scuttle glistening by the hearth rug. Something always drew her back to Granny Bailey's old living room. This was the scene of the happiest of her childhood memories.

The door bell rang and she primped her hair, straightened her tweed skirt and grey cardigan and wished she'd had a cigarette. She took a deep breath. Steady the Buffs!

They stood at the door like a bunch of windswept carol singers on a winter's night, out of breath, silent, as nervous as she was. Each one bowed and shook her hand firmly before she ushered them into the hall and down to the parlour. There was a golden-haired handsome boy with a steady nervous tic to his mouth; a tiny dark-haired woman who could be twenty or forty, so hunched and thin and pale was she. She clung on to another student, a girl with braids wrapped over her head. Three older men stood together. Finally, at the rear, was the sad-eyed young man she'd seen limping up the road. He was shivering, half stumbling into the room.

Once their coats were piled at the foot of the old staircase they went into the parlour. At the sight of the glowing fire their eyes lit up with delight and they all chattered joyfully, warming their hands, sniffing the wood smoke with obvious pleasure.

Iris felt herself relax a little. Everyone loved an open fire on a cold night and she pointed out to them where to sit while she collected pens and paper.

She smiled at their eager faces and pinned a label to her

cardigan. 'I am Iris. My name is Iris Bagshott... Bag... shott. My name is Iris. You say it, please.'

She gestured for them to repeat it slowly and smiled encouragingly as they attempted to copy her. Then she handed them each a pencil and paper on which to write their own name for her. She had been warned that the surname would be written first.

Nagy Peter... Kocsis Zoltan... Kocsis Georgy. Brothers evidently. Eva... Jozef... Magda... Ferenc. 'I am Peter. My name is...'

Over and over again she repeated the exercise. Only the short square-set young man with the slicked back hair remained silent. 'I am Iris... and you are Franz... Frank?' She was struggling to pronounce his name. For a brief second his lips curled into a smile at her efforts. The others laughed. 'Feri?'

He raised his hand in protest. '*Igen, angol*... Iris, I am Frank... ee?'

The ice was breaking and she passed around some biscuits, teaching them please and thank you in a group. They sipped the Camp coffee warily. Iris gathered that they liked their coffee black and strong, thick and in small cups. It was amazing what arm waving, mime and goodwill could do to aid communication but it was hard work for all of them nevertheless.

When the lights were lit around the house, Flora arrived in the jeep and bundled the students into the back. 'How did it go?' she whispered, as if they could understand a word she was saying.

'OK, I think.' Iris smiled shyly. 'It feels like we're climbing Everest. In three weeks we'll barely be in the foothills.'

'Just be thankful it's not you learning Hungarian. It's supposed to be fiendishly difficult.' Flora was leaning out of the window, cheeks raw in the bite of the wind.

'When you get back to camp, please ask the interpreter to see if they'd like to come for a proper English tea on Saturday, if they're free? The quicker we get on with these lessons the better.'

They all waved and practised their 'Goodbyes', calling down the path to the goodbye gate. Frankie lingered there, looking back over the yard and bowing awkwardly.

'*Danke*… Mees Ireese.'

Afterwards she cleared the room and poured herself a large sherry from the bottle she had been going to give to Henry Salt. Iris sat by the fire, exhausted but strangely satisfied. She found herself drifting off into wild dreams of dark eyes and handshakes and the smile on Frankie's face.

'Time to get yourself trimmed up for Christmas. Shift yourself, old girl, down to the bottom of the garden. You've got guests coming on Christmas Eve, guests who'll want to know all about ye olde English Yuletide.'

Iris often talked to herself as she went about her chores but down the garden path, searching for greenery, she turned round to make sure no one was listening. Just the robin on the gatepost and he didn't count.

There would be plenty of yew and woody rosemary wands, a few straggly box bushes and surely some holly at the bottom by the field. Then Iris spotted streamers of dark ivy, masses of it going spare. If she trimmed the mantelpiece with cotton wool and Christmas cards, wound ivy and holly berries around the brass candle sticks and bought a few red candles, it would brighten up the place immeasurably.

But whatever would she cook for her English group? Flora was not at home to guide her for she had whisked Henry and

James off to London to finish their shopping and take in a show, lucky things!

The group was going better than Iris had dared hope, such an interesting bunch of individuals. At first they had been lumped together in her mind as 'the refugees'. Now she was beginning to see them all separately, all with differing needs and abilities. After a promising start Frankie was the one causing her most concern. His attention was always wandering and his cough was dreadful.

They were on to money and sizes in their classes. The women were eager to buy clothes with their allowance, underwear and stockings instead of the terrible hand-me-downs from Flora's charity boxes. Iris cut out masses of adverts and pictures for them to label and price and rehearse the right coinage. It was proving a monumental task as the vagaries of English money continually caught them out. Her students needed to know about tanners and bobs and half dollars, florins and crowns. She borrowed a set of cardboard coins from the local school for them to fathom out and name. She did not want any of her group being cheated by the local shopkeepers who'd diddled the Yankee soldiers shamefully in the last war.

Iris decided to serve hot soup, then cold pork stand pie, chutney and potatoes in their jackets, followed by hot mince pies and cream, washed down with cider and hot ale and spice punch. That should warm everybody up. Numbers were a bit vague and she could squeeze out a few more portions if extras tagged along. She could not bear to think of any poor exile stuck up there in the dark forest when there was a British Christmas going on.

The depression she'd felt on her arrival had somehow evaporated with all the trekking to and from the camp, the classes and her festive preparations. She was far too busy now to bemoan her lot. Having Flora to chivvy her along had proved unexpectedly welcome as well, her ebullience balancing Iris's own natural reticence. Henry had had the measure of the way his wife could bulldoze her way through red tape, restrictions and flannel. She was becoming a true friend.

'Deck the hall with boughs of holly...' Why was she humming to herself on such a grey afternoon when darkness was falling? Iris wondered if there was still mistletoe in the orchard and searched the apple trees where the old swing was tied. She checked the rope and sat on the damp wooden seat, pushing herself off as she had done as a child, not caring if the whole world saw this middle-aged spinster playing games. The winter scene before her, once so familiar as to be invisible, suddenly sharpened into focus. You're lucky to have ended up back in such a place, she told herself. She saw the silvery tinges to the wood, the stark outline of arches and paths in the garden, the warm red brick of the cottage. It seemed all of a piece somehow.

There must be mistletoe in here somewhere. Iris leapt off the swing and rooted amongst the gnarled pear trees. There it was, nestling in the crook of one branch, dark sprigs with pearl berries. Enough to make a traditional ball for the hallway. What on earth am I bothering with mistletoe for at my age? Iris laughed but picked it just the same. Because underneath you're still the big kid with her dreams of bulging stockings and parties when it comes to Christmas...

How would she explain the custom to the group? But kissing under the mistletoe was as much a part of the ritual as plum pudding and Christmas crackers. Magda would help her out. Her English was better than the rest and she knew a little French. Magda wanted to be a teacher and had escaped over the border, leaving her family behind. She would be feeling dreadful at this time too.

As Iris dragged her sack of greenery up to the house she caught sight of some little white flowers poking through their dense green foliage: the Christmas roses. How could she have forgotten that bunch on the shade path which Mother always preserved for Christmas Day, placing them on the table in a china egg cup? Dad transplanted some to the fairy glen which he then promptly dug up. Primrose Path and Stinging Nettle Lane… It was years since she had remembered her own gardening days. I must come back here and pick some hellebores tomorrow in memory of the old days, she thought. Rituals should be followed in the festive season. It was one of the few bits of the magic still left to grown ups, after all.

The tightness in Ferenc's chest was not going away. Sometimes he could hardly breathe when he got out of his bunk. But nothing was going to keep him from that party, even if he had to crawl there on his hands and knees. Lessons in the old house were the sun around which his whole week revolved. They made this place bearable and the dark wintry nights flit past as he recalled the peace of that place.

As buildings went he had seen far prettier ones at home but there was something about the setting and the garden which lifted his dreary spirits. He longed to walk around it at leisure, not capture brief glimpses. His English was not good enough to ask for a tour, though, and Miss Iris might think him forward and ungrateful to want to see outside instead of inside. How could he explain he was used to open spaces and tilling his father's land, working hard to grow food, vegetables and fruit? A man could keep his family well fed in such a garden as this. In the war he saw many bombed out ruins and houses sliced in half, their empty shells decayed and forlorn. He knew not everyone in England lived in a house like this for he had seen their slums from the train, the backs of dreary little houses, black with soot. Iris Bagshott was obviously one of the privileged class and maybe he should despise such opulence but she was so kind and eager for them to learn. His thinking was very topsy-turvy now.

Joining the group had changed his perspective, forced him to mix and talk, forget the scenes of home imprinted on his brain. Familiar shapes and scents, like Ilona's face when he kissed her, so many scenes to be blotted out. When he tried to study he could lose himself in the exercise and forget his loneliness in the warmth of that room with its cheerful fire spitting sparks on to the hearth rug. He liked the other students. Peter was concerned for him and wanted him to see the doctor in the surgery hut for his racking cough but Ferenc wanted no fuss and no confinement. It was only a heavy cold. If he stayed warm he would be able to disguise his fever.

He wanted to take a gift to the party. It troubled him that he had nothing to give Iris and the Lady in the Jeep. He had nothing on him worth giving and the *palinka* was long since drunk. Was there nothing of Hungary in the camp, no souvenir of home? Only a few makeshift flags, scars and bullet wounds, bitter mementos indeed. And there was one special ingredient which was sorely missing from the flavour of the English food dished up so sloppily to them. Where would he find the magic Magyar spice paprika, the red dust of the orient which brightened up their stews, as typically as soured cream, Liptauer cheese and Tokaji? Yes. Surely someone had had the gumption to bring with them a taste of home?

He asked around the huts and people laughed at his request.

Do you think we had time to bring the kitchen jars with us? When you're swimming for your life, what good is a packet of paprika? We had other things to worry about. He yearned for this taste of home; thought of all the exiles missing from their family tables this festive season who might never again taste the sharp pungence of the spice. He trudged back to his hut and flopped down, feeling the familiar aching sadness creep over him as he watched the moon climb in the clear sky.

Later the men smartened up their shabby clothing, shaved and slicked back their hair with water. The group and some extra friends were driven down to Fridwell in a convoy of battered vehicles. Ferenc loved the moment when the forest track widened and the curtain of trees opened to reveal the plain below and the sloping edge on which the village was perched. He wanted to savour the moment when the car turned through the gate and he saw the smoke rising from the wide brick chimney. Once there he got out slowly to stretch his legs, his breath catching in the cold damp air. He felt the sky whirling round him and grabbed on to the wall to steady himself. Sweat was pouring from his brow and only will-power got him down the path and into the house, making for Miss Iris's sitting room.

When he saw the candles flickering in the half light and the greenery swathed around the pictures he recalled Christmas Eve in the old church at home before the Russians came. The room was crammed with visitors, a noisy cheerful gathering squashed together, but the crush was taking his breath away and he made for the door. Perhaps outside he could breathe. The lady had gone to so much trouble to please them, a table in the kitchen full of food, but he had no stomach for it.

He watched Iris shyly trying to introduce her students to a priest, looking neat in a winter dress the colour of ripe tomatoes. It suited her and with her wavy hair hanging loose on her shoulders she looked younger and more girlish, less severe. For the first time he looked at Miss Iris as a woman, not a teacher, and it disturbed him to be doing so. It felt disloyal, comparing her with others. She was no beauty but those dark eyes shone even though there was a sadness to them at times and he wondered how she had come to be living here alone with no man by her side. In his country it would not have been so. Perhaps the war had robbed her of her lover. He thought of Ilona far away. There was still no message from her though he had written and sent out a radio request for her to contact him.

Perhaps if he found his coat and took a breath of air, walked in the garden, it might clear his cotton wool head. There was a mound of coats on top of his own and he could scarcely lift them. The effort seemed to sap his last reserves of strength. He dropped them and made for the door in a paroxysm of coughing. He staggered out into the dusk as if he were floating, unaware that Iris and Peter were following behind, alarmed by the sound. 'He sick, very sick…' were the last words he heard.

The men carried him upstairs to a cold bedroom high in the roof. Sounds came and went from him. His limbs were strangely light and the ceiling circled round and round above his head. Ferenc sank back on the bed with relief and then felt nothing.

'I ought to put him in the Cottage Hospital,' said Doctor Mac who had threaded his way through the revellers. Having demolished the buffet they were now round the piano, singing the Hungarian carol *'manybol oz angyal'* with great gusto. He examined the man and shook his head.

'This chappie's not been taking good care of himself... his right lung is filling up. He needs watching... I'll ring for an ambulance.'

'On Christmas Eve, Doctor? Is that necessary? If he stayed put here wouldn't that be sufficient?' asked Iris, concerned that her charge would wake up to find himself in yet another strange place. 'I'm sure I can manage, with a few instructions.'

'That's awfully kind of you, me dear, but surely at Christmas you've enough on your plate? Rest and these antibiotics should do it.'

'My plate's not that full. I've time to be Florence Nightingale for a few days. The other students will help, I'm sure. None of them is doing much over Christmas either. But if he's in any danger then, of course, you know best.' Iris did not want to take any risk with Frankie's chest.

'Oh, he'll live. Yer old ma would be proud of you, Iris Bagshott. Not everyone would open their home to strangers on Christmas Eve.'

'I thought that was how the first Christmas happened, room at the inn and all that?'

The doctor raised his eyebrows over his glasses.

'He'll recover quicker in familiar surroundings with nurses who speak his own language but the journey back to camp would not be wise in his present state. The sick bay's a wee bit draughty up there.' Doctor Mac shut his case and bounded down the stairs to his next call. 'I'll be in to see him later. Merry Christmas tae one and all!'

He grabbed Magda and kissed her under the mistletoe, to the astonishment of the foreign guests who wondered if all English doctors did this.

Iris smiled and tried to explain. 'We kiss, so, and it brings peace on this house. Good luck.'

This they seemed to understand and the men winked and stood about in turn waiting for a kiss. Iris ushered them back into the kitchen to tell them the news about Frankie. 'He stays here. He is very sick.'

'We stay?' The group laughed while she looked shocked.

'Beds for Magda and Eva, *igen*… yes. *Nem* beds for you.'

'We sleep here,' said Georgy, pointing to the old sofa. 'All one and one all!' They nodded their heads and laughed.

'Where did you learn to say that?' Iris was so confused she sat down on the kitchen bench to mop her brow. What a strange loaves and fishes Christmas this was turning out to be. Friddy's Piece would be school and hospital, hostel and canteen. She would have to borrow some food from Flora. There was no time to dash into town for a chicken now. Thank God they would all be going to the Salts tomorrow!

Ferenc watched the chinks of morning light seep through the gap in the curtains. He stretched his legs under the covers and stared up at the old beams in his attic bedroom. What a strange dream, waking to find visitors at the foot of his bed: a grey nun-like figure, a child with golden curls like an angel on a Christmas tree, and a tall man in strange costume and fancy waistcoat. So many people trooping through his room on their way to where? Now he was fully awake. His mouth tasted foul and his beard was like sandpaper. Where was he? Then he remembered he was safe in the cottage.

He rose gingerly from the pillow. The tight feeling around his chest was gone. He inched himself slowly to the edge of the high bed and dangled his feet over the side. He could hear the noisy banter of his compatriots, his mother tongue interspersed with broken English, and was half mindful of anxious faces while the doctor examined him. How long had he been up here? Then Iris popped her head around the door and smiled.

'There is life at last! Good. Happy Christmas, Frankie.' She shouted down to the others and they bounded up the stairs to shake his hand and wish him well.

In the days following he made his way downstairs to join Peter, Zoltan, Eva and Magda, who stuffed him with Flora's leftovers, wine and brandy to build him up. The gang conversed in English and his head ached from trying to follow it. Peter was moving north to a hostel soon and Magda to Birmingham with Eva. They would all go back to the camp for the New Year celebrations but he must remain at Friddy's Piece until Doctor Mac gave him the all clear. He was stuffed like a turkey with strange spicey mixtures, including Granny's elderberry cough medicine which had fermented for years in the back of the larder, and made to rub his chest with Vic embrocation to ease his catarrh. Ferenc could not move without somebody waiting on him like a servant and began to feel embarrassed. How could he ever repay such kindness?

When the cottage was empty and all the visitors were out for a long walk in the crisp snow he sat by the fire with Iris, silent as she raked over the coals. How could he thank her? Watching the flames leap into golden light he came upon the first glimmer of an idea. He stood up and drew back the curtains. High above the garden the moon rose, not a paprika moon like the red-tinged ball he remembered from home but a silvery orb highlighting the tips of the branches, the roof of the barn. He mimed his intention and she smiled.

'You want to dig my garden?' she mimed back and they both laughed. 'Not yet, Frankie... but soon, when you are stronger.' Pointing to his chest. He raised his thumb. He understood. 'I dig garden…' And later that month he returned to do just that.

Ferenc spent all his spare time forking over the kitchen patch, pulling out weeds. 'We have shit?' he asked innocently one day, pointing to the ground. Iris fell about laughing at his words.

'*Nem*… We need manure for the soil.'

'Yes, horse shit and cow shit, yes?' Ferenc smiled.

'Horse dung and cow dung, Frankie.'

'Why you say dung, manure? It is shit, yes? I no understand why no shit?' He could not get over all these words meaning the same thing. He would never learn them all. He turned back to his digging.

Iris dug a hole and pointed down. 'When I'm angry, sad or do not understand… I dig hole and shout down it… see? Then I dig it over again. It makes me feel good.'

'You Crazy Horse!' was the only way Ferenc could reply.

They took Gertie down to Flora's stables to beg some well-rotted manure and lugged it back in the open boot to spread over the bare soil. Iris felt a twinge of excitement to see the old patch looking like it had under Granddad Bailey's care.

One by one she said her farewells to the students as they were dispersed across the Midlands. Soon another batch took their place for brief English lessons; new students bringing fresh news out of Hungary. It was getting harder now to escape and there were horrific tales of shootings and drownings. Ferenc sometimes sat in and acted as interpreter but Iris felt it was more like the blind leading the blind when he was in charge.

She became used to seeing him at work in her garden, clearing the ditches and trimming back the rampant hedge growth. He sorted out the chicken hut and cleared the pen for a batch of pullets in the spring. He took a fancy to Granddad's hut and carried a chair down so that he could smoke in peace and listen to the shortwave radio there. It was no real surprise when Henry and Flora came to tea one day and offered him a job in the S & B works. Henry had watched how conscientiously he had cleared the garden and struggled with his English lessons. He would fit in with the other men for he was quick to learn and eager to please. He would be a general workman and do some ferrying about as he had driven trucks in his army days in Hungary. Gertie was commandeered to give him driving practice and her poor gear box took a pasting as he constantly veered to the right when he was not concentrating.

'We ought to put a red flag on the bonnet when you're at the wheel,' Iris teased. 'Red flag! Danger! Stop! Yes?' He was getting to understand her teasing a little. He would pause and give her a soulful look and then the widest grin like a naughty boy caught out in the classroom. One of those looks would melt the coldest of hearts.

Sometimes he stayed late and she cooked an evening meal, once trying to copy a goulash recipe from a 'Round the World' cook book. It was a disaster for it was sloppy and she had put in ordinary pepper not paprika. Ferenc was very polite and tried to eat it but goulash it was not! Even the bottled sauerkraut tasted like cabbage in dishwater. For the first time he talked of home and his mother. 'I write letter to Mother for a... *Guylas*?' 'For a recipe, a list of all the things in a goulash.' Iris seized the opportunity to ask him about his home. 'You live with your mother and father, yes? You were a sports teacher in the school? You have girl friend, a fiancée?' She pointed to her ring finger.

'I have friend... Ilona... a teacher. She not come with me. I wait at station. She not come. Why she not come?' He bowed his head.

'You wrote to her, yes?'

'Yes, five letters. I not understand.'

Iris could see he was upset and did not pursue her questions. Sometimes she felt an Iron Curtain coming down between them. She knew that he was angry that no countries had come to Hungary's aid in the last days when Imre Nagy had cried to the west to intervene. 'I not understand' covered so many feelings and conflicts for Frankie. When he had gone back to his lodgings she felt the first twinges of jealousy flood over her that he had a sweetheart but brushed aside her own foolishness and smoked a packet of cigarettes to calm herself down.

Iris watched winter turn into spring and the days pull out. Her work at the camp dwindled. She discovered snowdrops and yellow aconites spreading like a carpet under the trees. The garden had been a backdrop to her activities before, somewhere to play and sit and think. Now it was taking on a life of its own. She began to look forward to the arrival of the primroses and marsh marigolds along the banks of the stream. She found her week was filled with supply teaching in nearby schools and that Saturday afternoons flashed past as she tidied up the herb patch and trimmed the yew arch back to shape again. She slashed the tired roses back to the base in the hope that if she fed them they might perk up and give her a surprise in the summer.

It had been so many years since she had bothered with outdoor work and the funny thing was that now she had soil on her fingers and felt the loam sifting grittily through them, it was no longer *a* garden but *her* garden. Suddenly all that was growing here was her responsibility, her baby, to do with as she pleased. What a surge of power it brought. I can shift things and change plants, she thought. I can see what comes up and execute, exile, imprison or liberate, as I please! There was always something coming up, going down, needing attention, and she found herself lingering over the borders to see what was happening there. She would take her class preparation to the window seat and look out over the garden, no longer with despair but with hope. It was her new friend, no, her childhood friend rediscovered.

On Sundays she would find Frankie hard at work somewhere, his black beret bobbing up and down, the wheelbarrow creaking along the gravel paths. She pottered about like Flora giving orders to Grumpy Greggs. The idea of herself as lady gardener with straw hat and trug was hilarious and she promptly donned a boiler suit and wellies to get stuck in with the great potato planting. Iris had read up in the old books that she should plant to a waxing moon and on Good Friday but it had bucketed down all day so the chittings had to wait to Easter Monday. Frankie was in a foul mood then, sullen, quiet and not himself. She had not asked him to help her but he felt vegetables were men's work and he must oversee the operation like a gaffer. In the flower beds he was a pussy cat but here the tiger was in control. '*Nem*!' He showed her how to plant a tuber and trench over the crop, stomping about the garden with a face like the wet Bank Holiday it was. Iris could have sworn she saw him digging a hole and shouting down it.

After the labours of the day they usually sat silently in the kitchen over cups of the Russian tea Frankie enjoyed. Iris rolled her neck to loosen its stiffness one day. Frankie stood up and proceeded to massage the strain from the back of her neck and shoulders.

'You like?'

She had no idea that touch could relax her so quickly, the firm strokes soothing away all her tension. How did he manage to do this? She was most impressed and tried to practise on his neck as they took their drinks to the fireside. She had learned to copy the feather strokes and sweeping circular movements, kneading the tension from his muscles. It was part of the silent rapport between them, the slow rhythm of the weekend. Even after Frankie had found lodgings in the city he would ride out on his bicycle every Sunday.

Tonight he was silent and drawn into himself. There would be no massage or conversation. The spark was gone from his eyes and he scarcely looked at her. Iris was puzzled and tried to probe this change of climate. 'You OK?'

'Yes. I go now, please. Thank you, Iris. Good dinner.'

The next week he came and went without her knowing, as if he had done his duty and fled straight away. Iris could not fathom why he would suddenly change overnight. Had he got bored or was it that he now had other fish to fry and preferred to spend his weekends with younger folk? She'd known it would happen one day. He was bound to want to hang around with pretty girls in dance halls. It was no skin off her nose. But as the week wore on and she bit off every kind comment in the staff rooms where she was a temporary supply teacher she realised her feelings were raw and wounded by his silence. It mattered very much when he did not come the next Sunday.

She'd prepared extra for lunch, just in case, watched the clock and fussed around the garden unable to concentrate. Finally she found herself sitting in his hut, sniffing stale Turkish cigarette smoke, wondering what he was doing and who he was with.

Every instinct told her that there was a woman behind this. What was going on? Why did she feel so let down, so bloody angry? She was frittering away a lovely spring afternoon with this futile sulking. Damn the knowing without words, that Bagshott bequest passed down to her; that nose for the truth of a matter. Frankie had a girlfriend and she was jealous. Oh, yes, silly old fool that she was, she had hankered after him and he had found her out. Now he was giving her the polite heave-ho as best as any poor sod could without the language to back him up. All these months he had just been humouring her, paying back some imagined debt in her garden. How stupid she was not to have realised earlier. How could any young man possibly look at her with lust or desire?

She caught sight of herself in the window pane. What a sight! Her eyebrows needed plucking, there was a slackening around her jaw line, crow's feet too. Standing with sagging breasts and rounded shoulders, Iris found herself, spade in hand, digging, digging into the border, shouting into the hole with tears running down her face: 'You silly old beggar, grow up!'

The Paprika Moon

❦

Ferenc stood on Trent Valley station platform waiting anxiously for the train to arrive. In his pocket was Ilona's letter, read and reread many times over. He could not believe she was coming to see him at last, that she had been two months in England at a place called Tidworth near London and was now staying in a hostel in Ealing. It had been such a shock to receive news of her arrival from mutual friends who had seen her by chance at a party. He'd wanted to burst with excitement at first but something was holding back his joy. He could not tell Miss Iris. Somehow once he told her that would be the end of the garden Sundays and the peaceful times working there. He would have to visit Ili at the weekends now and perhaps find a job closer to her. She had been brave enough to risk coming over alone and he must support her. She was his long-time sweetheart after all.

What if she didn't recognise him in his best mac and trilby hat? Was he not like any Englishman now, for he had a job and a place to live of his own. He went to night school to improve his English and one day might become a sports teacher again. The job in the motor works was mundane and sometimes boring but there was plenty of overtime and money to buy himself new shirts and fancy ties and football boots. He was going to join a local team. Ferenc no longer felt like a label with 'refugee' written on it in black ink. Now he was Frankie Hordas and soon he would have a wife to complete his dream.

He searched the compartments as the train drew into the platform, peering amongst the smoke and soot for his first sighting of Ili with her fair hair loosely braided, her dirndl skirt and ankle socks.

A woman stood before him smiling, a woman with red lipstick and painted eyes, with a ponytail and fringe like a dancer in the movies, her billowing skirts clinched at the waist with a thick belt, all curves and softness.

'Feri, how are you?' They kissed each other on the check and clung to each other.

'Ili, how you've changed…' He could not take in her new appearance. She whirled round and he could see the petticoats swishing under her skirt.

'If all these English girls can dress up as film stars so can I. You like it?' He was not sure. There was a harder, more spiky edge to her now and he felt oddly nervous. There were a hundred questions he needed to ask of her.

'Where shall we go… to a movie or dancing or both?' Ili was prancing down the platform, leaving him behind. 'Isn't it exciting? So much to do and see and now we can go anywhere we please without a permit. They even give me money to spend. Do you remember when we were students, we hadn't ten florints between us? It was no life, was it? Now I can go into London every day if I want to and there's always a party or a concert or friends to visit. I wish I'd come with you months ago but I was afraid.'

'How did you get out?' he asked when what he really

wanted to know was why she had not been brave enough to come with him.

'I walked with a group of other students fifty miles to the border and we slipped across one night...'

'How are my parents? And yours?'

'They manage and they understand. Don't look so serious, Feri. Life has to go on and we've seized our opportunity. There's no future for us back home. Come on, let's not waste the day. I'm starving!'

They ate in a cafe in the market place and wandered around the ancient Cathedral, feeding ducks in the park like any tourists. She was as polite to him as if he was a stranger not her Feri. 'Ilona, you've changed,' he faltered. 'I hardly recognise you. Why did you take so long to tell me you were here?'

'You know how it is when you first arrive. So much to sort out.' She was not looking him straight in the eye.

'But you could have come to the camp here. Given my name as next-of-kin? I have written you many letters and you never replied.'

'Feri, don't go on! I'm here now, aren't I?'

'Will you come and stay up here?' he asked gently, guessing her reply already.

'No fear! After London this is a hole. I'm registered at a college now and there's a group of us sharing digs together.'

'I see,' he replied, his heart thudding. 'Where do I fit into your plans, Ili?'

There was silence for a moment.

'I was going to write to you, honestly, but with one thing and another... Life is different here and there are so many people.'

'You've met someone else, I take it? Do I know him?'

'No. It's just that a group of us started going round together and I met Lazio at a party. He's a medical student and – well, we sort of hit it off.'

'I see. So I take it you are not expecting me to come down to London very often?'

'You'd always be welcome, Feri, but we can't turn the clock back, any of us. Things happen.'

In the whole of that long day she never once asked about his own journey to freedom, his experiences, his life now and his new friends. He was seeing his sweetheart for the first time as a rather selfish, silly young woman who was in love with her London life, not him. His illusions were shattered. He was talking to a stranger.

The hours dragged slowly by until she boarded the train and he pecked her on the cheek. 'Take care of yourself, Ili, and let me know how it goes…' His voice faded as she waved a farewell from the carriage window. He knew this was no *au revoir*. How could two people have grown so far apart in just six months? As he walked through the quiet suburbs to his lodgings, he felt a deep sadness but a strange sensation of relief as well. He had never wanted to settle near London. Cities did not interest him. He loved open spaces and woods and most of all the quiet peace of Iris Bagshott's garden and that kind and funny woman who lived there. That was the piece of England he loved most.

He watched the moon rising like a ball of red fire; his paprika moon rising again. A good omen.

Iris slaved all spring like a navvy in her garden, planting out, keeping busy every minute of her spare time. A garden takes no sides in any argument, it listens, is a great leveller, she thought. And sometimes it took her by surprise, imbuing her with that strange feeling of joy which transfigured everything she touched and did in it. She could feel the spirit of the place driving her on to create an arch here or make a new patch of planting there; not to be afraid to dig up the turf and create new beds and shapes. Such was the beauty of the soft opalescent light it made her linger outside in the evenings when she was not teaching at night school. Yes, she would settle for a comfortable old age here, sip her cocoa, listen to the wireless, buy a television maybe. Thoughts of Frankie had dulled merely to an ache. She could laugh at her own foolishness. Sometimes you have to accept a loss and let it go, she mused. Then the door bell rang and she strolled along the passage to see who it was.

Frankie was standing on the doorstep with a bunch of flowers, a bottle of red wine and a silly expression on his face.

'How go the potatoes?'

Iris smiled with genuine pleasure. 'Long time, no see.'

'Pardon?' He whipped off his trilby. 'I come see you, yes?'

'Come and see the garden. How nice that you're here again. Was it something I said?' Iris smiled, knowing that the poor man would not understand her words. They walked around the paths, nodding and pointing and miming to each other. He raced up to the vegetable patch to examine the potato haulms for blight. There was none. Had they not done it all by the book?

Later they drank his wine in the parlour and she quizzed him. 'Why have you come? It is many weeks. Did you go away?'

'I no understand. I see Ili. She in England now. She in London...'

'So you are going to marry her?'

'No. Ili have a new friend in London.'

'You are sad, yes?' She pointed to her heart. He shook his head. How could he explain his feelings? He had no words.

'No. I no sad. I am here. I dig garden.'

'You dig the garden!' sighed Iris. Here we go again, back to the garden of lovesick fools. It was going to have more shouting holes in it than a sieve but it was lovely to know he would be back once again.

They made so many mistakes that summer – planting too early, too late, in the wrong place or in the wrong soil that she began to wonder if they would be bankrupted by the garden. She was Queen of the flower beds and he was King of the vegetable patch and people in the village got used to seeing them bobbing around the garden together, two friends who enjoyed each other's company and often entertained a bunch of wild refugees who called at short notice and stayed overnight.

In the autumn they dug up their harvest and burned the haulms on the bonfire, pulled up the poppies and annuals and sorted out the pond again. It was back-breaking work. One afternoon, reeking of smoke, aching in every joint, Iris collapsed by the wellspring to sip some water. Frankie knelt beside her and began to massage her back. She sank down into the rhythm of his strokes, in no mind to resist. His massage was harder, firmer and more deliberate and he kept whispering her name like a chant. A surge of electricity shot through her limbs, unblocking that knowing she had felt for months. I love this man Frankie. He is the heart of my garden, she realised, jerking upright.

'You no like?' He looked puzzled.

'I like, but it's damp here now and it's your turn. Let's light a fire and go inside.'

Iris could not wait to lay her hands on his neck, to feel

each curly hair, soothe the tight muscles across his back. She worked her way slowly down to his shoulders.

Frankie grabbed her hand and kissed it, no longer out of gratitude but with desire. Iris paused and wrapped both her hands around him. They needed no language for what would follow next. Each caress was charged with a tension all its own as two nations united: King of the kitchen plot with the Queen of the flower beds, fused together with longing in the firelight. Who needed words when there was so much love?

'Iris Bagshott, I don't believe I'm hearing this!' said Flora, folding her arms across her cashmere twinset. 'Am I right in thinking that Frankie Hordas is living here... over the brush? Sleeping in your bed? Have you gone crazy? What will Fridwell think?'

'What it's no doubt been thinking for months before it actually happened. I was waiting for you to say... *at your age!* I know I'm forty-six and he's thirty-two, but so bloody what? Flora, how old are you and how old is dear Henry?' Iris was standing firm.

'That's not the same,' argued her friend.

'Tosh! As you say. Why is it right for a man and not a woman? We were friends and now we are lovers, the natural order of affairs. What's so wrong in that? We're free agents.'

'I thought he had a girl in Hungary?'

'Not any more. She lives in London and with someone else.'

'So he came to you for consolation? Just wait, he'll be off with some young thing ere long.' Flora puffed smoke in her face. 'It'll all end in tears, Iris. I care about you...'

'... making a fool of myself? Is that it? Henry can marry you but if I were to marry Frankie it would be obscene?'

'No, I didn't say that. It's just a bit unusual. It'll take some getting used to.' Flora was struggling for words.

'Are we so different from any other couple? For the first time in my life I smile everywhere I go. He gives me so much support and kindness, and he's taught me how to relax my body and… He's the sort of man you want to make love to with your eyes open.'

'Iris, please!'

'Don't be so prudish, Flora Salt. You know exactly what I mean.' Then Iris gasped, knowing full well her words could never apply to Henry and Flora. 'Frankie knows how muscles work. He can massage away a stiff back, any ache or pain. He has a real gift for it. I'd love to set him loose on poor Henry's back to see if he could ease away the stiffness. He learnt it from a coach in his football days.'

'Just you leave Henry's back where it is! Whatever will the poor chap say when he finds out?' Flora sat down and swigged back her sherry.

'He should be pleased that I've found someone unmarried, sensitive and kind; someone who has given me back my self-respect. Glad that I've discovered love in the heart of my garden. Tell him we've both fallen in love with my garden. We can't wait to get going on all our projects. Our garden doesn't care if we're young or old, English or Hungarian, so long as it's looked after. Because of it we've found each other. A little late in life for me, perhaps. It'll have to be our child, I fear.

'Be happy for me, Flora. I've so much to give to both of them. Now I'm looking on the world with loving eyes. It won't last, nothing does in this world, but for now… Don't look so horrified. I'm not going soft in the head. I'm happy. H.A.P.P.Y. Anyone would think you were jealous?'

'But I am, Iris. That's what's bothering me. I've never seen you so alive before. It's as if you've found part of yourself long since buried. When you came here last Christmas your eyes were dead. Whatever Frankie's done to you, he's taken years off you already, decades in fact, and I'm green with envy. I see before me a young lass in the first flush of passionate love, defying the world and convention, with all the pain of discovery, betrayal, sorrow before her. I'm sorry to be so cynical. I won't say another word.'

'Good, I should hate us to fall out. Just wish me well. I know the odds are stacked against us. I'm living for this moment, not when I'm sixty and he's… whatever. No one knows what the future holds for us.'

'So let's see what you've both been up to in this magical garden of yours?' Flora made for the door, anxious to be away from such a frank conversation. Her breezy change of subject could not hide her confusion and shock.

'Here up the steps is project one: the new kitchen beds and path. Ahead of you, round the corner, will be Frankie's rock and alpine garden which is a mud heap now. Project three will be unclogging the boggy pond and the stream in the bottom field, as well as tidying up the shade banks by the well. And then there's project four, restocking the orchard and rescuing that manky donkey from Longhall Manor School. Oh, and Frankie's shed's to be turned into a study. He's going to go to college when we've saved up a bit.'

'Enough! I'm exhausted already. You two have a lifetime of projects. I hope you've time to fit them all in before one of you conks out in the attempt. If you want any more cuttings from The Grange, you only have to ask.' Flora made for the gate across the fields, a short cut to her house down the stream path.

'Thanks, I'll take you up on that.' Iris waved. Only time

would tell how this garden would grow. She shivered as if someone had walked over her grave. Nothing was going to spoil the fun of it all, the planning, the heaving about, the satisfaction of creating a garden. Surely one of the greatest pleasures in a lifetime?

Goodnight

Iris

⁓⁓⁓⁓⁓

It's time to say goodnight to Frankie whose dust nourishes the rose 'Compassion', always the last stop on the tour. He was not for public display in the rose bed but tucked away close at hand to gossip to by the kitchen steps.

Ours was not one of those thunderbolt affairs; all flame and no substance. We grew towards each other like new grafting on old stock, didn't we? Iris pauses to dead head the bush.

We needed no ceremony to declare our love. Just seven good years and seven lean when his persistent cough wouldn't heal. No one told us about killer tobacco then. It should have been me to go first, not him. How can I leave this garden when Frankie is still here? She turns her face to the upstairs window where he used to sit, propped up with pillows, giving her orders for the day, too weak to come outside, putting a brave face on his dying. It was Frankie who taught her to make lists and never to hoe without carefully checking all the seedlings for interesting self-setters. 'Never miss a freebie,' he would chuckle.

How can I leave this garden when it's so much a part of me and mine, part of us? While I live so do both of us for a marriage of souls can't end until both parties are gone. It's been the best therapy for my grief. Let them all squabble over it when I'm fit only for fertiliser. I bet there'll be Bagshotts crawling out of the woodwork who've never darkened my door, hoping for a share of the spoils. I've made plans with my solicitor to stitch up their greedy purses. Pity we had no cuttings ourselves but a new century will bring fresh stock to the place. A new challenge for someone else.

How I longed to give you a child, Frankie, but it was always too late. Our child is this garden. Still, there've been plenty of little monkeys swinging in the orchard and riding the donkey, fishing in the pond, playing hide and seek in the shrubbery. James Bowman's brood, Peter Nagy's boys and Magda's girls. Do you remember how at each of our reunions they'd all troop in with bags full of baby gear, pushchairs and carrycots, and we'd show them all our work, presenting our garden like proud parents?

When Henry passed away, James took over the running of S & B Motors, Flora sold The Grange and now it is a guest house called 'Country Sunshine'. Flora and James transported half their garden up to Friddy's Piece for Iris to cram into her borders; the silk tassel bush, the *Viburnum farrerii* with its pink pompoms giving delicious winter scent, the *Kerria japonica* whose golden buttons sprout up the kitchen wall – so many Salt memories to cherish. Flora will be visiting soon to see her offspring.

This garden has been a labour of love, difficult to keep up but measured in many lifetimes. And mine's not over yet! So much to see to still, but the tour is over for tonight, Frankie. Time to call Lady in from the wild end, but first I must hammer this notice on to the gatepost. It's been burning a hole in my pocket. Then I can sleep in peace.

MISS BAGSHOTT WISHES IT TO BE KNOWN THAT
SHE DOES NOT INTEND TO SELL HER PLOT.
SHE IS QUITE WELL AND DOES NOT WISH TO BE
INTERRUPTED UNTIL OPEN DAY.

Tomorrow the For Sale sign would be coming down.
Iris smiles. That should warm the heart of the garden.

Acknowledgements

Thank you, all my gardening friends for your help in supplying me with information about the history of plants and gardening, especially Menna and Alan Picton who found the source of the Fridwell spring.

I am indebted to the following: The Lichfield Archive office for information on the medieval priory at Farewell, Staffs, the late Howard Clayton's excellent book on the Civil War in the Midlands: *Loyal and Ancient City*, the Hungarian social club of Rochdale for a warm welcome and to those willing to share personal experiences of their escape from Hungary in 1956.

The plant quotations are taken from *Culpeper's Complete Herbal*. I would like to thank the National Trust for permission to quote from Rudyard Kipling's poem 'The Glory of the Garden' and Barbara Thornton for her lovely illustrations. Most of all I must thank my husband, David, who was always able to locate a fine watering hole on our garden quests!

My story is fictitious. The setting is real. The house stands, the church flourishes, the stream flows but alas the garden grows only in my heart.